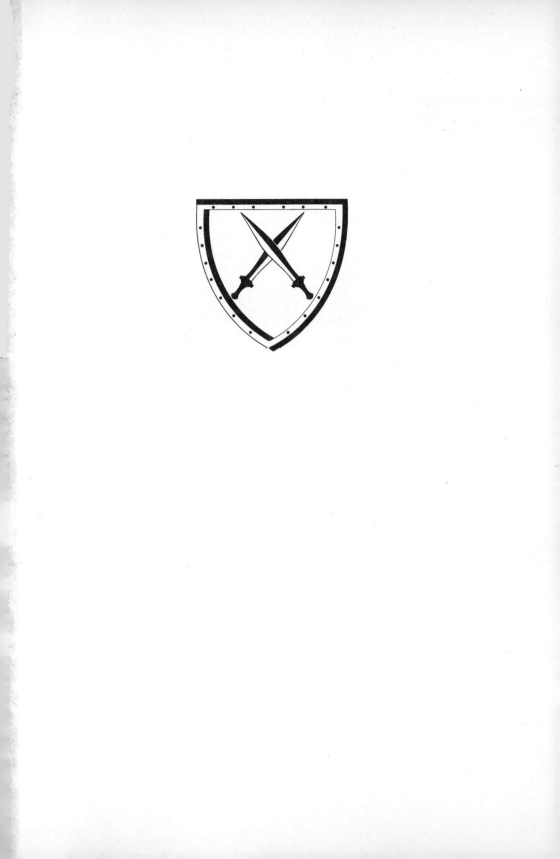

Titles by MERCEDES LACKEY
available from DAW Books:

THE NOVELS OF VALDEMAR:

THE HERALDS OF VALDEMAR
ARROWS OF THE QUEEN
ARROW'S FLIGHT
ARROW'S FALL

THE LAST HERALD-MAGE
MAGIC'S PAWN
MAGIC'S PROMISE
MAGIC'S PRICE

THE MAGE WINDS
WINDS OF FATE
WINDS OF CHANGE
WINDS OF FURY

THE MAGE STORMS
STORM WARNING
STORM RISING
STORM BREAKING

VOWS AND HONOR
THE OATHBOUND
OATHBREAKERS
OATHBLOOD

THE COLLEGIUM CHRONICLES
FOUNDATION
INTRIGUES
CHANGES
REDOUBT
BASTION

THE HERALD SPY
CLOSER TO HOME

BY THE SWORD
BRIGHTLY BURNING
TAKE A THIEF

EXILE'S HONOR
EXILE'S VALOR

VALDEMAR ANTHOLOGIES:
SWORD OF ICE
SUN IN GLORY
CROSSROADS
MOVING TARGETS
CHANGING THE WORLD
FINDING THE WAY
UNDER THE VALE
NO TRUE WAY

Written with **LARRY DIXON**:

THE MAGE WARS
THE BLACK GRYPHON
THE WHITE GRYPHON
THE SILVER GRYPHON

DARIAN'S TALE
OWLFLIGHT
OWLSIGHT
OWLKNIGHT

OTHER NOVELS:

GWENHWYFAR
THE BLACK SWAN

THE DRAGON JOUSTERS
JOUST
ALTA
SANCTUARY
AERIE

THE ELEMENTAL MASTERS
THE SERPENT'S SHADOW
THE GATES OF SLEEP
PHOENIX AND ASHES
THE WIZARD OF LONDON
RESERVED FOR THE CAT
UNNATURAL ISSUE
HOME FROM THE SEA
STEADFAST
BLOOD RED
FROM A HIGH TOWER*
Anthologies:
ELEMENTAL MAGIC
ELEMENTARY

*Coming soon from DAW Books

And don't miss
THE VALDEMAR COMPANION
edited by John Helfers and Denise Little

CLOSER TO HOME

THE HERALD SPY
BOOK ONE

MERCEDES LACKEY

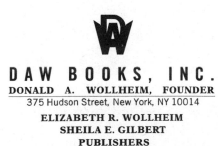

DAW BOOKS, INC.
DONALD A. WOLLHEIM, FOUNDER
375 Hudson Street, New York, NY 10014

ELIZABETH R. WOLLHEIM
SHEILA E. GILBERT
PUBLISHERS
www.dawbooks.com

*Dedicated to the memory of Shirley Dixon,
the best mother-in-law on the planet.*

The crow skimming the treetops with his mate cast an avid eye down to the ground below, looking for one last opportunity for a meal before taking to the branches for the night. It was about an hour to sunset, and although it was getting into autumn, the days here in the heart of Valdemar were still warm and the nights only pleasantly cool. Today had been perfect haying weather, cloudless, dry, and clear, and tonight was going to bring more of the same conditions. The crow approved of haying; it scared a lot of large and tasty insects and even rodents out where they were easy prey for a clever bird. It was certainly good weather for camping, which, it appeared, the owners of a most peculiar caravan were doing. The crow approved of camping, too, and headed in their direction. Caravans needed to be approached with caution, but sometimes there was food. Unwary toddlers could have their rusks snatched. There might be scraps or offal. Rarely, someone who appreciated crows might offer food freely!

Amily chuckled at the crow's thoughts. She was enjoying

1

riding along in his mind; it was purely a one-way excursion, as it was with all the animals whose eyes she used and whose thoughts she spied on. She hadn't told Mags about this Gift yet; she wanted to talk to someone at the Collegia who might have a better insight into it. It wasn't Animal Mindspeech. She couldn't control the creatures she spied on. At the moment it seemed of very little use, and she hadn't had it long.

Such caravans as the one standing below the crow tended to be at one extreme or the other—either very drab and utilitarian, the sort of thing used to move goods from one place to another and not meant to attract attention, or the very opposite, gaudily painted and elaborately ornamented. This one was . . . neither one, nor the other. It had been painted a plain white, except for the carvings that ornamented the roofline and the doors, and the shutters that could be closed over the windows to protect them from a storm, which had been painted dark blue. But at one point it had surely been painted as gaudily as you please, for there were designs of flowers and vines bleeding through the white paint. Faintly, but definitely there. It looked as if several coats had been applied, too. The original must have been truly powerful paint.

The caravan looked odd from this vantage. And the crow's eyes picked out a lot of details that Amily had missed. Maybe this Gift might be useful for scouting, or even spying, but how would you get the animal in question to go where you wanted, look at what you needed to see, or listen to what you wanted to hear? Amily supposed that you could just search for random creatures that were near what you wanted . . . but that could end in a lot of frustration.

Two handsome horses of the vanner breed grazed, hobbled, beside it, as did two beautiful white beasts that no one in all of Valdemar would ever mistake for anything other than Companions.

Well, that wasn't quite true. In the course of their Circuit, the six travelers had come across quite a few people who thought Companions were nothing more than white horses. Exceptionally trained white horses, but certainly no more than that. It irritated Mags and infuriated Jakyr, but Amily was used to people seeing only what they expected to see.

The crow found this even more promising, as he circled. He knew these white horses. Their riders were never cruel, often kind, and always well fed enough to offer a bite or two to a crow. The only question now was, did they like crows?

Amily chuckled silently. Of course she liked crows. Sometimes, before Bear had fixed her leg, crows had given her endless hours of amusement. They were among the first birds to come when she tossed bits of food, quickly learned not only to recognize that she wasn't a threat, but to recognize her even at a distance, and their antics made her laugh.

The humans were camped some distance away from the road, and had followed a track between two sheep-meadows to get here. The van was parked beside a neat little building which anyone in Valdemar would recognize as a Waystation, but the four people from the caravan were not making use of it at the moment. The door was closed, with the bar on the outside still in place. There was a well, a proper one, with a stone wall around it and a wooden canopy over it, with a wooden hatch to keep it clean when not in use. And they *had* made use of that, for the bucket suspended under the canopy was still wet. They were all sitting on rugs spread on the grass around a fire. It appeared that they had gotten their dinner elsewhere, perhaps at an inn further back down the road behind them, and had brought it along to enjoy *al fresco* here, for the little fire certainly wasn't serving any purpose other than to heat water for tea. Then again, given the young feast displayed on the rugs, there really was no need for a cooking fire now, and there were more than enough leftovers to serve for breakfast.

As the crow circled, his mate following him cautiously, Amily became aware that he really was *hungry, and it wasn't just corvid greed. She'd seen crows making off with their own body-weight in food and more, taking it elsewhere to cache it against a hungry day, but this fellow had a mostly-empty belly. She resolved to be generous.*

Most of the eating seemed to be over with, and letter-reading had begun while there was still light to read by.

Not that the crow knew what "letter-reading" was. Amily was the one that recognized what they were all doing. Well, all of them but her. She was lying back on the blanket with her hands under the back of her head and her eyes closed. It was very odd seeing herself like this. It was not like looking in a mirror at all.

The crow landed, his mate after him. His mate hung back, though; much more wary of humans than he was. One of the people—currently perusing one of a packet of letters—was a woman dressed in Bardic Scarlets. She looked to be of late middle-age, not yet starting to go gray, but just beginning to show character-lines in her face.

Melita looks very imposing through a crow's eyes.

A second, much younger woman, as quiet and brown as a sparrow, in fairly ordinary clothing (although her outfit featured breeches rather than a skirt), was lying on her back on the blanket, eyes closed.

Definitely very odd to see myself like this. A little unsettling too.

A third, a man in Herald Whites, about the same age as the first woman but with silver threading through the dark blond of his hair, was opening the last of his letters and gave a surprised chuckle when he saw the sealed envelope contained a second one.

I think I'll pretend to be napping a little longer, this is very interesting.

The fourth human, a young man, dark of eye and hair, but in gray clothing not unlike the Herald's, was packing up the leftovers. The crow gave a tentative *caw,* and he looked up, grinned and tossed a generous chunk of cheese in the crow's direction, and a second toward the crow's mate.

Both birds seized the bounty, and flew off. The crow was very well pleased. That cheese was enough to fill his belly for the night, and give plenty of time in the morning to find the next meal.

And I didn't have to be generous after all. Mags anticipated me! Amily opened her eyes and sat up, ready to see what Herald Jakyr had found in his letter that was so amusing.

———————

"Well, Mags," Herald Jakyr said aloud, making Mags, who had been watching the crows fly off with a half-grin on his face, look in his direction. "It seems someone found a clever way to track you down without giving you away."

Mags bit off an exclamation and took the sealed envelope, ripping it almost in half in his haste to get at it. "How in—" Mags said, and then plunged into the content of the several thick sheets of vellum that had been inside. With an amused smile, Amily took over the clearing-up where he had left off.

"Huh. This ain't from . . . anybody I know. But it's in Bey's tongue." He looked over the letter, which had very little writing on it. Then his eyes widened, and he pulled a bit of burning branch out of the fire. Holding the flame carefully under the vellum, he warmed each page up . . . and like magic, as the others watched too, tiny, brown writing appeared between the few scrawled lines.

"Mags, if you know that secret—" Jakyr said, when he'd closed the mouth that had dropped open in surprise.

"Wouldn't do us no good," Mags said shortly. "Needs a fruit we ain't got." He perused the letter, while Amily picked up the envelope and tried the same trick with it. Her attempt yielded nothing.

"Well?" Bard Melita (or just "Lita" to most) asked after a moment, with evident impatience. "What is it then?"

"Hang on, it's from Bey, and it's in . . . well, it's in Bey's tongue. I have to translate it, then puzzle it out." Mags' brows were creased with concentration—and then, relaxed with relief. "Well, he says the coast is clear, more or less. Nobody from the Sleepgivers is going to be looking for me no more."

"I assume there's more to this than the ruse we were planning on?" Herald Jakyr asked.

Mags nodded. "All right, let me take this one bit at a time. The first thing he writes is that he obviously got home safe. He says, once he got back home, he came up with a pretty fine story about comin' across the last of the lot that was supposed to be comin' for me at the Bastion, interceptin' him at the border to Karse."

Jakyr nodded. "That's a good, plausible story."

"Bey's clever that way." Mags puzzled through the next part of the letter. "This's why the letter's so long, he's got a mort of things to tell me. All right. He told them all the feller was caught by the Karsites, got wounded and was dyin'. Bey gave over his talisman to his pa to prove his tale." Mags scratched his head and looked up with a half-smile of rueful admiration. "Reckon he must've pulled a couple off the bodies afore we all pitched 'em down the hole in the cave we was livin' in. I shoulda thought of doin' that."

"You had more than a few things on your mind," Jakyr reminded him. "You also had no idea whether or not they could prove dangerous after the wearer was dead; Bey would know better about that than you. And Bey was practically born in subterfuge."

Mags shrugged. "Aye, well. So, Bey tells 'em all that this made-up feller told *Bey* that the bunch that was huntin' us killed us all, an' the Karsite demons killed the ones comin' back to report it. He's pretty pleased by the tale he spun, 'cause he says they all swallered it, and they reckon to steer well clear of Karse from now on. They don't know nothin' about handlin' their demons, he says, an' there's no reason no more t' go that way. He says he also dropped hints that 'Mags' is as common a name hereabouts as say, 'Daisy' or 'Rose' or 'Perry.' So he says I can use the name I'm used to. So, that's just the first bit. Give me a bit'f time . . ."

Bey wrote in a very florid style—and obliquely. It would probably take someone who had shared both his memories and his experiences to get the full message, which was, without a doubt, exactly what he had intended.

"Well," Mags continued, feeling once again that odd disconnect between the Bey he knew and rather liked, and the . . . entirely calculating and crafty fellow that he *also* knew, and didn't much like. "He says his pa was kinda sickish when he left, and by the time he got back, the word about me bein' dead and all kinda knocked him sideways. He says he got the feelin' his pa was just holdin' on to see if Bey had growed up enough to take over. So that pretty much settled him on doin' what we talked about, him talkin' to that girl he had in mind, an' scein' if he could count on her at his back an' all." He had to chuckle about the next part. "She called 'im a few choice kinds of an idiot, an' kissed 'im, an' he gets all coy about it, but seems like she'd been chasin' after him all this time an' he didn' have the wit t'see it. So they go to his pa an' get things all settled. Bey's pa an' her pa basically did everything but throw 'em at what passes fer a priest. An they ain't been married but a month an' his pa died."

"That's—terrible!" Amily exclaimed, as Lita shook her head. But Mags and Jakyr exchanged a little look, and Mags knew exactly what Jakyr was thinking—because he was thinking it himself. *I wonder how much Bey had a hand in seeing his pa off to the next world . . .*

It seemed Dallen was of the same mind. *:They are an entire nation—small, but a nation—of assassins. It seems perfectly likely to me.:*

In those memories he had shared with Bey, his cousin's relationship with the head of the Sleepgivers, his father, had been . . . ambiguous. He absolutely respected the old man. He absolutely was loyal to him. But . . . there was no love there. That had been reserved entirely for Bey's mother, who had died when he was a child. And Bey was ambitious. He had very definite ideas about steering the future of the Sleepgivers, plans that were unlikely to see fruition while his father was alive. *Would* he have given an old, sick man a little help across the threshold of death?

:He had plenty of practice in doing just that,: Dallen observed.

Mags sucked his lower lip thoughtfully, and decided to keep his thoughts on the matter between himself and Dallen. "Well, Bey says that between that tale he spun up, and that he's now the head of the clan—" He raised an eyebrow.

"There is no longer anyone interested in verifying that cock-and-bull, far-too-convenient story he told," Jakyr said dryly.

"Pretty much." Mags shrugged. "The whole idea of lookin' fer me was his Pa's anyway. I've no doubt a lot of 'em thought it was daft, tryin' to bring back someone that was raised a furriner. The more 'specially as they lost a *lot* of fellers tryin' t'do it. Ended up with a costly contract with Karse they canceled, an' that didn't turn out well fer 'em, neither. Hell, prolly half the clan thinks Bey snuck off t'kill me his own self."

"And without a doubt, the ones that think that admire him for it." Jakyr reached for a pocket pie he had left warming on a stone next to the fire, as Mags cut a last slice of bread and piled ham and pickled onions on top of it, before Amily could pack the loaf and ham away.

"An' if any of 'em hinted at it, he'd go all *shocked* like." Mags took a big bite of his concoction. "Well, t' get back t' this letter, there's some about how his gal is already workin' on a baby. There's a lotta stuff just meant fer me, remindin' me of stuff that should be in my head now. 'E said 'e waited a decent bit afore arrangin' t'hand the letter off to someone that'd give it to a Shin'a'in horsetrader 'e's got contact with." He shook his head with admiration. "Wish't I knew how 'e managed that. I didn' know th' Shin'a'in went that far."

Jakyr shrugged. "You never know what a Shin'a'in is likely to do. They'll go vast distances to ensure that a horse is properly placed—and equally vast distances to take one back if they discover it hasn't been."

Mags could only shake his head. "I dunno. I ain't run across any, jest some of their hand-work. All I know's what I read, which ain't much. Anyway, he says the horsetrader was t' pass it off to whoever's goin' north to Valdemar, and 'e's put you, Jakyr, as the one t'get the letter, 'cause ain't nobody down there knows who you are."

"There is a lot more to that letter than that," Jakyr pointed out. "You're barely half through it."

Mags had to chuckle again. "Well . . . I gotta say, other than remindin' me of stuff I shoulda got from his mem'ries that 'e says I might well need, the rest of it is . . . Bey's woman has got him tied in knots. Well, like my pa was for my ma, if the stories he tol' me are right. The rest of the letter is him goin' on about her. He says she pretty much hung the moon an' the stars. An' she's no little flower either; he says 'she's better at close-quarters combat than I am!' Which, you'll reckon, means real damn good."

"If she wants to keep her own children alive, I suspect she had better be," Lita observed shrewdly.

"He says here, 'e told her the truth 'bout me. Huh." Mag scratched his head, puzzled. "Wonder why."

"Possibly because this way she knows, for certain, that he trusts her. And possibly because it reassures her that no unexpected competition is going to show up. Probably both," Jakyr mused. He finished his pocket pie and poured hot water from the pot over the fire into the teapot. "Well! Who wants the Waystation? Because whoever wants to use it should probably open it up and give it a good airing before the sun goes down."

"We'll take it, Jakyr," said Amily, as she stowed the last of the food in a basket. "The wagon will probably be more comfortable, and we have younger bones." She motioned to Mags to stay where he was, and got up to take down the bar and open the door. She walked with strength, and a just barely perceptible limp, now. But Mags was not about to let her do all the work by herself. The rest of the letter could wait. Lita stowed the leftovers in the caravan while they worked, and Jakyr fetched more water and took care of the Companions and vanners for the night.

Mags joined Amily, opening up the shutters, then the windows themselves, then fetching one of the featherbeds and some bedding as Lita passed them to him from the caravan. He made up a small fire in the fireplace, then fetched in water while Amily swept the place out; he'd have done the sweeping, but she snatched the broom out of his hand. With a laugh, he left her to it while he got the water.

Since they were officially off-circuit, they didn't *have* to stay at Waystations, but Lita got unexpectedly . . . prim . . . when they were at inns. She would insist on sharing a room with Amily, leaving him to share with Jakyr, which was not the way he would have preferred things. He reasoned that she was just trying to preserve Amily's reputation (or perhaps her own!) but it was rather annoying to say the least. So when Jakyr started suggesting, right after two such incidents, that they might just as well use the Waystations, he had agreed immediately, and Amily had sided with the two men. Whoever felt most like doing the work of turning the Station out slept in it; more often than not it was Amily and Mags. The wagon was more comfortable for sleeping, as Amily had said, but it was stuffier, and a bit claustrophobic even with Bear and Lena gone. In any event, it was certainly pleasant to have the privacy, no matter which of the two places they spent the night.

By the time they had everything arranged to their satisfaction, Lita and Jakyr were already in the caravan, and there were lights burning inside, making the little windows around the top glow. There was still enough twilight to see by, but just barely, and the breeze was turning cool enough to close up the Waystation windows again. Mags made sure the campfire was out, and returned to the Station, where Amily had lit a lantern and arranged the bedding on the floor in front of the fire.

"We'll be home this time tomorrow," she said, as he stripped down and joined her in the blankets. "I'm not sure how I feel about that."

"Why?" he asked.

"Well . . . we haven't had to be anyone but Mags and Amily while we've been gone," she said, and sighed.

He realized immediately what she meant. "You'll be th' daughter of the King's Own. I'll be—well, not too many people are s'pposed to know I'm 'is student, but I *will* be that lad what almost got kilt a couple'a times, an' yer lad what intends t' marry ye." He held her close for a moment, but then moved just far enough away that he could look into her eyes. She looked worried. "An' that'll be th' problem, aye?"

"Among others. I suppose it is just as well that I wasn't Chosen after all." She made a face. "Because then people would be expecting *me* to be the next King's Own on top of all of that."

Mags could think of something he would much rather be doing right now than discussing all of this, but . . . *We ain't gonna do that until we talk about all of this.* "Aight," he said, and let her relax and put her head on his chest. "So, you been part'f alla this fer a lot longer'n me. Lay it all out fer me."

She was quiet, very quiet, which meant she was thinking hard. He watched the flames in the fireplace and listened to them crackle; caught the nearby hoot of an owl. *Funny how almost gettin' killed makes a feller enjoy just . . . quiet times . . .*

"Well, taking one thing at a time," Amily finally said,

"There's Father, all by himself. Without coming out and being . . ." he felt her cheek grow warm against his chest ". . . *blunt* about it, I made it as clear as I could in letters what we were to each other. He didn't seem surprised."

"He'd be pretty stupid if he was," Mags said dryly, "And your Da don't strike me as bein' stupid." *He* was a little surprised, though. He'd thought it was the sort of thing she would have wanted to say face to face. "Is thet somethin' thet was better left fer writin', though?"

She had to chuckle a little at that. "Well, when I'm telling him something I intend to do anyway, whether he likes it or not, I've always preferred to write to him about it, even when we were living in the same set of rooms."

"Are you gonna do that with me?" Mags asked after a moment. " 'Cause if it's all the same to you, I'd druther ye didn't. I like talkin' things over."

"*You* are not my father, the King's Own, and the King's spy," she pointed out. "Well, you're the King's spy but—"

"But not the King's Own, who's gonna have one set'f thoughts as jest Nikolas, one set as yer Da, and one set as th' King's Own," Mags filled in for her. "I reckon ye've been balancin' thet fer all yer life, so ye know best."

"Not always, but . . . well, I also didn't want him to get it from Bear and Lena's letters, or Jakyr's, or Lita's." She sighed. "Which, sooner or later, he probably would. I don't know he was reading their letters to their friends before their friends got them, but in his position, he certainly could have been. Plus, I am sure at least Jakyr and possibly Lita had been ordered to report directly back to him."

Ugh. I can understand that but . . . oh, that's a little uneasy-makin'. Am I gonna be readin' peoples' mail? Why that seemed more intrusive than merely knowing their secrets, he couldn't have told. Maybe it was because reading their mail seemed a lot like deliberately reading their thoughts. He could do that, too, but . . . it was wrong to do so, unless he was under direct orders. Well, probably the same went for mail-reading.

"I reckon I'm jest as glad I weren't ordered to report back t'him," he replied, deciding that, yes, if he had to, he would throttle down the feeling that he was doing something embarrassing and read other peoples' mail, if ordered. Such orders would only be coming from the King or Nikolas after all, and if he couldn't trust them, who could he trust? "Since ye didn' say anythin' I reckon he was all right with us?"

"He had to take the chance that *his* mail would be intercepted and read—not that I saw any signs of tampering—so he was a bit oblique, but yes." She sighed again. "So that hurdle was jumped moons ago. Father the King's Own, however . . . requires things of his daughter. I wasn't going to bring all this up until later."

He shrugged, ever so slightly, enough for her to feel it, not so much it would disturb her comfort. "Might's well git it over."

"Well, we were talking about getting married right away, and . . . he basically said that we were going to have to give people time to get used to the idea. And we were talking about doing the same thing that Bear and Lena did, and he made it very clear that no, we were going to have to—"

"Oh no," he groaned. "Dammit, a big show was the *last* thing—"

"Well, we're going to have to put one on," she said. And she didn't sound nearly as unhappy about it as Mags was.

:Of course she isn't, you dolt,: Dallen scolded him. *:She's been the little brown mouse in the corner all her life. Watching her friends in the wealthy and highborn get to sparkle and shine in lovely gowns, and be made much of, like the chief actresses in a popular play. And now, she will get to sparkle and shine and be made much of, herself.:*

:But I make much of her!: he protested.

"You're talking with Dallen, aren't you?" she asked. To his relief, she sounded amused.

"Uh. Yes?"

She giggled. "Don't let me interrupt you. When you get quiet like that, I know he's giving you a piece of his mind."

"Uh . . . right . . ."

:Oh yes. And only you and her father ever have. How did it feel to be the Kirball champion?:

:Uh . . . what?: Where had *that* come from?

:How did it feel to be the Kirball champion? You liked it, didn't you? You liked people looking at you with admiration?:

All right, now he saw what Dallen was getting at but—seriously? *:It was a stupid game? All right, maybe not a stupid game, I mean, we was learning about war and tactics and all but everybody else figgered it fer a game and—:*

:And nothing. You enjoyed being made much of, and there's nothing wrong with that. You didn't let it go to your head. This is just exactly the same thing. Everyone wants that, at least once in their lives. You see?:

And that was when he knew exactly what he should say. "Know what? I reckon that'll be fun."

She went very still. "You really mean that?"

He took a deep breath, and thought about how everyone looked forward to the Fairs and Festivals . . . and this would just be one more sort of Festival, right? Smaller, mostly for friends . . . aye, well, alla th' Collegia, pretty much but . . . friends, sure . . . and why not? "Aye," he said. "Who don't like a party?" His arms tightened around her. "It'll be great! Shoot, it'd be a damn shame t'throw away a good reason fer a shindig!"

She squirmed around in his arms and kissed him so enthusiastically he thought that the conversation was over for a few moments . . . but then she broke it off, breathlessly. "You don't mind that we'll have to—you know—wait for a while?"

"I—uh—what?" It took him a *long* moment to drag his mind back to the fact that she wasn't done yet. *Does Bey have to go through things like this? Do all fellers?*

"I don't mean . . . not *be* together." She flushed. "I mean, betrothed couples . . . it's done all the time but . . . there's supposed to be . . ."

"Huh?" Fortunately, there was something working in his head, because a moment later, a fragment from *somewhere*, Dallen, maybe, managed to shove itself into the front of his brain. "Oh . . . right. We cain't just do what we talked about, right. So there's gotta be a buncha formal stuff." He freed an arm so he could scratch his head in puzzlement. "I mean, I ain't so up on what we need t'do. On'y weddin's I ever saw was the Prince an' Princess, an' Bear and Lena's, on'y I never actually *saw* thet—"

"Father will probably tell us," she pointed out, and then relaxed and giggled a little. "Father will probably talk to whoever it is that figures out what sort of Court etiquette has to be satisfied and hand us our orders. If he hasn't got a handful of detailed instructions waiting for us now!"

Mags sighed. "He prolly does . . . on t'other hand, that'll make it easier. Like a dance, I reckon. Jest foller the steps, an' there ye are."

Too bad I ain't so good at dancin'.

He really, truly, did not want to think about what a complication this was going to bring to a situation that was *already* complicated. Because he was going to be going into Whites, which meant he'd be a Herald, which meant, instead of being a student, he'd actually have a job to do. A job he would be expected to turn up for. Heralds didn't just laze about. And Heralds couldn't go missing from their jobs, either. So his continued training, and his *work,* of being a clandestine agent, would have to be juggled along with the job.

At least Amily knew all about that sort of juggling, having watched her father do it for her entire life.

But further thought along those lines was shoved to the side. Amily had gone back to kissing him, and he was perfectly prepared to abandon *thinking* in favor of *feeling,* at least for a while.

Amily woke at dawn; she always woke at dawn. She had been relieved to discover that Mags was an early-riser too. This morning, though, she could tell he wasn't awake yet, and the makeshift bed was, for once, so comfortable she didn't feel like shifting yet. So she just curled up "spooned" against him, and considered their homecoming.

On the one hand, it was annoying that, once again, being the daughter of the King's Own was going to interfere with *her* life. On the other hand, she had long ago gotten over the notion that life was somehow supposed to be fair, and as *things interfering with her life* went, this one wasn't too bad. She wasn't one of the girls who'd dreamed about having an impressive wedding, nor really, had any of her friends been the sort who did, but she knew plenty of girls who came to Court, matchmaking parents in tow, who had apparently thought about nothing else for their entire lives. She had really just wanted to get married the way Lena and Bear had; quickly, quietly and privately.

But once again, it seemed that was the sort of thing that the daughter of the King's Own just didn't do. At least Mags was all right with that. And since both of them had good, stout senses of humor, and neither of them was likely to get at all stressed over things going wrong—which, they inevitably would—it would probably be a lot of fun. It would be a very good excuse to gather the friends together who had scattered across the face of Valdemar.

Anyway, according to her Father, it wouldn't, and couldn't, happen right away. So they wouldn't have to think about it for a while, and there would be time to make sure all the things that *would* go wrong got sorted out.

And somewhere, somehow, in all of that, she had to figure out this Gift she'd developed. *I wonder if it started when he began Mindspeaking at me.* Mags had a very rare Gift of

Mindspeech. He could speak to and be heard by anyone at all, whether they had the Gift or not. *I wonder if . . . if when something like that happens, it can knock loose any Gift you might have and set it going, like a stuck wheel.* Gifts were one thing she *hadn't* studied.

Mags was very still when he slept; he hardly moved at all. Maybe that was a habit left over from his horrible childhood, when he and all the rest of the orphans had slept together in a heap all winter long for warmth. Being squirmy probably got you exiled to the edge of the pile. She thought about getting up, but before she could make her mind up about it, she sensed he had gone from sleep to waking.

"Mornin', sunshine," he said. "Reckon soonest started, soonest done, aye?"

"Aye," she agreed, and put away her thoughts, for now, in favor of doing.

And so, for the third time in his life, Mags rode into Haven.

This time, he wasn't riding into the unknown. This time, he was not bringing more trouble with him.

This time, it really felt as if he was coming home.

The sight of Haven from afar, the irregular pool of buildings around the rise on which the Palace and Collegia were built, no longer struck him with awe or trepidation. They called it "the Hill," but from here, he could see it wasn't a hill, not as such. It was a gentle slope up to a higher level of the plain on which Haven stood. The river bisected the Palace grounds, separating the Palace and Collegia from Companion's Field, and then tumbled boisterously down to the town, and meandered through it and away.

Beyond the skirts of the city were farms spreading out all around, some with groves of fruit or nut trees, all of them with windbreaks of lines of trees planted along the hedges that marked the divisions into fields. There was no wild forest this near to Haven. But there were trees in plenty, and all of them were in autumn colors, though those colors were fading fast, and already some of the leaves were falling. Thrifty farmers were harvesting those leaves to heap up over their winter-hardy crops to protect them from the frost and winter cold. Mags wasn't anywhere near familiar enough with farming to know what crops could be kept—stored, really—right in the fields well into winter, but he knew there were some. Winter squashes, parsnips, and cabbages, he was certain of, because they made their appearance looking tasty and fresh all winter long in the markets. Out there in the fields, as they passed, there were farmers working, making mounds of leaves, brittle, aged straw and hay too old to use for fodder, weighing them down with a light layer of sand. They waved if they happened to look up and notice the Companions, but mostly they were too intent on their work to look up even for a moment. It wasn't as if the sight of Heralds and Companions was a nov-elty to anyone, this close to Haven.

Jakyr caught him eyeing the farmers; they exchanged a look, and Jakyr laughed.

"We'd all of us starve if we had to live on a farm. I have no idea what they're doing," the Herald said ruefully.

"Nor me. I'm a city girl," Lita said from the driver's bench of the caravan.

"I'm . . . mixed," Mags said. "I know every single sort of wild plant that can be eaten without givin' yerself a bellyache. But I dunno how t'grow a blessed thing. An' I dunno how to store any of it, neither. The mine kids ate whatever we could get our hands on an' never saved nothin'."

"Nobody can know everything," Jakyr said philosophically.

:And it is highly unlikely you will ever have to pass your-self off as a farmhand,: chuckled Dallen. :Intrigue of the sort you will have to investigate rarely takes place among the cab-bages.:

Well, that was true enough.

It was past time for the Harvest Fair, but Mags was not particularly disappointed. Truth to tell, he was of the mind that he was likely to be busy enough settling himself into his new duties and his new life without the distraction of a Fair.

:Nikolas has plans,: Dallen interjected.

:I'm certain he does.:

The air had that scent of old leaves and faint damp, tinged with woodsmoke, that Mags remembered even from his days as a mine-slave as the signature of autumn. Back then, the smell of ham and bacon curing had been a torment, but there had always been the chance that he would be able to get his hands on a scrap of meat or two, and there would be bones in the thin cabbage soup. And autumn meant nuts, if he could manage to get out into the woods while there was some light. So although autumn wasn't the "season of plenty" as far as his memories were concerned, it was, at least, the season of being less hungry. . . .

Somehow, no matter how he prospered, those days of terrible want never really left him.

But I *can leave* them, *and think about what I have now,* he reminded himself, and resolutely brought his attention back to the present.

Every smoke-house within sight of the road was going—and Mags was very glad that they'd had a fine breakfast, or the faint hint of bacony-goodness on the wind would have probably driven him insane.

"I, for one, will be glad to get off the road at last," Lita said, as Amily joined her on the driver's bench, closing the little hatch door behind her.

"I think we all will," Amily agreed. "Are you going to go back to being the head of Bardic Collegium?"

Lita shrugged. "That's not for me to say," she replied. "I'll leave it up to the senior staff. But . . . chances are, they'll put me back in the hot seat."

Jakyr snorted. "There's not much chance that they won't, Lita. You were too good at your job."

"Well . . . there's a little bit of politics involved. And more than a bit of reluctance on my part." She freed a hand to rub it across her eyes. "It would be a lot easier to just go back to being a senior instructor." She glanced sideways at Jakyr, who was wearing a rueful expression. "And just what are you thinking?"

"That it would be a lot easier to go be a senior instructor, because the last year taught me that I am nowhere near as young as I thought I was," he said, which startled Lita so much she unbalanced for a moment. He laughed at her. "What?" he demanded.

The vanners looked over their shoulders at her in bewilderment and stopped dead in the road. She chirruped to them and slapped their backs with the reins to get them going again.

"You?" she said.

He leveled a look at her. "Who was the one that was going on about second chances?"

She flushed, and looked away. Mags glanced at Amily, who just gave a little shrug.

:Don't ask me, I wasn't privy to the conversation,: Dallen declared.

Mags feigned shock. :What! Gossip you don't know? Inconceivable!:

Dallen snorted.

"And anyway, the Healers are probably going to insist that an old man like me needs more time to recover from getting perforated like a pincushion than I've had," he pointed out. "A couple of seasons as an instructor should tell us if I can change my roving ways without going insane."

"Going?" Lita said under her breath—but loud enough so everyone could hear.

Jakyr just chuckled—which was a very different reaction to the one he would have displayed on the journey out.

:Do you—: Mags asked Dallen, tentatively.

:I am not in the business of predicting the success or failure of romances,: Dallen said dryly.

Each time they topped a hill, the city was a little nearer. Mags judged they would probably reach the outskirts a bit after noon. It was going to be very strange to be at the Collegium again, but without Lena and Bear around. But it was going to be equally strange to be there and not be going to classes. . . .

On the other hand, that was going to be something of a relief as well. No more worrying about passing or failing something. No more studying! Well, not formal studying, anyway. He'd have to learn about things, surely, but he wouldn't be facing an examination at the end of it.

:No, but if you don't master what you are studying, you might face something a lot more serious than merely failing an examination,: Dallen pointed out.

:Thank you, Master Wet Blanket,: he retorted.

:I live to serve.:

It was *his* turn to snort.

"Well, I cannot wait for a proper hot bath, one I can just wallow in until the water turns cold," Amily laughed. "And since we'll be arriving before there is any sort of stampede for the bathing rooms, that is the very first thing I intend to get."

"That's my biggest complaint, I think, next to hard beds," Lita agreed. "Even when there is a bath-house in a village, or a bathing area in an inn, you never get to soak as long as you want because there is always someone tapping her foot and waiting for you to get out of the water."

"My featherbed. Meals I don't have to cook. Firewood I don't have to cut. Hot baths whenever I want them . . ." Amily sighed. "It's good to be back."

"Aye," Mags agreed, as they neared the edges of the city itself. " 'Tis."

To Mags' strangely mingled relief and disappointment, there was no one waiting to greet them as they came in through the side gate mostly used by Heralds. Part of him had been dreading that there would be a crowd gathered, and part of him had hoped there would be. But in fact, there was no one waiting at all. And . . . really, why should there be? By this time, most, if not all, of the Trainees who were about his age were in the Field themselves, having gotten their Whites, and now paired with a senior Herald to supervise their first months of work according to the new training system. He knew all of that from the letters they had all picked up at Guard-posts on their circuit, many of which had been from those same friends. There were people here still, teachers mostly, who knew him well—but this time of day was right in the middle of classes. He wouldn't want to disrupt classes just because he and Amily had turned up again.

And at the same time, it was a relief, because right at this moment, Mags just wanted to get settled in and not be fussed over.

All four of them already had their personal belongings packed in two bags each; not their clothing, which after so many months on the road was going to need a serious laundering, and in some cases, mending, before it was fit to wear again, but everything that was *not* clothing. When Lita pulled the caravan up to the stables, grooms came to take charge, and servants came to discover what was to go where.

Servants. . . . It was going to take some time to get used to this . . . he was a Herald now. Servants came and did things for him.

I'd better get used to it quickly. If I have to fit in with the wealthy or the highborn, I can't slip and go to do something for myself.

"Deal with the sorting out, Mags, would you?" Jakyr asked, and without waiting for a reply, he picked up one of his two bags and went around to the other side of the wagon. While Mags was sorting out what went where and with whom with the grooms and servants, Jakyr and Lita both vanished, and the grooms took the wagon and vanners away, leaving him with Amily and their bags.

"Well," he said, feeling suddenly very awkward. "I s'ppose you need to be getting back to your rooms—"

"Ah—" she said, a little awkwardly. "Father . . ."

And now he felt exceedingly stupid. Maybe *he* didn't have anyone who should be breaking off what they were doing to greet him but—

"Right, right!" he said hastily. "You go. Catch up with me somewhere later—"

"I'll meet you at your room in a candlemark or so," she said, and grinned. "After Father and I finish, *I* want a bath, and I expect you do, too."

He had to chuckle at that. "Reckon I need one too. Right. Meet you at m'room."

Another servant had showed up at this point, and at Amily's direction, picked up her bags and followed her, leaving

Mags to take his own and head for the stables, with Dallen following like some sort of enormous dog.

:Nothing like some sort of enormous dog, thank you very much.: With an indignant snort, Dallen trotted on ahead and put *himself* into the hands of a groom that appeared as if he had been summoned. *:You go get that bath. You were right. You need it.:*

Rather than taking offense, Mags just chuckled, opened the door to his stable room, and chucked his bags onto the bed. Then he blinked and stared. The room had . . . changed. It was still *his* room, because those were his books on the table and in the bookcase, but someone had been in here, vastly improving it. There was a brand new wardrobe up against the wall, instead of a chest for his clothing, and a brand new, larger bed with a big goosedown comforter on it. He raised an eyebrow at that, but the bed he'd been using *was* an old one, very much due for replacement.

It certainly did look as if someone had been hard at work in here. There were four chairs and a real table, and there was a padded bench with a padded back and two more chairs arranged in a group so people could sit and talk. The walls had been whitewashed, making things much lighter. Someone had also checked all the glazing on the window and re-puttied it, sealing it well against leaks and drafts, added shutters on the inside to be closed against the winter cold, and put up two sets of curtains—a heavy one, and a lighter one, presumably to let breezes in come summer. There were new rugs on the floor, and one of them was even made of sheepskin with the wool on, which would be nice for sprawling on. And, of course, that handsome new wardrobe.

He opened the wardrobe, and as he had expected, there were Whites in his size waiting for him. No disguises of course; those had been either stored down in Haven, or, if common enough, in the chest of his personal clothing. He raised the lid, and satisfied himself that nothing had been removed or disturbed—except that all of his Trainee Grays were gone. *Someone else is gonna get those nice sets of high-born Grays I got loaned,* he thought with a little regret. But, then again . . . he was a Herald now, and *all* Heralds had Dress Whites. There was probably something just as fancy waiting in the wardrobe.

He looked again at the waiting Whites, and suddenly became uncomfortably aware of the fact that, compared with the ones in the wardrobe, the uniform he was wearing was . . . a bit dingy. And a bit shabby. And Dallen was right, he was a bit dingy and shabby as well . . . just thinking about it made him begin to feel a bit itchy.

And that was all it took for him to seize a new set of clothing and everything that went with it and head for the bathing room.

Either Amily and her father had had quite a long talk, or she must have made good on her pledge to soak until the water turned cold, because he was clean, clothed, and back at his room, rearranging things to suit himself, when she arrived just as the dinner bell was ringing at the Collegium. "Do I still eat with the Trainees?" he wondered aloud, as she paused in the doorway to look with surprise at his changed quarters.

"If you want," she said. "It's up to you. Father does once in a while. When he is not eating with the Court, which is what he mostly does because he's King's Own, he eats in our rooms because he needs the quiet. But Father is a special case. Heralds between circuits can eat with the Court, in the Collegium dining hall, or in their rooms, or go down to inns in Haven. It really all depends on what they feel like at the time. There's no rules about it."

"Oh, that's too much to think about," he said with a laugh, as she made a face at him. "What do you want to do? Though

I think I'd rather not eat with the Court, if I am supposed to be keeping myself quiet and not be noticed."

She linked arms with him and pulled him toward the door. "We still have friends who are Trainees, and I expect they'd like to see us," she pointed out as he pulled the door shut behind them. Moving quietly, they passed by Dallen's stall on their way out. Mags had to chuckle; Dallen was fast asleep, with a little bit of hay sticking out of the corner of his mouth. It was oddly endearing.

Wish I could fall asleep that easily.

The weather was still outstanding, and as they neared Herald's Collegium, Mags sniffed appreciatively. It smelled as if tonight was a batter-fried fish night, something they rarely got at inns, and never made for themselves. "Oh! Fried fish!" Amily said with glee as she recognized the scent, and hurried her steps, tugging at his arm.

I guess things went good with her Da. . . . That was a profound relief.

Not that he wasn't completely certain that if Nikolas had disapproved of him and Amily being together he would have heard about it a *long* time ago. But . . . well . . . there was always that little bit of doubt. Because if there was anything that Mags was good at, it was doubt.

As it happened, it was Amily who had a great many friends still at the three Collegia, and not Mags—but Mags didn't actually mind, though it was *just* a little melancholy to sit down at the familiar tables and not have Bear and Lena to one side of him. Still, within moments all of Amily's acquaintances had taken him as one of their number, not minding the Whites at all, and he found their chatter vastly entertaining. It was relaxing to *not* have to be analyzing everything the people around him said, matching it to their tone of voice, and trying to figure out if they had some sort of hidden agenda.

Amily's friends all wanted to know how Bear and Lena were, expressing some envy that they had gotten what one of the Bardic Trainees described as "The softest job *ever!*" And Mags was happy to tell them that this posting was going to be a very nice position for both of them.

"A *Baron,*" the lad said, sighing. "I mean, she deserves it. But . . . a *Baron.* Did you see the castle?"

"Manor," Amily corrected with a laugh. "Yes, we did. Baron Burns—and isn't that alliterative?—has a manor that's almost the size of the Palace, I think. He's rather imposing to look at, tall and very, very dignified, but very easy in his ways. Lena is his new Court Bard, so she'll be doing whatever it is that Court Bards do—"

"Direct and rehearse the other musicians, write new pieces when the Baron wants them, perform," the boy—Rendall? Yes that was it—supplied. "Likely she'll be asked to play for the Baron's wife and her ladies every day. And if she doesn't perform herself, she'll be responsible for the music at supper every night, and if there's any dancing or anything after."

"That sounds like a lot of work," Amily said approvingly, as another friend, anxious to give them a proper welcome home, went to the serving hatch herself and brought back a heaping platter of fried fish so fresh it was smoking, and put it down on the table. Mags knew better than to snatch with his fingers when the fish was that hot; he used a pair of forks to fill his plate and Amily's with the hot fish, steamed greens, and fresh rolls.

"Well, it don't seem like work when you're doing what you *want* to be doing," Rendall said. "You know?"

"I reckon you're gonna make a good Bard," Mags said, as he blew on a piece of fish to cool it down. It occurred to him then, that maybe he shouldn't be worrying so much about what he was going to do now that he was a full Herald. If nothing else, he was going to be doing what he *wanted* to be doing.

Sure beats chipping sparklies out of rocks.

"Well, I, uh," Rendall said, blushing so hard it showed through his tan. "Thanks?"

Mags couldn't speak just then as he had a mouth full of luscious fish. He just nodded. "You're welcome," Amily said warmly, with an amused glance at Mags.

Their table began to fill up with people Mags certainly would consider his *friends,* even if they weren't as close as the folks who had been on his Kirball team, or Bear and Lena. Before he was halfway through his first plate of fish, it was starting to feel like a homecoming after all.

He had always liked this room, anyway. It was big, without being pretentious. Plain wooden walls and floor, one wall with enough plain glazed windows to allow plenty of light in the daytime. Boasting a high ceiling with exposed rafters, full of plain wooden tables and benches, with a few wooden chairs, it was a room that held a lot of good memories for him. He looked up and down the table at the mix of uniforms, and the cheerful faces, and knew why he was here.

These, too, were his friends, his brothers and sisters. This was where he belonged.

It wasn't possible to just slip away, not when you were the center of attention at an impromptu party, so Mags and Amily went the other direction, bidding a sort of formal goodnight to everyone still at the table.

"Tired already?" someone laughed.

"Matty, we've been on th'road for most of a year," Mags said, with exaggerated patience. "We've been sleepin' in Way-stations or bunks in a wagon. What d'you think?"

Matty laughed, and everyone else took it in good part; the group broke up, then, and once Mags and Amily got out into the hallway, he said what was *really* on his mind.

"I reckon it's about time to track down your Da." They both knew that Herald Nikolas would not have broken into his duties for anyone but his beloved daughter; his protégé could certainly wait for a more opportune time. But now dinner was about to be served for the Court, and that was not a "duty" as such. If they didn't make themselves available to Nikolas, he would surely come looking for them.

Amily's lips twitched a little nervously. "You're right. We might as well go to Herald's Wing. Have Dallen tell Rolan where we are, I suppose."

:Already done,: Dallen said sleepily. *:Rolan says Nikolas will be there shortly.:*

They left the Collegium through the doors that connected it to the Herald's Wing, where Heralds all had at least a little room for the times when they were not actually out on circuit. Most of them were out so much that the rooms were half or a quarter of the size of Mags' stable room and Spartan indeed, except, perhaps, for the quality of the bed. But the King's Own lived here full time, and had a suite of rooms that included separate accommodations for his daughter, and were situated nearest to the guarded door that led to the Palace proper.

When they arrived there, they discovered that someone had ordered wine to be brought, with three cups. On a little table near one of three chairs that had been grouped together stood the pitcher, the cups beside it, and water beading up on its side. Mags raised an eyebrow at Amily when they saw that; she just shrugged. They took seats, and waited.

What could have quickly become an awkward moment never had a chance to devolve. Nikolas himself pushed open the door within moments of their sitting down. They both got to their feet immediately, but he motioned to them to sit again. Quickly pouring wine for all three, Nikolas handed them cups, then took his own and dropped into his chair.

"Politics," he said in tones of disgust. "I'd rather be Willy the Weasel cheating my customers than sit through another interminable debate about nothing that matters."

Mags had to chuckle. "I see nothin's changed."

"Oh, everything has changed," Nikolas replied, and took a

long, slow drink of his wine. "Now that people are reasonably sure that the King or the Prince are not about to be murdered in their beds by shadowy assassins with uncanny abilities, they are now free to act like the self-centered fools they are." He grimaced. "Arguing over every last penny that comes out of their pockets in taxes, and arguing even more if it goes to something that doesn't directly benefit them. Idiots. Fortunately the last thing the King needs me for is handling these . . . people. But I still have to listen to them." He took another long drink of the wine. "Welcome back, Mags. I am very tired of having to be in two places at once. You could not have come back at a better time."

"Yessir," Mags said, diffidently. He wasn't certain what else to say. Fortunately Nikolas took that problem right away from him.

"First of all, you needn't stare at me as if you think I am likely to challenge you over the honor of my daughter," the King's Own said dryly. "Assuming that my dainty darling didn't rip my face off for being an overbearing father, I've had a year to get used to the idea that she isn't my little girl anymore, that she was never *my* little girl in the sense that I could control anything she set her mind to do. I just want you two to promise me two things."

"Yessir!" Mags said immediately, before Nikolas could even make his requests. He was so relieved that Amily's father was not taking this situation . . . poorly . . . that he would have promised just about anything.

Nikolas laughed. "Just be discreet, and I'd prefer you didn't actually get *married* for at least a year."

Since that was the very opposite of what Mags had expected the Herald would say, all that Mags could do was gape at him. It was Amily who frowned, and asked, more than a bit sharply, *"Why?* Or rather, why shouldn't we?"

Nikolas sighed. "As always, my dearest, there is nothing that happens in our lives without political ramifications. The

Prince and Princess have only been wed for a year. I'd like it to be two before anyone connected to the Throne has even the quietest of weddings. Then there is the personal consideration. I know you two have been through very trying and dangerous times together. I'd like to make sure your love affair can bear the boring and tedious times as well."

Mags blinked. He hadn't thought of that. It was a good point.

Amily looked rebellious for just a flash, but then, she shook her head. "I was going to argue, but dammit, Father, you're right. I've seen couples just turn . . . sour on each other when things were quiet and boring. Oh! Why do you always have to be right?"

"I'm not always, but I'm flattered you think I am," Nikolas said dryly. "Bear in mind that adversity can have the same effect, but that's usually financial adversity. . . ."

He left unsaid the obvious fact that no Herald would ever have to suffer financial adversity. Not while the country was ruled the way it was.

And if things changed that drastically, well, Mags didn't think there would *be* a Valdemar anymore.

Nikolas leaned back, his arms draped along the back and sides of the chair. "I know you two were concerned about, well, a father's inevitable reaction to the two of you pairing up, and you were correct to be concerned. It's a rather atavistic tendency of fathers to be overprotective of their daughters. But I had most of a year to cram my instincts down into a box and sit on them, and most of a year to remind myself daily that my daughter was intelligent, shrewd, and that I certainly did not *own* her."

Mags chuckled weakly. So far, he had barely wet his mouth with the wine, and only because his mouth was so dry with nervousness.

"I really don't have anyone to 'blame' but myself, seeing as I shoved you two together so much you would either have conceived a terrible hatred for each other, or the inevitable opposite." Nikolas smiled crookedly. "I got used to the fact that my poor crippled little girl was neither crippled nor little any-more, and she *certainly* didn't need anyone's pity. And I had a year to look over the young bucks at court and decide that I would probably attempt to kill half of them if they even *looked* at her, and she'd kill the other half before I got a chance to."

Amily was startled into a giggle.

"Then I reminded myself that although I had no objection and every trust in a young Herald, a young Herald—all except you, Mags—was going to be out in the Field most of his life, and that was no life for Amily. And so, gradually, I managed to reconcile myself to this, then even come to appreciate it. And here we are, painlessly sitting down together, and this time it is me telling you I'd like you to delay, just to be sure . . . but only delay the wedding." He sighed. "I remember being your age. Let's just leave it at that. Be discreet."

Amily made a mocking face at her father. "Honestly, Father, I think we have *some* self-control!"

"All right then, lecture over. Now, assignments. You are both old enough to take on fully adult responsibilities. Amily, you are officially attached to the Royal Chronicler. You made great progress in the Heraldic Archives, which fortunately has not been completely undone in your absence. Put it back in order, then do whatever the Royal Chronicler wants you to do." He smiled a little. "Now that the weather is turning, that won't be a hardship; you'll find yourself very glad to be snug in the Archives while poor Mags trudges about the city in all weathers. Mags, I want you to start establishing several per-sonas. Things you can drop into at a moment's notice, without attracting attention. I don't have anything in particular that I want you to investigate at the moment, though that is likely to change at a moment's notice, so it is best to get things in place now. Just establish things you can slip into and out of and keep your ear to the ground."

Mags nodded. He already had some ideas there. It would

be easy enough to impersonate a beggar again, for instance, and people looked right past beggars most of the time. "Is the pawn shop still in business?" he asked.

"Yes, and that will be one of your personas; I've been Willy the Weasel for as long as I have been doing what I do, and you've already got the Weasel's nephew well established. Use your own discretion about what else you establish, and let me know what you've done. If you need money for anything, come to me and I'll arrange it."

Mags straightened a little, and nodded. So, this was quite, quite serious now. Nikolas hadn't stipulated any budget; that meant that he was free to spend as much as he needed to. "Anything else I should be doing?" he asked.

"Well, obviously you have to have an official position as well as the clandestine one, so you'll be assigned as a Herald down in the City, attached to the Guard. *They* know that your investigations will take you off on cases that are not theirs, and they will expect you to have to excuse yourself most of the time. I worked with this exact Guardpost back before I became King's Own, and one of my best agents is one of their number. In fact, you know them, you've brought them pawned articles in the past."

Mags brightened a little at that; he did know them, and, more to the point, they knew him.

"I'll start right away, sir," he said immediately.

Nikolas nodded. "Good." He handed Mags a peculiar copper coin; it wasn't Valdemaran, but Mags wasn't familiar enough with coinage to know where it was from. "You'll get your assignment paperwork tomorrow; when you get it, ride down there, and give them this along with the mandate. They'll know what it means."

Mags stowed the coin in his belt-pouch, and finally took a real swallow of his wine. *Straight back to work,* he thought, with resignation. *Oh well. Nikolas works his own self like a mine-slavey, reckon he figures everybody else ought to, too.*

He wondered if Amily was feeling the same touch of resignation, or even resentment. If she was, she didn't show it, but as he had learned out there on the circuit, she was adept at disguising her feelings when she felt it was necessary.

————————

Amily was ruefully amused. Rueful, because, of course, it was inevitable that her father would put them straight to work—after they had *been* working for the entire year. Amused, for the same reason.

"Well, time to temper the bitter with the sweet," her father said, after emptying his wine cup. Then he stood up. "Come along you two," he said. "I've something to show you."

She exchanged a puzzled look with Mags, but both of them got up, and followed Nikolas. First, out of the Heralds' Wing and into the gardens, then across the gardens to Healer's Collegium. It was well after dark by this time, but the weather was still pleasant in the early evening, so the gardens were still kept completely illuminated for the benefit of those who wished to stroll in them. Amily wondered what on earth her father was taking them to Healer's Collegium for, especially at this late hour. He puzzled her even more by leading them in through the entrance to the part of the building that served as the winter conservatory for herbs and the quarters for whoever was in charge of tending those herbs. Until last year, that had been Bear. *Is he going to introduce us to Bear's successor?* she wondered.

But then, when they got into the living-quarters, she saw that all the lamps had been lit . . . and there, in the center of the main room, were *her* bags.

It took her a moment to grasp what this meant, but when she did, she felt her eyes widen. She turned to her father, still partly in shock, to see him grinning at her. And Mags was looking just as surprised as she was.

"You're an adult now, with an adult's responsibilities," Nikolas said, with a sort of rueful pleasure. "It's time you had quarters of your own. No one in Healer's knows how to tend the herbs as well as you do, since you helped Bear so much. So until they get someone up here who *does,* these rooms are yours."

She looked around at the sitting room, so familiar, and yet, without Bear and Lena's things here, unfamiliar. She thought of how she had, more than once, coveted this place, both for the privacy and for the proximity to growing things in the midst of winter.

"But when they find someone—?" she asked.

"By then we'll have figured out if you should get rooms with the Court officials, with the highborn, with Princess Lydia's ladies, or if you'll be married," he replied. "I'm inclined to think it will be the last, since herb-Healers seem disinclined to come to the Collegium, but you never know. The Princess put in a claim on you, so you might well end up lodged with her ladies, since the Princess outranks the Chronicler."

On the whole, Amily much preferred this arrangement. With its separate entrance to the outdoors, made so that someone going to and from the outdoor herb gardens would not track muck into the clean environs of the Collegium itself, she'd be able to come and go as she liked without anyone the wiser. That wouldn't be as easy, quartered with the ladies of the Princess' Court. She hoped that any herb-Healer teachers would stay away from Healer's until she didn't need these rooms anymore. It was more than worth the little work of tending and watering some plants for the unparalleled privacy.

"I had all your things moved here a couple of moons ago, but other than the obvious, I left it all for you to arrange to your liking," Nikolas continued. "So, I will leave you to it." Then that rueful smile was back. "You've both turned into adults on me," he said. "And every cautionary bit of advice I might have given you is either something Jak and Lita already told you, or something you've learned on your own. I'll just say this. You'll always be a hundred times stronger together than you are separately."

And with that, he left, and the two of them were alone. Alone in a place that was *hers,* with no one to snoop, however inadvertently, and no one to have to answer to. Mags suddenly grinned at her. "How 'bout we set things to rights here, then decide what to do?"

That seemed like a perfect idea to her.

———————

"Scared?" he asked, as they walked back to his room at the stable—because as nice as the new rooms were, she wanted the *complete* privacy that the stable provided, at least for a while.

"Yes. No. Both." She sighed. "It's not as if I haven't done this work before but this time—"

He nodded. "Aye, I get it. This time, it's different. Before, if ye didn't feel good that day, or ye just wanted t'do something else, well, it was all volunteer, and no one was lookin' over yer shoulder. Now . . . now it's a job."

"Yes! Exactly." She made a face. "I used to wonder how the ladies of the Court could bear not having anything useful to do, but all of a sudden, I have this very stupid envy of them."

"Ain't stupid, but look at it this way. We're doin' stuff we like t'do. Ain't too many people get that." He squeezed her hand, and she squeezed it back. *He's right.* "But that don't mean we can't wish we was idle rich and highborn, sometimes!"

She had to laugh. *He's right about that, too!*

"Even Father's had days when he just wanted to run off and fish," she confessed.

"The only reason I don't get as many of them days, is because the best part of my life started when I come here," he reminded her.

By this point they had reached the stables and gone inside. Even as a tiny child, she had loved the Companions' Stable; it was everything that was wonderful and comforting about any stable, but without any of the drawbacks associated with having *horses* in one. The only time anyone needed to muck out a Companion's stall was if they'd all been shut into the building by dreadful weather. Right now the only scents in the air were the pleasant ones of clean beast, straw, and hay. There were dim lanterns at each end of the stable, and the Companions themselves dozed in the soft, filtered light.

Despite the fact that she knew very well they were surrounded by curious, sometimes mischievous minds, it still felt as if she had far more privacy from prying than she would have back at Healer's Collegium.

And that is probably a ridiculous illusion, she thought, laughing at herself a little. *But I'll cherish it while I can.*

In the morning, as they both got dressed, Mags wondered if he should be the one to point out that the bathing rooms were *up at the Collegia,* not down here . . . when Amily finished pulling on her boots and said, "Bother. The bathing rooms are going to be a long trudge when it gets any colder."

"Sometimes I wonder if you got some sort of Mindspeech Gift you haven't figured out you got," he replied.

She started a little, and turned to look at him, brown eyes wide. "Why do you say that?"

" 'Cause, missy, seems like you read m'mind all the time." He leaned over, planted a kiss on her nose, and stood up, stamping his own boots into place. "So, I crave anything for breakfast *but* porridge." Porridge had been a staple on the road, both what they cooked in the Waystations overnight, and what inns served. He always reminded himself, whenever it was burned, or full of lumps, or congealed and cold, that back in the mines he would have cheerfully licked the bowl clean . . . but he was mightily tired of the stuff.

"Mhm," she agreed, nodding her head. "Flatcakes, I was thinking."

"Sausage-and-egg pie."

"Fruit soup with cream."

"Bacon, cooked perfect an' not burnt up or limp!"

Naming foods they would like to see offered up for breakfast occupied them all the way to the dining hall.

They parted once they were both fed, conscious of their new duties. Since Nikolas hadn't been specific about what he intended for Mags last night, Mags had the feeling he was going to rectify that this morning, so he wanted to report to the King's Own before the Herald needed to join the King for *his* official duties.

He found Nikolas, as he had expected, setting aside the dishes from his own meal, in his quarters. The door was standing open; Rolan, of course, would have told Nikolas that he was coming.

"I believe," the King's Own said, meditatively, "That I shall make the extra bedroom into an office. Do you know, I have never actually had one?"

"That don't seem right," Mags observed, waiting a moment in the doorway for an actual invitation to come in. "Even Stablemaster has an office."

"Well, I never seemed to be able to stop moving long enough to need one." Nikolas chuckled. "Perhaps with my girl operating on her own responsibility, one less responsibility of my own will allow me to sit in one place long enough to document things properly. Close the door, come in, sit down. I have a particular assignment I want you to take on."

Mags did as he was told, taking one of the comfortable chairs opposite Nikolas; he had the feeling that, whatever it was that Nikolas wanted him to do, it was going to be challenging.

"You've been gone long enough that you've fallen out of the minds of people here in the Court as the Kirball champion. In fact, they have a new one. Diffcrent from you, of course, but young Robin, in *his* way, is probably better than you were. This means the courtiers have forgotten what you look like," Nikolas said, his eyes unreadable. Which meant, as Mags knew, that he was going to be adamant about this job, and he was not going to accept "I can't do that" as an answer. "I need someone *of* the Court, *in* the Court, high enough to become a confidant, but not so high that he's a rival. And considered trustworthy and apolitical so no one will worry about telling him things for fear they might get to ears they shouldn't."

Mags blinked. Become a courtier? That was a pretty tall order. "Don't you have to be born into the highborn families?" he askcd, cautiously, and consciously shaping his speech to lose every vestige of his lowly origins, choosing his words and inflection with care. "Granted, now we know who my parents were, and they would certainly *qualify,* but I very much doubt such a . . . sensational parentage would allow me to be as innocuous as you'd prefer."

He knew Nikolas well enough by now to sce the very slight relaxation in his posture that told him he'd given the King's Own the right answer. "I have that sorted. You're going to be the cousin of one of my informants from the early days of my being the King's spy. He is perfectly happy with this arrangement. He has a couple of rooms in the oldest part of the Palace, which you will ostensibly share. We'll supply you with a wardrobe. All you have to do is establish a persona."

Mags chuckled. "That'll be easy enough. Something a little like the Weasel's tough-lad nephew, tempered for the manners of the Court. I'll hide in plain sight; shallow enough no one would suspect me of deeper motives, enough of a wit to be amusing, a bit of a brawler but not a bully, and a bit of a hard drinker but not a wastrel." Although he had never spent time in the actual Court circles, he'd observed the younger relatives of those who were at Court to keep the favor of the King, or on business, or there for their own reasons. He knew the kind of young man who was readily taken in as a friend by the others—someone high enough in birth to be considered a peer, not high enough to be considered a rival . . . and all those things he'd mentioned to Nikolas. Someone who was universally considered to be good company. "I'll probably need to spend . . . what I consider to be too much money," he added. "More often than not, I'll be paying for drinks . . . and other things." This was where his knowledge of the less savory parts of Haven would come in handy. He knew all the good taverns. He knew all the taverns these young men would consider to be risky enough to be adventurous, but where, in fact, he could alert the Guard so that there was no actual risk to them at all. And, of course, he knew the brothels.

Nikolas raised an amused eyebrow. "Is this something we don't tell Amily about?" he asked.

Mags had to laugh. "Oh no. This is something we *do* tell her about. The last thing I need is for her to find out about any misadventures from someone else." Besides . . . he knew the brothels, and he knew the ones where he could pay a girl for her time and get . . . say . . . a perfectly innocent candlemark or two in a thorough-going backrub, and there would not be one word said to give the fact away that he hadn't gotten far more. In fact, he rather hoped for a couple of those occasions. There were several houses of pleasure where the ladies were quite good at that sort of thing.

For that matter, I know a couple where I can ask a lady advice about . . . well . . . how to please another lady.

Nikolas questioned him more closely about his idea, making cautious suggestions. It took them awhile, but eventually Mags was more than satisfied with the character he was about to inhabit. It was utterly unlike "Mags"; the "Mags" that the people of the Court knew was amiable, very athletic, very focused on his beloved game, and . . . not very bright. This new character was sharp-witted, clever, and quick. *My biggest problem is going to be coming up with enough clever speeches.*

"All right then. I'll tell Lord Tyler that we're going to set this up, and he'll begin planting the seeds for your 'arrival.' Have you got a name you want to use?"

Mags thought about that for a moment. "Magnus," he said. "It's close enough to 'Mags' that I'll answer to it even if I'm half-stunned, or I actually *do* have to get somewhat tipsy."

Nikolas made a note of that. "All right, then, for now, down into Haven to the Guard Post and present yourself to them. I'll be seeing you later."

———————

As Amily had somewhat suspected, the Chronicler merely acknowledged that she had been assigned to his office and told her to go back to putting the Heraldic Archives to rights. "And don't trouble yourself to come back until it's finished," he added. "I know your work, why should I waste your time, and most importantly, *mine,* hanging over your shoulder? It will take as long as it will take. Off with you, young woman!"

And that pretty much left her free to set her own pace and her own hours, which was exactly what she had been hoping for. Not because she intended to shirk—but because there were things she wanted to see to that were not under the heading of "working for the Chronicler."

Like . . . the little matter of this Gift of hers.

It seemed to her that the logical place to go to ask about it was not to the Heralds. She'd lived in and around Heralds all her life, had read quite a lot of the reports in the Archives, and never had she seen anything about a Gift like this one. Rarely, there was a Herald with Animal Mindspeech—but those Heralds could actually talk to animals, and understand clearly what they were thinking, as if it was all in words. They didn't passively "ride" in an animal's mind, sensing what it was feeling and getting a general, fuzzy notion of its thoughts. Further-more, because the communication was two-way, they could generally persuade an animal to do what they wanted it to.

No . . . this seemed more like something a Healer would have. A Gift like this would be very useful to someone who specialized in Healing animals. A Healer would be able to tell what was hurting, or feeling bad, and where, if he had a Gift like this. And he would be able to tell when his efforts at soothing his patient were working.

So, as soon as the Chronicler had dismissed her, it was back to Healer's Collegium she went. At this time of day, she hoped, things had settled down enough that she could find someone to talk to who could tell her who would know these things.

As luck would have it, one of the first Healers she saw who was not looking busy was also someone she knew. Healer Daymon, one of the ones Bear had recruited to apply Healing treatments to her leg once the physical operation had been completed, was standing, chatting to one of the assistants, his posture relaxed. *Ha. Caught him in a moment of gossip! Good, then he won't mind my interrupting.*

Daymon, a tall, lanky, lantern-jawed fellow with a winning smile, spotted her first and grinned at her, waving her over as the young man he had been talking to went on his way. "Amily, I had heard you were back from your great adventure! How was life in a trader's caravan?"

"Not as bad as it could have been," she observed. "Though it's nothing I'd care to experience for any longer. Daymon, who would I talk to about Gifts?"

He raised one sandy eyebrow. "Now why would you want to know about Gifts? Have you suddenly gotten one?" He said it as if he thought it was a joke, but the other eyebrow rose to join the first when she nodded.

"Not *suddenly,* it came on over the course of several months, and I *think* that I absorbed enough, being around

Healers and Heralds as long as I have, that I've got it under proper control. But I want to be sure, and I want to find out if anyone has ever had something like it." She paused expectantly.

"Well, obviously it isn't something dangerous and spectacular . . ." Daymon crossed his arms over his chest, and regarded her from his superior height.

She laughed up at him. "No, in fact, it's minor and anticlimactic. I can see and hear what animals do. That's all. I have to concentrate to do it, and it's *so* weak a Gift that when birds wake me up in the morning, it's because they are singing, not because my head suddenly fills with images of delicious worms."

"That's a disturbing image I'd like to forget," Daymon laughed. "All right, I know exactly who to take you to. Come along!"

He led her down the corridor. Healer's Collegium and the associated House of Healing were very light and bright inside; everything was painted white or light colors, whitewashed, or white-tiled. This was the better to see and eradicate every speck of dirt, of course. In fact, the only part of Healers' that was *not* painted and tiled that way was the hothouse and the living quarters attached to it. Amily was rather glad about that. She didn't *dislike* the brightness, but it wasn't exactly what she considered to be homey. The rooms she had taken over from Bear were all light-colored wood, floor, walls and ceiling, something she considered much more home-like. Rather like the inside of the caravan, actually, but with plenty of room.

But Daymon took her on past the part where humans were tended to, cared for, and mended, and into the smaller part of the House of Healing where animals were tended. People did not often bring animals here; only when they were rare, expensive, or very much beloved. Still, someone needed to train Healers in how to take care of animals as well as people. Here, at least, Healers were taught that there was no Healing task that was beneath them.

Daymon seemed to know exactly where he was going, as he led Amily unerringly to the part of the building where there were a few stalls devoted to animals donkey-sized and larger. There he found who he was looking for: a gray-haired, gray-bearded man in robes so old and faded they were more gray than green. He was tending a foal, and from the look of things, had just finished feeding it, when Daymon hailed him.

"Elked!" he said, and the old man looked up. "We've got a pretty little conundrum for you to wrap your head around."

"I'm fond of puzzles," Elked replied, and patted the foal, who folded his legs under himself and settled back into the straw of his bedding. He tucked the bottle he had been using to feed the youngster into a kind of leather holder at his belt, and stood up.

"Well, young Amily here—you've heard of Amily, Nikolas' daughter?" At Elked's nod, Daymon went on. "Amily seems to have grown a sort of minor Gift; like Animal Mindspeech, but not."

At Daymon's gesture, Amily took over, explaining as best she could what she was experiencing. Elked listened closely, then questioned her even more closely about whether she knew how to shield, how she was doing so—all the proper questions, so far as she was concerned. And she was able to answer him to his satisfaction, at least insofar as her ability to protect herself from her own Gift was concerned.

"Well, this is a pretty little puzzle," he said, tucking his thumbs into his belt. "I'm not going to test you, as I don't think like a dog or a bird—" he chuckled "—but everything you have told me so far suggests that you have things properly under control. As for the Gift itself . . ." here he shook his head. "I reckon me a time or two when a Healer's had something like that. Not often, mind; when someone has Animal Mindspeech it generally works both ways. But 'tis a useful enough Gift. If you're in the woods, you can see if the birds and beasts are wary or no. You can see if a dog is yapping his fool head off about nothing, or a stranger. If you want to know about what's going on somewhere within your range, you just cast about for a bird or a beast, and see through their eyes. Maybe you can't persuade 'em to go look *for* you, but you can generally find a sparrow or a mouse about."

"Oh—" Amily said, chagrined that she hadn't thought of that. "I thought it was useless!"

"Nothing on earth, in the heavens, or in the waters is useless, my lass," Elked said, and patted her on the head like a child. Then again, she probably seemed like a child to him. "Now if you have trouble with it, come to me, I'll get you sorted out in a trice. But you've got a sound head on your shoulders, and 'tis obvious you were listening when others had their lessons, or talked about them. I think you'll be fine."

"But—why should it wait until *now* to turn up?" she asked. "Don't Gifts usually appear younger than this?"

He pulled meditatively at his beard for a moment, thinking. "Well, that's generally true, but not always," he replied. "And you've been hanging about with that Mags lad, right? The one that can Mindspeak to everyone?"

"Yes—would that make a difference?" she asked curiously.

"It's a funny thing, that particular Gift. Doesn't come up that strong very often. And when the one that has it spends a lot of time Mindspeaking to someone who don't—if the one that don't has *any* little hint of Gift, that Mindspeaking seems to bring it out. Like watering a seed that's been dormant." She felt her eyes widening and he nodded.

"If anyone would know that, Elked would," Daymon said in confirmation. "There's no one in all three Collegia who's spent more time studying Gifts."

Amily spent a little more time questioning the old Healer closely, but by the time she was finished, she was satisfied with his answers. And determined to make as much use out of what she'd been Gifted with as she could.

It was definitely winter now, and no mistake about it. There wasn't snow on the ground yet, but only because it got barely warm enough by day for most of it to melt off, although you could find thin drifts of white in shadowed corners. The trees were bare, and down in the town as well as up at the Palace, the fallen leaves had been taken away, except in Companion's Field. In Haven, well *nothing* went to waste. Leaves went to stuff mattresses, or to be thriftily used to start fires. The dead leaves from the Palace that hadn't been heaped over the flower beds had been taken down into Haven for precisely that reason.

Gray stone and gray weathered wood below and gray sky above, and a wind to chill even the warmest nature. Mags wished he was back up at Haven already, and tucked up at a fire.

Mags wasn't spending much time in his own room, now that it was really cold. No one seemed to notice when he came and went from Amily's rooms, so they had both decided this fit her father's definition of "discreet." The plain fact was, now that he wasn't the Kirball champion, no one found him very interesting. And Amily's notoriety from being kidnapped and all had worn off in the time they'd been gone. There was just nothing interesting about either of them as long as they kept quiet, and kept themselves to themselves.

He, for one was finding it very beneficial to be in the same building as the little things that made life more comfortable—like hot baths and indoor privies. And Amily had arranged to have a little iron stove set up on one of the hearths, instead of having an open fire, so they could even cook for themselves when they didn't want to trudge over to Herald's Collegium and the big dining hall. That was something he had never had the advantage of in the stable. Both of them had gotten plenty of practice in cookery while on Circuit, and with a much greater variety of things available—and an entire greenhouse full of herbs—it wasn't that hard to put something tasty together.

It had been over one of those self-made breakfasts of oat porridge that Amily had told him about her new Gift.

She had explained that she wanted to be sure it wasn't something that would fade in time, and that she had it in hand before she told him.

He'd been surprised by the revelation, but not at all surprised that she had identified it, learned what it could do, learned how to handle it, gone to an expert, and dealt with it all with complete competence. "I wish it was more useful," she had sighed.

And he had chuckled. "Takes more smarts and more skill t'get the most out of a little than it does to get *something* out of a lot. I betcha ye'll figger out how t' do more with this than some'f the strong Mindspeakers can with everything they got."

She was right, though; it seemed to be of very limited use. Anything smaller than a rabbit just didn't hear human voices in a way that allowed her to make sense of what was being said. But it did provide them bits of amusement, when she had spied on some of the Princess' Ladies-In-Waiting up to a little harmless mischief, watching them through the eyes of a pampered, spoiled lapdog.

As for Mags, he was slowly establishing a sort of routine. He had created all the new personas Nikolas thought he needed.

Three were mere sketches, a set of hands in servant's livery, one in the household of one of the Great Lords of State, one in the household of a *very* wealthy, but not highborn courtier, and one in the Royal Household itself. As he knew, when a household was not well-regulated, servants came and went all the time. At this point in time, it seemed that servants were less plentiful than unfilled positions, and as a result, a well-trained servant could find himself a new job as often as he liked. And at any rate, when things were busy—which was likely the time when Mags himself would want to overhear things—no one ever looked at a servant's *face,* not even the people who were supposed to be keeping track. He could slip in at a feast, for instance, and no one would notice as long as he knew what he was doing and he was in the right livery.

He had Willy the Weasel's street-tough nephew, of course, and re-established Harkon in very little time at all. People remembered Harkon and respected his brawling ability. "Willy" himself—Nikolas—rarely went down to the pawnshop anymore. Harkon could swagger in for a few candlemarks, whenever the two fellows Nikolas had acting as the hired help "needed a more expert eye at assessing goods than their own"—or, in translation, when someone had information rather than goods to sell. At the moment, that wasn't often. And if the need arose for him to pursue the gleaning of intelligence more vigorously, he could take over the night shift entirely.

Then there was "Magnus," the young cousin of Lord Chipman. "Magnus" was probably the most fun; Mags got to be convivial, apparently reckless, and a spinner of tall tales. He also got to be the fellow who bought most of the rounds at the taverns down in Haven. Magnus was very slowly ingratiating himself with his fellow highborn lads, the younger sons, the ones with too much time on their hands and not a lot to fill it, with winter coming on and outdoor pastimes out of the question. "Magnus" explained his familiarity with Haven as due to living there in an overcrowded household, and he was grateful to his "uncle" for inviting him up to share his space at Court. The others were restless, spoiling for something to do, preferably something with a touch of trouble about it. Magnus was more than willing to provide the illusion of trouble without the substance. He hadn't led an expedition to a brothel yet, but that was just a matter of time.

One benefit that hadn't occurred to him at the time of inventing "Magnus," but certainly was making itself apparent now, was his ability to throw a good bit of custom in the way of deserving innkeepers. When you could stroll into a tavern with a handful of your cronies, throw a big handful of silver on the table, and order drinks and meals—the fact that you had paid *in advance* meant that an innkeeper struggling on the edge of profit could afford to send a lad out for better provender than he had on hand. That, in turn, would make "Magnus'" friends come back on their own—and the profit from that one night would have made it possible for the innkeeper to be prepared for another such incursion. Injecting a little more prosperity into some of the less-prosperous parts of Haven always made him feel a little happier.

At the moment, no one stood out as a *real* trouble maker—someone with a vicious streak, or someone who had ulterior motives for being at Court. Then again, that didn't mean there wasn't someone like that among the courtiers, it only meant that circumstances, which were confining "Magnus" to the lowest circles, hadn't thrown him into contact with trouble yet.

On the whole he would rather that trouble didn't rear its head until he had himself more firmly established anyway.

Then there was his "real" job . . .

Which he was on his way back from at this moment, with his head hunched into his shoulders, his cloak wrapped firmly about himself, making himself as small against the wind as he could, given he was on Dallen's back.

There was always a need for Heralds down in Haven. The Prince, for instance, was on duty at the Great Magistrate's Court of Appeals every afternoon; this was the court you could have your case taken to if you appealed the verdict from your first trial. Other Heralds were either on duty or could be called on at need for the district courts. Mags was one of those; he had a couple of days in the fortnight when he was on duty, and *technically* he could be called down from the Hill in an emergency, but practically speaking, the officers of the court knew to call on someone else.

The job itself was not all that difficult; he invoked the Truth Spell when it was needed to sort something out. Cases that required the use of a Truth Spell were saved until he was on duty. Most cases in the court that he served . . . well . . . didn't need anything nearly that complicated. People in that part of Haven were generally caught red-handed in whatever they'd done, from theft to murder. And his mere presence in the courtroom tended to make the truth come out anyway. It was civil cases where his talent tended to be needed, and in his district they didn't get a lot of those. After all, in order to press a civil case, you had to be literate enough to file it, had to take time out from your work to plead it before a magistrate (who decided whether it was worth taking to court), then had to take time out from your work for the trial. You had to have *motivation* to file a civil case against someone when you were poor.

Today, however, had been one of those days. It had been a situation where a quarrel between neighbors had turned into a feud, which had escalated into actual damages on either side. Each side claimed the other in the wrong, and it had taken using the Truth Spell not only on the claimants, but on the witnesses. *That* had been a right mess, and he figured he had more than earned his dinner today by the time it was all over.

It was bitter, bitter cold today, with that strong wind, and he couldn't wait to get back in the warm. Granted, it wasn't as wretched as it had been up in the Bastion, but it was bad enough, and he wasn't in his warm Field uniform, he was in Whites that were designed for winters where you weren't at risk of freezing to death if you took a wrong turning.

He was bundled up in his warmest cloak, relying entirely on Dallen to handle where they were going. The wind was behind them, at least, rather than trying to rip the edges of the cloak away from his body, but it was howling right up the street, being funneled by the buildings on either side. There wasn't much traffic on the street; this was an area of residences, mostly. Two- and three-story, narrow houses, packed closely enough together that neighbors could pass things between their passage-facing windows.

Dallen wasn't plodding, but he wasn't moving briskly, either. You didn't want to move too quickly through here. There was no telling when a little might dart out of one of those narrow passages right under your nose.

They were approaching his least favorite bridge over the river, which was still several blocks away, but already he was thinking glumly about how much worse it was going to be with the wind coming at him from *every* direction, which it always did on that bridge. Not to mention the spray from the rapids underneath. The best he could hope for was that there wouldn't be a glaze of ice on the stones.

The parapets at either side were barely knee high, and he never liked crossing it even in the best of weather. He knew *why* they were so low, of course; huge drays had to come down this street, bringing oversized goods up to the wealthier parts of Haven. This was the only bridge like it in the entire city for that reason, and the only place where the river could be crossed by such oversized vehicles. The river was on the downhill slope at this point in town, and looking at the foaming water from the arch of stone always made him feel as if he was likely to topple into it. When there was more than just a few patchy spots of ice on the thing, he'd go halfway across town to avoid crossing it.

He glanced up from under his hood, and saw they were practically the only people in sight. In fact, there was just one single person starting across the bridge ahead of him, afoot, shoulders hunched against the wind. He immediately felt sorry for the poor beggar, having to plod wherever he was going afoot in this weather. At least sitting atop Dallen there was a warm spot where his legs clutched Dallen's barrel.

And then, with no warning whatsoever, he heard the scream of a horse somewhere ahead, a crashing noise, and the clatter of hooves on stone. His head jerked up in immediate reaction, and he felt Dallen's startled reaction beneath him.

The hell? His first reaction was to try and figure out where the noise was coming from, because it didn't sound good!

From one of the side-streets ahead, a maddened horse, trailing the remains of a smashed cart, careened around the corner and down the street, heading toward the bridge.

Instinctively, Mags rose in the stirrups, shouting and waving. Useless, of course; they were too far away.

The fellow crossing the bridge never had a chance. The runaway galloped toward him, remains of the cart swinging wildly from side to side behind it, and shouldered into him just as he turned. He was sent staggering backward toward the parapet as Mags watched in horror, and the ruined cart finished the job by swinging into him and knocking him over the side!

But there was worse . . .

For in his head as the man was hit and fell, he heard an inarticulate shriek for help followed by silence as the man hit the water. And that inarticulate shriek had been in a *very* familiar Mindvoice.

Nikolas!

Years, now, of working together until their response to emergency was at the level of instinct had the two of them acting even as the runaway horse clattered off the end of the bridge and around another corner.

Dallen launched into a frantic run, as Mags made himself small in the saddle and held on with everything he had. Desperately, he cleared his head, and he tried to Call Nikolas . . . and got no response. Nothing.

Let him only be unconscious. . . .

But even if his mentor was "just" unconscious, he couldn't last for long in the foaming tumble of water down below, as the river dropped down the Hill.

Dallen plunged down the bank to the edge of the river, pivoted on his heels with a sideways wrench that would have thrown an inexperienced rider out of the saddle and threw himself along the narrow path beside the churning water while Mags strained his hands holding onto the saddle and his eyes trying to catch sight of a body. As his heart froze, he saw nothing . . . nothing . . . and then, just a glimpse, a bit of back and an arm, limply tumbling along in the water.

:There's a place where it eddies a bit ahead. That's our best chance,: Dallen said. Mags trusted him; Dallen's knowledge of every nook and cranny of Haven was phenomenal. If they didn't manage to fish Nikolas out soon. . . .

Oh gods, what do I tell Amily?

But he still wasn't getting any response from Nikolas, despite his repeated mental calls. His stomach roiled with fear. This was a Herald's worst nightmare; to know *a friend* as well as one of your own was in peril.

Somehow Dallen put on a little more speed, moving with

uncanny agility along the rough, boulder-riddled path. Now, more than ever, Mags blessed those hours and hours spent practicing and playing on the Kirball field. Without that practice, even Dallen would never have learned that kind of agility.

Dallen's hooves rang on the stone and hard-packed earth of the path, and the wind whipped at them. Mags reached up and unfastened his cloak, letting it be carried away into the river. When they hit the water, the dragging weight of it would be the very last thing he needed, and it *could* rip him right off Dallen's back, or worse, get wrapped around Dallen and doom them both.

:Don't leave my back,: Dallen said.

:Won't,: he promised. Together, they had a chance; Dallen was infinitely stronger than he was, as well as larger, the better to plunge through the current. But if he got torn away from Dallen . . . there'd be two helpless bodies in the tumbling rapids.

He felt Dallen suddenly gather under him, and knew that, although he couldn't see it, they were nearing the place where Dallen thought they might be able to get Nikolas. He looked ahead; no sign of the Herald—

:Behind—:

He snatched a look over his shoulder, caught a glimpse of a tumbling back and head, and saw that they had gotten slightly ahead of their target. He kept his eyes locked on the body, as Dallen leapt into the water.

They hit with a shock that was like being hit by lightning.

The cold drove all the breath out of him, but he was ready for that, and fought for a breath as he strained upward to keep his head above the water. He had expected to be plunged under the water completely, but somehow—maybe because Dallen was so big he *couldn't* go under the water—they got soaked, but kept their heads high enough to breathe. And Dallen had timed his entrance perfectly, for Nikolas literally tumbled into Mags' arms in the next moment.

He grabbed and hauled the Herald over Dallen's withers in front of him, and as the water threatened to tear the limp and heavy body away from him, he flung himself over Nikolas, and hung on to the Herald and the saddle with every bit of strength in his arms, trying to keep the body pinned against Dallen's withers with the weight of his own body. Dallen half-swam, half-leapt toward the bank, trying to use the current as much as he could.

It seemed to take forever . . . surging up, getting a breath, falling back, getting soaked, over and over again. Waves beating at them and the current trying to tear them apart. His arms were on fire with cold and agony, his lungs burned from the water he couldn't help but breathe in, and the cold had penetrated every bit of him.

Then Dallen heaved up onto the bank, front legs, then a scramble and the hind legs. Only the high back of the saddle kept him and Nikolas from pitching back into the river. Then they were up on the bank, and safe, and Mags and Nikolas slid down off Dallen's back—not entirely voluntarily.

Mags hit the ground beside Nikolas' unresponsive body, and rolled his mentor onto his back. He was white as marble, not breathing, and when Mags put his ear to Nikolas' chest, he couldn't hear a heartbeat.

Amily was bundled up to her eyes and halfway between Healer's Collegium and the Guard Archives when suddenly the place exploded with frantic activity. Heralds and trainees erupted from every door in sight, and Companions raced out of the Field and Stable to join them. Amily felt her heart leap into her throat—for something terrible was surely happening!

And then, suddenly, Rolan raced up to skid to a halt beside her. She looked up at him with relief. "Rolan! What—" she began.

And then she heard the voice, in her mind, heavy with grief and sympathy. *:I'm sorry, little one. I am so very, very sorry—:*

And then she looked with shock into his blue, blue eyes . . . fell into them . . .

:I am so sorry it is this way for you, Amily. I Choose you.:

———————

Mags didn't hesitate, not for a moment. Not when Bear had drilled him for weeks on *exactly* what he needed to do in a case like this. Once spring had come, Bear had taught them all, him, Amily, Lena, Jak and Lita. The Breath of Life. Where Bear had learned it, he hadn't said . . .

That didn't matter, not right now. All that mattered was Nikolas, and what he *had* to do, because he was *not* going to go home and tell Amily that—

No. It was *not* going to be that way!

Mags tilted Nikolas to one side, with his head on the downward side of the slope of the bank so that all the water ran out of his lungs. Then he rolled Nikolas back onto his back, put both hands over Nikolas' breastbone and began pumping with all of his weight behind each push. Thirty pumps, and then he paused, tilted Nikolas' head back, pinched off his nose, and breathed twice into his open mouth and down his throat, feeling Nikolas' chest rise with the breath he blew in. Then he went back to pumping; thirty pumps, then another two breaths. Thirty pumps, two breaths. Over and over again, keeping count only of those thirty pumps and not how long it was taking. Because it didn't matter. He would do this forever. All the while swearing quietly and prodding Nikolas' mind frantically with his own.

We have a chance. We have a chance. That water is cold, and cold water holds off death for a little while . . .

That was what Bear had told him, anyway.

Dallen lay down next to Nikolas' body, and in a moment,

he was radiating so much heat that his coat steamed, warming the two of them. That gave him more strength. Dallen wouldn't have done that if there was no hope, would he?

There was a clamor in the distance, but he ignored it. There was nothing for him now but this single task, and he must, he *must* do it until Nikolas came back to them.

Thirty pumps, two breaths. Thirty pumps, two breaths. Mags was fiercely determined to keep it up until someone tore him away. . . .

Then—

: . . . Mags?: came a weak, thread of a thought. His heart leapt.

:Nikolas!: he "shouted."

And that was when something huge and white *shoved* him away with its head, so that he fell over sideways, and he heard another Mindvoice in his head. A female one; one he didn't recognize.

:Live, Chosen! LIVE, Nikolas!:

"Rolan—" he gasped, but of course he knew it wasn't Rolan, not with *that* Mindvoice.

And in the next moment, Nikolas coughed, coughed again, began to breathe on his own, and they were *all* swarmed by Healers and Heralds and. . . .

Mags just got out of the way. On the whole, it seemed best. He fell over Dallan's back, and just lay there quietly for a while as Dallen radiated heat with all his might, until Nikolas and the strange Companion were taken away and someone noticed he was still there.

———

Mags got offers of half a dozen cloaks; he took one at random, and he and Dallen managed to drag themselves back up to the Collegium. Dallen got taken away to be warmed up inside and out . . . and so was Mags. Not before he made sure that Amily was with her father; that was only right and proper. And not before he had learned that Rolan had Chosen Amily, which *sort of* explained why Nikolas had a new Companion. But once he knew that Amily and her father were together and Nikolas was being tended to by nearly every Healer in the Collegium, he did the only smart thing there was to do.

He got himself into a hot bath, boiled until the water started to cool, and ran more hot water in. Once he actually was feeling *too* warm, he got dressed and went to the kitchen and ate hot bread and slices of meat straight off the spit and a huge mug of some herbal concoction that Cook swore "will set ye right square up." Then he sat in the kitchen with his head on his arms and baked in the warmth while the work bustled on around him. He might even have dozed a little; no one stirred him.

Eventually, he felt like himself and prodded Dallen.

:You all right?:

The reply was steeped in contentment. *:I cannot believe we made it all come round right.:*

:Me neither. You hurt anything?:

:Just strains and some bruising. They'd have poulticed me to my withers if I'd let them. I'm going to sleep now. The Healers are done with Nikolas. Amily has had her cry and now she's just sitting there in disbelief that things turned out the way they did. The King is having a conference, and you'll need to go shout some sense in them shortly.:

He sighed, and raised his head from his arms. A glance out the window showed him the sun had gone down. It appeared that, for the larger view, everything was, more or less, sorted out. But that didn't mean things were any less upsetting or confusing.

Nikolas had, by every possible standard, died. A quick check with some of the other Companions—he didn't want to further send already upset Heralds into a worse state by asking them about it—filled him in on what he didn't already know, and put everything in order for him. Two of the un-paired Companions from the Field had taken it on themselves to give him a fairly exact rendition of the events. Nikolas had died. There was no question about that. The Death Bell had even gotten off four strokes before abruptly ceasing to ring. Rolan had Chosen Amily.

But then . . . Mags had brought Nikolas back, and Nikolas had promptly been Chosen by that new Companion, Evory. Mags had the shrewd notion that it was Evory's fierce spirit that had "persuaded" Nikolas not to give up and die any-way . . . but there was no telling for certain, and Evory wasn't talking about it.

The King was upset—both because his very good friend Nikolas had very nearly been lost forever, and at least in part because now his Monarch's Own Herald was *not* his very good friend Nikolas, but an unknown and untried *girl*. Amily was a great deal more than upset, and most understandably, because suddenly she was not only Chosen (which she would have been happy about under other circumstances) but because it was Rolan who had Chosen her, and because her father had very nearly died. The entirety of Herald's Collegium was upset, because something like this had *never* happened before, not in the entire history of Valdemar. Things *were*, or *were not*. When the Monarch's Own died, he had the good sense to *stay dead* and not get resurrected to be Chosen again by a different Companion. Of course, no one was crass enough to put it that way, but it was clear enough that was, more or less, the way their troubled and muddled thinking was going. Everyone was concentrating on what had "gone wrong" and not on the bloody *miracle* they'd all been given.

Well, Mags couldn't do anything about that. But he damned well could do something about the most important person, bar her father and himself, in Amily's life.

He asked for, and got, a tiny glass of distilled spirits from the cook, and he downed it, even though it nearly made him choke.

And with that to bolster his courage (without being enough to muddle his thoughts) he headed straight for the Royal Suite in the Palace, every stride ringing with determination.

And given his Whites and the look on his face, not even the Guards at the door to the King's Chambers stopped him when he stalked up to the door and wrenched it open.

Silence fell immediately, with that sense that a moment earlier, people had nearly been shouting.

"—what—" said someone into that silence.

King Kyril looked up from the huddle of Heralds and officials as Mags let the door fall shut behind him. Prince Sedric opened his mouth as if to speak. Mags cut them all off.

"This here is just about *enough* of all the makin' out this is some kinda calamity!" he thundered. " 'Cause it *ain't.*"

The room went deathly still. Because . . . well, Herald or not . . . who ever would talk to the *King* that way?

Right now . . . with the woman he loved being tied in knots, and everyone acting as if it was somehow her *fault* that this had happened and if she wanted to, she could just somehow give Rolan back, Mags would have spoken to gods themselves this way.

"So Rolan Chose Amily? *How's that matter?"* he continued, doing his best to imitate the most stern old priest of a stern religion he had ever heard or seen. "For godsake, it ain't like you *lost* Nikolas! In fact, you got the best thing that could ever've happened! We got a bleedin' *miracle,"* he continued, repeating his own thoughts.

As they all stared at him in shock at that pronouncement, he continued with what he had worked out on the way. "You got Amily, an' she's watched her pa do the job of King's Own since she was old enough t'walk. You think she ain't got a good idea of what she needs t'do? Not like when the King's Own *dies,* an' the Companion goes and Chooses some youngling what ain't ever heard of Heralds! An' Nikolas is bloody *alive.* You got her pa *here to advise 'er.* Ye figgered that out yet? 'Tis another bleedin' *miracle!* You got th' old King's Own right here in person t' *advise* the new King's Own, and that's *aside* of havin' Rolan to advise 'er! You got her pa fit to work, not paralyzed or feeble-minded, but in a fortnight or so he'll be walkin' around sensible, an' now he's free t' do everythin' he *wasn't* altogether free t'do before!"

Now, a great many of those advisors had no idea what Mags was talking about. But those who knew that Nikolas had been the King's personal intelligence agent and spy suddenly got wide eyes . . . and the King himself looked as if Mags had struck him in the head, he was so dumbfounded by what apparently was a revelation. Prince Sedric, however, was nodding.

"Majesty—" he went on, pointing at the King. "Ye still got yer best friend, *alive,* an' fit t' do his work. Amily's still got her pa. Ye got a King's Own what's gonna . . . I gotta be blunt here . . . *outlive you,* barrin' accident. Which means Sedric's gonna get a seasoned King's Own, when th' time comes, which I hope ain't soon. Oh, an' I got more, cause I know Amily, an' you don't. Amily might be the best-read King's Own in the history of *ever,* on account of she knows them Chronicles like only a Chronicler does. I swear, she's read 'em all. If there's a solution that worked in the past, she'll either know it, or know where to look for it. Which, Valdemar ain't often had. So?"

He paused for breath, and stood there, a little belligerently, fists on hips, staring them all down.

Finally King Kyril blinked three or four times, and took a deep breath himself. By this time, Mags was a master at reading peoples' faces and posture, and he could practically see the tension running out of the King. As he had figured, they had all gotten themselves tied in knots, wrangling over how all this stuff that had never happened before absolutely had to be *bad* . . . and to be fair, most things that "had never happened before" *had* tended to be bad of late. But he had just jarred them all out of that nonsense, and in good time, too. Now they'd all be able to come at this *thinking,* instead of feeling.

"So," the King said, in his quiet, bass voice. "Thank you for delivering all of us from our foolishness, Herald Mags. You have rightly pointed out that not only is this *not* a calamity, it is the best possible outcome we could have had from what nearly was a tragedy, and we have been blessed by the gods themselves to still have Herald Nikolas among us."

Prince Sedric caught Mags' eye, and slowly winked. Mags felt the tension drain out of himself.

"Well then, beg pardon for interruptin' yer Majesty," he said with a low bow. "I'll just let m'self out."

And he did.

———————————

". . . I would give any amount of money to have seen their faces," Nikolas said, from the depths of his bed.

He had not emerged from his ordeal unscathed. Virtually every bit of him was battered and bruised. His left arm was broken in two places, and had been splinted and bound up against his chest. His lungs hurt him when he breathed, although the Healers were making sure they Healed without his also getting pneumonia. And his head had taken several hard knocks. But given what *could* have been . . .

Mags shrugged. "King's Companion tol' Dallen, and Dallen tol' me, that they were all workin' themselves up to some sorta panic. Someone had to go in there and point out that it not only weren't a disaster, it was anythin' but."

Amily left her father's side long enough to give him an embrace and a kiss that warmed him right down to his toes. She said nothing, but then, she didn't have to. Her heart and spirits were battered and sore from everything she had been through in the last several candlemarks, and the fact that without being asked he had dealt with something she was in no state to . . .

. . . "grateful" was not nearly a potent enough word for how she felt right now, and they both knew it, and both felt it.

"Really, things is better *now* than they was afore, except for you havin' been rolled down the river an' nearly dyin' an' all," he finished, sitting himself down in a comfortable chair and helping himself to some of Nikolas' uneaten dinner. "It's good for me too! Bad 'nuff to have lost the King's Own, but losin' Amily's pa, an' losin' m'teacher too?" He shook his head, and stuffed a buttered roll, whole, into his mouth. "I'd'a been a right mess." He'd have held it together for Amily's sake, but . . . it wouldn't have been easy.

"Rolan says this is why I was never Chosen," Amily said, in a small voice. "I was always supposed to be King's Own eventually, and since I was doing so well without being Chosen, no Companion ever wanted to . . . to just be the second best, I suppose. He also says that this wasn't supposed to happen for a long, long time."

"It's very difficult to describe how I am feeling right now," Nikolas said into the silence. "Grateful past words to still be *alive,* just to start with. Getting used to a . . . much closer bond with Evory than I had with Rolan . . . and I wouldn't have thought that was even possible. But also feeling a little lost. I've always been the King's Own. Just at the moment, I am not at all sure I know how to be . . . just a Herald." He looked at both of them out of blackened eyes, forlornly.

But Mags just snorted, before Nikolas could get himself talked into feeling depressed about the change his life had just taken. "How many times've you wished you *wasn't* King's Own when ye had to be two places at once?" he asked, logically. "So. Now you ain't got that problem no more. 'Stead'a havin' t' divide yerself between two jobs, ye can do one *really, really* well."

Nikolas tilted his head painfully to one side, and looked at him oddly. "When did you suddenly become a wise old Herald?" he asked. "Who are you, and what did you do with Mags, who had no answers to anything?"

Mags only laughed.

He finally persuaded Amily to leave her father in the capable hands of a Healer's assistant, and come to bed. And before she went to bed, he made her a sort of breakfast-dinner out of what they had on hand in her rooms, making sure she ate every bite of it.

"I'm feeling . . . bruised," she confessed, as he settled into bed beside her, and took her in his arms, knowing that tonight the last thing she would want was anything *other* than simple comfort.

"Reckon that's as good a way of puttin' it as any," he agreed. "Ye got about as rough a beatin' inside as yer pa got outside."

"I have to keep reminding myself that Rolan would *not* Choose someone who wasn't right for the job . . ." she said, her voice trailing off. But then, out of nowhere, her face lit up with a joyous smile. "Oh *Mags!* I've been *Chosen!* Can you believe it? I've been *Chosen!*"

He chuckled, kissed her, and held her tight. "Yer the kindest, bestest gal on the Hill, th' Queen an' Princess not excepted," he told her firmly. "An' Rolan hisself told ye the only reason ye ain't been Chosen till now was 'cause they was savin' ye t'be King's Own. So there. Believe it. An' don't worry about not bein' up to the job. Ye got yer pa. Ye got Rolan. Ye got *yerself,* sweeting. I just bragged all over ye t' the King's face, tellin' him you know them Chronicles better'n anyone but the Chronicler, an' if someone ever came up with an answer for anything, you know right where it is. Yer tough. Yer smart. Yer brave. Yer Nikolas' proper daughter."

With the smile still on her face, she broke down and cried a little, for relief as much as anything, he thought. And then she went to sleep.

After a long, long while, so did he.

Amily woke up in a panic. Her reaction to panic, however, had been born from years of not being able to move quickly; she froze. With her eyes tight shut, she identified where she was (in bed, with Mags a solid, warm weight next to her) and which bed she was in (her own, in the rooms in Healer's Collegium) and what time it was (by the sounds in the building, just past the morning bells). When her mind and memory caught up with the rest of her, she realized she had a very good reason to wake up in a panic.

I'm the King's Own! I should *be in a panic!*

She kept her eyes shut, and her body still, and let herself take comfort from Mags' presence while she tried to sort herself out. Part of her wished devoutly she could go back to sleep . . . the rest of her wished devoutly she could go back in time to the day before yesterday.

Because, although she had dreamed for—well as long as she could remember—about finally being Chosen, the last thing she had ever wanted to be was King's Own, and not just because it would mean her father was dead. Being Chosen was both wonderful and terrifying, in equal measure, but the wonderful part, she thought, would make up for all that. Being Chosen as King's Own . . .

She had to remind herself, over and over, for a while, that her father was *not* dead.

It helped . . . but not as much as she hoped.

The enormous weight of responsibility on her felt spiritually crushing. Being a Herald was responsibility enough! This—

:Rolan!: she thought, desperately, still with her eyes squeezed tight, a few tears of desperation leaking out from her eyelids.

:Chosen?: the grave voice replied. *:Before you ask, this can't be undone.:*

:Why not?: she demanded. *:Plenty of impossible things happened yesterday, why not one more?:*

:Principally, because in order to attempt to undo it, we'd have to asphyxiate you and then attempt to bring you back to life,: Rolan replied dryly. *:I don't think that is an optimal idea. When death severs the bonds, and new bonds are made, the only way to sever them again is death or repudiation. And do trust me, my love, repudiation is not something you want to experience.:*

At the moment, she wasn't altogether sure of that. . . .

:You can take my word for it. It's soul-shattering. I simply won't repudiate you, so you can put the idea out of your mind.: The Mindvoice softened a good bit. *:Besides, you haven't asked me how I feel about all this.:*

Well, that was true enough. She tried to take deep breaths. Breathing deeply was supposed to help with panic. And she listened with all her being to what Rolan had to say.

:Nikolas was always serving two masters—his task as King's Spy and his task as King's Own. I have you all to myself, and I rather like that.:

She opened her eyes to the darkness of the room and blinked a little. That was . . . a surprise. She'd expected Rolan to prefer her father over her.

:I don't prefer either of you as people. You are both wonderful, and I am pleased to have bonded with both of you. I do prefer not having my Herald juggle two jobs. I do prefer not being in a situation where I am forced to sit idly while my Herald puts himself in danger without me near enough to quickly come to the rescue. Yesterday was just the latest of those, and it very nearly ended horribly.: His Mindvoice turned soothing. *:I have every confidence in you, Chosen. If I didn't, I would never have Chosen you myself.:*

She set her chin stubbornly. *:But I don't know anything about being King's Own!:*

There was a distinct sense of a snort. *:Of course you do. Now you're just being stubborn, and I am not going to sit here and tell you what you already know, when you know you know it, and I know you know it, and you know that I know you know it.:*

Now that made her smile a little. Rolan continued. *:And you might think about this, while you are thinking. In what other capacity would you and Mags be able to stay in Haven most of the time?:*

She bit her lip. She hadn't thought of that. If she had been Chosen in the usual way . . .

:Even the Heralds serving in the City Courts get rotated out into the Field unless they are handicapped in some way. You're very fortunate. Mags may get sent out of Haven from time to time, but it will not be often and never be for long. He'll take over Nikolas' network of Kingdom-wide agents, and add to it himself, and he will rely on them for anything outside of Haven for the most part. That only makes sense. A spy is only as effective as the extent to which he fits in where he is at, and is both able to penetrate suspect's lives, and be invisible. That's unlikely to happen when you are an outsider.

Your father has spent years building and maintaining his dif-
ferent characters in Haven itself. Doing the same is just not
possible if you are gallivanting all over the landscape, and
that doesn't even take into account the difficulties of a stranger
coming into an insular community and trying to establish
himself as an agent. It is much better to have operatives
planted everywhere, and rely on them. And that is what Mags
will do. You two will be able to spend the majority of your time
together.:

She considered all of that. *:So . . . he'll leave only when he*
has to see something in person, for himself?:

:Or when his operative asks for help. Which could be risky
for anyone but a Herald—there is always the chance that the
operative has turned.: Rolan didn't trouble to explain, and
indeed, Amily could think of any number of ways that a Herald could determine something had gone wrong with such a
situation . . . not the least of which, for Mags, who was such
a very powerful Mindspeaker, it was vanishingly unlikely that
anyone would be able to fool him for long.

:But . . . : She stopped herself before she began a plaint
about how she *couldn't possibly* do what her father had done
as King's Own. She already knew the answer to that. Or, answers, rather. Her father was right here to advise her. This was
the same problem every new Monarch's Own faced, and somehow they all managed *without* having their predecessor there
to help. And for once, she had all the advantages. Not only did
she know the Court very, very well, she knew the history of
Valdemar very well, she had Rolan, she had her predecessor—
and she still had her father. She had the King's Spy. Spies! Her
father and Mags!

Really . . . the only thing she could possibly claim was *I*
don't want to!

And just what kind of a feeble complaint was that when
this was almost what she had wanted for so very long? Oh,

here she was, like a child getting a sweet, and deciding petu-
lantly that instead of a honey-sweet, she wanted a cherry-
sweet!

:What if I make a mistake?: she finally said.

*:Everyone makes mistakes. I make mistakes. If you make a
mistake, we'll admit to it, own it, and then fix it.:*

What possible answer could she have to that?

So she got up—without disturbing Mags, which was hardly
surprising considering everything he had gone through yesterday—and got dressed. It seemed very strange to think that
in a candlemark or two . . . she'd be wearing this clothing only
rarely. And in a candlemark or two, the person who had always tried to be the least conspicuous person in a room would
be one of the most. *:Now what do I do?:* she asked Rolan.

*:You report to Herald's Collegium and the Dean. He will
guide you from there.:*

Mags woke to find himself alone, and a quick glance at the
windows told him he'd slept . . . late. So did his stomach.
There was full morning light out there, even if it was gray and
overcast, and his stomach was decidedly empty. He closed his
eyes to concentrate a little.

:Dallen—where's—:

*:With the Dean. Getting Whites, since they've decided that
there is nothing in particular she needs in the way of classes and
really, after everything that happened yesterday, having her go
straight into Whites without being a Trainee first is the* least *of
the violations of protocol,:* Dallen said, with a distinct sense of
amusement. *:And from there, I do not know, but she will probably be much too busy to think of anything but anxiety.:*

Poor Amily! To be thrown, not only into the job of being a
Herald, but the most difficult job of being a Herald that there

was! His first impulse was to rush to her side and cushion and support her through all of that.

:Don't, she won't thank you for it,: Dallen advised.

His second impulse was to do it anyway . . . but when had Dallen ever given him bad advice when it came to Amily?

:I suppose you could consider the lack of advice I gave you for some time to be "bad" advice,: Dallen pointed out.

:So now you want me to go against your advice? Make up your mind, horse,: he scoffed, and stretched, winced a great deal, and opened his eyes again.

:If you feel as bruised as I feel, I am sorry for you,: Dallen said. *:Nikolas, however, feels much worse. And that is what he deserves, for being such an idiot as to have been afoot on a day like that. Even if he was going incognito.:*

Mags was just glad they could joke about it. The more he thought about what *could* have happened . . . well, his blood ran cold.

He got up, trying not to move too quickly, and got dressed. More than ever, he appreciated Amily's lovely rooms here at Healer's. The bedroom was small, but then, it was only used for sleeping, but it was cozy and warm, and this morning his bruises were deeply thankful for that.

As he dressed, he was keeping his thoughts to himself, because he wasn't entirely certain he wanted Dallen to be privy to them just yet.

It was amazing, wonderful, and uplifting to think that Amily had been Chosen at last. The problem only came when he thought about the fact that she had been Chosen to be King's Own. Life was difficult enough, being a Herald. But . . .

Like it or not, he was going to be sharing her a lot. Not just with her Companion, which at least was something they had in common, but with the King . . . the Prince . . . who knew how many other people!

How much privacy would they have *now?*

Would Nikolas even allow them to get married now?

Second and third thoughts and doubts went through his mind, and he let them. Because in the back of his mind, he knew that he might as well get them over with now rather than later. Somehow he was going to have to think through all of this, and convince himself that everything was going to be fine—or, well, as fine as things could be, between two Heralds, given what life for a Herald was like—before he saw Amily again. If he couldn't convince himself, how could he possibly convince her?

It was worrisome, though. It would have been hard enough with only one of them being a Herald. With both . . . it would be very difficult, one reason why Heralds seldom married each other. But Amily was the King's Own, and a very great deal of her time was not going to be hers.

Kinda funny how Nikolas wanted us t'be sure we could handle bein' bored . . . one thing's for sure now, we ain't never gonna have the time t'be bored. At least, Amily ain't.

He sighed, stretched his aching muscles one more time, then tied up his boots. Time to get up and get moving. He had a lot to do.

At least there was this; thanks to Rolan and Dallen, they would *always* be able to find each other, no matter how busy they were. And that was no inconsiderable thing.

First things first: best to go to Nikolas and find out what he was working on that had had him down in Haven, in civilian garb, without Rolan. Then find out if it was something he was going to need to take over. Because Nikolas was not getting out of bed soon, and when he did, it was going to be a while before he could use that arm.

He took himself off to the bathing room here at Healers for a quick wash, then went looking for food since last night he had used everything they had in the room to make supper. Looking pathetic and begging at the Collegium kitchen for sausage and biscuits got him fed, and a couple of apple pocket pies into the bargain. As he headed back to Healers, he prodded Dallen. *:Guess what I got?:*

He could practically *feel* Dallen salivating, and made a quick change of destination. After all, he could get more later, when he went begging for storable food.

Or . . . if Amily's all tied up, I can go down to the market and get stuff, and get pies at that one liddle stand. . . .

:What are we doing, after you bring me my pies?: the Companion asked, as he reached the stable door.

:Yer gonna talk to that Evory and find out if Nikolas is awake, an' if the Healers left him clear-headed enough to fill me in on what he *was doin'.:* The door was shut tight against the cold, and the fireplaces—or more properly, ovens—at either end of the stable were going, keeping the interior warm. He slipped inside quickly, to avoid letting too much cold air in. Dallen was in his usual stall, right by Mags' old room. The Companion hung his head over the wall of the stall and stared at Mags' pocket purposefully.

"Keep yer hair on, horse," Mags laughed, and extracted the pies.

:I like Evory. I've always like Evory. She's sensible, she doesn't panic, and she's steady. It won't take her long to learn what she needs to in order to support a Herald who might technically be out of immediate reach a great deal of the time. And she says, Nikolas is awake, just finishing breakfast, and will be in fit shape to talk to you in a little while.:

The stable was quiet and dark with all the hatches and doors closed. It was like that in winter; thanks to the ovens built into either end, it never got *cold,* but it was cool enough that the few Companions who were still lazing about in their stalls this morning were wearing their blankets. Dallen had been double-blanketed, to prevent him from stiffening up after yesterday's fright. He looked as if he planned to stay in, and Mags didn't blame him in the least. He deserved a couple days' rest after what had been a truly heroic rescue.

"I wanta get to know her m'self," Mags pointed out. "Gonna be easier if I can talk to her direct when I need to." Mags had an unusually strong Gift of Mindspeech; he could actually hear the thoughts of those who didn't have the Gift themselves, and speak into their minds and be heard and understood. He could speak directly to almost every Companion—he had to temporize that with "almost," because he hadn't actually tried to speak directly to too many of them; the closest he had gotten was a direct, and widespread "shout" to anything and anyone with the Gift to hear him. But it helped to get to know the Companions, so he could recognize their individual Mindvoices.

:Right now, if she was allowed, she would go sleep on a rug in his room,: Dallen said dryly. *:Not that I blame her. This situation has unsettled everyone, but having your Chosen nearly die on you at the same time you Chose him . . . that's particularly . . . horrid.:*

Mags fed Dallen the second pie, thinking that Dallen was, if anything, understating the case. *:Has to be a first time for everythin',:* he said philosophically, and took his leave. *:I think what's mostly unsettled folks, when they start rememberin' again that we oughta be happy Nikolas is alive, is that it* is *the first time. 'Member how upset people was when things got changed to the Collegium way of bringin' up Trainees? An' that was with Bardic an' Healers already havin' that right there, workin'.:*

:True, that,: Dallen said, as Mags made his way back toward his original destination, pulling his cloak tight around him against the wind. *:No one runs from anything quite like they run from change.:*

Nikolas was nibbling on a piece of buttered bread when Mags arrived, looking as if he had next to no appetite. But he perked up when Mags came in the door and flung himself down in a chair. "Fine mess ye got yerself into," Mags said without preamble. "I thought *I* was the one s'pposed t'get into all the scrapes."

Nikolas looked . . . thoroughly battered. His left arm was in a sling, heavily bandaged, possibly splinted under the bandages. Most of his face was interesting shades of black, blue, purple and green. Mags really didn't want to think about what his body looked like under the loose, warm flannel smock they had put him in. The only things he didn't seem to have were cuts and gashes.

Nikolas shook his head very, very slightly. It probably hurt to move it even a little bit, despite whatever the Healers had poured into him in the way of potions. "Not only can I still scarcely believe what happened, I'm befuddled to think it was a stupid *accident."*

"No doubt?" Mags asked. He, himself, had been pretty certain it *had* been an accident—after all, he had seen most of it, and he could not for a moment imagine how anyone could have orchestrated such a thing—but he was glad to hear it directly from Nikolas.

"None at all," Nikolas replied, and grimaced. "Just a plain, stupid accident. I have a very considerate Healer in charge of my case; he brought me the Guard report this morning as soon as I was awake, knowing I was going to be fretting about it."

"Well, that's only sensible," Mags pointed out. "Usually when the King's Own gets dead, if it ain't sickness or old age, someone was after him."

"Not a shred of doubt," Nikolas confirmed. "Someone was moving a barrel of roof-tiles up to a second floor to mend a roof. A dog chased a cat between the legs of the fellow on the end of the rope, and he let go. The barrel crashed down into a cart, and some of the tiles hit the horse, battering and terrifying it, as if the crash behind it hadn't frightened it enough. And you know the rest. A pure, uncalculated accident. Even with the ability to compel animals to do something, I doubt it could have been pulled off deliberately. There were just too many variables there."

"Loony," Mags agreed. "Given how many people is usually shootin' at us an' the like, seems impossible."

"And yet—" said Nikolas.

"And yet," Mags agreed. "Well. I went an' read th' Council a sermon on countin' yer blessin's last night. Ev'one from the King on down had themselves in a fizz about what happened, an' all they could think about was disasters. I put 'em in mind of how it weren't anything like a disaster, an' did it a bit forceful. Hope it didn't come amiss." Truth to tell, he wasn't worried about *any* of what he had done, including the rather rude way he had spoken to the King. He wasn't in the least repentant. "Can't say I wouldn' do it again."

Nikolas managed a bit of a smile. "I'd have done the same. From what I understand they were panicking like a lot of chickens with a snake in the henhouse."

Well that was an apt simile, since a snake wouldn't be able to do anything worse than eat a few eggs, and if the silly hens would stop squawking and flapping, and work together, they'd be able to peck at it and drive it out . . .

They sat for a moment in silence together. Mags took a moment to cast his eye critically over the room, but found nothing to complain about. The walls had been painted a cheerful yellow, the usual tiled floor covered with a warm rug, and the window had heavy curtains that could be closed if the light made Nikolas' head ache—which it just might, considering. This was one of the rooms with a little iron stove inside the fireplace, which would keep the heat even, and there was plenty of wood there. The bedside table had been left with fruit and a pitcher of water. Mags was satisfied that the Herald was being properly pampered.

"Somethin' like," Mags agreed. "Ain't heard a peep 'bout it this mornin', so I reckon they're settled for now. So, I pretty much know yer hurtin' an' given th' choice, ye'd drink somethin' nasty an' sleep, but I gotta know what was on yer plate when ye went over the side of the bridge, an' I gotta make some arrangements t' handle it."

Which, of course, he did. Amily and Rolan would deal with the matters concerning the King's Own, but when it came to the matters concerning the King's Spy—that was all on Mags now.

"I didn't have much. It's mostly been King's Own business to concern myself with, now that it's coming on winter, and people are leaving their estates now that Harvest is over and settling in at Court. Just two things, really. There's someone with the nasty habit of blackmail in the Court, and he has got several people in knots." Nikolas sighed. "Of course, if they would stop climbing into beds they didn't belong in, or at least, if they are in arranged marriages, they'd had the good sense to arrange things properly with their spouses, there wouldn't *be* a problem."

Mags nodded. That was par for the course for the Winter Court—or, well, it was par for the course without a blackmailer. Marriage for love was not the norm among the highborn and the wealthy. And when people didn't marry for love . . . it was easy to predict what would happen next. The Seneschal made it his business to know just who was having assignations with whom, or at least the ones that were open secrets, and for those who were quartered in the Palace rather than fine houses up on the Hill, he arranged the assignment of rooms and suites to make things more discreet.

"So far, all he's asked for is money," Nikolas continued, "But there's always the concern he'll ask for something else, so I need you to find him."

Mags nodded. "Ye got anywhere with it?"

Nikolas shook his head, and finished the last bite of his bread and butter. "No, so you might just as well start with a fresh eye. No one but Kyril knows I was investigating. You might as well tell the Seneschal at this point, you will probably need his help."

Well that made things cleaner, if not easier.

"Anythin' else?" Mags asked. "Ye said there was two things."

"The reason I was in civilian clothing and afoot without

Rolan. There's a newish thief-master down in Haven who uses children." This time the hint of a smile on Nikolas' face was . . . interesting. If Nikolas hadn't been a Herald, Mags might have said there was a touch of cruelty there. "If he was a good master, I'd leave it for the Guard, but he's not. I've heard some things that made me want to pound a head. As soon as I find him, I'm taking those children away from him and recruiting them as intelligence agents."

"Coo! That's a right good idea!" Mags already knew what such thief-masters were like—stories might paint them as father figures, even kindly, but in reality they were generally vicious, and the children served them out of fear, not knowing that escape was possible. In fact, he'd pulled that particular act himself. He'd despised himself for it then, though he had never actually harmed the children in question, but here was a chance to put the balance right. "Since it looks like yer gonna be laid up fer a while, I'll handle that 'un too."

He already had a good idea of what he wanted to do. It would need money—but that was not a problem now. The Seneschal would learn he was Nikolas' adjunct, if the man didn't know already, and that meant that the Crown's purse was open to him.

Nikolas heaved a sigh of very real relief. "That eases my mind. I didn't want that situation to go too deeply into winter. I want those children out of that situation before their master can use freezing them as yet another punishment. From what I've heard of the man. . . ."

Nikolas didn't have to continue. He and Mags had worked the dark side of Haven more than enough to know some of the things that went on right under the noses of the Guard and the Heralds. The law-keepers couldn't be everywhere at once, and, unfortunately, it seemed that there would ever and always be people who only wanted to hurt and exploit others, and would find ways to do so.

"Huh." Mags pondered that. "Reckon I'll put that on m'plate first. Gimme the details, what ye got of 'em, anyway."

"I don't have much," Nikolas admitted. "It won't take long."

So it proved; Nikolas had no more than the neighborhood in which the thief-master was headquartered, and the fact that the boys were working, not as cutpurses or pickpockets, but as burglars, presumably rooftop-runners. When he heard that, Mags grinned.

"Yes, I know," Nikolas said, just a little crossly. "That couldn't be better for you, could it?"

"Hey now, ain't my fault I'm still a squib, an' still pretty good on the tiles," Mags protested. And it was true, really, although good food and good treatment had rectified some of the stunting that years of privation had given him, he was still undersized by the standards of the Heralds, most of whom— well, as children, the Trainees coming into the Collegium were generally used to eating a lot more, more often, and better than he had been.

He'd made up for some of that, but he still was never going to be anything but . . . short.

Nikolas sighed. "Forgive me. I'm a bit out of sorts."

"If I'd had a yesterday like yours, I'd be more'n a bit outa sorts," Mags assured him, getting up. "Hey, look on th' bright side. You ain't had any time to yerself in years. Now ye get to take some. So take some. Sleep, read, sleep some more, have long chats with yer new Companion, and sleep. Mebbe learn t'—I dunno, braid horsehair like I do. Or somethin' else with yer hands. Play draughts. Get a dartboard."

"I—" Nikolas began, then looked a little stunned. "You have a point."

"Glad ye see it my way." He waved his hand at his erstwhile mentor. "Be back t'check on ye later."

Because right now, he was going to go talk to the Seneschal and arrange to get some funds for his new project.

Amily kept her back very straight and her expression as enigmatic as she could. Now, sitting in what had been her father's chair next to King Kyril, was the time to keep anyone on the Council who didn't *know* her guessing about her.

She had never, ever expected to be in the Council Chamber, and certainly not in this chair.

This was the Greater Council Chamber, since this was a meeting of the full Council. She had already been confirmed as the new King's Own, and the full story of yesterday had been related and dissected and discussed until everyone was *completely* convinced it had been nothing more serious than an almost-tragic accident.

This was a relatively simple room; it held the great Council table, shaped like a circle with a piece missing, so that pages could enter the center of the circle and refresh water and winecups, and the plates of fruit and bread that stood at intervals, without having to reach over anyone's shoulders. The East side was all tall windows. The West side held a great fireplace, and she was very glad for its warmth. The North and South walls held identical maps of Valdemar drawn on light canvas. At need, tokens representing troops or other important things moving through the Kingdom could be pinned onto the canvas. The only tokens there now were troops stationed along the Karsite Border.

Right now, since her situation had been dealt with, the business before the Council was completely routine, and nothing that the King's Own needed to intrude into: tallies of emergency winter supplies for the Guard, and for the Heralds in the Field. She'd seen these tallies in the Chronicles, going back for years, and there was nothing out of the ordinary in them—

"Wait!" she suddenly said, into the middle of the dry recitation.

Silence descended on the room, and the eyes of every

Councilor at the table were suddenly on her. Finally King Kyril spoke.

"Herald Amily?" he said, dryly. "Was there something amiss?"

"The tallies for hay and straw," she said. "For the Heralds. What were they again?"

Now all eyes turned down the table to the fellow who had been reading out the tallies and having them automatically approved. He cleared his throat, and the tone in which he did so was strongly disapproving. He read them again, a bit louder than he needed to. "They are, to the bale, exactly the same as last year, with an increase for ten new Heralds in the Field," he added, his voice icy.

"And the Guard supplies the Waystations from those supplies, does it not?" she persisted.

He laughed shortly. "As everyone knows. But—"

"But there are *twenty-three* more Heralds in the Field this winter than last," she pointed out. "Not ten. It's the first lot of the big influx that made us go to the Collegium system in the first place. They're paired with senior Heralds, which means each of the Waystations on thirteen more circuits will need double the hay, and half again as much straw. You need to check the rest of your supplies for the Waystations too, although I think from what I remember they're all right. It was just the hay and straw tallies that seemed off to me."

The man's mouth dropped open, and snapped shut again.

"Why didn't someone notice until now?" asked the Seneschal, his face crossed with an expression of mixed irritation and disgust.

She just shrugged. "Things happen. It's all right, it's been noticed now."

The King nodded slightly. "Easily mended. Now, shall we continue?"

The tallies went on, but Amily was still thinking about the

discrepancy. *:Was that an accident . . . or something else?:* she asked Rolan.

There was some silence while Rolan considered her question. *:Well,:* he replied. *:It seems odd that every other tally was correct. Hay and straw are not dreadfully expensive this time of year . . . :*

:But when the supply falls short, at the end of winter?: she persisted. *:Isn't that when they are at their most expensive?:*

:And the shortfall would obviously have to be made up. Well spotted. I'll pass that on to the Seneschal's Herald.:

Unfortunately Amily couldn't talk to Leveret, the Seneschal's Herald, herself, the way her father could have—she *still* could only Mindspeak to Rolan. But that was all right; the suggestion that someone somewhere in that chain of procurement might be looking to feather his own nest would still get to the Seneschal as soon as there was a bit of a lull.

She settled back in her chair, and listened attentively to the rest of the Council meeting.

At least now no one was looking at her as if they thought she didn't belong. *One hurdle down. A thousand more to go.*

Mags surveyed the interior of the shop to the left of the Weasel's pawnshop with a great deal of satisfaction. The four oil lamps mounted to the walls lit up the place very nicely. Mind, people in this part of Haven rarely owned *one* oil lamp, much less four, but he wanted to minimize the risk of fire . . . and no one who didn't actually belong here was ever going to see the inside.

His little group of hired workmen had done their work well, and incuriously. The shop had been refurbished to a state most homes in this part of Haven never saw.

What had been the front of the shop had been turned into one large living space. The walls, which had been falling to bits, had gotten the plaster chipped off and replastered, then painted white. The wooden floor had been repaired and sanded so that the floorboards were nice and smooth. Overhead, the ceiling had been redone as well. The room would not have been out of place in a tradesman's house now. What had been a separate back-of-the-shop and store-room had been opened up so that the first floor was all one room; this was because the only source of heat, the fireplace at the rear, would otherwise not be able to properly warm the entire place.

Fortunately the chimney had been in good shape, although someone in the past had attempted to put in a sort of pottery "stove," perhaps in an attempt to economize on fuel. That had been removed, the fireplace had been repaired, the original pot-hooks put back in, and the original oven built into the side of it cleaned out and made fit for use again. The hearthstone had been replaced, the chimney swept. Next to the fireplace, a compact little kitchen had been installed, along with a stone sink, and an indoor pump to the same well the pawn shop used. These were all things most people who lived in this part of Haven did not have, but Mags was determined that *his* gang would never be tempted to sell their skills elsewhere, and these comparative luxuries would guarantee that.

The room was only sparsely furnished, outside of the table and cupboards for the kitchen and four benches. There were chests along one wall filled with a good assortment of used clothing in many sizes, and bedrolls and pillows along the other wall. There was only one bed—more of a frame with a straw-stuffed mattress—and that was reserved for the adult who would be in charge here. If she hadn't been as old as she was, he probably wouldn't have bothered with a bed for her, either; around here, everyone was accustomed to padding the floor with what they could and sleeping together in a huge pile, fully clothed, covered with anything they could find to keep them warm. This would be a considerable step upward for all of his recruits.

There was a pull-down staircase to the attic in the middle of the ceiling. The attic had also been refurbished and made weather-tight, and had also been supplied with bedrolls and pillows. Mags figured, based on his own experience as a mine-slave, better have too much bedding than too little.

The cellars had been freed of vermin, a "shop cat" had been

acquired, and the cellars fitted out with a well-stocked set of pantries, as well as other storage.

Everything was in readiness. Now he just had to make his moves.

While this place was being rebuilt, Mags had not been idle. He now knew exactly where that gang of young thieves was working, and who was in charge. It was going to give him a great deal of pleasure to take over from this particular thief-master. All he needed to know was where they were living, and he could make his move.

There was a tap at the door, a pause, two taps, another pause, and a scratch. That was the salutation he had been waiting for. Mags immediately went to the door, unlocked it, and opened it.

There were four people waiting just outside in the light from the lantern outside the door. One was a slightly stoop-backed old woman, who looked as if she was wearing every skirt, shirt, apron and shawl she owned. Which, of course, she was. But if her clothing was tattered, nearly worn to bits, and faded, it was also clean. Her gray hair was bound in a single neat braid down her back. And the dark eyes nestled in her wrinkled face were both shrewd and kind.

Clinging to her were three children of indeterminate age and sex; all three had shoulder-length hair, and all three were huddled in a hodge-podge of cast-off clothing far too big for them.

"Right on time, Aunty Minda," he said with satisfaction. "Come in, tell me if anythin's lackin'."

When he had conceived of this plan in the first place, he had known that there was one particular thing—or rather, person—that he could not do without. He was going to need a sort of "mother" for the youngsters, since he couldn't be there all the time, and he certainly couldn't leave them to fend for themselves. So he had his ear to the ground, so to speak, wait-ing and watching for the right sort of person to turn up. It had to be someone who was a denizen of these streets herself, so nothing the younglings said or did would be a shock—and so that, if correction or punishment needed to be meted out, the person in question would be able to apply something that would impress the miscreant with the gravity of the situation without abusing him. It had to be someone who liked boys— and someone with the right set of mothering instincts. It also had to be someone who was in need herself. . . .

Unfortunately in this part of Haven, that last was not all that hard to come by; it was all the other qualifications that had made for problems. There were any number of habitual drunks, any number of women who were too sick to keep track of one lively youngster, much less a houseful, any number whose notion of "correction" was to mete out beatings hard enough to scar.

But with the help of the local Guardsman on this beat, he'd found the perfect match.

"Aunty" Minda was well known for being a mother-figure to any child hereabouts who needed one. She was now a beggar, though not by choice; she was just too old to continue working as a scrubbing-woman. She had collected three cast-off children who begged with her, and had been protecting and feeding them as well as she could. But the attic room in which they all lived left a lot to be desired; it was not so bad in summer, but now that winter was here, she and the children were very likely to freeze to death.

When Mags had approached her with his proposition, she had been embarrassingly grateful.

And she'd had one caveat that clinched her in his mind as perfect for the job.

"This bain't a den'o'thieves now, be it?" she'd asked, "Because if 'tis . . ." her lip had quivered, and she'd looked half-stricken, but she still continued ". . . if 'tis, I cain't hev no part of it."

Mags had laughed. "Now, Aunty . . . I don't ast where peo-

ple get the stuff they sells us, but thievin' it m'self is astin' fer
a rope necklace! Nah, I'm branchin' out. Gonna hire out boys
as messengers an' such . . . and hev 'em keep their ears open
an mouths shut 'cept t'me. Uncle Weasel says sometimes
words is worth more'n sparklies, an' he's right."

That had satisfied the old woman, though only the gods
knew if she objected to being in charge of a theft ring because
stealing was *wrong,* or because *she* would get in as much
trouble with the law as the young thieves did.

It really didn't matter to him. What mattered was she'd
keep his recruits from backsliding.

Minda edged in through the door, the three little ones
pressed up against her, and Mags shut it behind her. The four
of them took in the state of their new home with expressions
more befitting someone who was viewing a palace than the
former shop. All four of them had eyes wide with wonder; the
littles all stared at that warm, big fire burning in the fireplace
at the rear, with its heaps of logs next to it. Minda was taking
in everything.

"Oo-aye, Master Harkon," Minda said, finally, "This—this
here's a wonder!"

"Dunno 'bout a *wonder,* Aunty, but it's good an' tight,
she'll be warm and cozy all winter, and none-so-bad come
summer. So settle yerselves in; 'tis yours, an' anythin' ye
need, ye come see me or the lads next door." Minda was not
aware that Mags was a Herald, of course. Not yet, anyway. So
far as she knew the plan was for Harkon to take over the gang
of thieves, bring the youngsters here for her to care for, and
employ them as overt messengers and covert information-
gatherers. *Everyone* knew that Willy the Weasel and his
nephew bought information. *Everyone* presumed they sold it
on—no one knew to whom, but that wasn't the sort of thing
the Weasel would ever want someone to know. Possibly he
engaged in a spot of blackmail now and again, but people who
were as poverty-stricken as those hereabouts saw nothing

wrong with blackmail. Only people with far more money than *they* had ever did things they could be blackmailed over, which just went to show that those who considered themselves "better" often didn't have the morals of a cat. And if they didn't want to be blackmailed, why then, they shouldn't be doing things they could be blackmailed *for.* And well done to Harkon and the Weasel for getting a bit out of them. This next step would just be cutting out the middleman, so to speak.

It was possible that one day Mags would take Minda and even some of the younglings into his confidence, but for now, the scheme would work just fine without any of them knowing who he really was. And the added benefit was that there would be one more lot of Haven's poorest who would be a little better off for it all.

"Here's yer key," Mag said, handing over one of the three iron keys he'd had made. "It opens the front an' the back door. Food's in cellar, an' so's the wood for the fire. Don't waste any, but don't stint, neither. Here's yer household money fer the fortnight." He put a leather pouch heavy with coppers and some silver into the hand that was holding the key. "Anythin' that's lackin', ye go get i' market. But keep good track. That'll have t' last ye the fortnight. I'm givin' ye thet long t' get things t'where ye like 'em, afore I bring in the rest."

After haunting these streets as much as he had, Mags knew pretty much to the penny how much it was going to cost to keep Minda and her three orphans for a fortnight, and there was that, and just a little more, for the odd sweet or treat.

"So now, ye settle in," he concluded. "There's stuff t'wear in them chests, Minda, the bed be fer ye, an' ye three littles figger out where ye want t'sleep. Next time I see ye, it'll be with a pack'f lads, so reckon ye best settle in quick as ye can."

With that, he left, before Minda could start gushing gratitude—*or* start asking too many questions.

By the stars, it was near midnight. Down on the streets, things were quiet. This was a residential street, in an area of tall, narrow houses so close together that people could open their windows and pass each other a pint of beer. Most people here were skilled craftsmen, prosperous, though not wealthy, prosperous enough to belong to Guilds. Their roofs were in fine repair, with not a loose tile nor a missing slate to make footing hazardous.

It was bitter cold up here on the roof, but Mags had the advantage of being pressed against the warm bricks of a chimney out of the wind while he waited for his quarry to show himself.

This was a set-up, a trap. Mags was going to catch himself a young thief. He'd made sure—by selling him the information himself!—that Gripper, the thief-master to these boys, had heard that the stone-carving owner of this house had gotten an unexpected bonus for finishing a job early, and had invested the money in a fine silver vase. This was the sort of thing Gripper's "lads" were adept at stealing; small enough to carry away easily, large enough for a fine profit. Mags knew that it wouldn't be long before the Gripper sent one of his boys to fetch it, and he'd been up here for three nights, waiting. Amily had been very patient about sleeping alone these three nights—but then, she'd had plenty to keep her occupied too.

Mags was listening very closely as well as keeping watch. He wasn't certain which of the boys was going to be sent to snatch this particular prize, but whoever it was, he was not going to be good enough to get past Mags.

Even above the whistle of the wind among the chimneys, Mags picked up the sound of feet slipping a little on the tiles. A moment later, he caught sight of what he was watching for, a moving shadow edging along the roof-line, heading for the gable window. Then the shadow disappeared under the edge of the roof, and Mags heard the sound of the window being opened, bit by tiny bit. When the sounds ceased, there was a long pause, and then a faint *thump.*

Moving far more silently than his quarry could, Mags followed; he made his way down the slope of the roof, swung over the roof-edge and in through the still-open window before the boy had any idea he was even there.

And once inside, he slammed the interior shutters closed and dropped a bar over them, putting his back to them. "Now, boys!" he said aloud, and the two former actors who worked at the pawnshop each unhooded the lanterns they'd been holding, flooding the attic room with light.

Frozen about a length away from Mags was a skinny little lad with hair as black as soot, and ragged clothing to match. The look in his eyes was of absolute panic, when he realized that he was trapped.

Aha! Luck was with him. This was one Mags actually knew, although the boy didn't know *him.* Even better. When he came out with the lad's name, well, it would seem as if the man who'd trapped him here had supernatural powers.

"Don' even twitch, Coot," he growled. "You ain't goin' nowhere 'till we lets ye."

With a moan of terror and despair, the boy collapsed into a quivering knot on the floor. This was perfect. Coot was *not* at all brave, and was about as likely to fly as he was to try and make a break for it now that he'd been caught.

Right now, the last thing in the lad's mind was that he'd been ambushed. He more likely thought that Mags and his two accomplices were servants of the owner of the place.

"Don' kill me!" the boy moaned through chattering teeth as Mags approached, slowly and deliberately, making sure each footfall was audible. "Don' kill me!"

"Got no plan t' kill ye, Coot," Mags replied, squatting down on his heels next to his captive. "Got other plans, altogether. . . ."

———————

The night was fading fast. It had taken some clever talking, and Coot was practically soiling himself with fear before it was over, but now Mags and the boy were strolling along a noisome street behind the tanner's district. The street was not paved. The air stank from the tanning yards. Rent was the cheapest in all of Haven, and more than half the buildings were empty at any one time. No one lived here who had other options, and the buildings showed it. They were in such bad repair that they leaned to one side or the other—to the point where it looked very much as if that leaning into each other was the only thing keeping them from tumbling down. Mags would never, ever roof-run around here; he'd be taking his life in his hands if he tried.

Mags had endured worse smells—and tonight, there was no wind, so the worst of the stink was staying put and not wafting over this street. But it did say something about this district that not even starlings would nest in the ramshackle eaves.

Mags had one arm over the lad's shoulders—outwardly friendly, but in reality as a precaution to keep him from running. Beneath his false camaraderie, he could feel Coot shaking as if he had a fever. "Now remember," Mags repeated, for the twentieth time. "We go up t' door. Ye tell 'em thet I'm here 'cause I got some business wi' t'Gripper. Thet's all ye need t'say. I'll do the rest."

Coot nodded frantically.

Mags squeezed his shoulder. Hard. Not so hard as to hurt him, but enough to make him feel how strong Mags was. "Jest do what I tol' ye. Nothin' more. Nothin' less. Do thet, an' ye'll be glad. Don't, an' ye'll be sorry, but not fer long."

Coot's trembling redoubled.

By this point they had reached the ramshackle building Coot had indicated was where the gang was quartered. It was nearly dawn, so all the members of the gang should be back by now, and Gripper was probably wondering where Coot was—or had already assumed Coot had been caught. If this had been Mags' gang, there would have been someone keeping a watch out—but the Gripper was not nearly as clever as he thought he was, for he didn't keep watches.

The more fool he.

Mags let go of Coot at the door, and the lad went up and knocked in a simple pattern. A section of the door slid aside, and a pair of eyes stared suspiciously at them. Mags came in for nothing more than a cursory glance. Coot got a full-on stare. Whoever Gripper had on door-watch was an idiot.

"Yer late," said a muffled voice. "Gripper ain't half mad."

If this had been Mags' gang . . . Mags would have assumed by now that Coot had been caught and was spilling his guts to the Guard. He'd have packed everyone up and moved them to another hideout. Evidently Gripper was no smarter than the boy he'd put on door-guard.

"I got . . . I got summun t'see Gripper," Coot stammered, shaking all over. " 'E says 'e gots somethin'—"

"Of int'rest," Mags finished smoothly, stepping up to the door. "Ye knows Willy th'Weasel?"

"Aye . . ." the voice replied cautiously.

"I be Harkon. I got business w' Gripper." He grabbed Coot's upper arm, and both pushed him aside and held onto him. "Ye gonna lemme in?"

Whatever the boy on the other side thought of what Mags had said, he was smart enough to figure out that the flimsy door was not going to protect him from "Harkon" if "Harkon" decided to come through it. And "Harkon" had more than a bit of a reputation as a tough. The boy opened it quickly. Mags shoved Coot inside, and followed, taking in his surroundings quickly.

That . . . was another new thing, since getting all those Sleepgiver memories from his cousin. He'd always been good at assessing things, what with Nikolas' training and all, but now—

Now, he could take in *everything* in the space of a heartbeat or two.

Like the shop he'd set up for his new "gang," this building was a single room, though whether it had always been that way, or whether it had been gutted, it was impossible to tell. Unlike the shop, the second floor—or attic—was gone, leaving only the rafters and a few boards here and there to show where it had been. Mags had no doubt that when it rained there were more leaks than solid roof. This place was as much a wreck on the inside as it was on the outside.

The floor was hard-packed dirt, so there was no cellar, which meant everything this gang owned was right here in this room. The fireplace at the far end—which had a number of missing bricks—let out as much smoke as it did heat and light. There was no hearthstone, no cranes for pots to hang over the fire, and not even a couple of pots by the fire. There was no sign of anything like a kitchen, but then, who among this lot would even know how to cook? Mags suspected they bought everything they ate at cookshops, or stole it out of the trash. Maybe they "cooked" what they could steal or buy on sticks over the fire. He shuddered to think of what they were getting.

Light was provided by crude torches stuck in makeshift holders along the walls, and he was astonished that they hadn't yet managed to set fire to the place.

Lounging next to the fire on a sort of throne made of boxes, ragged cushions and tattered blankets full of holes was Gripper. The rest of the boys were huddled on the piles of rags along the wall that probably served them as beds; some gaped at Mags with scraps of food clutched in their hands.

Gripper slowly sat up, glaring at the intruder, as Coot scuttled to one side.

Gripper wasn't tall, but he was heavily muscled; if there had ever been any doubt in Mags' mind that Gripper held his sway over his gang by use of his fists, that doubt was over now. Mags judged him to be no more than a couple years older than he himself was, but those years had been very hard on Gripper. His nose had been broken more than once, he had no more than half his teeth and the ones in front were jagged and broken. His long, greasy hair was scraped back into a matted tail tied with a piece of leather thong, impossible to tell what color it was. His clothing consisted of several layers of food-stained tunics, over leather trews. It didn't look as if he had ever taken anything off, much less washed it. It was all held to his body with a thick leather belt that held two knives.

"'Allo, Gripper," Mags said, easily, hooking both thumbs into his own belt, and taking a relaxed posture.

Gripper grunted, frowning. "Yer pretty free with m'name, seein' as I don' know ye. Ye tol' Berk ye had business wif me, an' I don' remember no business wif the likes of yew."

"Oh, I got business all right," Mags replied, carelessly. "I'll make it short, so ye unnerstand me. I'm takin' yer gang."

Gripper stared at him for a moment, as if he couldn't understand what Mags had said. And then he burst out laughing.

"Yew!" Another howl of laughter emerged from that caricature of a mouth. "Yew! Why yew ain't—"

And then Gripper wasn't laughing anymore, he was gasping for breath. Using the techniques he had acquired and practiced of how the Sleepgivers fought—on the rare occasions that they actually fought someone openly, that is—Mags had crossed the space between them in two flips before Gripper had even been aware he was moving, ending by driving both feet into Gripper's gut. Bouncing backward in another flip as Gripper fell back onto his improvised "throne," Mags landed on his feet and charged forward again, delivering a flurry of hard blows to Gripper's stomach and chest. Gripper wasn't even able to fight back; he was too busy trying to get a breath. He couldn't even gasp. Mags didn't care.

Mags grabbed his greasy tunic, hauled the now purple-faced, pop-eyed gang leader to his feet, and spun both of them in a half-circle. Then he hauled back and punched Gripper in the chin so hard that the man lifted right up off his feet and measured his own length on the dirt floor.

And once down, he didn't move.

There was a long moment of incredulous silence from the boys ranged along the walls. Then, with an hysterical yell, Coot charged in from the side and began raining blows with fists and feet on the prone Gripper. A heartbeat later, every boy in the building was kicking, hitting or pummeling the now unconscious "master" thief, letting out pent-up rage that had been held in for far too long.

Given the little that Mags had learned about the man, it seemed no more than a fraction of the punishment he'd earned.

Mags let them have their way. After what he had heard, he frankly did not care if they murdered the man. He sat on a box and let them wear themselves out.

When the last of them had delivered the last, weary kick to the pulped mess on the floor, he cleared his throat.

Eleven pairs of eyes were instantly riveted on him.

"No more beatin's, no more gettin' locked out by night. Real beds," he said into the silence. "New clothes fer ev'rbody. Reg'lar meals, an' no shit 'bout makin' a quota afore ye et. No quotas, 'tall. New job. Once't yer cleaned up an' lookin' right, yer messenger runners. On'y, ye keep yer eyes an' ears open, an ye hear *anythin'* innerestin', ye come straight back an' tell. If'n it's good stuff, I pay ye. Elsewise, ye keep yer messenger penny. Who's in?"

———————

If there had been anyone out in the street to see the odd parade, Mags and his new gang would have made a strange sight, him leading the way and a tumble of eleven skinny ragamuffins trailing along behind him. However, he took care to take a path to Aunt Minda's little home that was likely to be deserted. He didn't mind a couple people seeing them, but he would rather that folks didn't get too curious.

He also hadn't let the boys bring anything from their previous "home" other than a couple of personal possessions. He'd left word with the Guard that they were to check Gripper's hideout at dawn, and he wanted the Guard to find whatever the boys had stolen that night, plus whatever else Gripper had squirreled away from previous thefts. Gripper had still been breathing when they'd all left. Mags was no Healer, but he thought that Gripper was likely to survive the candlemark or so until the Guard found him. After that? It was not his problem.

Once at their destination, Mags unlocked the door and threw it wide. The boys at the front of the group gasped at the sight that met them. The rest crowded forward to see, until the whole mass tumbled inside.

Aunty Minda had stood up from her bed, a smile of welcome on her weathered old face, and her arms spread wide. "Ah, come to Aunty, my little chickens!" she called, and to Mags' intense pleasure, as he closed and locked the door behind his new gang, not a boy hesitated to come closer. Some, the three or four youngest, actually burst into tears and flung themselves at Minda's skirts. The others came forward shyly, or hesitantly, or with pretended boldness. But all of them responded positively to the old woman.

In almost no time at all, she had them all seated around her and digging into big bowls of cabbage stew with chunks of brown barley bread. She and Mags had conferred earnestly together on just what the boys' first meals should be—he, with the experience of having starved, and she, with the experience of feeding the starving—and they had settled on this as least likely to harm them, most likely to fill their bellies in a satisfying manner.

And *now,* now that they were feasting themselves as they probably had not eaten in months, if not years, now that they were warm, now that they saw with their own eyes that what Mags had promised was true, he stood up and cleared his throat.

Once again, he was the center of attention for eleven boys.

"This's how it'll be," he said, sternly. "Aunty Minda's yer keeper. Ye don't obey, yer out. Ye make her mad, yer out. Gods help ye if ye hurt her, 'cause I'll beat ye bloody an' *then* throw ye out. Ye bring trouble here, yer out. Ye bring the law here, yer out. Anybody cain't hold with any of that?"

Eleven heads shook "no," a couple of them violently.

"Tha's good." He nodded. "Now. I'm gonna leave ye with Aunty fer some days. She's gonna turn ye inta summat people'll trust t'carry messages, while I get it set up wi' inn-keepers an' suchlike. Ye do what she tells. She tells ye t'scrub yer skin off, then off it comes. No arguments. While she gets ye fit, ye sleeps, eats, gets some meat on yer bones so ye're fit t'run like the wind when yer told t'run. Ye all good with that?"

Eleven heads bobbed so hard he had to suppress a burst of laughter.

"Aunty?" He raised his eyes to meet Minda's. "This still suit ye?"

"Oh aye," she said, softly, from the middle of the crowd of somewhat noisome younglings. "Oh aye, Marster Harkon. It suits."

He nodded brusquely. "Then I'll be off. Be back when I'm back. An' when I'm back, ye best be ready t'work."

He turned and headed for the door.

Only to be hit from behind by four of the boys, who plastered themselves to him, babbling incoherent thanks. One of them was even crying.

One of them was Coot.

He hardly knew what to do at that point . . . *this* was not something he had anticipated happening. It felt . . . good. But uncomfortable at the same time. He patted their filthy heads and shoulders awkwardly, until at last Aunty called "Time for seconds!" and began dishing out second helpings of bread and stew. Only then, they peeled themselves off him, and went back to their newly-refilled bowls.

He waved goodbye at the door, and hurried out, before the tears stinging his eyes could actually fall. After all, he was supposed to become their taskmaster. It wouldn't do to show any weakness.

:Looks like we did better than we had thought, Chosen,: Dallen said thoughtfully, as he made his way as swiftly and silently as he could, heading for the inn where he could resume his Whites. *:I expected more resistance or rebellion. I certainly expected to lose at least a third of them who wouldn't be willing to serve another master.:*

:Aye,: Mags replied, his jaw clenching. *:All of which makes me think . . . Gripper was worse than we thought. I'm beginning to regret not killing him.:*

He expected a rebuke from Dallen for that rather un-Heraldic thought. And he got one . . . sort of. *:He's not worth you getting his blood on your hands. And besides . . . :*

There was a long pause.

:Besides what?:

:Under the circumstances . . . surviving this is going to be much, much worse for him. Prison is not going to be kind to him.:

That teased a ghost of a smile from him.

:Aye,: he replied. *:You're probably right.:*

:Oh, aren't I always?:

———————

"Damn and blast," said the King with irritation, as he tossed a letter aside. Amily immediately set aside the notes she had been taking on another missive. She was just as glad to; it was long, repetitive, and concerned a situation within Duke Perrin's family that there was *no way* the King was going to interfere with. The Duke, however, seemed under the impression if he repeated himself enough, the King would cave in.

This, evidently, had been one of her father's duties; to sit in the King's study with him over breakfast, and distill things like Duke Perrin's letter down to a few sentences. She didn't mind the sitting in the study; it was possibly the most comfortable room in the entire Palace; small, cozy and warm, with a pair of chairs that allowed one to sit at ease. She very much enjoyed the breakfast; obviously the King got the best of the best. But she was by no means certain she was . . . competent enough to tell what was important in these letters, and what was not.

Then again, maybe nothing is, and he already knows that. Maybe he's testing my ability to cut straight to the heart of a matter.

"Majesty?" she said. "Is there something I can help with?"

King Kyril rubbed his eyes with his right hand, then pinched the bridge of his nose between his thumb and forefinger. "No, nothing you can *help* with," he said with a sigh. "But something you need to know about. Lord Kaltar gave notice a fortnight ago that he intended to bring his family up to their manor in Haven for the Midwinter Court."

"I remember," she nodded.

"Well, *this* letter is from Lord Leverance. Who intends to bring *his* household up to *their* manor for the Midwinter Court." The King actually stabbed the offending letter with a paper-knife. "Kaltar's household will be here within a day, so it's too late to let *him* know, and Leverance's letter was sent the day they set off, so it's too late to stop *them.*" The King removed the letter opener and stabbed the letter a second time. Now she knew why his desk was scarred with knife-marks. *"Damn and blast."*

Amily was fully in sympathy with the King's feelings.

Everyone knew of the feud between the two families—although the number of people who knew the actual cause of the feud could probably be counted on the fingers of one hand. It had been going on for at least as long as Amily had been alive.

For almost ten years, the King had managed to keep the two families apart, but it appeared that either by accident or malicious design, that was not going to be the case anymore. Privately, Amily expected that it was malicious design. Probably, so did the King.

It would accomplish nothing to say so, however.

"Well . . . why are they *saying* they are coming?" she asked, for she had not been privy to the contents of those letters.

"Matchmaking," Kyril said, sitting up a little straighter, and turning to eye her. "Lord Kaltar of House Raeylen has an only son he wants to marry off, and I have no idea what he's looking for in a girl for the boy. Lord Leverance of House Chendlar has three daughters, and I *do* know what he is looking for; he wants a lad with money and no land for one of them, who'd be willing to give up his own family name and adopt Chendlar."

Amily blinked. "Is that likely?"

Kyril snorted. "Chendlar isn't that exalted a name. That's what the feud's about. Before you were born, Leverance's sister was offered to Kaltar, rather bluntly, and Kaltar's father was . . . less than diplomatic about the rejection, and Leverance's father was just as harsh about the rebuttal. I believe that words like *If you'd spent less time siring bastards and more time tending your fields you might not live in a hall that sings in seventy voices when the wind blows,* and *I have bitches with better pedigrees* were exchanged."

Amily winced. "But. . . ."

"But yes, under ordinary circumstances, that would simply turn the families into enemies without the bloodshed. Unfortunately, one of those aforementioned bastards decided to prove . . . something . . . to the old man. I'm not sure what the young fool was thinking, maybe that he would avenge the insult, but the short story is the idiot got himself killed, and the feud escalated." Kyril ran his hand over his face in exasperation. "It spilled over into the streets more than once, to the point where my father had to assign the Guard to supervise every move every member of the households made outside of their manors."

"Perhaps with children in need of appropriate spouses, they'll confine themselves to sour faces and muttered insults?" Amily suggested, without much hope. Then a thought occurred to her. "Perhaps you could insinuate someone into each household—friends for the son and the daughters? Then you'd at least get some warning if something was about to boil over. Mags has 'Magnus,' who would probably do very well for that task."

"Mags would certainly do as a local friend for the son," the King agreed, and tapped his fingers on his desk, thinking. "In fact . . . he might actually be able to *prevent* some of those hotheads from starting altercations, if he manages to get enough influence on the boy." He gave Amily a long, speculative look. "Who would you suggest for the daughters?"

"Lady Dia Jorthun," Amily said promptly. "She's not so pretty that they'd consider her competition, and given her own lineage and marriage, they'd consider themselves flattered and lucky that she was taking an interest in them. And she was part of our little circle that kept Nikolas informed of what was going on among the children of the courtiers. She knows not only how to hold her tongue, but how to get other girls to confide in her."

The King made a note. "Lady Dia it is. I'll speak to her myself, I know I can leave Mags up to you." He let out his breath in something that was not quite a sigh. "This Midwinter Court is not going to be *easy,* but we just might be able to keep things from exploding into duels and fistfights."

"From the sound of things, Majesty," Amily said slowly. "I think I would be grateful to keep it *just* to fistfights."

The King grimaced. "You're probably right. But we'll see. You never know what's likely to happen."

Well, if there was ever a statement Amily was going to agree with wholeheartedly . . . it was that.

"Harkon" returned to the shop at midday, on the fourth day after he had dropped the boys off with Aunty Minda. He was pleased to find the door locked, and used his key, after giving the signal-knock he had taught Minda.

But the door was opened for him, before he could push it open, and when he stepped inside, he had to repress a grin, for he scarcely recognized the younglings he had recruited.

Or would it be better to have said, "rescued"?

They'd all had their hair cut short, no surprise there; he'd have been astonished if anyone could have dragged even the coarsest comb through those matted locks. They were all now—inadvertently—blonds. The preparation for head lice Minda had intended to use on them had that effect, or so she had told him. Well, the blond hair would grow out, and meanwhile, it gave them a sort of pleasing uniformity.

He'd caught them at their midday meal of bread and thick, bean soup, and already they looked significantly better than they had when he'd last seen them. They were all staring at him with expressions ranging from wariness to veiled fear, but he waved a dismissive hand at them. "Gerron wi' yer food," he said. "Aunty, a word."

Minda left her chair beside the fire, and he led her over to a bit of bench near the door. "Well?" he said. "How're they shapin' up?"

"A few troubles," the old woman said candidly. "Nay as many as we thought. There was some sass, but afore I could even say ary a word, one or another'f the other lads smacked th' barstard acrost the head!"

He nodded. That was a very good sign. "An thievin'?" he persisted. "When ye let 'em out?"

"Nay so much as a pin," she told him, sounding surprised herself. "I think their marster give 'em the cald grue about yon Guard. 'Struth, they spent a good bit of first day beggin' me t' tell 'em they *warn't* goin' thievin'!"

"Well good," he replied grimly. "Thet means I ain't gonna have ta give 'em the cald grue m'self."

He stood up and strolled over to the boys, who stopped eating, some with the spoons halfway to their mouths, staring at him in apprehension.

He looked them over carefully. The assorted used garments he'd bought for them, he'd purchased with an eye to making them look as uniform as possible. So they were all in plain black trews, and plain black tunics. Or—well, as "black" as used clothing could get, which meant a sort of charcoal gray. *Nothing* like Trainee Grays, of course. They'd all been supplied with thick felt boots with leather soles—felt was cheaper than leather, and with a couple of pairs of socks, a lot more forgiving, so the sizes didn't need to be even close. And they'd all gotten black belts of heavy canvas, with messenger pouches to match. Under their tunics, they all had thick woolen sweaters knitted out of odds and ends of leftover yarn, or yarn salvaged by unraveling an older sweater and knitting it up again into a new one, so various drab colors peeked out at collars and cuffs. Hanging up on hooks along one wall were the wool-lined, canvas capes they would wear when they went outside.

None of these clothes fitted *well*. In fact, it looked as if Aunty had erred on the side of "too large," since shirt-sleeves and trews were rolled up and tied in place, and tunics held in with belts. Fortunately, all of those trews would have drawstring waistbands, but every one of these boys could probably have smuggled a bushel of apples in his pants. There were patches and darned places on every garment. Nevertheless, this was probably the warmest, best-dressed, and most comfortable they'd all been in their short lives.

"So," he said, raking them with his glance. "Ye've shaped up. Minda says ye ain't givin' her much trouble. Tha's good, I won't have ta toss any'f ye out."

The looks of relief that spread across the hunger-pinched faces told him everything he needed to know.

"Now, from whut I know, ye're all roof-runners, aye?" he asked.

The boys exchanged wary looks. Finally Coot spoke up. "Aye, Cap'n," he said, giving Mags the title common to those who ran theft rings.

Mags nodded. "Here's whut I wanta know. Are ye *fast?* Cuz I need boys whut's fast. If ye ain't fast, I'm holdin' ye back till ye *get* fast. That means no extree dosh, no special favors, jest bed an' bowl."

He was met with surprised blinking. It had never even occurred to them that he was going to give them anything other than the food, clothing and beds he had already! He nodded as they slowly came to understand what being in *this* gang was going to mean.

Still eating, they huddled up for a moment, speaking to each other in low, urgent voices. He suppressed a grin, as he could sense what all this meant. Aunty Minda had put the fear in them, all right, fear of being thrown out! He'd chosen exactly the right woman for the job.

After a few moments of talking, the boys turned back to him. He dug out a little notebook and a bit of pencil and waited, pencil poised above a blank page. One by one, they stated their names—or more precisely, the name Gripper had given them—and what it was they could do.

"Aight," he said, when they were done, perusing the page. "Grub, Flea, Ash, an Jo. Yer gettin' held out fer now." The four boys named looked disappointed, but also as if they had pretty much expected this. "Yer job—" he continued, pointing the pencil at them "—is t'practice runnin'. Tha's what ye do. When yer fast, ye'll join the crew. Rest of ye, I got three inns that'll take ye on messenger's bench."

In the simplest possible terms, he described what their job would be—which wasn't really at all difficult. Take a message, run it to where it was supposed to go, get confirmation and run back. "But there'll be lads that'll try an' cheat ye," he warned. "So, *allus* get yer penny afore the start. *Never* agree t'get paid on t'other end. An' never, *ever,* get inter a race, where feller says 'e'll hire two on ye, an' on'y pay the one thet gets there fastest. Unnerstand?"

They all nodded.

"Now, that there's the open part've job. Like Weasel's shop next door, all open an 'bove board. Right?" He chuckled, and so did they, because everyone knew that the Weasel was a fence as well as a pawnbroker. "So, on the quiet-like. Ye keep yer ears open. Ye hear summat 'bout a man's business, ye tell t'me. Ye hear summat about summun or somethin' gettin' nicked, ye tell me. *Anythin'* that seems innerestin', ye tell me. If I like it, ye gets t'keep yer messenger penny. An' t'make it easier, Aunty Minda's gonna teach ye readin' an' writin' arfter supper."

He had expected some groans, but instead, he got nothing but perked up heads and nods. After a moment, he realized why. These boys knew they couldn't be messengers forever; a grown man couldn't run as fast as a fleet and agile boy, especially not one that could scamper over rooftops to avoid problems in the streets, or take short cuts over fences and between parked carts. But a boy that knew how to read and write—well, he could get himself another respectable sort of job when he outgrew being a messenger. He could work at a shop, or in a tavern. He could work for a stall-keeper who was himself illiterate. There were scores of things he could do as long as he was literate. A boy that knew how to read and write would never go hungry again.

That . . . had never occurred to him. Not until this moment, when he saw it in their faces, the moment that he told them that they actually *had* a future, because he was going to give them something that no one could steal from them, and that would always be useful.

He hadn't thought about that at the mine, when he'd been indifferently taught reading and writing by his master's daughter. But then, at the mine, he'd never thought he would ever be free of the mine. And *he* hadn't known the value of what he was being taught. These boys did.

"Aight. T'morrow I'll come for ye. Show ye yer stations. Aunty Minda'll give ye summat t'eat fer nuncheon, an' *save* it, don' go gobblin' it, 'cause thet's all ye get till supper. An' don't go thinkin' ye kin hold back pennies; innkeeper'll be keepin' track."

He wouldn't, of course. The innkeeper had more than enough to do without keeping track of which messenger boys were going out. But the boys wouldn't know that, and Mags was not inclined to lose any money for Minda, who was the beneficiary of this little business.

"I'll be back at supper t'hear if'n ye got summut of innerest fer me. Arfter that, yer on yer own. Ye kin choose t'slack off, but that means no chancet fer pennies, aye?"

"Aye, Cap'n," came the chorus. The boys all looked determined. And really, they *should* be. They had gone from being virtual slaves, to this. They'd be fools not to appreciate it.

And if there was one thing Mags was sure of, it was that no boy who was a fool had survived for long under Gripper.

This was by no means one of the finest manors on the Hill. It was also in the section where the manors themselves were rather close together, with nothing in the way of lawn or ornamental foliage in the front, although they did have very nice long gardens in the rear. The gray stone building was old, and had not been renovated in the last hundred years, at least. To enter the manor, you had only to go up a set of five steps and you were right at the double wooden doors that marked the entrance.

And once admitted, you found yourself in a somewhat dark anteroom that did not boast any sort of heat-source. Lord Leverance had elected to meet Amily there, and thus far, no one in the family was moving from the spot, although the three daughters were looking chilly and uncomfortable. *At least I am still in my nice warm cloak,* she thought, pitying the girls. All three looked very like their mother, with brown eyes, round, doll-like faces, and brown hair. Lady Leverance did not look particularly pleased to be standing about in the cold antechamber either, but she, at least, had a much warmer wool-plush overgown than her daughters. Looking from the eldest to her mother and back again, Amily guessed that her Ladyship had been no more than fourteen or fifteen when she'd had her first child. And from the research she had done in the Archives, Amily already knew it had been an arranged marriage. There was no love there . . . although there was no loathing either.

Still, her Ladyship seemed friendly enough. Unlike his Lordship.

Amily was holding tightly to her mask of serenity, even though "serene" was the last thing she felt in the face of Lord Leverance's obvious and blatant disapproval of her. But he didn't dare *say* anything. She was the King's Own, after all, and having her turn up to welcome his Lordship to Haven and the Winter Court was the highest possible honor, short of sending the Prince or Princess Royal.

But she could tell he didn't approve of her, and she thought she knew why. She was young, and female. Or perhaps the level of disapproval was reserved more for the "female" part than the "young," but put together, they represented both change and a reversal of what he considered to be the proper social order, and he was not at all pleased.

She just hoped that what she had to say next was going to sweeten all this sourness, as she finished reciting the official message of welcome.

"And as a token of his esteem, the King would also like to offer you the services of Dia, Lady Jorthun as an aid to your marital negotiations this season. She's the wife of Lord Jorthun of Ayersmark," she added, at the moment of blankness that crossed Lord Leverance's face.

Well, he might not have recognized Jorthun's name, but he *certainly* recognized Jorthun's Duchy of Ayersmark. His disapproval vanished in an instant—because, basically, the King had just sent along the lady ranked just below the Princess Royal in the Court to help with his matchmaking.

Dia stepped forward, a smile on her pretty face. She was dressed expensively and exquisitely, her overgown of thick blue velvet, the sleeves lined in mink, the collar and hem trimmed in the same fur, a muff of blue velvet and mink, and her undergown of quilted and embroidered samite. There was absolutely no doubt that she was not sloughing off Lord Leverance and his family by wearing her second-best.

In the past year, Dia had not only scored the marriage-coup of the decade, she had matured into a gorgeous woman. Or, perhaps the first had been the result of the second. In any event, she had also matured into something else—*the* person one called on when one wanted to make a stir on the social scene, because Dia knew everyone, and everyone owed her social favors. Her friendship with the Princess Royal didn't hurt her standing in the least, and neither did the fact that she and her husband absolutely adored one another.

"I'm here for one thing and one thing only," Dia said, as Lord Leverance bowed deeply to her. "And on His Majesty's express orders." She turned to Leverance's three daughters. "I am here to get you into *all* of the *best* Midwinter parties!" She dimpled. "If there is an important party you miss, it will only be because you had the bad taste to fall ill."

If the import of this was lost on the girls—other than the excitement of being escorted into the season's finest social events—it was *not* lost on either Leverance or his wife, who gasped, and then curtseyed deeply to Dia, clutching her hand in gratitude. "Your Ladyship!" Lady Leverance babbled. "You are too kind—you are too generous—we are most grateful!"

"Oh, nonsense," Dia said, tugging on Lady Leverance's hand to get her to rise. "I'm nothing of the sort. I'm only too happy to oblige. *You* may come to regret my so-called 'kindness' after a fortnight of trotting from one party to another!" She raised one eyebrow, shrewdly. "I hope you understand that there will be *at least* two, and possibly as many as four every day."

At just that moment, before her Ladyship could respond to that, one of the chief reasons why Amily had recruited Dia's help poked his little head out of the hole in the front of her muff made precisely for that purpose. Lord Leverance politely ignored the . . . intruder . . . but all three girls gasped and Lady Leverance stared.

"Oh! What is that?" asked the youngest, Violetta, (who was, in Amily's opinion, the prettiest and by far the best tempered of the three). "It's *adorable!*"

"He is a warming-spaniel," Dia said with authority. "They are especially bred and trained to be unobtrusive. They stay in your muff to keep your hands warm, and when you are sitting, they come and sit under your dress to keep your feet warm. They are *all* the thing. I breed them myself—or rather, my dog-man does, and trains them."

Violetta had, by this time, come close to Dia and was coaxing the little dog to stick his head out of her muff again. "He's the sweetest thing I ever saw!" she said artlessly. "But what . . . when he has to go . . . you know?"

"He lets you know he needs to, you put down the muff so he can get out, and he goes off to the nearest spot of earth to take care of matters," Dia said, in her most kindly of voices. "Then he comes right back. Would you like to see him out of the muff?"

"Oh yes, please!" cried the girl, and Dia obliged by bringing the dog out in her right hand. It was a tiny spaniel with long, silky golden hair, and enormous brown eyes, scarcely the size of a puppy even though it was obviously full-grown.

Now, all of this was absolutely the truth. These tiny lapdogs *were* all the rage, they *had* been bred for exactly this purpose, and Dia *did* raise and train them. In fact, her dogs were much sought after. But Dia hadn't brought the dog here by accident.

Dia handed him over to Violetta, who was instantly crooning over him, obviously completely smitten.

Which was precisely what Amily wanted.

"Well, I can see you know dogs," said Dia, with a pleasant laugh. "And Star clearly likes you. Would you like to have him?"

"Oh, more than anything! Please, *could* I?" There was no doubt that Violetta had fallen completely head over heels with the little dog; she looked to her parents with entreaty, her huge brown eyes wide with pleading.

"Out of the question—" began her mother. "I cannot possibly allow you to—"

"Oh, but you must," Dia replied firmly . . . so firmly that her tone reminded Lady Leverance immediately who outranked whom, here. "First of all, it will establish your family as being educated in the current modes. Second, I would be ever so pleased to place one of my dogs with someone who so clearly will give him the love he needs. He's not one I have grown attached to, yet; he's one of the latest litter, just now finished with his training. I insist that you take him, Violetta. He will be my Midwinter's Gift to you." She turned to the other two sisters. "Would either of you like a dog as well?"

The eldest, Brigette, shook her head, as did the middle sister, Aleniel. "You are very kind, Lady Dia," Brigette said for both of them, "But neither of us are . . . good with animals." The look of faint distaste on her face spoke volumes. *Never had pets even as children, and don't want them.* This wasn't all that unusual, actually; many of the highborn looked on animals as things you ate or things you used, and never understood emotional attachments to them. Then again, these were often the same sorts of people who never formed very strong emotional attachments to other human beings. As children, they seldom saw their parents, were brought up by nurses, governesses and tutors, went into arranged marriages, and in their turn gave over *their* children to nurses, governesses and tutors. They went through their lives as if they were pieces on a giant game-board. But, given that they were often moved about by their parents or overlords as if they actually *were* mere playing pieces . . . this was certainly understandable.

"Well, then, I shall have to find a more conventional Midwinter's Gift for you two. Something special for new undergowns, perhaps," Dia said carelessly, and it was obvious from their expressions that the girls themselves found that a much more pleasing prospect than being given a dog. "Now! Herald Amily, since your duty has been done, you can get along to the Palace. The young ladies and their mother and I have some important discussions to engage in . . . and some equally important reviewing of their wardrobes."

Amily retreated at once, with a formal bow, and allowed the Leverance's manservant to show her out.

Rolan was waiting for her at the front door. He had trotted off on his own after delivering her—probably to Master Soren's stable, where he knew that he would be properly tended to. And he had brought himself back now that she was finished. It was probably just as well he had done so. She wasn't at all sure that these people properly understood what a Companion was.

:That went well,: Rolan observed, sidling up to the steps to make it easier for her to mount.

:Very well,: she agreed, mounting him; he turned his head to the road and trotted back up to the Palace. *:I was afraid Dia was going to have to spend a lot of time coaxing one of those girls to take that dog, rather than the young one practically stealing it from her.:*

Rolan was clearly pleased. Well, so was she. *:And now you have eyes and ears in the household.:*

It was rather more than that. Now Amily had the means to know exactly *what* animals were in the household, and where they were likely to be. And if the dog wasn't positioned somewhere she wanted to spy, she might well be able to use some other animal instead; through the dog's eyes, ears, and nose, she would know where every animal was in the household. When she had suggested this ploy to Mags and her father, both had been keen for her to try it out.

She left Rolan in the care of the stablemen and went straight to her rooms. She wanted to see as much as she could before something came up to interrupt her.

Mags was out . . . she had a good idea where. This was perfect. She settled down in her favorite chair at the fire, closed her eyes, and hunted for the very familiar mind of that little dog.

She found him, comfortably nestled against a pair of feet in embroidered woolen slippers. She knew they were wool because he smelled the wool; not Dia's feet then, so he must be with Violetta. By paying close attention to the sounds—which were nothing *but* random sounds to the little dog—she was easily able to translate the sounds into words. It seemed that the ladies were at the end of a conversation on fashion.

"Now I think we need to go to his Lordship and break the news on what expenses he is going to face." That was Dia's voice. The little dog picked up his ears at the sound, but did not stir. He had been set down by the new person, and unless he needed to take a walk, he was not moving.

"It will be less than he feared, but more than he likes," replied an older woman. That must be Lady Leverance.

"Well, isn't that always *the case with men?"* asked Dia with a laugh. *"If they had their way, we would wear the same gown, winter and summer, feast or fireside, until it fell apart. And then they would ask us why we didn't just patch it back together."*

All five of the woman laughed at that. *"Come girls,"* said her Ladyship in tones of authority. *"Let's see to this, while we have dear Dia with us and he cannot argue for fear of looking like a miser."*

Oh, so she was "dear Dia" already, was she? That was a good sign. It meant Dia was amused, and not affronted, that she had told them to use her given name. Dia might have been kind enough to volunteer—and she had certainly played this sort of game more than once back in the day when Amily and her friends were Nikolas' eyes and ears among the courtiers' children, but . . .

Well, there was a limit to what Dia would do if she was bored or irritated by her erstwhile charges. But if she was enjoying the work—well, she'd definitely extend herself.

The dog saw a hand reach under the skirts, and snuggled into it. Violetta brought him out and tucked him into the crook of her arm in lieu of a muff. She kept slowly stroking his head as they walked; the dog was half-hypnotized with pleasure, which was the hallmark of the breed. As they walked, the dog unconsciously analyzed everything he was smelling, and Amily "read" what it was that he got.

Mice; well that was no surprise, given how long the house had been shut up, untenanted. And the family must have known that, for the dog also scented a number of cats. Two in the kitchen, which was very smart of the cook, but there also seemed to be a cellar cat, and three cats allowed to prowl the rest of the manor. Even though these didn't seem to be pets in any sense, it was pretty clear that Amily could probably find a cat or two she could use if the dog wasn't in a position to eavesdrop on what she wanted to hear.

But then, they all entered the study, and Amily felt such a wash of relief that it was a good thing she was sitting. For the dog not only scented but *saw* an enormous, aged mastiff at the fire, and as they entered, Lord Leverance said, indulgently, *"Put your puppy down for Lion to smell, Via. I want him to know the little thing isn't a rat to be shaken to bits if he sees the pup without you."*

Violetta laughed. *"Poppa, Lion is the kindest dog that ever was to puppies, and you know it."* But she did put the dog down in front of the mastiff's nose.

The little dog knew instantly from the mastiff's scent and

the thudding of his tail on the hearth-rug that this was a friend. They sniffed noses, and then the mastiff gave the pup a single, somewhat sloppy lick with a tongue that was nearly the size the little dog was. Even though this tumbled him end over end, much to the amusement of the humans, the pup raced back to the mastiff and began licking one of its floppy ears with great determination.

Meanwhile the humans were talking about the clothing the girls would need. This was nothing Amily was even remotely interested in. Ah, but the mastiff, however . . .

She slipped into his mind, familiarizing herself with it so she could find him immediately. This was a very old dog; his joints ached unless he was basking in the sun or in front of the fire. He was his master's favorite hunting dog. There were vague memories of tremendous bear and boar hunts in his mind. Now in his old age, his master indulged this great champion of his pack with a place on the hearthrug of his study and the pick of the leftovers and trimmings from the kitchen.

Anything that went on in this room, he would be here to hear. This was precisely what Amily needed.

And if Dia hadn't brought the spaniel, she would never have known it.

She withdrew from the mastiff's mind and slowly "woke" herself up. She had a lot to report, to her father, and to Mags.

But it would be to her father, first. Still confined to his bed, he was the easiest to get to, after all!

Mags ghosted along the rooftops in the dusk, following the little group of young men headed up by Lord Kaltar's only son, Brand. They had all left the manor just after supper, as he had expected they would. What group of young men, newly come to Haven, could be expected to hang about the family hall when there was a city full of pleasures to explore? Particularly when none of them had been here when they were old enough to partake in those pleasures?

Mags, in his persona of "Magnus," had already made Brand's acquaintance—and, far more to the point, had already established his palate for good wine and his eye for a pretty woman. His plan now was to wait until they were trying to choose a tavern or an inn, "happen" upon them, and steer them to a place of *his* choosing.

As they wandered down the road, Mags had no trouble keeping track of all of them. They were exceedingly careless young men, and it was a good thing that they were in a group, or they would have been easy prey for footpads and cutpurses. But no thief or ruffian was going to approach a group of ten or so, all of them armed, not even if they were drunk. And they weren't drunk, yet.

It hadn't been at all difficult to discover their plans for the evening. Lord Kaltar had made it quite clear yesterday that he was going to entertain a group of his own cronies at his manor after dinner. The manor was not all that large, and the younger members of the family had been . . . strongly encouraged to take their presence elsewhere for the evening. The young men had been amused and vocal about it all afternoon, and Mags had commiserated. So the heir to the House and his cousins and their friends were free once the last of dinner had been cleared away.

Now, as of this afternoon, they'd had no plans, which was typical of the youngest members of the Court. But being as they were young men, and were likely to take this first completely unsupervised evening as a chance to enjoy themselves without restraint, it was pretty obvious to Mags what they were likely to do. So Mags had simply ridden Dallen down to the point where the first street of inns and taverns branched off from the main route through Haven, sent Dallen home again, and waited on the nearest roof. He didn't think that the group would actually pick any of these, or want to—they were all expensive and, more to the point, sedate. But this would be a good place to suggest his choice when they were inevitably disappointed with what was on offer on this street.

Though the light from the windows of the half dozen inns on this street was welcoming, as were the scents of food wafting from them, there were no great peals of laughter, or the sound of dancing, and the music that could be heard was decidedly. . . .sedate.

Mags paused on the roof just above them, crouched on the eaves. Literally "eavesdropping." They didn't even look up to see him. "My grandfather would drink here," said one young wag, as they came to the last place on the street. "But I certainly have no desire to do so."

"Nor I," agreed Brand, sounding disappointed. "We'd be better off going back to the manor."

"Oh gods," groaned one of the others. "You know that the girls are going to try to get us to join them, and if there is anything more tedious than playing at courtly games with your cousins, I don't know what it is."

"It's a damn shame we're too insignificant to join the Prince's Court," someone else grumbled. "At least we'd be playing at courtly games with girls we don't know."

"There's *much* more of the city!" someone else objected, as Mags climbed up and over to reach the roof of the stable, well out of sight. The voices faded as he did so. "Surely there must . . ."

They were still discussing the matter when he came around the street corner ahead of them. He stopped, shading his eyes with his hand, and peering at the group in the rather dim light of the lanterns on either side of the inn doors, as if he had no idea who they were. "Ho!" he cried. "By the gods, Brand, is that you? And Rafe, and Sevast and Byll?" He began walking rapidly toward them.

Brand turned as he came up to the group. "Magnus!" he said, "Please tell me there is more to this city than—this!" He waved his hands expansively at the street around them.

"Piff. This?" Mags said scornfully. "This is where you quarter your grandfather if there's no room left in your manor. This is where the rich old merchants take their friends for business meetings. This is where you take your *wife* for a night of so-called entertainment. Or your daughter. Or you take your auntie here, when she wants to hear some music. You don't come here for *fun* unless you're over the age of fifty. Or you're henpecked. You want a night on the tiles, my lad, you want to see the best part of Haven by night, you've come to the right man!"

Brand looked at him in confusion. "Night . . . on the tiles?" he said doubtfully. Clearly, he had not the slightest clue what Mags meant.

Mags laughed. "Look up. All our roofs are made with tiles. No thatching allowed in the entire city. One spark from a chimney fire and half a quarter would be ablaze. So, where do tomcats spend their evenings?"

"Oh! On the roof!" Brand replied with a laugh. "Yes, a night on the tiles is exactly what we want. With she-cats! Pretty, willing, amorous she-cats!"

"Ah now . . ." Mags wagged his finger at the young man. "Now you listen to me, all of you, because this is important. This isn't your country house where you can do what you like with the maidservant or a village girl, pay her off with a bit of jewelry and be done with it. Now, I can *take* you to a place where you'll get drink *and* your wick dipped, but you'll be paying for it. In good hard coin."

Brand gaped at him. "You're—serious!"

"Never more so. The fine art of lovemaking, that's a profession, here. You can pay for a cheap rut in an alley up against the side of a building for a copper bit, or you can spend *gold* buying a fine apartment and fine gowns and fine food and finer jewels for a courtesan who'll make your head spin, but one way or another, you'll be paying for it." He wagged his head back and forth. "That's the way of the world in the big city, lads. Unless you happen to find yourself a lady in the court who's a widow, or one with an elderly husband. Or one who's not to her taste. Or a husband whose taste is for something other than ladies if you catch my meaning."

Brand blinked.

"I know for a fact your father told you the servants of the King are not to be touched," Mags continued. "And as for your own—"

"Ugh," Brand said, making a face. "There's not a toothsome one in the lot."

"A-purpose. Never doubt it. So, unless you manage to find an accommodating lady in the Court, you'll be paying for it." Mags grinned. "Now, don't worry, I shan't take you to any place so lofty your purses will weep. And . . . just between you and me, if you behave yourself, don't make a spectacle, and don't go *wasting* your ready, your father will be refilling your purse often enough you'll have no complaint. A man likes to know his son is a man, eh?"

"Do you think so?" Brand asked eagerly.

"Just remember, part of being a gentleman and not making a spectacle is to pay," Mags cautioned. "And if you don't pay what's agreed on, the Guard or the Watch *will* be called, and instead of a nice warm bed and a cuddlesome wench, you'll be spending the night in a cold jail cell with some half dozen ruffians, and Lord Kaltar will be called in the morning and rather than having your purse refilled, it'll be taken from you. On the other hand . . ." He allowed a big, slow smile to spread over his face. "You can take it from me that these nymphs of the night know tricks your village girl never dreamed of, and they're worth every silver piece. So, what's it to be? Just a night of drinking, or drinking and debauchery?"

There was never any doubt what they would choose. And Mags had already prepared for that. He wouldn't take them to the *best* brothel in the city; he was well aware of the general state of their purses, and knew that there was no way they could indulge themselves there. But they wouldn't know how to behave in the best brothel in the city; the courtesans there were highly talented in many areas, and the sort of man that patronized them was one who preferred his inamoratas to have conversation and wit—and a level of expertise in love-making that these boys wouldn't appreciate. The one where he was going to take them would suit their mood as well as their purses much better.

It was a bit of a walk, but these were people that were well used to walking. Those who lived most of their time on their country estates walked furlongs every day. It probably would never even occur to them to ride a horse down into the city. And it wasn't as if there wasn't plenty for them to look at on the way down, even in the dim light from the windows and lanterns, and the occasional street-lantern. They passed through one night-market, open for the benefit of those who were working all day long, and the lads gawked at the people buying and selling at what, to them, was a ridiculous hour to be doing anything of the kind.

Finally they arrived at Mags' destination; it looked just like a very handsome inn, three stories tall, all the windows softly lighted, a stout door, and the sounds of laughter and music coming muffled through the walls . . . except that there was a guard on the door, there was no sign of a stable, and the sign over the door merely showed a crescent moon, though the name on the sign was "Flora's."

As the others paused in confusion, Mags went up to the guard, who greeted him by name. "Evening, Master Magnus," the man said. "Friends, or relations?"

"Lord Brand and his cousins, new come to Haven. I promised to take them for a night of entertainment," Mags said. He had been here before, as Magnus, although the lady he had visited knew him as Mags. She was one of Nikolas' informants, although Mags had not been introduced to her until *after* his return to Haven as a full Herald.

The guard looked them over, silently counting. "I believe we can accommodate you, Master Magnus," he replied, and opened the door. Magnus waved them all in; Brand went first, followed by the rest, with Mags bringing up the rear.

They entered into the common room, which was not unlike the common room of an inn, whitewashed walls, polished wooden floor, a ceiling with exposed beams, with tables and benches, a good fire at one end, and the bar at the other, with a trio of musicians holding forth in one corner. There were several differences, however. The benches were comfortably padded. The serving girls were attired in chemises so thin as to be almost transparent, and skirts hiked up to show plenty of leg. And there were other girls scattered among the customers in a variety of costumes that you would never see a lady wearing elsewhere in the city.

There was a red-haired wench in what looked like the robes of some religious order or other . . . except the robes were open to the waist, and slit up to mid-thigh. There was a girl with her hair loose under a crown of ivy, in the sort of gown girls in the country wore, except the neck was pulled so low as to be barely covering her nipples, and the skirt was hiked as high as the serving-girls' were. There were several girls in a parody of mens' clothing—one dressed as a Guardsman, one as a horse-tamer, and one all in black leather with a hand-crossbow at her hip. The other women were wearing more typical female costume, but it was diaphanous, or otherwise revealing. Mags kept his grin to himself, as Brand and the others looked about themselves with their eyes nearly popping out of their heads.

A lady of middle years—the only one wearing a conventional, modest gown of a very fine blue wool, with an under-gown of pristine white linen—approached them, and on spotting Mags, came straight to him. "Master Magnus," she said with obvious pleasure. "It has been too long."

"Ah, lovely Flora," he replied, bowing over her hand. "It

has. But I make up for my dereliction by bringing you a bevy of guests."

"So I see." Flora cast her eyes over the entire group. "Gentlemen, welcome. I trust that you will not be offended when I make it known to you that there are rules in my establishment. If there are any you find . . . restricting . . . I can and will recommend another house that will suit you."

The rules were, Mags was pretty certain, nothing that the lads were going to object to. Flora was very protective of her girls; her girls, in turn, were utterly loyal.

After the rules, came the prices . . . and if the men were a bit surprised to have all of that laid out so boldly and without apology, the presence of the girls gathering around the group certainly quelled any hesitation on their part. And it didn't take long before choices had been made, purses had been brought out, and the group was scattered to the private rooms above.

All but Mags.

"Nothing for you, tonight, Master Magnus?" Flora asked, archly.

Mags shook his head. *"Someone* needs to keep an entirely sober head to get this gaggle of country geese gathered up and safely back in their roost before dawn," he pointed out. "There will be other times."

Flora laughed, took his hand and tucked it in the crook of her elbow. "Then in that case, you will allow an old woman to come take you off for just a glass or two of wine and a good gossip."

"I would gladly allow an old woman to do so, if I actually saw one in front of me," Mags replied, which made her laugh. "But I will be happier if it is you, dear lady."

Flora, as well as her girl Lissande, was actually one of Nikolas' informants—another excellent reason to have brought the group here. He could kill two birds with the proverbial single stone; get her latest report under the guise of "gossip," and cement his friendship with Brand and his cousins.

It was going to be a long night, but at least it would be a fruitful one.

———————

"Shouldn't I be—" Nikolas began.

"No," Amily and Mags said, firmly, and at the same time. They exchanged a look, and Mags gave Amily a nod of deference, silently signaling, "He's *your* father."

"Father, you might have had all the attention from Healers that anyone could ask for, but the fact is, you have been abusing yourself and your body for as long as I have been alive, and now your body is going to take revenge on you for it if you don't give yourself a proper long rest." She was gratified to see that Nikolas looked properly guilty. "It was all I could do to persuade the Healers to let you come back to your own rooms for a full recovery. Winter is *not* the best time for someone who got the sort of shock you did to try and come back from it."

Nikolas had been set up in his sitting room with everything he needed, including some things the Healers had thought would work well to help him get his muscle strength and endurance back. There was a set of wooden stairs he was supposed to run up and down—there were only four of them, but the Healers seemed to think that was enough for now. There was a set of thick iron bars he was supposed to use to exercise his arms. He was using both more than he was supposed to, but the Healers had told Amily that this probably wasn't going to cause any real harm, that he'd just wear himself out and that would *force* him to rest. She was a little dubious about this, but they were Healers, and she was not.

But he wasn't content with exercising in his rooms, or even "running" up and down the corridor. He wanted to be out there, down in Haven.

"I'm not doing any good cooped up in my rooms like this," he fretted.

Amily looked over at Mags and shrugged. But Mags blinked, as if he had suddenly gotten a very good idea.

"How old's Willy the Weasel?" he asked.

Nikolas shrugged. "Older than I actually am, chronologically. Probably about as old as I *feel* right now. Why?"

" 'Cause ain't no reason why you can't go mind the shop. Ye kin sit there, just as well as here. Ye'll have one of the lads there in case ye need something done that ye can't manage. An' I'm just a shout away by Mindspeech." Mags looked terribly pleased with himself for coming up with this idea. Amily wanted to smack him with a stick for a moment, but then the look of mingled relief and pleasure on her father's face made her relent.

So instead of objecting as she wanted to, she simply sat there and watched the two of them work through every possible difficulty that either could think of. Her father's normally forgettable face took on an entirely new aspect when he was animated like this, and she could see in him the oddly attractive man that her mother had fallen in love with. As for Mags, the wiry, dark-haired man *she* loved had a tendency to lose every bit of the restraint that had been drilled into him, so that he not only talked with his hands, but with his entire body.

As she listened, she began to relax. Cooped up under the orders of the Healers, with no freedom in sight, her father had been completely unrealistic about his abilities. But now, planning things with Mags, he was being absolutely, utterly honest. There was no way he would be able to make the walk from his usual point of disguise to the shop. Mags suggested a place *he* was using now, much nearer, a storage shed. "I'll get the Weasel's stuff from the inn and set her up for ye," he said. "It'll mean two changes; Nikolas to Goodman Brody, an' take a chair from th' inn, then Brody to the Weasel."

And so it went. It was clear, seeing how anxious lines left her father's face, that this was a good idea. Maybe he wouldn't recover as fast . . . but maybe he would recover *more* quickly.

When the last detail was hammered out to their satisfaction, Nikolas turned to her. "And how are you progressing with Lord Leverance?" he asked, without any preamble at all.

She grinned. "Lord Leverance's good old mastiff has a very keen nose. Every time his Lordship is disturbed or in a temper, the dog knows it. And when the dog knows, I know. So if Leverance actually decides to *plan* trouble, we'll not only have warning, we'll know what it is." Then she shrugged. "Unplanned trouble—well—there isn't much we can do about that."

"This is all I can ask for," her father said, and made a wry face. "Let's just hope that shepherding three daughters to parties is going to exhaust the old bastard. I remember the last time he brought his family here. He didn't engineer any confrontations at Court but down in Haven. . . ." He shook his head. "The Healers were furious."

"I haven't gotten into Brand's select circle yet," said Mags. "It's all relatives. But I think I can get there. I took him and his entourage to Flora's." He grinned. "She gave them something to think about besides looking for Leverance's men and starting quarrels."

"I shall have to see that Flora gets something in gratitude from the Crown if she can keep that lot of young troublemakers too exhausted to move," Nikolas said wryly. "It could be you've hit upon the most effective solution for dealing with this feud yet."

"Congratulate me if it works," said Mags, with a sigh. "Only if it works."

7

As Violetta sat with her sisters beside the fire in the tiny solar they shared with their mother, she decided that she had never been happier, or more excited, in her life.

She *loved* being in Haven. She loved going to Court, even if Aleniel and Brigette complained that they weren't really seeing and being seen by the *really important* people. She loved it anyway, the dancing, the music, all the beautiful gowns, and the *men!* All she had ever been around before were her cousins who were, well, *cousins.* And yes, within certain degrees of separation it was all right to marry a distant cousin but . . . no. Not when you had known these boys all your life, and you knew all their faults. And they knew yours, which was always off-putting. These were all strangers to her, these young men. Their faces were even subtly different from those of her cousins. There was a certain *look* to the family, and these young men didn't have it. And they all *talked* to her, and said flattering things, and were polite. The cousins tended to talk down to her, never flattered her, and often were anything other than polite. But, she supposed, that was to be expected. The cousins were all people who had seen her fall and bruise herself and scrape her knees, knew how long it had taken her to learn to dance, had shared lessons and teased her, and pulled silly and sometimes slightly cruel pranks on her. It was only to be expected that they looked at her, and saw, not a young woman of marriageable—or at least, betrothable—age, but little Vi, who never could keep her hose tied up, or her hair in proper braids, and who, until two years ago, had been as clumsy as a calf. All these lovely, strange young men saw someone who—if she had the right dower, or the right connections— might be a good match. They also saw a lady new to them, and perhaps, if her mirror wasn't lying, was very pretty. Someone they certainly wanted to flirt with, dance with, be seen with.

It didn't matter, not at all, that Aleniel and Brigette had gotten the new gowns, and her "new" gowns were ones cut down and remade from the ones they had discarded. Violetta's new gowns were new enough, no one *here* had ever seen the gowns they had been remade from, and she had new chemises, because the chemises they had brought from home were all wrong for the necklines of the new gowns. Lady Dia had descended with a veritable horde of seamstresses, and between them and the servants, the three girls had new wardrobes with the latest touches within days. Father had grumbled at the cost, but not with that crease between his eyebrows that meant the cost really *was* worrying. And thanks to Lady Dia's cleverness, there were trims and ornaments that could be interchanged, corselets and belts and cinchers that could be swapped about among the three of them that would make it possible to create the illusion that they had many more gowns than they really did. Father had liked that part a great deal.

She was glad of that. Lady Dia was manipulating Father with great skill but she had no idea that under the skin of the man who was being indulgent with his daughters, and very indulgent to the youngest, was another man entirely. Violetta had seen him in a rage, and more than once. He'd beaten servants half to death when they marred or destroyed something valuable. He'd sent all of them running to lock themselves in their rooms—Mother too!—when he'd been angered over something important. No, it was a good idea to make Father happy about saving money, since he was likely to be in a constant state of concealed irritation that Lord Kaltar was also here in Haven for the Midwinter Season.

And *she* had that adorable little dog, Star, that Lady Dia had given her! Violetta loved animals, and always had, but she'd been told that none of her pets from home could come to Haven. Which was fair, really, since most of them were cats, and they would fight with the resident cats of the Haven manor-house, and the rest were creatures unsuitable for the manor-house like a pair of rabbits, and a squirrel. Father had brought the only dog; his great mastiff that went with him everywhere, but the mastiff never left Father's side. She had been missing all her pets, and this little dog was utterly, utterly perfect in every possible way, and gave her something to love that loved her back. Not only was she allowed to take him with her everywhere, she was *expected* to take him with her everywhere. He was as quiet as a little toy, perfectly behaved, and loved fondling and attention. He slept in a proper little bed on the kitchen hearth at night with no fuss. He was even using the door in the kitchen, made in the middle of the human door for the cats to come and go, when he needed to go out.

Right now, he was sleeping on her feet, keeping them warm, as she plied her needle in the company of her older sisters, hoping to finish the embroidery made to tack on the square neckline of one of her new-old gowns in time to wear it to the first of the Midwinter parties this very evening. Although—if she didn't, it would not be bad, she would just have to wear one of the fur neck-pieces instead. Lady Dia was escorting them, and Violetta knew that her sisters would have nothing to complain about. This time, they absolutely would be in the company of the "best" people, and many of those people would be young men who had not yet had marriages arranged. Of course, there was very little chance at all that Aleniel and Brigette would be allowed to choose a husband for themselves; marriage was too important to be left to young people. But at least, they would have the opportunity to look over, and be looked over in turn, and get to know something about the young men available before a betrothal took place. And if they were *very* lucky, and there was more than one suitor (or rather, the suitor's parents, more likely) applying for their hands, they might be asked if they preferred one over the other.

That was just how it was, of course. Still . . .

Violetta couldn't help but dream that, for her, it might be different. After all, once her two older sisters had made advantageous marriages—which they would, because they were both pretty, and had good dowries—she might be given leeway to choose for herself. She already knew she was Father's favorite, although when it came to things like clothing allowances, he was either strictly impartial or favored the other two. But he indulged her in so many other things—like all her pets—that she couldn't help but realize that he favored her.

So she might be able to be the one of the three who would get to choose, not for advantage, but for another reason. And she daydreamed that there might be a handsome, kind, gentle young man who would love her on sight, as she would love him. . . .

"And there is Violetta, dreaming about being the heroine of a ballad again," said Brigette, with a laugh, as her hands dropped into her lap and she forgot to take her stitches.

"She might as well," Aleniel observed. "Once Father has *us* well established, it won't matter that her dower is half of what ours is. There are plenty of third and fourth sons out there who would be quite happy with a pittance and a place in Father's court. When the alternative is joining the Guard, or some Temple or other, or being the redundant and expendable fellow to send out to do unpleasant things, a pretty young wife, a modest income, and a guaranteed place at the Court Royal isn't so bad." This was said without any acrimony whatsoever; Aleniel was by far the most practical of the three of them, and had no inclination for romance. She never had, in fact, and so far as Violetta could tell, that was just her nature.

"I hope," she continued thoughtfully, "That Father finds me a nice, wealthy old Duke or Count. The older the better, so long as he doesn't have any children by a previous marriage. That would suit me very well. I shall do my duty to him with such enthusiasm that an heir is sure to follow . . . and he will most certainly die a happy man, leaving me free to follow my fancy." She smiled. "And in the meantime, because I shall tend his ills and do everything in my power to make him feel he has gotten a great bargain in me, I expect I shall lead a very cosseted and indulged life."

Violetta nodded. *Pragmatic* didn't even begin to describe Aleniel. Some might think her cold if they ever listened to her speak frankly. Although she never *did* speak frankly, except to her sisters and Mother and Father. For strangers, she was cordial, and cheerful, and she had been practicing the arts of being charming and seeming warm for the past year and more, ever since Father had determined on coming here this Midwinter.

For her part, Violetta didn't think she was cold, no matter how she spoke. She was just extremely practical, and always had been, for as long as Violetta could remember. When she chose fabric for a gown, it was always something that would wear well and could last through at least one turning. When she chose a dish at dinner, she always calculated whether or not she would look graceful eating it. And from the time they all began to speak of husbands, it had been Aleniel's plan to wed an old, titled, rich man.

To that end, she had set out to make herself into the sort of spouse that would best please an old, titled, rich man. She had never undertaken to learn something without having first decided it could be used to her advantage. She never bothered with learning a musical instrument, for instance, but *did* learn everything she could about creating medicines in the still-room, because an old man would appreciate someone who could soothe his ills much more than someone who could plink out a tune. Her embroidery was superb—a very highly prized skill, since beautiful embroidery made a fine gown worth a great deal more. She knew dozens of card and board games, the better to amuse an old man who might be disinclined to leave the comfort of his own hearth. She had a strong, clear reading voice for the same purpose.

And her self-control was . . . epic. She never raised her voice, no matter how angry she might be, and no matter how angry she might be, she never showed it. She never lost her temper. She was always serene on the surface.

Violetta actually admired her sister; she always thought it must take an enormous amount of discipline to deny yourself things you might *want* to do so you could learn things that would serve a more useful purpose. And of course, Aleniel was going to give whoever became her husband an absolutely honest bargain. On his side, there would be wealth and rank. On her side, her beauty, her accomplishments, and the promise of an heir. She would, Violetta knew, be absolutely and completely faithful to her husband for as long as he was alive. She would pledge her sworn word to that at the altar, and she never, ever broke her word.

Aleniel had what seemed to Violetta to be an almost inhuman patience. She had no trouble at all waiting what seemed an *impossibly* long time to Violetta for something that had been promised. She had been perfectly frank with her sisters—if not to their parents—that her plans did *not* include lovers until after her husband was safely in his grave. She was perfectly ready to wait for however long that took.

But then, she had always been perfectly ready to wait for anything she really wanted. She'd demonstrated that over and over again as a child.

For instance, there was a beautiful, absolutely perfect place on the estate to swim; a sun-warmed pool, with clear waters, mossy banks to lie on, fed by a little stream with a waterfall. But the girls were forbidden to go there alone. They had to take with them a particular trio of female mercenaries their father employed for various escort and guard duties on the girls and their mother. Many had been the time that she and Brigette had lost patience, waiting for the mercenaries to finish escorting their mother to market, or visiting the cottagers, or some other task that Father felt required an escort. She and Brigette would wander off to some other pursuit, but Aleniel would sit there, reading or sewing or some other useful thing, no matter how warm the day, patient. And her patience would always be rewarded. She would get her swim and return home in time for dinner or bed, cool and comfortable, while Violetta and Brigette would have to make do with sponging down with a basin of tepid water instead of having the refreshing swim that they longed for.

So Violetta had absolutely no doubt that Aleniel would do exactly as she pledged. It was as certain as it was that the fire at their feet was hot.

"Well, I'll be perfectly happy to find father has got me either a second son in a landed family, or a nice, wealthy merchant," Brigette said firmly. "Not just any merchant, of course. It will have to be a Guildmaster." She set a few more stitches thoughtfully; her embroidery was absolutely fabulous, and she was creating a lozenge containing the family crest of a gold rampant lion on blue to appliqué to one of her new gowns, using real gold bullion for the lion's mane. "It would be lovely if it were someone in the Jeweler's Guild . . . or the Cloth Merchants. Just imagine having the free run of the warehouses!"

Brigette was not as pragmatic as Aleniel, Violetta knew, but she *was* practical, and she loved beautiful things. "Just imagine being your husband's showpiece!" Aleniel replied, with no rancor whatsoever. "You are pretty enough to show off anything to good effect, and your husband would be a fool not to drape you in whatever he wished to sell and take you to Court and festivities as often as possible."

"That . . . would be wonderful," sighed Brigette, as her eyes turned dreamy. Violetta knew that in her imagination, she saw herself gowned and jeweled to perfection, the envy of every woman who saw her. As long as she could have beautiful things, Violetta knew she was indifferent to what her husband looked like. Well, almost indifferent—but unlike Aleniel, Brigette was unlikely to find herself married to a sick, smelly old man. It would more likely be a man of quite mature years, but still vigorous enough to run his business and run it well. And given that her marriage would be to someone who was marrying into the highborn, acquiring a title of nobility for his offspring if not himself, it was very unlikely that she'd be married off to someone who wasn't suitable, presentable, and pleasant.

They all three sewed a little more, basking in the warmth of the fine fire.

"And we know what Vi wants, don't we?" Aleniel exchanged a look of amusement with her sister. "A beautiful young man, who writes her terrible poems, and caterwauls under her window, and whispers ridiculous things into her ear." She put her embroidery down in her lap and struck a pose. *"Oh Violetta, Violetta! Your sweetness puts the flowers to shame, and your eyes teach candles to burn brighter!"*

Brigette also dropped her embroidery and put the back of her hand to her forehead, dramatically. *"I swear by sun and moon and stars, never have I seen a maid more fair, and never was fair maid more kind!"*

"Oh *stop,*" Violetta protested, as her sisters giggled. She blushed, because, to be honest, that was exactly what she wanted. Only she of the three of them *believed* in the love-ballads that the Bards sang. Only she of the three of them hoped she could marry for love, not advantage.

Only she had no avarice for fine jewels, or expensive gowns, or a great manor. *So long as we do not go hungry or ragged or cold, I would marry a farmer if he loved me and I loved him.* She didn't dare say that out loud, of course. Her sisters would first laugh at her, and then make it their business to disabuse her of those ideas.

Well . . . as long as Father doesn't plan to marry me off to one of the cousins . . . There wasn't a single one of them she loved, and there were quite a few of them she didn't much *like,* but that would be Father's idea of kindness, so she never had to leave home, and she and her husband could set up their household as part of Father's greater household. If he got that idea in his head, she really had no idea how she would talk him out of it.

Still . . . if that had been his plan, he wouldn't be letting her go along to these parties with her sisters, now, would he? He'd save the expense of the gowns and all and keep her home.

So she listened to her sisters outline their plans for this evening, and daydreamed, thinking about meeting someone's eyes in a dance, and having the world change . . . and the fire crackled pleasantly, the work under her hands was soothing, and her new pet poked his little nose out from under her skirt and made her smile.

Listening to the girls gossip away about the sorts of young men they were hunting sounded exactly like listening to a lot of young men plotting a day of game hunting! Amily wasn't certain whether to find that amusing or appalling. She did make a note to ask Dia or one of the others if *all* the young ladies of the Court were like this . . . though she had the sinking feeling that most of them probably were. And . . . looking at it pragmatically, she knew she shouldn't be surprised at this. Getting married well was their *business,* the thing they had been trained for from the time they were very small.

She was just grateful that she wasn't one of them.

Her own fire crackled just as pleasantly at her feet, and the more time she spent in these rooms, the more she appreciated Bear's taste in furnishings. The chair she was in was extremely comfortable; exactly the sort of thing that you needed, if you were going to be concentrating on Mindhearing . . . making sense of what came through a dog's ears!

Well I am obviously not going to learn anything from Violetta's pup, she thought, *At least not tonight.* It was time to move to the mind of the old mastiff, and see if his master was having a conversation with any of his underlings that would be useful to overhear. She opened her eyes and rubbed them a bit, then shifted a little to make herself more comfortable. Closing her eyes again, she sent out her thoughts, searching for the familiar mind of the old dog.

The mastiff was easy to find for her now, and she settled in to discover that, rather than drowsing as he usually did, the old dog was very much awake and alert.

And that was because the master's little sanctum was full of his men. And he was delivering a stern lecture to them. Or rather, *at* them; it was pretty obvious from his tone that he was laying down the law rather thickly, and was going to brook no dissent.

". . . don't want my girls' chances spoiled because you hotheads can't keep your tempers if one of you idiots sees someone of House Raeylen and starts something."

There was grumbling at this, immediately, grumbling which began to rise in volume.

And this insubordination, enraged the mastiff's master. The mastiff heard the anger in his master's voice, and scented it as well. His hackles came up and he tensed, although he was too well-trained to growl without being commanded to.

Lord Leverance, in the meantime, raised his voice and shouted them down. *"I am the head of House Chendlar, and by all that is holy, you will obey me, you young fools! Once I have marriages arranged, at least for Aleniel and Brigette, you can do as you like, but until then if you attend these Midwinter parties, you will keep your swords in your sheathes and your challenges behind your teeth! Because if you don't, I can beat you to a bloody pulp, throw you out on your asses and leave you to join the Guard or find some other fool's bread to eat! Do I make myself clear?"*

Amily was more than a bit startled by this. There had been *no* sign of this formidable temper in the man she had met. But then again, a temper like this wasn't something you showed to your superiors. It was something you kept hidden, and only displayed to your subordinates.

Small wonder all the servants in Lord Leverance's house treated him with total respect. That respect was probably born of fear.

There was muttering, but it all followed the general pattern of "Aye, my Lord," or "As you will, my Lord." It was clear this pack of relations had seen his temper at work as well, and they were not about to chance evoking it. For her part, Amily was . . . well not precisely *delighted,* since it was quite clear that Lord Leverance had no intention of actually giving up the feud, but at least somewhat relieved that he was attempting to keep blood from being shed for the time being. *I wonder if I ought to advise the King that he shouldn't allow any betrothals to take place until* after *Leverance takes his family and goes home . . .*

But that would scarcely be fair to the girls, who hadn't done anything, and didn't deserve to be punished. And the eldest two really, truly wanted those betrothals.

Although a part of Amily was completely revolted by the idea that they defined themselves by their ability to make a "good" marriage. And that once married, they would define their own worth by how "worthy" their husbands were. She tried to remind herself that this was how they had been trained, and that they didn't know any different, and that they couldn't miss what they weren't aware existed.

And by that reasoning, it is perfectly acceptable for people to keep slaves, if that was how they were raised, they aren't abused, and they don't know any better. No. No, I can't accept that is right. I may have to accept that this is what those girls want, but I don't have to accept that this is right.

And she would, by all that was holy, work to change it.

But she had work to do. She went back to concentrating on the dog and what she was hearing through his ears and seeing through his eyes.

Having laid down the law, Lord Leverance dismissed his men. He sat in silence for a moment, brooding into the fire. The dog got up and sat down beside his master, laying his enormous head on the man's knee. Leverance smiled a little, and gave the mastiff a rough caress. *"You, at least, I can count on, old man,"* he said to the dog, who, of course, only understood the words "old man" as being one of the things Leverance called him, and thudded his tail on the floor. *"I know when I give you an order, I can count on you to obey it. Those hot-headed fools . . . I am not so sure. I swear, there are times that if I could replace them, one and all, with dogs, I would."*

The mastiff nudged his master's hand, and Leverance chuckled a little. *"All right, old man. Go and lie down. I have to attend this infernal party as it's the first of the lot, but after this, you'll have me all to yourself while her Ladyship and Lady Dia deal with this confounded nonsense. It would be much easier if we all did the sensible thing, and treated this marrying off business like a Hiring Fair. We should assemble all the parents with children to marry off in an enormous room and conduct this properly in a businesslike fashion."* He sighed. *"Well, we can't so . . . keep the hearth-rug warm, old man. It will be a late night for me."*

And with that, he got up to leave. Amily disengaged herself from the old dog's mind and debated going to the King . . .

:You don't need to go to the King,: Rolan reminded her. *:You have me. I've already passed the information on to him, or at least, what's relevant.:*

One less thing to have to worry about, then. For a change!

Which only left her with several hundred others. Time to get dressed in her own version of finery, and join the rest of the Court . . . or rather, the ones who were not attending the particular Midwinter party that the three girls were going to, nor any of the other three being held tonight—none of which had nearly the cachet of the first. The courtiers in attendance at this evening's very subdued gathering would be insulted if she and at least *one* of the Royals were not there.

:You'll be fine. It's the Princess. You can play that game where you say rude things about the people dancing atten-dance on her and both try not to laugh,: Rolan said with amusement. *:Oh, the King gives you leave to relieve Duke Erdenval of his pocket-money at cards. Kyril says he's over-due for a fleecing.:*

Well, that was something, anyway.

She wondered how Mags was faring.

———————

It was dark. It was cold. There was snow piled up on both sides of the street, which at least made it easier to *see* the sides of the street; you generally didn't want to stumble too far to either side because of the gutters, and what they usually con-tained. Mags was holding up a very drunk heir to House Raeylen, as Brand sang a song in praise of Flora's prettiest girl, declaring his love for her aloud between verses. Mags could only roll his eyes—and not just because Brand was very loud, and *very* drunk. Lelage was—at least by every account that Mags had heard—an extremely talented young lady in her chosen profession. She was also, by every standard, a stunning beauty, and she stayed with Flora in no small part out of loyalty and friendship, because she certainly could have gone out on her own, or to any of the really exclusive houses of amusement in the city. At Flora's, her services were reserved exclusively for four and only four gentlemen, none of whom were Brand, nor were likely to be, since he couldn't afford the services of an "exclusive" girl. But Brand had seen her and was smitten, and never mind that she was . . . well . . . a whore. At the moment, enflamed with desire as he was, that apparently didn't matter.

Then again, for people in Brand's circles, the difference between a girl who sold her services and a girl whose marriage was a commercial commodity was, at least in Mags' mind, largely semantics. It might be that Brand was either clever enough, or cynical enough, to see it the same way.

Still, even as beautiful as Lelage was, Mags couldn't quite figure out why Brand was so obsessed with her. There were plenty of girls at Flora's who were pretty, and "talented," and were inclined to give a handsome young man a bit of a discount because he was more pleasant to deal with than some of their other customers.

Maybe it was just that she was unattainable. Maybe it was because she accepted his compliments, and his serenades, without even hinting that she found them laughable or distasteful. She *had* made it quite clear to Brand that she could not, and would not, reciprocate in any way.

Maybe the fact that she didn't outright tell him to bugger off makes him think that he has some sort of chance with her. Though the gods only know what he thinks he would do with her. He can't afford her, and she's not going to take him on for what he can *afford.*

"Listen, my lad," Mags said, his breath steaming in the cold air, when Brand came to the end of the last verse, and finally fell silent, and his steps became a bit firmer. "Your father is not going to like hearing any of this nonsense. Not the whoring, but that you're in love with a whore. That's all very well, just don't say it out loud."

"But Magnus . . ." Brand groaned. "She'sh driving me *mad!*"

"Madder, country-boy. You were already mad." Mags slapped Brand's cheeks lightly with his free hand. "I'm not saying you can't be in love with her, I'm saying you need to shut your face about it. Just keep it to yourself. Remember that once you're married, you'll have your own household and your own money and you can do what you like with it. And if you're still in love with Lelage, that'll make things very different."

As he had expected, Brand was *not* drunk enough or in love enough to even consider marrying Lelage. The reminder that marriage would make it possible for him to become one of Lelage's exclusive clients—or even her *only* client—cheered him up immediately. Lord Kaltar had one kept woman himself on his estate, tucked away in a snug little cottage where his wife would never find her. Mags knew this, thanks to his own ghosting around the manor and eavesdropping on conversations all over the domicile. His Lordship would not deny his only son the same. And any wife who found out about his dalliance would probably just be grateful that her husband was keeping a courtesan, and not sleeping around the Court itself. For a young man as handsome as Brand, the latter would be pitifully easy and could cause all sorts of unpleasant complications.

Brand was of the darkly-handsome-and-brooding sort, although his looks belied his temperament; he wasn't "broody" at all. In Mags' experience, until he had seen Lelage, Brand was generally very cheerful. And why shouldn't he be? He was the *only* heir, he was an only child, his mother gave him anything he wanted and his father—well, Mags had seen no evidence yet that his father had any intention of curbing his son's activities as long as they remained within reasonable bounds. Certainly Brand's purse was heavy enough when they all went out drinking or to Flora's, and that silver could only be coming from his Lordship.

Now Brand was cheerfully singing what he could remember of snatches of other songs, rather than that ballad to the beauty of Lelage. Not *exactly* love-songs, or at least, not the sort that a well-bred young man would sing to an equally well-bred young lady. Still, Lelage, if she could hear him now, would probably be amused. And would probably top his bawdy ballads with one of her own.

At least his singing was no longer at the top of his lungs. Although this wasn't an unsafe neighborhood, it wasn't a safe one either. And tonight, it was just Mags and two of Brand's cousins, rather than the ten or a dozen he usually brought along on his trips into Haven. Mags wasn't tired, not even half-supporting Brand's weight, but he had been hoping to make better time through this part of town.

I'm going to be glad when we get up to—

The sounds of footsteps on the pavement made him look up. And his hackles went up.

The street ahead had just been blocked by five men.

"And what have we here? A songbird!" said the one in front sarcastically.

From the way that they had spaced themselves out, and the way they held themselves, they were practiced fighters. Five men with hoods casting their features into shadow, and scarves wrapped around the lower halves of their faces. Two of them had cudgels, two had knives, and the one in front had a cheap sword.

Hell.

Brand suddenly stopped singing, and straightened, pulling away from Mags. Not completely sober . . . but the shock of being accosted by street thugs had sobered him up, at least somewhat.

This wasn't necessarily a good thing. The last thing Mags wanted was for him to tangle with street fighters. He was in no condition to handle himself, and although he was something of a brawler, as Mags knew from practicing with him, he had no notion of the sort of dirty tricks these thugs would pull. And the two cousins with them were not in much better shape than Brand.

"I'd ask for the contents of your purses, but from the state of you, I expect you've spent them bare." The leader gestured with his sword, pointing to his own feet. "So instead, you four can come along with us, like good boys, and tell us who your parents are. Don't worry, it won't be uncomfortable, and I am sure you'll be back with them by—"

:Dallen.:

:Understood.:

Mags didn't bother to pull out his own sword; that would take too long and would telegraph that he was sober. Instead, while the leader was still speaking, he made a running leap at the leftmost thug, tackling him and bringing him to the ground before the man could bring up the cudgel. The back of the thug's head hit the cobblestones with a *crack,* but Mags took no chances; he struck the thug's chin with the heel of his right hand, driving it back onto the stones a second time, then he rolled to the left, off the body and onto his feet. He just barely grazed the snowbank on the left doing so.

It's a damn good thing there's a full moon.

Now he drew his sword, and used it to fend off one of the two with knives as the thug recovered from his surprise and charged. These men were brutal street-brawlers, and Mags had no intention of giving any of them second chances. He parried the second thug's overhand blow, spun with the momentum, and brought the sword up in a savage cut at the wrist of the man's knife hand. He didn't chop the hand off— his sword wasn't heavy enough to do something like that— but the thug dropped his knife with a shriek and staggered away, clutching at the spurting wound.

Lucky shot for me. Got the artery. Not so lucky for him.

But now the other thug with the knife, and the leader with the sword, were coming at him. He dropped under the sword-swing, and reached for the wrist of the knife-wielder, who was charging from the side. Twisting on his own axis, he pulled the knife-man into an uncontrolled fall, and cut at the side of the swordsman at the same time. The swordsman barely parried the blow; the knife-man was so off-balance that he went face-first onto the street. He was out of the fight for the moment, leaving Mags to concentrate on the leader.

By this time there was shouting at both ends of the street. Dallen—or the Heralds he'd warned—had roused the Guard and the Watch. Mags parried another swing from the swordsman, got a moment of breathing room and kicked the head of the prone knife-man to make sure he stayed down. Out of the corner of his eye he could see Brand's cousins tussling with the remaining cudgel-man. He wasn't worried about that one; it was two-to-one, and unless one of the cousins was wildly unlucky, the worst that would befall them was a broken bone.

There was more shouting, and it finally dawned on the swordsman that the shouting meant *he* was in trouble. He cast a look full of venom at Mags, disengaged and took to his heels, leaving behind his four companions-in-crime.

Mags reversed his grip on his sword, ran the few paces to where the cousins were still fighting with the last of the thugs, waited until he got a clear shot, and smacked the would-be kidnapper behind the ear with the pommel-nut. The man went down like a stone.

The cousins staggered back, panting heavily, and that was when the first of the Watch reached them, along with a Guardsman. "Sir! Are you all right?" the Guardsman asked urgently, peering at him in the moonlight.

Dress well, and they will always assume you are the victim, not the perpetrator, Mags thought cynically. But at least tonight that was working in their favor.

"We're uninjured, which is more than I can say about these

blackguards. The leader went that way," Mags said, pointing down the street. "But you'll never catch him. He probably knows the back alleys like a cat."

"Don't matter, sir. We'll find out who he is from his *friends* here," said the Guardsman, as the Watch set about securing their prisoners. "Robbers?"

Mags nodded. "I'm afraid we were making ourselves a little too obvious," he said ruefully, as more of the Watch and a couple more Guardsmen arrived and began collecting Mags' victims. "My friend was serenading the moon, after celebrating with a good deal of wine."

"This part of town, milord, if you are going to be . . . ah . . . *obvious,* you had better do so with a couple of bodyguards or in a larger group," the Guardsman said tactfully. "Still, you seem to have come off all right."

"Largely because they were expecting all of us to be drunk," Mags replied. "By the time they realized I wasn't, I'd laid two of them out. Thanks for the timely rescue; their leader is a swordsman, and probably wouldn't have been as easy to handle as his thugs."

One of the Watch fetched a torch, and another made notes in a book as Mags gave his account of what had happened, and a now-more-sober Brand and his cousins corroborated it as best they could. The Watch offered an escort of two of their number back up as far as where the streets became—as the Watch put it—"more polite-like," and Brand accepted it.

No longer needing to lean on Mags to steady himself, Brand walked silently next to him for several blocks before speaking.

"You—"

"Don't say I saved your life, because I didn't," Mags interrupted. "You heard him yourself; he had no intention of doing anything other than holding us briefly for ransom. He'd have sent his demands to Lord Kaltar, and we'd have been found, safe and probably tied up and possibly unconscious, within a couple of candlemarks of ransom being handed over. I just saved you some inconvenience."

"And acute embarrassment, and explaining myself to my father, and the tedium of thereafter having to take an escort with me wherever I go. So I am still deeply in your debt," Brand replied. "Magnus, where in the name of the gods did you ever learn to fight like that? You moved like a cat!"

"Here—" Mags replied, waving a hand to indicate the streets around them. "All of your fancy swordmasters aren't worth a clipped copper out here. This isn't the first time I've put down a footpad. Although—" he added, with a frown "—it's the first time one's threatened to kidnap me for ransom. I wonder where they got *that* idea from?"

"Well it's one I hope you nipped in the bud," said one of the two cousins, who was nursing a bruised shoulder.

"So do I," Mags agreed.

:Though we know very well where they got that idea from,: Dallen said grimly. *:The Sleepgivers put a lot of notions into the heads of the local criminals; notions I would just as soon got driven out again.:*

Dallen was most probably right. Kidnapping had been almost unheard of here in Haven until the Sleepgiver assassins had turned up. Mags didn't like it at all. *:Tell Amily about this through Rolan,:* he told his Companion. *:The King needs to know; in the morning when she meets with him is probably soon enough, but I'll let her be the judge of that.:*

:Done,: Dallen replied.

"You're very quiet," Brand said at that moment.

"Catching my breath. And thinking. It's probably best if we take this good fellow's advice from now on." He nodded at the Watch who had come with them. "It's not that hard to convince the rest to come with us. Is it?"

But here Brand sighed heavily. "Harder than you think," he said. "The Midwinter parties started tonight. Not—" he added "—that they're things that are anything but dead boring, most of them. But the lads have parents and the parents are expecting them to be trotted out to show their paces and their teeth."

Mags nodded sagely. "That's not anything I have to worry about," he admitted. "I live on the generosity of my uncle. I'm not exactly a shining matrimonial prospect."

Brand sighed heavily. "Well . . . I am. So I'll *have* to go to some of these things. But my father laments that they are *not the best ones.* I assume by this he means that the families giving the *best ones* are a cut or two above us, and wouldn't deign to invite us."

Mags laughed at that. "So? We invite ourselves! If you want."

Brand looked at him incredulously. "You can do that?"

:Dallen, can we do that?:

:It's done all the time. You wear masks, and don't stay long, and don't get into trouble. The guards at the door look you over, and if your clothing is fine enough, they'll let you in without an invitation.:

"It's done all the time, as long as you wear a mask and don't cause any trouble," Mags said, repeating what Dallen had told him. "After all, in our circles, these parties are all about marrying daughters off. There are lots of girls, not so many men. Having a brief surge of mysterious young men come in to dance and flirt harmlessly and have some wine takes the tedium out of the evening for everyone. You just don't stay long."

"That sounds like fun, actually," Brand admitted. "More fun than being an actual guest."

:We can get a list of what parties are when, and where. The evening ones, anyway.:

"I can get a list of what's being given, when and where," Mags told him, with a slap on Brand's shoulder. "You just leave it up to me. It won't be nearly as much fun as a night at Flora's, but your father will probably approve. And you might get a look at some pretty thing you wouldn't mind being leg-shackled to, and put a word in your father's ear about her. The girls of a family all go in a gaggle, like a flock of sparrows, and even though you won't have a chance with the eldest, you might with one of her younger sisters."

"Huh!" said Brand. "I might at that!" He grinned at Mags, just as they reached the area the Watch deemed safe, and their escort turned back with a salute. "Magnus, you are the best fellow I've met since I got here!"

"Happy to be of service," Mags said, with only a touch of irony.

8

The little dressing room was warm, very well lit and . . . a bit dazzling, since there were four gowns hanging on the wall, besides the one that Lydia had finally chosen, and all of them were stunning. And there was a casket of jewelry open on the dressing table that had made Amily blink. Of all of the things that Amily had expected to do when she became King's Own, overseeing the dressing of the Crown Princess was not one.

But it was certainly the most pleasant job she'd been set since she got the position. And, at least at the moment, the most relaxing. She hadn't really had to do anything except suggest that, given the huge crowds that were going to be in the Palace tonight, the lightest of the gowns that Lydia's hand-maiden had selected was probably going to be the most practical. Lydia herself, having grown up in the household of a Guild Master, had a fine eye for fabric, color, and design. There was not a gown that she owned that was not flattering.

It's kind of a relief to be a Herald, Amily reflected. *I never have to worry about what to wear, or the color of it.*

In this case the gown in question was deep blue, trimmed in silver, and all the jewelry Lydia was wearing was silver with sapphires. She watched as Princess Lydia's servant put a beaded veil with a simple coronet over her hair. Now that she was married, like all married women, Lydia was expected to keep her hair beneath a coif or a veil of some sort. Only Heralds, Bards and Healers could escape that particular custom, at least among the women at Court. "I know this is horrible of me to ask you to help me with all the guests," Princess Lydia said, apologetically. "But you know how awful my memory is."

"Since I've known you *forever,* yes I do," Amily laughed, as the servant hid a smile. "Really, Lydia, you should stop apologizing. There are plenty of things you excel at; you shouldn't be expected to be a paragon at *everything.*"

Lydia's dressing-room was adjacent to the bedchamber she shared with the Prince. It was a very small room; the clothing closet attached to it was actually larger than the room itself was—the dressing room was just barely big enough for Lydia, her handmaiden, and Amily. This evening was the Midwinter Reception of the full Court; everyone was going to be here—or at least, representatives of every notable family were going to be here, since inviting all of the cousins and uncles and aunts would fill the Palace five times over. As it was, the festivities were going to spill out all over the public rooms of the Palace. Not just the Great Hall, but the Throne Room, the Lesser Throne Room, the Greater Audience Chamber, the Lesser Audience Chamber, the Feast Hall . . . and the Royal Family was expected to mingle.

Needless to say, just in case of trouble, there were Guards in practically every alcove. After years of dealing with the Sleepgiver assassins, no one was taking any chances on anything going wrong.

Not that Lydia—and, for that matter, the King and the Prince—couldn't take care of themselves. Lydia had been taking lessons in fighting for much longer than Amily, and the

King and the Crown Prince were both Heralds so it was a given that they knew how to defend themselves. Still, it was better to be safe, and as a consequence, not only were there Guards everywhere, there were plenty of Heralds in Formal Whites, instructors at the Collegium and the Heralds serving Haven itself, circulating in the areas where one of the Royals would be as well.

Technically, Amily should have been with the King. But the Healers had finally allowed Nikolas some more freedom to move about, and he had taken his customary position by Kyril's side, which suited Amily just fine. Most of the people here were used to Nikolas as the King's Own. Kyril was used to having his old friend at his side, and this was not the best time to change that arrangement. And, last of all, there were plenty of people here who would probably be confused at seeing a young woman where they expected Nikolas. Anyway, she was getting the far more interesting job of helping her dear friend Lydia remember just who in the nine hells she was talking to when total strangers came up to her, rather than just standing at Kyril's elbow and trying to look as if she actually belonged there.

:All that studying in the Archives is proving to be useful,: she observed to Rolan with amusement.

:This is something Nikolas never needed to deal with,: Rolan replied, with equal amusement. *:The King has a ridiculously encyclopedic memory for the important people of his realm.:*

This would be the first time that Lydia had performed this particular duty of the Princess Royal, and she was understandably nervous. Last year, as a newlywed, she had been able to stick by her husband's side and merely smile and nod as needed. This year, however, she had to play her part alone, seeing and being seen, with a pleasant word to anyone who approached her. And, possibly, being asked to put in a very political comment or two . . .

That would be via Amily and Rolan. Rolan was watching through Amily's eyes, and if something needed to be said, he would prompt Amily, who would murmur in Lydia's ear.

"We'll do fine," Amily said reassuringly. "When have you ever known me to miss a question when we played 'guess who that guest is' at your father's parties?"

"Never," Lydia sighed. "I don't know how you do it."

"Well, it wasn't that hard," Amily confessed, as Lydia stood up. "No one ever paid attention to me at any of your parties, which gave me plenty of opportunity to study them. And anyone who was a stranger was someone you generally mentioned beforehand, so I knew who to watch for. And now, well, I have Rolan to prompt me if I don't recognize a family device."

"I wish I did," Lydia said ruefully. "All right then, time for my performance."

Almost any other young woman would have asked "How do I look?" and probably with some anxiety. But not Lydia, which was one of the things that endeared her to Amily. Not that Lydia was indifferent to her appearance; she knew she was attractive, and she enjoyed wearing lovely things. But she didn't get obsessed with them, and when, as now, she had the services of a servant whose *entire* job was to make her look like the Princess that she was, she assumed that the servant would *do* that job and dismissed her own appearance from her mind in favor of more important things—like her duties.

"The King is relying on you and Sedric to keep Lord Kaltar and Lord Leverance apart," Amily reminded her. "That's far more important than remembering whose name is what, and it's something I can't do. You, on the other hand, have high rank and an amazing command of pure charm. You've been assigned Lord Leverance, and the plan is to try and keep him in the Throne Room. If need be, and he acts as if he thinks he needs to go elsewhere, you can take him on a personal tour of the Long Gallery. Sedric will keep Lord Kaltar away from both rooms."

"I will certainly do my best, if I have to seize his arm and drag him away by force," Lydia said firmly. "All right, let's go take up our station."

The formal receptions for each of the guests had taken place over the past several days, both to keep certain parties separated—there were other folks who had disagreements going, though none so prone to bloodshed as the one between Leverance and Kaltar—and to keep from exhausting people with long receiving lines. This meant that each member of the Royal Family could just take up his or her place, and remain within a relatively small orbit. And unless someone was absolutely *determined* to greet every member of the Royals, there was no particular reason to leave the room to which he'd been sent by the doorkeeper.

That was the theory, anyway. In practice, while there would be musicians and Bards everywhere, there would only be dancing in the Great Hall, so anyone who wanted to dance would have to go there. A potential problem, but fortunately, one that had already been solved in at least one case.

For as it happened, both Lord Kaltar and Lord Leverance had been rather vocal about not wanting to dance; Amily had learned Leverance's preference through his dog, and Mags had learned Kaltar's through eavesdropping. Probably the three girls would want to, and possibly Brand, but they were all counting on Brand's youth and inexperience—and the presence of the Guards—and the presence of the Royal Family—to keep him from making any sort of fuss if he encountered Leverance's girls or their mother. Not that he'd likely recognize them, but he might recognize the embroidered lions they wore. The mobs of cousins had *not* been invited, and had not expected invitations. But there were other Midwinter parties being held for those who did not have a coveted invitation . . . and . . . well, Amily had a pretty shrewd notion that Flora's, The Compass Rose, and other establishments down in Haven would be busy.

For that matter, the cousins might well host a pair of impromptu gatherings themselves, at the two manors. After all there would be no supervising eyes to monitor the food and drink, and none of the servants would dare contradict their orders.

Lydia and Amily entered the Throne room from a private corridor that connected it with the Royal Suite, and the sound, the scents, and the blaze of light practically struck them in the face as a Guard opened the door for them. In fact, the Throne Room was so crowded that it didn't really need much heating; the sheer press of bodies was making it warm. Lydia threaded her way gracefully toward the Throne with Amily right at her elbow, since the dais made a good place for her to take up a stand and gave her some clear space at her back. As soon as she was in place, people began making their way toward her.

As she smiled and said pleasantries, smiled and spoke compliments, and Amily kept a sharp eye out for Lord Leverance, Amily reflected that she didn't envy her friend at all. *If this is being a Royal . . . it is an honor I can very much live without.*

Violetta stood a little behind her older sisters and looked out over the Great Hall of the Palace, feeling breathless. This one room alone was half the size of their entire manor here in the city! The ceiling was hidden in shadows, it was so high, even though the room blazed with light from all the candles in sconces mounted around the room. And the press of people was enough to take her breath away. She felt very much the country-girl, and did her best not to gawk. She couldn't imagine how Brigette and Aleniel were managing to look so serene and unimpressed.

The air was thick with perfume, and the sight of all of the gorgeous gowns and jewels left her dazzled. She had been persuaded to leave her little dog Star behind, and now she was glad she had; the poor little thing would have been in danger of being trampled in the crowd, and obviously if she was going to dance—and oh, how she hoped she would be asked to dance!—she couldn't carry her muff to keep him safely in. Still, she wished she had the comfort of his dear little warm body, because at the moment she was feeling significantly overwhelmed.

She had been half-terrified that none of the dances would be anything that she knew. After all, they lived out in the country, and like fashions, dances changed and the change began here, at Court. But she was relieved to see that their dancing-master actually did live up to his boast of "being able to teach every popular step," because she'd watched three dances so far, and they were all ones she knew so well she could do them sleepwalking. Just now, the dance was a stately pavane, and the partners swirled and bowed, turned and paced, separated and rejoined in patterns she knew by heart.

Mother was standing beside them like a veritable dragon, with Lady Dia beside *her,* whispering in her ear every time a young man approached Brigette or Aleniel. All it took was a single warning glance to send the "unsuitable" away before they even got within greeting distance. But after three young men had been sent packing, a fourth proved to be worthy, and was beckoned onward with a smile and a nod.

Knowing who he had to placate, he bowed over Mother's hand. "If I might have the pleasure of your daughter's company in the dance?" he asked politely, as the pavane ended, and the musicians paused before starting a new number. "I believe it will be a gigue, if that is permissible?"

Mother smiled and gestured, and he offered his hand to Aleniel. Brigette looked faintly disappointed, but a moment later a middle-aged fellow in tawny velvet, with a Guildmaster's chain around his neck, appeared as if conjured, and begged to take Brigette onto the floor. She beamed at him, he beamed at her, and Mother beamed beatifically at both of them.

No one came for Violetta by the time the music started. *I suppose I look too young,* she thought, doing her best to hide her disappointment. The gown that she'd chosen was the best she owned, a lovely red brocade over an embroidered saffron chemise . . . but it did hide her breasts and made her look as slender as a boy. But if she had chosen any of the other gowns in her chest, Mother would not have approved. Either they were not grand enough for an occasion like this, or they had defects that would be readily visible in this light, or their necklines were cut lower and the bodices tighter than Mother thought proper for this particular occasion.

"Mother, may I get some water?" she asked, interrupting a conversation between Mother and Lady Dia, which seemed to be centered about the middle-aged man who was partnering Brigette with reasonable skill, if not much grace. There were tables with ewers of cold water and goblets along the windows that formed one wall of this room, and suddenly she was feeling much too warm.

"Go ahead dear," Mother said absently. "Do not get out of my sight, and do not accept any invitations to dance. If someone asks you, send him to speak to me."

"Yes, Mother," she sighed with resignation, and wound her way through the crowd until she could reach one of the tables. A servant there handed her a goblet of cold water before she could ask for it, and she turned, sipping it, to watch the dancing from this vantage.

And that was when she saw him.

He was . . . beautiful. He looked like a poet. He danced as gracefully as a deer. He was dark, broodingly handsome, and could not be more than two or three years older than she. He was, in every way, exactly the sort of young man she had dreamed of. She couldn't take her eyes off of him, and when at the end of the dance he bowed over his partner's hand, escorted her back to *her* waiting mother, and then headed straight for *her,* she thought she was going to faint.

And then . . . he addressed the servant, asking for water, without even glancing at her.

He downed the goblet in a single gulp, handed it back, murmured a polite, "Excuse me," to everyone around the table, and went back to the crowd at the edge of the dancing, taking another girl out for the next number.

Not her.

He had never even noticed her.

Of course he didn't notice me! The last girl he had danced with, and the one he was dancing with now, didn't look like children! She felt herself blushing hotly with acute embarrassment, even though nothing had happened, and he hadn't actually *snubbed* her, he'd simply not seen her. But oh, it hurt. It hurt desperately.

She clutched her goblet and sipped at it to ease her parched throat, and watched him dance. *Who is he?* she wondered. *I must know.*

She listened as carefully as she could to the gossip among those standing near her. The young man was certainly attracting a lot of attention; she overheard more than one person wonder aloud who he was. But no one around her seemed to have any idea, although the few girls *without* their mothers certainly were not backward in their open admiration of him.

"He dances like a dancing master," murmured one. "I wish he'd ask me."

"He must be one of the people just here for Midwinter Court," said her friend, sounding disappointed. In the next moment, she revealed why. "With so many of us here, you and I probably won't even find out his name until after he's gone."

"If I were wedded to *him,* I wouldn't even *care* if I was stuck in some damp, cold manor in the back of nowhere," confessed another.

Violetta nursed that goblet of water for as long as she dared, before her mother's increasingly frequent and commanding glances turned into a stare. With regret she handed it back to the servant, and returned to her mother's side.

Her sisters kept getting satisfactory partners, at least by Mother's standards, and she kept getting none. Most of them were decidedly not handsome or young, but Mother was radiating maternal satisfaction every time Brigette and Aleniel stepped out to dance, probably due to what Lady Dia was whispering in her ear.

All last night, her dreams had been about *herself* doing the dancing, and not just her sisters. And yet, now that she had that beautiful young man to watch, she was not completely discontented with her lot.

She tried to reason out what he must be like, watching him closely and analyzing everything he did. She wished she could hear what he was saying, but from the reactions of his partners, it was probably all the usual polite blandishments. Still, he was careful with his partners, watching them and matching his steps to theirs. He never seemed to overstep his boundaries. Out there on the dance floor there *were* men who were too forward, or indifferent, or careless; she could tell it by the reactions of the ladies they were dancing with. But he was none of these things.

He must be here, like we are. Looking for a wife—or at least, his parents are looking for one for him. Which meant, if his rank wasn't too high, she had a chance. Even if he hadn't noticed her, she still had a chance. If only, oh, *if only,* he was a younger son with no chance of an inheritance! Because if Brigette and Aleniel married well, that meant that it would be *her* husband that would inherit, if he agreed to take the name of Raeylen. That inheritance would be nothing to sneeze at, especially not for a younger son with no prospects of his own.

She hated thinking like that . . . it was so cold and unromantic . . . but it gave her hope.

She filled her gaze with him, feeling feverish; his dark eyes flashing in the candlelight. His black hair, falling like silk to his shoulders. The face of a melancholy poet. He was dressed simply, but elegantly, in a parti-colored tunic of brown and saffron, with matching trews that fit him so closely they were nearly hosen, and soft brown boots. He was wearing no jewelry. Did that mean he was of limited means, or that he was indifferent to show? She couldn't tell.

In her head, she was writing a letter to him, although at the moment it was a tumble of confused phrases. *He will never see me in this crowd, but if I can get his attention with my words . . . there might be a chance.* She wished she could slip away to some quiet place, write it all out, and somehow get it into his hand. . . .

Mother noticed, at long last, how quiet she was, and turned to her. "Violetta, are you overtired? Feverish?" She put the back of her hand to Violetta's brow, somewhat to Violetta's embarrassment.

"It's just . . . very loud, Mother," she said, untruthfully. "And I feel lost among all these people. Is there someplace quiet I could go for a little, do you think?"

Her mother pursed up her lips a little, but then it seemed to occur to her that Violetta wasn't getting any dancing partners anyway. Violetta could almost see her thinking, calculating. After all, if Violetta left for a bit, that would be less competition for Brigette and Aleniel, and it would be much easier to keep track of two girls than three.

Mother turned to Lady Dia.

"My Lady, can you keep an eye on the older girls for a moment?" she asked, with just the proper amount of humility. "I would not ask, but it seems Violetta is a bit overheated, and would like to find somewhere to sit quietly—"

"Oh, my dear, I know just the thing," Lady Dia said immediately, with a laugh. "She isn't the only youngster to find this annual fete a little overwhelming. I'll take her to the Palace Library myself, no one will bother her there, and it is child's play to find your way back here. She won't even need an escort back, it's only two rooms away and there are Guards everywhere."

Before Mother could do more than utter a few words of thanks, Lady Dia had tucked Violetta's hand into the crook of her elbow and they were making their way out of the Great Hall. Jewels flashed in the candlelight, gold and silver embroidery gleamed, and fabrics of every color swirled in and out of their path.

"Now pay attention, but I promise you will be able to find your way back simply by listening for the music," Lady Dia told her, as they left the Great Hall by a side door, and turned to the left. "This is the Throne Room—see the Princess Royal over there at the end?" The room they had just entered was about half the size of the Great Hall, but had the same high ceiling, and the same wood-paneled walls. The main difference was that every other panel boasted a beautiful tapestry hanging of the arms of the Kingdom, the winged horse rampant, with broken chains, in white on blue. By walking on tiptoe, Violetta could just see the top of the Princess' head, and the head of someone right beside her. She vaguely remembered what the Princess looked like from when she and her sisters were presented two days ago. Beautiful, of course, and so very dignified and composed. *Could I ever be that calm and confident?* She and Dia crossed the foot of the Throne Room, and came to a wooden door; this one was closed, with a Guard at it. Dia nodded at the man, who nodded respectfully back. Evidently he recognized her. Even in this crush! *Does everyone at Court know Lady Dia?*

"The young lady is feeling a little overwhelmed, and would like to sit in the quiet for a little," Dia said. "Is anyone using the Library who would be disturbed by her being there?"

The Guard—who was almost as old as Father, gray-bearded and very dignified in his blue-and-silver uniform—smiled at her with an understanding look on his face. "No one is in

there at all, Lady Dia, and she is welcome to go sit for a while."
He nodded to Violetta. "I imagine your head is swimming a
little, eh, milady?"

"Just a little," Violetta lied, stammering a bit, because her
head wasn't exactly swimming. Then she added something
truthful, to give some veracity to Lady Dia's claim. "I've never
seen so many people in one place in my life."

"You should see one of the Great Fairs, or one of the Collegia summer gatherings. There's twice that many people at a
summer gathering, and the population of Haven almost dou-
bles for a Great Fair," the Guard told her, opening the door for
them. "Now, just you go and sit down in there. Read a little if
you like. Come out when you feel better."

Dia led her into a dimly lit room that held more bookshelves
and books and stacks of papers than Violetta had ever dreamed
existed. Granted, since Father wasn't much of a reader, most
of the books in the household were *hers,* with the exception
of a few in her father's office. But the mere sight of all of these
was a little intimidating. How could anyone ever read all of
these?

*Oh now, don't be so naïve. One person doesn't have to read
all of them. The Palace is full of people.*

There was no fire here. But there *was* brickwork that looked
like the back of a hearth, with chairs and little writing desks
with lit candles fixed to the top of them next to it. When Dia
brought her over to it, Violetta realized it was radiating heat.
There must be a fire or an oven of sorts on the other side of
that brick mass, to heat this room. Which made sense; you
wouldn't want an actual open fire in a room so full of paper.

"Now just rest there until you feel yourself again," Dia
said, kindly. "Then come back to the Great Hall. I'll make sure
we don't move from where you left us, but in case you can't
find us anyway, just ask a page for me. Or, if you decide you
would rather not rejoin us, you can send a page with a message to me and just stay here and read."

Lady Dia left her alone in that quiet place, closing the door softly behind her. It was surprisingly quiet in fact, with the distant sound of music and voices muffled thoroughly by the thick walls and all of the books.

Under any other circumstances, Violetta would have been content to just sit there for, well hours. She hadn't realized that all the heat and the noise had been giving her a headache until she sat down in one of the chairs beside a writing desk. There were probably hundreds of books of poetry and romances here that she had never read, never even *heard* of, probably, and although she didn't know where in all of these shelves such things might be found, it would be pleasant to look for them.

But then she realized that right next to her was a writing desk that had been set up for anyone who needed it . . . and on it were an ink pot, quill pens, a basin of sand, and palimpsest paper—paper that had been scraped of former writing, so you could use it for notes without spoiling good, clean paper. In short, everything she had been longing for less than a quarter candlemark ago.

She actually *could* write that letter to that beautiful young man! And get it into his hands, too! All she had to do was find a page or a servant, and there were *lots* of them in the Great Hall. No page would question a lady; most of them were very young children and would never even think to do so. Not only that, but Mother would never know what she had done! And if there was any chance that he had overlooked her by accident, or had been given orders which young ladies he was to dance with, at least he would know how she felt—and most importantly, who she was!

Feverishly she set to work, picking the cleanest piece of paper she could find, and dipping a new quill carefully into the ink. The things she had thought to say tumbled about in her mind. How would he react to this? Women were not supposed to be the ones approaching men! But then . . . *young* women were not supposed to be doing any approaching at all. That was for their parents to arrange.

Never mind. What was the worst that would happen? He would laugh at this, or regard it with disgust, and throw it in the fire. She had nothing to lose.

Forgive my audacity, my wretched boldness, but I know no other way in which I may tell you what is in my heart. I know I may deserve your reproach and your scorn for daring to write to you in this way. For you do not know me, as I do not know you; I only saw you a little while ago, and yet, in the moment that I first saw you, I was transfixed, I was rendered mute, as my heart leapt and said, "He is the one! He, and no other!" I do not know if you are an angel who will take pity on me, or a devil come to tempt me. I am torn with doubt, filled with agony that only you can resolve. Is this mere infatuation, or the recognition of a true lifebond? I do not know! In one moment, I rejoice that I came here this night and saw you! In the next, I sigh with bitter suffering that ever I came and ever I saw your face. I am young, too young perhaps, and I have never known anything like this in all my short life. This fever, this inexperience, torments me! And yet I know, there is no other than you, not one on earth, to whom I would give my heart. I feel that this is ordained, that the gods themselves decreed that I must love you, or why else would I be so tossed by the waves of these emotions? It is my fate; all my life until now was merely waiting for the moment when first I saw you. I did not know you, and yet I have loved you all my life.

Her throat closed, and a wretched knot formed there, making it impossible to swallow. Her eyes burned, then spilled. She began to cry, tears streaking her face as her pen raced across the paper. At least her flawless penmanship remained the same, no matter how her vision blurred with falling tears.

Whatever my destiny is to be, I consign it to your hands, and to your honor. I beg your protection and understanding of this impulse. And I feel, I know, you will not betray me. I feel in my heart that you and you alone could fathom what is in mine. No one else understands me; they hear my words, but they never listen. I shall wither alone and misunderstood, unless you save me. Oh, give me reason to hope! I know that such boldness deserves reproach and scorn rather than reward, but let the love that I offer you unconditionally and with both hands be my excuse!

I dare not read this through; my heart sinks, leaden with the fear that you will think me a little fool and my love worthy only of ridicule. And yet, I know in my heart that you are good and honorable. Give me but a whisper of hope, a drop of sympathy, for I am yours, forever, past death itself. Violetta, youngest daughter of Lord Leverance, House Chendlar.

It was done. She sanded it and dried it quickly. There was sealing-wax in a small drawer of the desk; she folded the letter small, melted the wax at the shielded candle on the desk, and sealed it, using her pendant instead of a sealing ring.

Then, she waited. She used the hem of her chemise to dry her eyes, and went to a window and put her fevered head against the glass to cool it and her eyes. *I don't think anyone will notice that I have been crying. If my eyes are red, I will say it is from the perfumes, or the smoke from the candles.* She hid the letter in her sleeve, and, trembling at her own audacity, went to the door.

The same Guard was there and he smiled at her as she emerged. "Feeling better, young milady?" he asked.

Unable to speak at the moment, she nodded, dropping her gaze as if she was shy. It wasn't a ruse, actually, she *felt* shy and terribly vulnerable, and afraid. He closed the door behind her and resumed his position, as she made her way back across the bottom of the Throne Room to the Great Hall. Since she was alone, she was able to dart between people much more easily than when she and Lady Dia had been coming along arm-in-arm.

The Great Hall was just as crowded as before. Instead of

going directly to her mother, she edged her way along the side of the room nearest the door, watching for the beautiful young man, hoping he would be near where she last saw him. At last she spotted him, in conversation with an older woman. From his posture, she didn't think they were related. A moment later, the old lady laughed and hit him lightly with a fan that she carried; she must be someone of higher rank than he who was flirting harmlessly with him. She had seen Mother flirt with Cousin Talbot in this way, many times. He seemed to be amused; at least, he was smiling at her, and leaning low to murmur things to her that made her laugh again. Violetta swallowed hard, and fought down a terrible wave of jealousy, but oh, she would have given anything to have had him smile at her like that.

She looked about and found a page, leaning against the wall near another table, this one laden with empty goblets discarded by those who had gone too far from the water table. This was a little boy of about eight or nine, in a blue and silver uniform that was a miniature version of the Guard uniform; he was perfect, much too young to dare to question her or refuse to do her bidding. And, fortunately, she had a little purse on her chatelaine that had a few coins in it, which would ensure he did what she asked quickly. She took a silver piece out of the purse, and tapped the page's shoulder. He turned, and before he could say anything, she pointed at the beautiful young man.

"Do you see that dark-haired man, speaking with the old lady in green velvet?" she asked. "The one with the green fan?"

"Aye, milady," the little boy replied, with a bit of a bow. "Is there—"

She pressed the letter and the coin into his hand. "Take this letter to him please," she said, shaking in her shoes at her own audacity.

The page looked at the letter and the coin, pocketed the latter, and immediately began making his way across the room to where the young man was.

Now completely terrified at what she had just done, she withdrew into the crowd a little, watching him from behind a portly old woman's broad skirts. She could barely see him, and she knew where he was and what he looked like. It wasn't very likely that he would be able to spot her.

The page reached him at last, got his attention, and handed him the letter.

The young man looked at it with a quizzical expression and asked the page something. The boy turned to look where she had been, but she was no longer in sight. He replied, and shrugged, and made his way back to the spot where she had found him, taking up his station again. Clearly, now that his task was completed, the page had no interest in trying to find her. The young man gazed after him for a moment, then shrugged himself, and put the letter in his sleeve, unopened.

He didn't cast it aside! She thought that her heart was going to pound its way out of her chest, it was beating so quickly.

Faint and lightheaded with emotion, Violetta went back to the Library. "I am not as well as I thought," she said to the sympathetic Guard, who readily let her back in.

"I'll find a page, and you can send a note to Lady Dia," he said, and he was as good as his word. As she sat down to write out a note to her mother the door opened again and another little page, a girl this time, entered.

I think I have had too much excitement, she wrote. *But this Library is quiet and I am as comfortable as I would be at the manor, so please do not cut anything short. I will be here when you are ready to leave.* She simply folded it in half, no messing about with sealing wax this time, and gave it to the little girl.

And there she remained, almost afraid to come out, until Lady Dia and her mother and her two very satisfied sisters came for her, and collected Father from the Throne Room, and they all made their way back home together. If this really *had* been home, they would, of course, have walked. It wasn't all *that* far from the Palace to their town-manor, not by country standards. But things weren't done that way here. They had arrived by carriage, and they returned by carriage. Brigette and Aleniel more than made up for her silence with their chatter. No one seemed to think they needed to find out if she was all right or not . . . which perfectly suited her. Because what could she say? *I saw the boy I will love forever* . . . that would hardly go over well. Or she could lie, and say that the crowd had overwhelmed her.

But she didn't have to say anything. They all entered the manor; the cousins were, for the most part, not back from the parties they had been invited to, so the manor was blessedly quiet. Leaving Mother, Father, Lady Dia, Brigette and Aleniel to discuss all the potential suitors her sisters had danced with, she said she was tired and went up to her room.

Once there, she let the maid undress her, but she tossed restlessly, aching with hope and weeping with fear, until morning, with the only comfort she could find being in the warmth and love of her little dog.

"And how was yer night, m'love?" Mags asked, as Amily came in, very late indeed. He had actually expected her much earlier; evidently the Princess' duties had kept her in attendance at the fete for much longer than he had thought they would.

Then again . . . I never went to any Royal functions. I reckon the Royals don't get to leave till the last guest gets carted out.

"Without incident," she said, throwing herself down in a chair. "Too warm. Very loud. Many, many, boring people. You didn't miss anything."

"Kinda thought as much. Such things don't seem like my sort of do. Unless ye got me in a servant's tabard, keepin' my ears open." He was tired, so he wasn't making any attempt to clean up his speech to Amily's level. He had been at the predictably raucous drinking-party held at Lord Kaltar's manor, in the absence of his Lordship and his wife and son. "Gotta say, 'tis a good thing I reckon bein' drunk's a waste of m'time, or I'd be sore right now, havin' t'stay sober while the lads around me drink like fish."

Amily laughed a little. "I hope your evening was also without incident, but I expect it was the exact opposite." She pulled off her boots, and wiggled her toes in front of the fire. Mags was already in his oldest and most comfortable trews and a knitted tunic; in a few moments, he had made some cheese-toast at the fire, and passed it to her. She took it with a sigh of gratitude, and accepted the mug of cider he handed her with a smile.

"Well, the hijinks started with the lads decidin' to see if the chimney in the Hall could be climbed." He sighed. "I got t'it just in time t'get the stuff off th' mantle an' inta the hands of the servants." The servants, of course, had not dared to rebuke the cousins, nor even dash up to the hearth in an attempt to save anything breakable. "Why no one broke his fool neck, I got no ideer. So then they got the bright ideer to climb atop each others' shoulders an' whack at each other with cushions. That wasn' so bad. You know, like fightin' on horseback, on'y with pillows an' usin' each other as horses. On'y one cushion bust, so that wasn't too bad, an' it weren't stuffed with feathers but with hay, so it weren't so bad t'clean up. That was when I reckoned I could start on a buncha stories an' get 'em boastin'. I got th' cook t'make salty eats; pickles an' salted cheese-toast, stuff that'd make 'em thirsty. An' I doctored their hard cider wi' brandy. I reckoned the faster I got 'em too drunk t'move, the better it'd be. That pretty much solved the problem; by the time his Lordship an' all got home, half of 'em had stumbled up t'bed an' the rest was sprawled all over the Hall, snorin'."

Amily choked on a laugh, as he passed the image on to Rolan, and Rolan passed it to her. It really had been funny. The cousins were laid out in the boneless contortions that only the very drunk could manage, and Mags imagined that between the heavy hangovers and the cramped muscles they would have in the morning, they were going to get punishment enough for their mischief.

"Her Ladyship weren't too pleased, but his Lordship laughed, and said he reckoned that there was gonna be green faces in th' mornin'." He paused. "But then . . . well, I got back here an' stayed awake t'talk with ye, 'cause I don't rightly know what t'do about this. Me an' Brand stayed down by th' fire, him t' get some food an' drink afore he went to bed, an' he remembered somethin' and pulled a letter outa his sleeve. I asked him what 'twas, and he allowed that he didn't know. Some page said a lady said t'give it to 'im."

"It was probably from a restless wife looking for Midwinter fling," Amily said, with a shrug. "I saw a dozen such delivered just while I was *watching* for such things. The gods only know how many people up at Court went to the 'wrong' beds last night."

"Well, so I reckoned, and so I tol' him, so he laughed and cracked it open an' started t'read it, an' his face changed. I ast him what was wrong, an' he got irritated. 'It's a stupid letter from a child who should know better,' he says, and flings it in the fire and picks up his mug an' says, 'I'm goin' t'bed,' an does. Well the fire wasn't even coals at that point so . . ." He shrugged. "I'm the King's spy. I fished it out. Hadn't even begun to burn, but I hunted up some scraps of paper in his lordship's study an' tossed them in an' made sure those *did.* Just in case he came back down t'make sure it'd burned."

Now he handed Amily the letter. "So. Here 'tis."

She read it through, her eyes going wide. "Oh," she said, faintly. "My. Is Brand—"

"I don' think he's gonna do anythin' 'bout it. But if he asks me, I'll say he's best off keepin' dead mum. That *he'll* look like a pure fool, with some liddle girl all love-lorn after him, an' worst of all, it bein' Leverance's daughter. An' that his pa is sure to figger he encouraged it somehow, and be riled about it." He shrugged. "If that don't work, I'll tell him mebbe it was all made up by some'un else entirely t'make him look like a mortal fool if he said somethin' 'bout it. I cain't see any good could come outa this, an' what's th' point of shamin' the girl?"

"That's exactly what you should say," Amily said soberly. "In fact, the more you emphasize that his father will take this poorly, or that he has someone who is trying to make a fool out of him, the better off you are. We are. Violetta isn't exactly a . . . little girl. She is certainly marriageable age. I can all too clearly imagine Lord Kaltar deciding to take some revenge on Lord Leverance by making the letter public, or at least making the fact that it was sent public. The poor child would never live down the shame. Mags, I am so very glad that you brought me this." She folded it up and put it in a safe place over the mantelpiece. "I will have to show this to the King, and then I think we will destroy it."

"Prolly all for the best." Mags huffed out a breath. "Were you ever that . . ." he groped for words.

"Innocent? Idealistic?" she suggested. "Romantic?"

"Somethin' like that." He pondered. What he wanted to say was *were you ever that much of a damn little fool,* but that was cruel, and really, who knew what was going through the child's mind? Poor thing, it might actually be a lifebond, though if it was, it was very one-sided. That happened, and the result was usually unhappy for everyone.

"No. I was far too sensible. But I was *living* at the Court and steeped to my eyebrows in intrigue, thanks to Father." She sighed. "I can certainly see how a naïve young woman, fresh from a country estate, who has been sheltered all her life could be." She made a face. "Do I dare tell Dia about this?"

"We've been trustin' Dia for a long time. Though Dia might well wanta march up there an' give the girl a good shakin'," Mags said. "I think ye better."

"Hmm. This gives me an idea. This might actually have turned out for the best."

Mags couldn't imagine *how,* but then, he wasn't Amily.

"In that case . . ." He waggled his eyebrows at her suggestively. She laughed.

"Yes, I think so. This will all have to wait until morning anyway."

Amily and the King were alone in the King's study, as they always were, first thing in the morning. Like her father, Amily shared breakfast with Kyril, combining eating and working, a small table between them, and food and papers spread out over the top of it. She had waited until after they were finished eating, but before Kyril managed to bring up anything *more* serious, before presenting him with Violetta's letter, along with an explanation of how Mags had gotten it, what Mags had done, and what they had discussed.

There was a very long pause, during which the King's face took on an expression of mingled exasperation and alarm, while he read it.

When he was done, King Kyril folded the letter with a muttered curse and looked up at Amily. "You and Mags were absolutely right to bring this to me immediately," he said. "And Mags' ideas to keep that hothead Brand from saying anything about this are precisely what we need. Dear gods." He threw the folded letter into the hottest part of the fire in his study and watched it burn. "That little idiot could have ignited the feud all over again. Only think what might have happened if Brand was actually more cunning than he is!"

"Or if his father had gotten wind of this," Amily agreed, grimly. "The first thing that went through my mind was that Brand might have decided to lure the child somewhere and—well, best not to think of what could have happened. It would certainly have been very ugly. I'm still worried that he *might* think of that; I don't know him, and I don't know if he has that sort of mind. I've been trying to think of some way to distract him so he forgets the letter ever existed."

"You would think there would be distractions in plenty," the King said, dryly. "He's a very good looking lad, and there are many ladies with wandering eyes here at Court."

"Yes, but are there any *beauties* with wandering eyes and complaisant husbands?" Amily replied, a little shocked at herself for even suggesting such a thing. "That's what we need for a distraction."

Kyril raised one sandy-gray eyebrow. "My dear King's Own . . . I am the King of Valdemar. *I* cannot exactly go to certain ladies of negotiable virtue and suggest they should throw themselves at Brand, now, can I?"

She had to laugh. "No, and neither can I. But Mags could, and so could my father."

"Nikolas is probably better schooled to make that particular suggestion, especially now that he is no longer King's Own," the King agreed. "And he also probably has a better idea which of them is bored with her current inamorata and likely to be hunting for something fresher." He smiled at Amily. "While I was . . . rather unhappy to lose my old friend as my right hand, I have to admit that *not* having him be King's Own is turning out to be extremely useful. And having both him *and* Mags available to do things I would rather not ask other Heralds to do is changing things for the better."

"I can't believe we're saying things like this," she murmured, half to herself. "This isn't what I thought . . . ruling . . . was about."

The King patted her hand. "It isn't always swords or laws, my dear. Sometimes it's just plain manipulation. Ugly perhaps, but it does get things done." He picked up a stack of papers from his desk, and evened their edges. "Now. About getting things done. Do you feel sufficiently prepared for the meeting with the heads of all the Guilds this afternoon?"

In the morning, Violetta told herself that there could not possibly be a response from the young man yet; it was much too early. Who knew when he would read the letter anyway? But she told everyone that she was feeling ill, and stayed home from the afternoon party at Lord and Lady Abrogin's manor, because *that* would be the perfect time, not only for him to send back his reply, but for her to intercept it without worrying that Mother would get it first. And it wasn't really a lie, either. She was nauseous with anxiety, waiting for his reply, and wondering what it would be.

But there was no reply. The only letters that arrived were for Mother or Father. And as the afternoon turned to evening, and as the rest of her family returned and began the business of getting ready for the evening open-house at Master Soren's, her anxious sickness turned to real illness. He hadn't replied, because he wasn't going to reply. She had poured out her heart for nothing—except, perhaps, ridicule.

No, surely he is too kind to share it to make fun of me. He probably threw it in the fire. . . .

But her stomach was utterly in revolt now, her head hurt so much that she could scarcely stand it, and she took to her bed. Mother came to check on her, diagnosed "overwrought nerves," and suggested that bed was the best place for her for a day or two. "Too many parties with too many people in too short a time for you, Violetta," she said with authority. "You are exhausted. You aren't used to this sort of excitement."

Since that was exactly what she wanted, she meekly agreed. Her old nurse put her to bed, tucking her in as if she had been a child. Silence fell over the manor as first Mother and her sisters left, then the cousins, and then, at last, Father. There was no one left—well, perhaps the odd cousin or two who was still suffering from over-indulging last night, but no one else but the servants.

If she hadn't felt so miserable, she might have actually enjoyed herself. Although this room was a fraction of the size of the one she had back home, she didn't have to share it with her sisters. It was a tiny little wood-paneled thing with one window and a small fireplace, and just enough room for the curtained bed, the chest of her dresses and the chest of her chemises. The bed had its own little lamp, and places in the headboard to store her favorite books. At home, Mother always had her working at something and she never got a chance to stay in bed and read and daydream.

Her old nurse brought her up a mess of cooked apples and honey in beaten cream, but she had no appetite for it and sent it back. *That* brought up the cook herself, along with her nurse. Both of them fussed over her a little, which was oddly comforting, and the cook brought her brandy and cream and honey and told her to drink it down.

Violetta had never had brandy before, but the drink was warm and soon she was a little tipsy and very drowsy. Her stomach still ached, and so did her heart and her head, but she felt as if she might be able to sleep.

But just as she was thinking about putting out the candle, her nurse returned. "Oh poppet," the old woman said, "I know you're not feeling well, but Lady Dia is here and I told her to come right up!"

"Oh—" Violetta began, but before she could say the word "no," Lady Dia was already in her tiny bedroom.

"You can leave us alone, Nurse," Dia said, firmly, and although she did not actually, physically *push* Nurse out, somehow, with her sheer force of personality, she *impelled* Nurse to leave, and firmly shut the nice thick door behind her. Then she stuffed a handkerchief into the keyhole, to prevent listening.

She walked the three paces it took, and sat down on the foot of the bed, and looked at Violetta so sternly that Violetta shrank back against her pillows. She had never seen this expression on Lady Dia's face before. It was controlled, and focused, anger. Not rage; Lady Dia was completely in control of her emotions and herself. This was . . . implacable.

"I am *exceedingly* angry with you, young lady!" Dia said, in a quiet, but furious voice, as Violetta quailed and felt her eyes filling with tears just in pure self-defense. Lady Dia not only *looked* angry, but little Star, the tiny dog, clearly felt that she was angry, for the pup cowered and whimpered, and tried to hide in Violetta's bedclothes. "I have seen toddlers in this Court that display more sense, and more forethought, than you did last night. Of all the thoughtless, inconsiderate, *foolish* things you could have done, you chose to perform the one thoughtless, inconsiderate, foolish thing that could have brought permanent disgrace to you, reflected disgrace to your sisters, and bloodshed to your family!"

Now Violetta's mouth dropped open in shock, because she could not imagine what it was that Lady Dia thought she had done! She hadn't insulted anyone—she hadn't even spoken to anyone! She'd been quiet and deferential, and spent most of the time in the Library! And Lady Dia and that Guardsman had told her it was all right to be there! "But—what—"

"That *letter!*" Dia hissed, leaning closer, so that Violetta instinctively tried to make herself smaller and clutched the bedclothes up to her chest. "That incredibly *foolish* letter! It was bad enough to send something like that to a strange man you know absolutely nothing about—that alone could have disgraced you forever! And not just if he had merely made it public, which not a few young men would have done! But let's just discuss that, first, shall we?"

Before Violetta could say anything, Dia continued ahead; clearly this was not going to be any sort of "discussion," since it was going to be Dia talking and Violetta listening. Not that she could have said anything. Her throat was so choked she could not have gotten a single word out.

"Now, suppose the man you sent it to had decided to share it with his friends. And he could have had many reasons to do so. He could have wanted to prove—in the event that you were planning to cry rape on him, that it was you who approached him. He could have thought it was funny, or flattering. He might simply want to shame you, since you *clearly* were feeling no shame when you sent it to him. What do you think would happen when that letter got out?" It was a rhetorical question; Violetta had no idea, and Dia did. "I can tell you. *First* of all, you would be utterly, utterly disgraced. Really, child, what woman, outside of a tale, would *ever* send such a thing to a man she didn't know? Only someone with no sense, or no morals, or looking to entrap a man. The entire Court would know, within days, if not hours. You are not of high enough rank for the King to intervene. No one would offer to marry you, at least not anyone here at Court, or connected enough with the Court to have heard about this. *If* you were lucky, someone very far from Court, who never planned on going to Court, might be induced to take you off your parents' hands. But unless he was very old, ignorant, or careless, it would cost them an enormous dower."

Violetta blanched at that. She had already heard, at great length, how her dower was going to have to be smaller than her sisters'. Any addition to her bride-price would have to come at their expense, and she knew what her sisters would have to say about that.

Dia nodded grimly. "I think that would be very unlikely. So what other courses of action could there be? Well, one of your cousins might be induced to marry you, on the condition he became your father's heir. But you would never be able to set foot outside your own lands again, and even so, your infamy would probably be known, and even your servants would be aware of it. Possibly they might get you off their hands by wedding you to some wealthy farmer or other, and I *know* how those weddings generally go. Your husband would never let you forget he did you a favor. He might verbally berate you, he might beat you, no one would lift a finger to help you. Even if he did not abuse you, you would learn what it is like to labor like any farm wife, and like any farm wife, you would be giving birth every year, and there would be no nurses to help you tend to your growing brood."

Violetta was cursed with a very good imagination, and as Dia spoke she could *see* all this in her mind's eye. She sat there, frozen, unable to move.

"But say your father didn't care to unload you on a farmer, or a cousin," Dia continued, as Violetta wondered what could possibly be worse than that. "Your parents would not only punish you in every possible way they could, there is the very real possibility that they would declare that for some reason you had gone mad and lock you up until they could take you home. Where you would be locked up in your room, forbidden to leave."

Violetta felt herself grow cold. "But—why?"

"Because if they said you had gone mad, and people believed it, they'd feel sorry for the rest of the family and *your sisters* would not lose *their* chances at good marriages as well as you," Dia said grimly. "And believe me, I have seen people declare their children insane for less reason."

"But I—" Violetta said, her voice breaking. She hadn't meant for any of that to happen! In the tales, no young man would be so cruel, so unthinking, so unchivalrous as to betray her by making her letter public! Why would he? What could he possibly gain?

But Dia had already told her what he could gain. He could protect himself from someone who might be trying to trap him. He could gain notoriety of the sort he *wanted,* among his friends, showing that girls were practically throwing themselves at his feet. And his reputation would not only emerge unscathed, it might emerge enhanced.

"But you, you *stupid* girl, didn't even bother to think of anyone but yourself, did you?" Dia went on, running right over the top of her. "And that is just the *least* harmful of all the things that could have happened. What if he had sent you a letter back telling you to come to him? You'd have gone without a second thought, wouldn't you?"

Violetta's face must have betrayed that she would have done exactly that, for Lady Dia snorted with disgust.

"And then, he would have had his way with you and *if you were lucky* left you to explain why you had gone and met a man alone and gotten deflowered," she said, shocking Violetta with her blunt language. "He most certainly *would not* have married you! And then your father would have had to either challenge him—a very bad idea, might I add, since if *I* were this young man, I would insist on Lord Leverance taking up the challenge himself, since he would be easy for me to kill—or take the case before the King—another bad idea, since that would put the King in quite an untenable position, and would require a trial, complete with Truth Spells, in which you would be revealed to be the foolish little idiot that you are. And then, well, we are back to what would happen if the young man revealed the letter, and all those consequences. He would be punished for taking advantage of you, yes, but not for rape, because you threw yourself at him. And so far as husbands for your sisters were concerned, well, they would evaporate. And as for you, not even a swineherd would marry you once you'd been ruined. Oh, and let's not forget that if your father challenged this man, your father would be *dead.*"

Tears overflowed from Violetta's eyes and burned their way down her cheeks. "But he wouldn't—I could tell he wouldn't hurt me—"

"No, you little idiot, you could *not* tell. You did not suddenly become Gifted. In fact, I can tell you for a fact that you have never been more wrong about something in your entire life. Because you didn't even bother to find out *who* he was before you sent that damned letter. Brand, son of Lord Kaltar, of House Raeylen." Dia folded her arms over her chest and glared as the tears practically froze on Violetta's cheeks.

Her mind nearly exploded. She felt dizzy. She wanted to die, right there, on the spot. "Oh no—"

"Oh *yes,*" said Dia. "And it must be true that the gods look after the foolish and the idiotic, because it is purely a matter of sheer accident that Brand was more than a little drunk when he read your letter, and he threw it in the fire. A friend of mine happened to be there at the time, and Brand told *him* about it, briefly, before staggering up to bed."

"He threw it in the fire?" she faltered. Surely her heart was going to break . . . all her heartfelt words, and he threw them in the fire. . . .

And then, her head caught up with her heart, and she quailed inside. Lady Dia was right! She was a fool! How could she even be *thinking* that, now that she knew who he was . . . and what he could do to her . . .

"You are also *mortally* lucky that I have discussed you girls with my friend, and he knows all about you," said Dia, sternly. "He is a dear young man, and he feels very sorry for you, and felt he had to protect you. If Brand even remembers reading it, my friend is going to convince him it was some other girl—one who doesn't actually exist."

Before Violetta could feel any relief at all, Lady Dia took both her shoulders in her hands, and shook her, hard. "Now you *listen* to me, you little fool. Your idiocy came within a hair of destroying your whole family. Because Lord Kaltar would *certainly* have used that letter to ruin you, your father would *certainly* have challenged him, and depending on whether or not the King managed to get things in hand, your father and Lord Kaltar would *certainly* have dueled, or their champions would, and no matter what else happened, your actions would have completely disgraced your family, stirred up the feud again, and there would be *someone's* blood on your hands! The King would have had to act, and very probably he would have confiscated *both* estates, leaving both families too impoverished to continue this quarrel."

By this point, Violetta was so overcome with horror that she couldn't even speak. Dia glared at her in silence for a good long time before nodding. "Now. What are you going to do about this? I *strongly* suggest the first thing is to spend a substantial amount of time this evening thanking those gods that kept your foolishness in check."

The tears began anew, and Violetta bowed her head. "Yes, Lady Dia," she whispered. Any tipsiness the brandy had given her had burned away, and all she felt now was a roil of emotions, all of them terrible. Misery, mostly. Along with guilt, terror, heartbreak, and grief. To think that she had fallen in love with . . . the son of her father's worst enemy! Oh, the bitter pain of it! He could not be more unattainable if he lived on the moon! Only the fact that he had been drunk had kept disaster from befalling all of them.

"Are you going to tell Mother and Father?" she gulped, still not looking up.

She nearly fainted with relief when Dia said, "No. It will serve no purpose except to upset them, and they do not deserve that. For all *I* know, your father might choose to do something foolish anyway, using you as his excuse." She shook her head. "Even if he did not, they would certainly lock you away as mad. My friend is the soul of discretion and has been entrusted with more weighty secrets than you have years. He'll keep this one for you; he told me he feels sorry for you, the gods only know why. I suppose because you are young, pretty, and innocent." She sniffed. "You certainly don't deserve such considerate treatment after the improper way you have behaved. *I* am certainly not going to go out of my way to try and find you a good husband now, and I strongly advise that you stay quiet and unobtrusive for the rest of your visit here. And if you have even a morsel of decency about you, you will avoid young Brand like the enemy he is. Is that understood?"

"Yes, Lady Dia," Violetta whispered, now thoroughly chastised.

"Good." Lady Dia stood up, walked to the door, with every thumb-length of her rigid with disapproval, and put one hand on the door-handle. "I'm bitterly disappointed in you, Violetta. I thought after the good care you were giving my little dog that you were a sensible, careful, thoughtful and capable young lady. I am very sorry to discover that I was wrong."

And with that, she left. Violetta could only blow out her candle and collapse into a puddle of pure misery among her bedclothes.

There was a knock at the outer door to Amily's rooms—the one that led out into the snow-covered gardens, not the one that led into Healers Collegium. She knew who it was; Dia had promised to come straight here after having "a little talk" with Violetta.

Dia was moderately—but only moderately—annoyed that she had missed one of Soren's Open House nights to deliver the lecture. Unfortunately, because she was serving as escort to the three girls, she was going to miss all the rest, but Soren was making it up to her by including her and her husband in his Midwinter Night gathering. She was, however, just as furious as she had sounded at Violetta's behavior.

Amily understood that, objectively, but part of her felt a great deal of sympathy for the poor girl. After all, she'd evidently been raised in a very protective environment but given the freedom to read and dwell on whatever romantic nonsense she could get her hands on.

"That was more than a bit strong, Dia," was Amily's greeting to her friend as she let Dia in. She'd been "listening in" on Dia's lecture to Violetta through the dog, of course. Dia shrugged, and took off her cloak, handing it to Amily. Together they made their way through the warm and green-smelling darkness of the hothouses and into the living area proper.

Mags was waiting for them. He'd built up the fire, arranged the most comfortable of their seats at it, and had gone and begged some pocket pies at the kitchen. They had both reckoned that Dia would need the refreshment. The little sitting room looked particularly inviting and restful.

"I wanted it strong," Dia said, a touch of iron in her voice. "That girl is . . . not *spoiled,* precisely, but she's been indulged. She needed a good shaking up, or she most certainly will get herself into some trouble, and possibly, some harm. There are plenty of young wastrels in the Court who would happily have taken advantage of her and discarded her afterward."

"Yes but . . ." Amily paused, groping through her thoughts. "Getting married shouldn't be a girl's only option! I *know* that the Guard is open to women—for all we know she is a good enough scholar she could be a teacher or—"

But Dia interrupted her. "Don't be absurd. She's nothing like suited for the Guard, as you well know. As for anything else, well perhaps that might come into play if we hadn't managed to save her from her own folly, but we did. She is still the daughter of Lord Leverance. She'll do what she is told to do, or face being cast out . . . and face it, unless you or I or the King takes an interest in her, and helps her build a new life, she is woefully unequipped to fend for herself. Marriage is the only option Violetta's parents are going to give her," Dia pointed out, settling herself at the fire, and removing the over-shoes that had kept her dainty embroidered slippers from the snow. "Really, she isn't even aware there *are* other options, and having been around her for many days now, I don't think she would consider the other options as anything other than ranging from unpleasant to outright horrifying."

"Girl's in love with love," Mags observed, coming in from the tiny room that served them as a pantry with a bottle of wine and three glasses. "Leastwise, thet's what it sounds like t'me." He handed glasses to Amily and Dia, and poured wine for all three of them. "Mind, I ain't got no experience about girls like that, not direct, but reckon there might be a couple in the Court. They ain't naïve 'nuff to go writin' letters like Violetta did, but I hear tell there's an artist or two does a brisk trade in liddle tiny portraits that kin be hid easy . . ." He shrugged.

Amily made a face, and passed the plate of pocket-pies to Dia, who took one of the savory ones. "You're probably right," she agreed. "I've seen enough like her here at Court. You're right, Mags, there are no few young ladies who moon and sigh over portraits they have no right to possess." She had to laugh a little. "In fact, some of them have portraits of musicians and actors and moon and sigh over them! Fortunately for us all, they have the sense to confine their obsession to mooning and sighing."

Dia rolled her eyes. "Good spirits and ministers of grace, defend us. I suppose I should be thankful she didn't fall in love with one of *them.* I very much doubt that things would have turned out the way they did. In fact, I would be shuddering with horror at the thought if that foolish child hadn't already exhausted all my emotions for one night."

Amily shrugged. "Well, she's had a good fright, and thanks to you and Mags, no harm has come from it."

Mags gave them both a self-satisfied grin; Amily thought

that he looked very pleased with himself. "I was savin' my best news till Dia got here. Had m'talk with Brand afore he left for a party. Managed t'convince Brand thet if'n 'e said anythin', what with the letter bein' gone, 'is pa would likely be mad as hops over him bein' played fer a fool, an' he better not say anythin' *at all* if he don't wanta get in trouble."

Amily tilted her head to the side. "I don't follow," she said doubtfully.

"Neither do I," Dia confirmed, and held out her glass for a refill. "Enlighten us, Mags. Speak at length, and eloquently. I really want to understand what you did. This sounds clever."

"I ast him . . ." Mags cleared his throat, and took on the cultured accents of "Magnus."

"'How likely is it that any girl of good breeding would write a letter like that to a stranger? Really, Brand, I think you are being played here.' An' he had t'agree that it weren't likely it come from Violetta." He tilted his glass at Dia and waited for her—and Amily—to make the proper conclusions.

Amily did first—and waited for Dia to figure it out. It didn't take long. "Oh!" Dia exclaimed, and laughed. "Of course! It would be someone trying to lure him into making a fool of himself. No matter how he responded to it—if he even made it public among his friends—if he did anything other than ignore the thing, he'd open himself to ridicule. Whoever had 'forged' that letter would make it all public, and he would look like an idiot for falling for such a ridiculous ruse!"

"And ain't no feller Brand's age takes t'bein' made t'look foolish." Mags nodded. "Talked it over with yer pa, Amily, an' he reckoned 'twas a good approach, an' it worked. Letter's gone, King burned it, so there's nothin' fer nobody t'find now. Even if 'e decides t'tell his pa anyway, it'd on'y be Brand's word, he ain't got no proof. An' thanks t'Dia, the girl's gonna keep shut of him, so he's got no way t'get to her."

"That we know of," Dia cautioned, but sipped her wine and relaxed. "I like the girl. I just wish she had . . . I don't know . . .

more sense and less sensitivity. At least she's not as hardened as her sisters. They are unbelievably cynical about this matter of husband hunting."

"They don't have any reason not to be," Amily pointed out. "They evidently don't know of—or don't care for—any of the other options that a woman has for herself either. All three of those girls have been raised to believe that the only thing that they can *do* is make a good marriage. And by a 'good marriage,' I mean one that brings them rank, wealth, or both. That would make anyone with intelligence cynical, and I will say, none of these girls are stupid. Not even Violetta."

Dia shrugged; well, after all, she'd spent her entire life in the Court, and Lord Leverance's daughters were by far and away not the only ones to be plotting the same course for their lives. She reiterated what Amily already knew. "They know they are commodities; everything they have been taught tells them that. When that's what you are taught by people you have no reason to distrust, you believe it the way you believe in your religion. You can't blame them for being interested in making sure the deal they get gives them the most advantages, and the most privileges."

"That might be true for the two oldest—but you know yourself Violetta is not hardened, nor cynical." Amily gave her friend a long and level look. "And maybe her parents had no reason to ever educate her in the fact that marriage is not the only thing a woman can do, but she's *here* now, and she's not stupid, and I think she ought to at least get some idea of what else is possible. Maybe *that* will catch her imagination and get her thinking about what she can be, rather than what's in the pages of those romances."

Dia eyed Amily, and sighed. "I *know* what you are thinking at me, you remorseless wench. I'll try and drop some hints in the girl's flower-like ear that she has other options, what they are, and how she might wheedle her parents around to them. But don't blame me if she doesn't listen. Mags was right, she's in love with love, and there isn't much that is going to convince her that happiness lies in any other direction than the arms of a handsome man."

"Now," Amily appended.

Dia snorted. "In my opinion—*ever.*"

Mags was happy to get away from the Court whenever he could, tending to his little crop of budding spies. He was altogether pleased with them; the three who'd been dubious had weeded themselves out, by violating one or another of the rules. His band of faithful had recruited more like themselves. Now he had a solid little group, and it was time for the next step. Nikolas concurred. *"And it is appropriate,"* he'd said. *"New year . . . new life."*

He'd already revealed who and what he was to Aunty Minda. He had figured that she would take it well, but he hadn't expected her full reaction, which had been both amusing and embarrassing. She hadn't been afraid of him or what he represented—why should she have been, when she had never broken the law in all of her life?—but she had very nearly treated him like some form of royalty, bowing and making her children kneel, until he'd told her in no uncertain terms that if she kept doing that, he'd have to get down on his own knees just to speak to her.

Then he'd done it.

That had made her laugh, and they had a good long talk that went on for well over a candlemark. He already knew much about her sad life; it had been one long struggle until now, never getting ahead, never managing to do more than stay one step away from homelessness and starvation. Until that moment, however, he had never known how much she idolized Heralds— and for no good reason as far as he could tell, since until he'd come along, no Herald had ever done anything for *her.*

He'd told her what he wanted and needed from his little gang—how he planned to take care of them, and how he planned they could work for him. And as he had hoped, she had some ideas.

Now it was time to tell the gang of—children, not boys, since he'd discovered to his surprise there were two girls in disguise among them. He'd advised the girls to stay in disguise; they were more likely to get messenger jobs that way, and less likely to have to be on guard against someone trying to abuse them.

He came in as they were eating dinner, locking the door behind himself just in case one or more of them took fright and tried to bolt, wrapped up in his usual faded cloak. The former shop had a home-like scent to it, of good food, strong soap, and drying laundry. There was a faint hum of conversation, but not much. Children who had been starved took their food very seriously, and seldom mixed talking and eating. He was pleased to see how they had progressed in the time he'd had them here. They no longer looked like they were starving, and they no longer *ate* like it, either. They were seated on their bedrolls, quietly and steadily spooning up another of Aunty Minda's tasty stews, with thick slices of buttered bread to sop up the gravy, and heavy mugs of some herbal tea. They gave him nods and waves of greeting when he came in, but by now they knew that he, too, considered eating to be serious business, and they should take care of it so long as they remained respectful.

He cleared his throat, though, and instantly got their attention. "I got somethin' t'tell ye," he said, gravely. "Fust of all,
ye need t'know, all this time I been testin' all of ye."

Wary looks met this pronouncement. He didn't blame them
for being wary. None of them were stupid, and all of them
must be thinking *testing us for what?* They would have been
hard-put to guess, since they already knew he had no inten-
tions of making them steal again.

"I still want ye as messengers," he said, "An' I still want ye
gettin' me whatever ye kin hear or find out 'bout. But ye need
t'know why I want ye t'do that. So—this's why."

He opened his cloak, untied it at the neck and dropped it to
the floor, standing there in his Whites.

Twenty-one pairs—he had nearly doubled his "gang"—of
the biggest, roundest eyes he had ever seen in his life stared
at him in utter astonishment. Twenty-one spoons clattered
into twenty-one bowls. Twenty-one mouths dropped open.

Utter silence fell, and he wondered if they were just going
to sit there until *he* said something else. Then, after a very,
very long time, one voice timidly squeaked, "Do th'Weasel
know 'bout this?"

He grinned. Trust the girl to think of that. The Weasel
scared her half to death, and fascinated her at the same time.
"Who d'ye think was my Herald-teacher?" he said to little
Mai.

It took them a while to get over their shock. He'd expected
that, and just went and got a stool, sitting on it in the middle
of the floor so he wasn't looming over them anymore. "Now, I
reckon if ye think on't, ye'll get why I *need* all of ye t'be eyes
an' ears all over town," he said, gravely, as if they were all
adults. Because, really, these children were not children at all,
for exactly the same reason that *he* had never been a child.
From the time they had been old enough to walk and talk,
they'd been doing some form of work or another. And when
they lost their parents—however that had happened—the only

way they kept food in their mouths was by their own efforts. There was no "childhood" for younglings such as these. Only varying degrees of work.

So they understood him almost as well as adults would. They thought ahead, and considered what they were going to do, almost as well as adults. And he couldn't help but contrast these unchildlike children with Violetta . . . because there was not a single one of them who would not have gone to *any* length to find out everything there was to discover about Brand before approaching him. If Violetta had had the sense of these younglings, that letter would never have been thought of, much less written.

"Same as ye said afore, Cap'n," said Mai. "Nobody thinks nothin' 'bout us. We kin come an' go, an' people blab in front'f us alla time."

He nodded. "People don't pay no more heed t'littles than if they was bugs. We Heralds cain't be ev'where, an' no matter what ye heerd, Mind-Magic ain't all that."

That pronouncement was met with skeptical looks. He shrugged. "Use yer noggins. There's a mort'o people in Haven, an' even if we *could* lissen to 'em all, which we *cain't,* it'd make about as much sense as tryin' t'hear summun in a Fair Crowd, aye? Think 'bout it. Ye dunno who t'listen fer, an' ye dunno where 'e is, an' ye gotta pick 'im out talkin' in a crush." He shook his head. "Cain't be done. An' even when ye know who t'listen fer? Ye gotta be sorta close to 'im t'listen. So what're ye gonna do? Foller 'im around day an' night?"

He sat there and let them think that over for a while. Some sucked thoughtfully on their lower lips, some went back to spooning up their dinner, but more slowly, and now with their eyes on him. When he finally thought he saw understanding, at least of a sort, in all of their faces, he picked up his narrative.

"Aight then. So, long as ye kin run messages, ye got jest th' same as I offered ye afore. An ye bring me what ye hear.

But see, there's more t'the deal than there was afore, cause now ye know what I am." They looked puzzled.

"Th' reason I tell ye this now is 'cause I want ye t'know when ye get too big t'play messenger, I ain't gonna throw ye out on th' street, on account of *now* ye're way more valuable t'me. No . . . when yer too big t'run, there's gonna be new jobs for ye." He paused again, and let that sink in. The littlest and youngest—well, that didn't mean all that much to them. They couldn't, at the moment, think of a time when they wouldn't be doing this for him; yes, they thought ahead like adults, but not *that* far ahead. And after all, it would be several years before they were too old to run messages. They couldn't even picture what it would be like to be an adolescent, much less what it would be like to have an adult job. But the oldest—ah, he saw relief just light up their faces. *They* were thinking about that already. They were already aware that a time was coming, within a year or two, three at the most, when they would no longer be able to do this job, and depending on their outlook on life, they were either trying hard *not* to think about what would happen when that time came, or were frantically trying to figure out what they could possibly do.

He had just changed that for them. In fact, he had changed their lives. They knew they were secure, possibly for the first time in their entire lives. He could see it in their eyes, the relief, the gratitude.

It made him feel good, but he didn't dwell on that. This was what had been done for him, when he realized he was *here* at the Collegium, and he belonged here. In a way, he was just paying all that back.

"Now, I dunno what ye'll do," he went on. "Th' job ye get'll depend on what yer good at. Some on ye'll go next door, t'Weasel's shop, an' work there. Some on ye'll get good jobs in tavern, mebbe an inn . . . jobs ye weren't never gonna get, without it was me or Weasel givin' ye th' nod, eh? Some . . . mebbe somethin' ye cain't even guess right now, on account of we dunno what yer good at yet. Whatever it is, ye'll go right on he'pin' me by listenin'. An' ye gotta bed an' food here with Aunty, 'till ye *want* and *kin* go out on yer own." He added that last, because he saw some anxiety creeping in again. The menial jobs in inns rarely gave the boys who had them beds as good as this, or food as filling and nourishing. Potboys and spit-boys, for instance, if they lived at the inn, generally slept on the kitchen floor and got the scraps rather than regular meals. So there was relief to hear that they would still have their "home."

"Ye're gonna have jobs fer life," he added. "An' thet's th' way 'tis. Ye'll niver, *ever* go hungry or cold agin."

The twenty-one pairs of eyes widened, and many filled with silent tears. He managed a smile for them, although it was very hard for him not to tear up, too. Oh, how he knew this feeling. He'd experienced it himself.

"Now, here's t'other thing," he continued. "Aunty Minda's been teachin' all on ye yer letters and numbers aye?"

All twenty-one heads nodded, as did those of Minda's own children. That had been a pleasant surprise, actually, to discover that not only was Minda quite literate, but she was a good basic teacher.

"Well, she's a-gonna tell me if'n any of ye are real good at that. An' if ye want, 'stead of running messages, ye'll be a-goin' t' real school harf the day, an' ye'll get same pay as ye'd get if ye was runnin' messages." Now, this was something unexpected for the children. They knew you could get basic letters and numbers at any temple, and anyone who employed children either had to arrange for these basic classes himself or send the children for at least a couple of candlemarks of teaching once a day. That was a given. And that was what they had been getting with Aunty Minda.

But schooling—real school, with books and paper and pens and learning more than how to spell out the words you most needed and how to work out if you had enough money to pay for something—cost money. Eyes widened once again, at the announcement that good students would be going there, and took on a look of stunned shock when the children realized that they weren't going to *lose* anything by occupying a desk.

"Well, makes sense, don't it?" he asked them. "Figger we needs all kinda people listenin' in all kinda places."

They nodded, because obviously it *did* make sense.

"I ain't quite done. T'other think I wantcher t'do is keep eye out fer more kiddies we kin trust, an' bring 'em here like ye already done." He narrowed his gaze and raked them all with it, looking as stern as possible. "Ye *don'* tell 'em nothin' 'cept I got a messenger pack. Ye *don'* tell 'em what we're doin', nor what I be. An ye *don'* bring 'em here 'less they're kiddies ye'd trust t'hold yer money. If ye cain't trust 'em wif yer coppers, I don' want 'em here."

That had seemed the simplest way to designate who to trust—and who not to. And it seemed to resonate with them; he caught several of them nodding.

He sat back on his stool now, and let his expression settle into one of anticipation. "Awright. Ye got questions? Ast 'em."

They did not bombard him with them; he hadn't expected them to. These were children who had been abused, oppressed, and dominated. They expected the worst at every turn. The Heralds Whites he wore had been, for varying lengths of time in their lives, the symbol of danger. They might not *fear* him, because they knew the man, their "Cap'n," who wore the Whites. But they were still cautious, wary of antagonizing him. In their world, asking too many questions could earn you very harsh treatment indeed.

But they had had weeks of good food, good treatment, and mothering nurture. He had treated them right. They'd *seen* him beat their abusive master within an inch of his life, then turn around and deliver them into what must have seemed like paradise. They had lost a good deal of their fear, and their wariness was, at this point, the wariness of a creature that doesn't want to ruin a good thing.

So, slowly, they thought of and asked their questions. Why, mostly. *Why are you doing this? Why would we go to school? Why do you want more kiddies?* They wanted motives; they needed to understand that he had reasons they could relate to for doing what he was doing. He put it all very simply, in materialistic terms, rather than moralistic ones. Although they were, on the whole, surprisingly *good* children, they weren't very moral yet. Aunty Minda was seeing to that part of their education, slowly cultivating empathy, sympathy, and other positive virtues in them. He was more than ever glad he had found her. Interestingly, with the good food and good treatment, *she* was looking younger, about half the age he had thought she was when he'd come across her. But if he could answer their questions in simple terms of *what is this worth to me, to the Heralds,* they understood it much better. Commerce, oh, they knew well, having been commodities themselves.

So to *why are you doing this?* he answered *because information is as valuable as food or drink, and sometimes more,* and gave them simple examples. *Why us?* was answered just as simply: *because you're all smart, and you stick with your Cap'n.* "Loyalty" was not a *word* they knew yet, though they were very familiar with the concept. *Why do you want more kiddies?* brought a laugh from him, and the answer of *When ye git too big, I'ma gonna need more messengers, feather-head!* And that made them laugh and smile.

Why are we going to school? had an equally simple answer. *So you can write down what you hear and see right when you hear and see it. The longer you wait to tell me things, the more you are going to forget.* Never mind all the altruistic reasons, or suggesting that if they were clever enough, they could become—well—almost anything! They had no concept of that sort of future. They looked at clerks, at artificers, at people in skilled trades as if they were an entirely different species. No one they knew had ever risen that high. They had no idea they could.

Well, they're not much different from me when Dallen found me. Reckon I turned out all right.

They also didn't ask too many questions about their future. This didn't surprise him in the least. They had been so down-trodden they no longer had the capacity to wish, or to dream— or at least, to do so beyond wishing and dreaming for the next good meal, a warmer tunic, maybe a sweet treat. They'd get that back; when children no longer lived in fear and privation, the ability to *hope* was one of the first things to return. From his own experience, he knew that children were surprisingly resilient. They would learn to dream again, and dream of a future. But not just now.

Finally, when the last of the questions seemed to have been asked, he got up. "Yer gonna be fine," he said gravely, once again reassuring them. "Now, tomorrow'll be jest like t'day, an' day afore that. Ain't nothin' changed 'cept what ye know. I'm still yer Cap'n. Aunty Minda's still yer boss an' yer ma. Any-thin' ye need, ye ast Aunty Minda for, an' if there be trouble, ye go next door t'Weasel's shop an' tell 'em there what's what. Keep runnin' messages, an' bringin' whatcher learn t'me, an—"

"Cap'n Herald?" said little Ash, who had only just begun message running last week. Until then, he hadn't, in Mags' opinion, been strong enough to have the endurance for it.

"Aye?" he replied.

"I heerd somethin' t'day." Ash twisted his hands together anxiously. "I got sat by some fellers as was all wearin' same sorta stuff. Same colors. Same kinda trews an' all. Even same kinda boots."

"That there's a *livery,*" said Coot with authority. "It means they all b'long t' th' same lor'ship." Mags smothered a smile. Of all of them, Coot had come the farthest, the fastest. He had the most confidence, and was the first to learn anything new. He was one of the ones that Mags had high hopes for.

" 'Xactly right, Coot," Mags commended. "So what'd you hear, Ash?"

"Well . . . they kep' talkin' 'bout a Lord . . . Kalten? Karan?" The little boy screwed up his face, trying to remember.

"Kaltar?" Mags asked, feeling a sense of . . . well, it wasn't quite excitement, because whatever it was that Ash had over-heard, it was unlikely to be anything good, if it involved Lord Leverance's servants and Lord Kaltar's servants. While so far the policy of keeping their Lordships' families well apart had been working—aside from that slip with Violetta—there was no way to keep their households separated. At least, not with-out some fairly egregious edicts he was pretty certain neither Lord would stand for.

"Aye, Cap'n!" the child said, his face clearing. "That'd be it! They figgered out Kaltar's gang goes t' Flag an' Flagon most nights. They been workin' up th' balls t' go arter 'em."

Mags wanted to kiss the child and kick every one of those servants of Lord Leverance repeatedly. *Of all the stupid . . .* He supposed that *they* must think that picking an altercation with Kaltar's underlings would get them favor in their mas-ter's eyes. And for all he knew, it *would*.

"Ash, that is damn *good* listenin'," he said, and dug out a copper bit which he gave to the boy. There was no harm in reinforcing the fact that the deal he had made with them when this all began was still in force. Good information was still getting rewarded, regardless of the fact that Mags was a Herald. Ash took the coin, his face lighting up. Mags looked him and the two younglings that ran message out of the Bird in the Hand square in the faces. "Aight, we got us a situation here, where I gotta know stuff, an' know it right away. So, I tell ye what. I'm a-gonna hev me a word wi' the Guard Post near th' Bird i' Hand. Ash, Bet, an' Silas, ye knows where thet is, aye?"

All three of the boys stationed at the Bird in the Hand nod-ded solemnly. Of course they did. Given their past, they probably knew the location of every single Guard Post anywhere they roamed.

"Ye three keep listenin' t'them men. Whut we got, we got us a feud between two gangs, an' ye know what thet means. On'y these two gangs is gonna hev more'n rocks an' fists and mebbe knives, an' if they tussle, people're gonna get hurt. I reckon they're gonna need some beer-balls afore they go marchin' on these other fellers, so they're gonna be drinkin' afore they go break heads." More solemn nods; these boys were no strangers to street violence or clashing gangs. They knew exactly how this sort of thing worked. "When they go a-marchin', you go run t'Guard Post. Tell 'em what's what. There's a siller piece for one that gets there fust, copper fer t'other two. Aye, 'tis that important."

Eyes truly widened over that. He rather doubted these children had ever held a silver piece in their hands in their lives— though their former master had probably had a hoard of them. "Aye, Cap'n!" all three chorused.

Mags stood up. "Aight. Now ye all know. Ye know how much good knowin' is wuth t'me. Ye know whut I be. Ye know yer *my* gang, an' I'm gonna take care on ye."

He went over to the door and unlocked it. "Get a good sleep," he told them all. "An' don' get too jealous uv Ash an' Bet an' Silas. They's gonna be other jobs that'll earn siller fer the rest uv ye, an' that's a fact. Keep ears open an' eyes sharp."

He wrapped himself up in his cloak, hiding every trace of his Whites except the bottom bits of his boots—and in the snow outside it was unlikely that would be noticed. Just before he stepped out the door, he took a look back inside.

They'd all grabbed their bowls and bread and were gathering around Aunty Minda, who was patiently answering the questions they hadn't dared ask him. But he didn't see any signs of apprehension or fear—just a little anxiety, which was to be expected. This was change, *big* change, and in their experience, change was seldom good. They needed to hear their "mother" tell them otherwise.

He smiled a little to himself, and left them to it.

:Everything has gone to plan, then?: Dallen asked.

:Aye, 'cept for that fool feud.: He sighed, and closed the door against the cold, moving out into the snow, pulling his cloak tighter against the freezing wind. It was, of course, snowing again. The street-sweepers wouldn't clear it off until morning, at least not in this part of town, so he would be slogging through it until he got to the stable where Dallen was waiting. *:I need t'figger out some way of findin' out when those idjits start fightin'. Somethin' tells me I need t' be there when it happens.:*

:Ask at the Guard Post. Or suggest something to them. I suspect they would have absolutely no problem with sending you some sort of simple "yes, the fight is on" message.:

He blinked, thinking about that a moment. Because it didn't need to be a detailed message; he already *knew* where the proposed ambush was going to happen. He only needed to be alerted when it was starting—which meant he needed a very, very simple signal of some kind.

Like . . . the sort of simple signal the Sleepgivers often used when they were communicating across a city, or across the countryside. Colored smoke.

Once again, Bey's shared memories were saving the day. *Bloody hell . . . thenkee, Bey. Hope mine are comin' in as handy fer you.*

———

This was the first time Mags had *ever* gone to a real afternoon Midwinter party. For that matter, until last night he had never gone to a real *evening* Midwinter party. He had discovered last night that the evening parties were a mix of dancing, eating, and drinking, with a room to one side devoted to card playing, and the card playing was really only for the chaperones. Up until now, the only things he had ever attended at Midwinter were several days of Master Soren's "open house," which wasn't the same thing as these elegant parties at all.

Compared to the open house . . . these formal parties were pretty dull stuff. Master Soren always took care to invite a mix of people based on how interesting they were, not on their rank, so the conversation was lively, and people always had a good time. He had good musicians, and people could dance if they chose, or listen if they chose. There were games—board games, dice games, and cards—laid out, so people could make use of them if they chose, but there were no "organized" games that everyone was harassed into playing. In fact, until he had come to this party, Mags had had no idea that people even did that to their guests.

But . . . well, it seemed that they did. And like everyone else, he had basically been told he was going to be playing them when he arrived. Oh it had been *phrased* politely: "You'll be joining everyone for the games, of course." But it was pretty clear that if you didn't join in, you were violating some sort of unspoken code. He had no doubt that those who did not follow the code were not given invitations to other such festivities. That would hardly matter to him . . . except that he was trying very hard to keep track of Brand, and it was easier to do so from among the guests than among the servants.

He was not the only one who didn't think much of this form of entertainment. While some people were enjoying the spectacle of a blindfolded young man in the middle of this manse's Great Hall, groping wildly in the air, trying to catch someone, it was pretty clear that others were utterly bored and forcing their laughter.

Not some of the young ladies, though; the blindfolded fellow was Brand, and there were no few of them who were not trying too hard to evade him.

Well . . . this Midwinter season might be the last time that they would have the thrill of doing such a thing with a good looking fellow their own age. By this time next year, at least if their parents got their way, these young women would be married and pregnant. And that would be the end of their freedom, until their children were grown. No parties of this sort at Midwinter, but rather staid dinner parties at which there was low-key music and the same entertainers that everyone else had hired, because you didn't deviate from the accepted formula for a party.

As Mags watched Brand slowly fumble his way across the floor, chasing the errant brush of a sleeve or a whiff of scent, he reflected on the things Amily had told him about girls in the highborn and wealthy circles.

They were eyes-deep in very specific lessons from the time they were old enough to walk; all things calculated to make them desirable as spouses, not things they might want to learn. When they reached adolescence, they were immediately considered to be marriage-fodder. Some were actually betrothed earlier than that, but the Crown frowned on child-marriages—fourteen was the youngest that was considered "reasonable." Once they turned fourteen, husbands would be sought, and if not found, every Midwinter Season was spent here at Court seeking one, until the girl got to her twenties. At that point, it was felt that she never would, and she had best join some religious order or resign herself to whatever use the family cared to make of her; usually as governess to some other sibling's children. During that period between fourteen and oblivion, was a girl's only taste of (relative) freedom. She could dance and flirt and play games with young men she didn't know. She got new clothing every Midwinter. She went to two parties every day during the Season. She got to see the capital, and if her parents were indulgent enough, got to do things like attend plays and the Midwinter Fair.

Then, once married, that ended. She was expected to handle her husband's household if he had inherited; if his parents were still alive she was expected to tend to him and serve as her mother-in-law's chief handmaiden. It was possible her husband would be much older than she was, and if so, she was expected to be his nurse if he required that. If he had young children by a previous marriage, she was expected to supervise them. Her household duties could range from few to dawn-to-dusk, depending on the wealth of her husband and how many servants she had—but even if she had many servants, she was expected to supervise them. And she was expected to produce, at the very least, "an heir and a spare." The days of dancing and attending parties were over, until *her* children were grown and married. Unless, of course, she married a man much older than she was; she could expect to outlive him, and possibly become a very wealthy widow while still young . . . and no few of these young ladies were hoping for just that. Or, they were hoping that their husbands would have no more interest in them than they had in him, and once the "heir and spare" were dutifully produced, their spouses would look the other way if there were . . . shenanigans. Just as *they* would pretend their husband was not up to shenanigans of his own. In either of these cases, they would be going to the parties that Brand preferred to attend . . . the ones where certain messages were exchanged, and late at night, certain doors were left unlocked.

Now, these girls knew that, all of it. Dia had made it quite clear to Mags that the ones as romantic and idealistic as Violetta were very few and far between. So in this brief interlude of relative freedom, they were enjoying the illusion, well aware that it was an illusion, that there was any hope one of these young men would fall in love with them. Unlike Violetta, they knew this was all staged as carefully as any play. If they married *any* of the young men here, it would be negotiated by their respective parents, not the random lightning-strike of romance.

This party had about thirty young people about Brand's

age, and roughly half that many parents. *Probably all the girls brought chaperones, or were brought by one,* Mags thought, considering the faces around him. *The lads are reckoned as not needing watchdogs.* He considered the group around him with a detached eye, and it occurred to him that these afternoon parties were meant to exhaust nervous energy and keep the young people out of trouble, rather than form the backbone of the serious marriage-marketeering. If you had to go to a supervised, chaperoned event in the afternoon, and you spent all morning getting ready for it, then there was no time for you to slip off to any unsupervised liaisons before you had to return to get ready for the more serious, evening party. He suspected that was the theory at work, anyway. There would probably be servants stationed anywhere that a young couple might try to find a moment of illicit privacy. Of course, the servants would do nothing themselves; they'd go get someone of appropriate rank to interrupt.

Glory. I am so glad I'm me, an' not them. He'd thought that courting Amily and becoming lovers had been complicated and fraught with a lot of "busy-bodying"! He'd had *no* idea!

A trio of musicians played a piece he supposed would be considered "lively" by the standards of people who were, in his estimation, severely overdressed for any exertion, what with their under-dresses and tunics, over-dresses and tunics, extra sleeves, neck ruffs, and who knew what-all was underpinning what was visible. It almost seemed as if the more money you had, the more clothing you wore.

Well, unless you are very poor. Then in winter at least you wear every stitch you own, all at once.

By the standards of the Trainees of all three Collegia and their celebrations, this music was exceedingly tame, so had the dancing been, and so were the games.

So far, they had been coerced into this game, into one in which a blindfolded victim was supposed to stick a tail onto a painted Companion, and a race in which the participants balanced boiled eggs in spoons while they attempted to run across the length of the Great Hall. If these things were supposed to be amusing, Mags couldn't see it. On the whole he was entirely glad that he'd never had to go to any of these parties before, and he was not looking forward to the fact that he'd probably have to go to them in the future. Or at least, he would as long as he still looked like a "young" man. *Well, maybe not nearly as many. The only reason I'm here now is to keep Brand from running across one of the House Chendlar cousins.*

He'd more-or-less been told to get into every official party that Brand attended, because it was entirely possible that the young men of House Chendlar would decide to invite themselves. This happened all the time; young men would decide to don masks and bluff their way into a party where there happened to be girls they were interested in. As long as they behaved themselves, this was basically winked at.

Thus far, none of the lesser members of the two feuding Houses had crossed paths. Mags was there to make sure that if it happened, it was only paths that crossed.

He really would rather have been watching in case the signal came telling him that there was about to be a brawl between Raeylen and Chendlar, but Dallen was standing by, already tacked up, and watching from just outside the Palace walls. Others were, too, but Dallen would be able to get down here and get him to the scene of combat faster than anyone else could get there.

At least he had been invited on his own, and not as part of Brand's entourage of new friends from Court. That meant he could leave—

:Mags! Red smoke!:

He managed not to jump. But his heart started to race, and he clamped down on his immediate reaction to run out the nearest door.

All right, he told himself. *No need to hurry.* In fact, he didn't strictly need to be there, although he wanted to in order to keep a careful eye on everything and coordinate the response. The smoke meant that the would-be combatants had just now set off from the Bird in the Hand. The little lads were *quick,* and could get from the tavern to the Guard Station in almost no time at all. The Bird in the Hand was a brisk half candlemark walk to the Flag and Flagon if you kept up your pace. They probably would not be setting that fast a pace; they'd all have some liquor in them, and they'd be egging each other on, which was going to slow them down.

He had time. And he was not going to be alone down there. The Guard was already mustering, and the Prince was also aware of the signal and for all Mags knew, he was probably out the Palace Gate at this point.

He carefully eased himself out of the crowd around Brand, and slipped off to the side. Making his way to the antechamber where the guests' cloaks had been left, he found it unattended, a piece of luck he was very grateful for. He really did not want to have to go out into the cold without a cloak. *Now . . . how to get out . . .*

:I'm almost there. Are you going to suit up?: Dallen had a uniform in his saddlebag, but there was no time to change into Whites, and he wasn't sure he wanted to. He needed to blend with the crowd that would inevitably gather, not stand out from them. He'd be able to do more if he *didn't* look like a Herald. *:I don't think so. Let's do this incognito.:*

He couldn't leave by the front door; there was a servant stationed there, and he didn't want to be noticed. But there was a door into the gardens, and a gate at the back of the kitchen gardens into an alley, and thanks to scouting out this manor beforehand, he knew where both were. Within a few moments, he was *in* that alley. If it had been night, he'd have been running along the tops of the walls that separated each manor from the next, but he would be terribly conspicuous if he did that in broad daylight. Not to mention that there was ice on the tops of these walls; at the speed he needed to be going, he'd likely slip and kill himself. Snow was coming down; big fat flakes falling out of a gray sky that looked like a dome of slate. *Too bad it isn't rain.* Rain would certainly discourage most of these idiots from trying to start a brawl.

:Next street.:

Dallen was at full run, and so was he; he was running on the edge of the alley where the snow hadn't gotten packed down into ice. That was all very well for delivery people and the collectors of refuse, who could use sledges on the ice, but not so good for a running man. Dallen got to the intersection of the alley and the street before he did; skidded to a halt and waited while he raced toward his Companion.

Mags vaulted into the saddle, settled in without bothering with the stirrups, and they were off. Dallen was running the fine line between "not going to kill ourselves on this icy street" and "my god, we are going to die." If they hadn't spent so much time together in Kirball practice. . . .

They pounded down the Hill, and fortunately there was no one out to see the incongruous sight of an apparent highborn riding a Companion at breakneck speed. People were either attending parties, at Court, or getting ready for evening festivities. But the Flag and Flagon was not *too* far down off the Hill; it was just off the main street with all the expensive inns that served those who did not have, or did not want manors for brief visits to Haven. A working-man's tavern, and not an inn at all, it was popular with the servants who served all those highborn. Mags dismounted a good block away, and came up to the inn via the back alley way.

Just as well that he did; as the snow got heavier, he came around the corner into the yard where drinkers could sit in fine weather, and nearly ran into a mob. It was clear that someone had warned the servants of House Raeylen that trouble was on the march, for they had left their benches in the tavern, and were gathering in front of it, weapons in hand.

Mags got himself atop a pile of shoveled snow and surveyed them quickly. No one was paying any attention to him, or to any of the other people who were gathering at the sight of what looked like it was going to be interesting trouble. *Idiots. Why is it there can never be a fight without people wanting to get in the way of it?* Most of the weapons were improvised; clubs, for the most part. But there were enough knives in the crowd to do some serious damage. And he could hear the mob coming from the direction of the Bird in the Hand now.

There was no sign of the Guard or the Watch.

:Dallen, we need help now.:

:I know. Help is on the way.:

The mob turned a corner and stopped. Clearly, it had not occurred to the men of House Chendlar that their enemies might have had some warning they were coming.

For a long time, the two groups just stared at each other. Then, at some signal Mags never saw, House Raeylen charged.

Just as the help arrived.

Pounding into the inn square from the Hill came at least two dozen Herald Trainees, with a couple of their instructors, all charging into the incipient melee at full speed. Anyone who saw them started scrambling out of the way. Anyone who didn't, and was *in* the way, soon found himself bowled over by a mount that knew precisely how to apply his momentum and his shoulder to an opponent on foot without hurting him too much.

It was the Kirball teams, of course—or rather, the Trainees that played on the teams. They must have been out practicing, which meant they were already in the saddle and "armored" up when Dallen's call for help came. And they were all well acquainted with a good scuffle.

Without a moment of hesitation, they waded in; once they cleared the center of the space, mostly all they did was shove in between any people who were fighting who were in serious danger of actually injuring one another. From the sidelines,

Mags assisted by pelting combatants with snowballs aimed
straight for the face. They couldn't hurt each other if they
couldn't see. Once other bystanders saw what he was doing,
they did the same. And so far as Mags was concerned, it really
didn't matter at all if the bystanders were on one side or the
other, as long as the snowballs kept flying. Any interference
was good interference.

Either the combatants on both sides were so worked up—
or so drunk—that the fact they were being yelled at by Heralds
and Trainees, and shouldered aside by Companions didn't reg-
ister, or they just didn't *care.* It was possible, of course, that
they actually did not care. Not everyone held Heralds in high
esteem, as he had discovered when out on circuit. Within
Haven . . . and near it . . . definitely. But the further you got
from the capital, the more likely it became that you would run
into people who respected Heralds not at all.

It seemed to take forever, but it probably wasn't more than
a quarter candlemark before the Guard and the Watch arrived.
Once they did, the Trainees backed off, allowing the men with
authority and experience to wade in and separate the fighters—
by force and with the weighted cudgels they were armed with,
at need. One or two had to be physically separated, and by the
time they'd gotten both sides sorted out and herded up into
two groups under guard, there was a flourish of trumpets, and
Prince Sedric rode up, surrounded by Guards.

Mags judged it prudent to leave. So did Dallen. *:Best if your
face isn't seen by anyone who can recognize it, Chosen,:* the
Companion said. *:I'll be in the alley. Duck into the stable,
change into your Whites, and let's go somewhere warm, dry,
and preferably with ale and pocket pies.:*

Amily rode in the entourage with Prince Sedric down to break up the riot . . . although by the time they got there, the riot was well over and the combatants separated into two groups under guard.

The Prince had ordered them all to go at the trot, not at the gallop. "I am not letting these idiots think their tantrums warrant immediate attention," he had told Amily, when she looked at him askance. "Mags has gotten some help to break things up, and the Guard and Watch can put them in order." His Companion had stamped a hoof to emphasize that. "Let them wait in the cold and the snow. Maybe it will cool their hot heads. If they have minor hurts, all the better. The truth is, it's their masters I want to deal with, not them."

So they trotted down to the tavern, with an entourage, but not a big one. He had come with not one, but *four* Guards with trumpets, and as they trotted into the area in front of a working-man's tavern, the trumpeters were blowing full fanfares at such volume there was no mistaking someone very important was about to arrive.

Amily didn't know what the Prince intended other than making a spectacular entrance, so she just followed his lead. The riders all arranged themselves in a line, opposite the two groups of men, with herself and the Prince at the center. There was evidence of fighting, but it wasn't as bad as she had thought it would be. There was some blood on the churned-up snow, being covered even now by more snow falling on it. Men were nursing black eyes and possibly cracked skulls, there seemed to be a couple with broken arms and shoulder-blades, and plenty were cut—but she couldn't see where any-one had been stabbed. There was a Healer working among them—and scolding each one under his breath as he gave them some basic tending. She had the feeling he was giving them more than a few pieces of his mind.

Finally the Healer was done, looked from one group to the other, and snarled "And tell your foolish masters that if they want any more tending for you idiots, they had better come hat in hand and prepared to grovel for it." Then he turned on his heel and left. Amily saw the Prince smother a smile with his hand. And silence fell, as thick as the snow that was building up on the ground, and on the heads and shoulders of everyone here. She had expected the Prince to launch into a lecture, but he did nothing of the sort. In fact, he just—waited. And mean-while, the servants of both Houses grew quieter and more ner-vous. Her hands got colder, so she put them against Rolan's neck under his mane to warm them up. He didn't seem to mind.

Finally, what the Prince was waiting for arrived.

An escort of Guards brought with them two mounted men. Amily knew them both on sight, of course. Lord Leverance and Lord Kaltar, the former already in his evening finery (but of course; he had three daughters to marry off) and the latter bundled up to his eyes in a cloak that did not quite conceal the fact that he was wearing armor.

Well . . . that's curious. Still, it was only padded armor. Perhaps he had been sparring.

:Or perhaps he knew this was coming and he intended some wicked mischief,: Rolan observed suspiciously.

It appeared that the Prince had ordered the Guard to bring their Lordships here, regardless of what they were doing at the time, in order to hold them accountable for the actions of their men. Amily breathed in the freezing air, sharply. This was something of a gamble. . . .

Then again, they weren't high enough, nor did they have allies enough, to make trouble for the Crown if they were offended. At least, not overt trouble. . . .

:Covert, however, yes,: Rolan agreed. *:I would not have made this move. But . . . I am not the one wearing the coronet, either.:* Amily sighed internally. Yet one more thing for Mags and her father to keep an eye on. *Father might be best for this. Somehow manage to become their crony in two different personas. . . .*

But Prince Sedric's voice broke her out of her own thoughts.

"My lords!" the Prince said, his voice ripe with indignation. "I ask you, what is the meaning of this brute spectacle that played out here not a candlemark ago? Why were our peaceful streets turned into a battleground? What madness is this? It is Midwinter, the Festival of Peace! Will you turn it into a Feast of War?"

Amily was watching both of them closely, and it seemed to her that *both* of them showed just a fleeting glimpse of something other than the feigned surprise that spread over their faces. *There is something going on here. Something none of us have guessed.* She was just as glad that her Gift didn't extend to reading human minds now . . . because the temptation to dig into their heads without their permission just might have been too great.

"Your Highness, I protest!" Leverance said, in a loud voice. "How could you think I had any knowledge of this? You can see for yourself that I was interrupted in preparing for Lord Jornan's fete this evening!"

"And I was sparring with my Weaponsmaster," Kaltar said smoothly. He glared at Leverance, accusingly. "But if this man has instructed his servants to do what he himself does not dare—"

"Enough!" the Prince roared, interrupting Kaltar before he finished, and without a doubt, provoked Leverance into a duel, as was his intention. He turned to the Captain of the Guard troop, and the Chief Watch. "Have you witnesses?"

At this point, Amily felt the best thing she could do would be to look as solemn and stone-faced as possible and take a lot of mental notes. She was very glad that she was seated in a Companion's saddle, though. Rolan was almost as good as a stove.

:Thank you for seeing my true value,: Rolan chuckled. She forced herself not to smile.

They both stepped forward and bowed. "We have, your Highness," said the Captain, as the Watch gestured to two of his men, who went into the tavern and brought out two men in server's aprons. "And have sent for witnesses from the Bird in the Hand."

Slowly, and with much "and then what happened?" the two servers told their story—which was remarkably brief, considering how long it took them to tell it. At least they corroborated each other.

"They been hearin' how t'other lord's men was a-gonna come down an' break some heads—"

There was a long pause. The Chief Watch poked the second man in the ribs with an elbow. "And then what happened?"

He started a little, and took up the thread. "—aye, an' Marster Jon, he tol' 'em, don't you make no pother here! Or you ain't never drinkin' here agin!"

Another pause. The Guard Captain nudged the first man. "And then what happened?"

"An' they larfed, an' said then they'd take it 'street, but no dogs was gonna make them turn tail an' slink back home!"

A very long silence. With a sigh, the Chief Constable elbowed the second again. "And then what happened?"

"An' Marster Jon, he tol' 'em, you leave it t'Guard, m'lads! You tell th' Guard!"

They seemed to think that was all they needed to say. The Chief of the Watch fixed the first man with a stern frown. "And then what happened?"

"An' they said they would, but they looked all sideways, an' we knew they wouldn't—"

By the time they were finished the innkeeper from the Bird in the Hand had arrived, and with him one of *his* servers, a skinny little wench with a decided mind of her own, who took very little time to speak her piece.

"Oh yes," she said, hands on hips, surveying the now chastened servants. "Oh yes. I know this lot—" and she pointed down the line of Leverance's men. "A week an' more it's been, and every day, drinking up courage an' tellin' each other how they were going to break the heads of more idiots like themselves! They started to bring knives and clubs with them to drink, and today they finally made up their minds to go and be fools and start a ruckus! Men are idiots! I've said it afore, and I'll say it again! Can't get three of them in a room with beer without two of them buttin' heads!"

The innkeeper, with much bowing and scraping to the Prince, corroborated every word. Then the wench decided to repeat it. At that point, the Prince turned to Amily.

"Can you cast the Truth Spell?" he asked, quietly. "We'll need one on Kaltar and one on Leverance, so it will take both of us."

"I can, Highness," she murmured, *very* glad now that Rolan had been ruthlessly drilling her in the only bit of conventional Heraldic Magic she could perform. It seemed that her ability to ride in the minds of animals was close enough to Mindspeech for her to make the Truth Spell work. In fact, that was one of the *first* things Rolan and the Dean had insisted she learn. She just didn't think she'd have to use it so soon.

:You always have to do things before you think you are ready,: Rolan observed. *:That's just life.:*

:Thank you, master philosopher,: she replied dryly, before returning her attention to the Prince.

"Good. Coercive, or just detection?" he pressed.

"I haven't been doing this long," she reminded him. "Detection . . . I actually haven't tried coercion and—"

"Don't try it now," he ordered to her relief. "Coercion needs a lot of practice under controlled conditions. Detection will serve our purposes. You take Leverance, I'll take Kaltar."

He turned his attention to the two highborn, wearing his most implacable expression. "My lords, the King's Own and I are going to impose the Truth Spell on you. This is not a request. You will speak the truth as you know it, or you will find that I am as harsh as my father can be."

:An interesting way to put that,: Rolan said with amusement; Amily didn't smile, but she agreed with her Companion, since in all the time she had been growing up at Court, she had never known King Kyril to do anything anyone would consider *harsh*.

Then again . . . that was not a lie. Sedric would certainly be as harsh as Kyril. Sedric took strongly after his father, who was a master at implying things that were not true, while speaking the literal truth. Then again, Sedric was serving as the Herald-on-duty in the Central Courts. He was probably getting a lot of examples of just that from lawyers.

But this was no time for thinking about anything else but the task at hand, which was to cast the only bit of "real" magic that had survived the death of the last of the Herald-Mages. She half-closed her eyes, and recited a little rhyme in her head nine times, all the while envisioning a wisp of blue fog with blue eyes in the middle of it settling over Lord Leverance. As she finished the last of her nine repetitions, his Lordship began to glow within a nimbus of dim, faintly pulsing, blue light.

The citizens of Haven who were still here had likely all seen this before—and even if they hadn't, they were not about to betray their ignorance by showing it. But the two crowds of servants hadn't, and if the silence had been deep before, it was so quiet now that Amily could actually hear the snowflakes falling on her hood with faint ticking sounds. They were transfixed by the sight of their masters glowing with light, and no source of that light to be seen. And they looked terrified.

Lord Leverance was glowing much more strongly, and Sedric began with him first. "Lord Leverance, were you aware that your servants planned to ambush the servants of Lord Kaltar here?"

The man set his jaw, and grated out, "I was not." The glow did not waver.

But that was all he said. Amily mistrusted it. Sedric needed to learn how to question a suspect better. Leverance had probably *technically* spoken the truth: he wasn't aware his servants were planning on starting a brawl *here*. That didn't mean he wasn't aware they were planning on starting a fight, nor that he himself had not suggested that very thing.

Well, maybe that was Sedric's intention—to see if these two were as good at telling the truth to suit their own purposes as he was. In any case, it was too late to advise him now. Sedric had moved his gaze to Kaltar. "Lord Kaltar. Were you made aware that your servants knew they were in danger?"

"No, Highness," the old man said raising his chin. "I was not. But I did give them leave to defend themselves if they felt they needed to when we first arrived. If nothing else, there are footpads and robbers in the streets of this city."

:*More honest than his foe,*: Rolan observed dispassionately.

"Well, they do *not* have leave now!" Sedric snapped. "Now hear me! Both of you! From this moment, your servants are *forbidden* to carry anything larger than an eating-knife! No cudgels, no clubs, no long knives, and by *heaven* no swords or bows or even a stone-sling! But there is more, my lords. Should there be brawling and fisticuffs in our streets, their positions in your household here are *forfeit.* You may send them home if you choose, but they will no longer serve you *here.* You will hire new servants who are citizens of Haven and can be trusted not to act like barbarians when there is a drop or two of liquor in them!"

There were gasps all around, and some of the men turned very pale indeed. Amily might have felt sorry for them if she had not been so angry with them—she didn't know how likely it was that either of the highborn nobles would actually send their servants back to their home estates. But she *did* know that it would be an expensive proposition, both to provide for that, and to hire an entire new staff.

Which meant both lords would probably pack up everything and go home, if their servants started brawling, rather than going to the expense and difficulty of hiring an entire new household full of servants.

At Midwinter. When the servants that could still be hired were probably not worth having, and those who were worth having would know they could ask for and get better wages. No, their Lordships would probably decide just to pack up and go home.

Without achieving the goal they had come here to accomplish; getting spouses for their offspring.

Coming here in the first place was an expense; she knew for a fact that although both of the Lords had and maintained manors here in the capital, they also both—until now—had rented them out for several years running to other highborn who did not have such a convenience. So not only was coming here an expense, they had actually lost some income by doing so this year.

Which meant that getting their children properly matched was very important to them.

And when highborn like Leverance and Kaltar were thwarted in something very important, they very seldom blamed themselves or their own actions. They almost always took it out on their underlings.

Things would not be very pleasant—for the menservants at least—in either household if that happened. This threat alone should keep the servants from brawling in the street.

"Am I clear?" Sedric demanded. You could have cut the silence and spread it like butter, it was so thick.

Both of the lords nodded grimly. Sedric dismissed his Truth Spell; taking that as her cue, Amily closed her eyes and imagined the eyes of the wisp closing, and the fog lifting. When she opened her own eyes, the blue glow was gone.

"You have our permission to take your men and return to your manors," Sedric continued. *"But!"* he snapped, as the men began to stir, "Lord Leverance, you will go *first,* as you clearly have an important engagement to attend. You will take King's Own Herald Amily with you. Lord Kaltar, you and your men will follow, when I hear from Amily that all of Leverance's people are behind his walls."

:Oh that will do wonders for Kaltar's temper,: Rolan said, with grim amusement. *:Being made to wait in the cold, while his rival gets back to his nice warm manor . . . I suspect Sedric does not believe the story that he was sparring and means to punish him for lying.:*

:Let's hope it's enough to teach him to keep leashes on his dogs,: she replied.

———

Amily accompanied Lord Leverance as she had been ordered; she hadn't quite known what to expect. Initially, his Lordship had been polite, but did not seem to have changed his opinion of her.

Of course, part of that opinion was that he still did not quite believe she actually was the King's Own . . . but at least he made some attempt at conversation, even if he was (unconsciously, perhaps) talking down to her.

She ignored that, politely, and to fill the very awkward silence, pointed out which manse, manor or mansion belonged to whom all the way up the Hill. She carefully took the path that avoided the street on which Lord Kaltar's establishment had been built. Lord Leverance kept his horse to a walk; obviously he intended to keep Lord Kaltar waiting in the cold for as long as humanly possible.

"I hadn't quite realized how many . . . er . . . self-made men there were on the Hill," Leverance said, after she'd pointed out Master Soren's home, reminded him that Soren's niece Lydia was now the Princess Royal and wife to Sedric, and also reminded him that Soren held open house all during the Midwinter Season. "I hadn't opened up the house for the Season in . . . well . . . since my marriage. I don't recall so many being here then. . . ."

"Oh they were there, I just suspect you didn't cross paths with them much," Amily said. "There are very few who feel they can afford to spend the Season in leisure. Their business often picks up during the Season, rather than shutting down, even those that deal in foodstuffs. So usually, they don't hold parties, or only hold one and that just for chosen business associates. And when their sons and daughters attend fetes, if you didn't already know who their parents were, you'd be hard-pressed to tell them from the highborn." She allowed herself a tiny smile. "If anything, they tend to be better-dressed than their highborn friends."

He actually laughed a little at that. "I suppose that would be true. And there's no shame in marrying into such a family. My daughter Brigette has her heart set on it, in fact."

The snow was still falling and showing no signs it was going to stop soon, and she wondered how Lord Kaltar was faring. Probably fuming.

:He is. Sedric is amused. He doesn't mind being out in the snow, since otherwise he would be attending a Court session intended only to tender Midwinter Greetings to him and Lydia. Poor Lydia is having to stand in for both of them.: Amily smiled; now she was getting the same sort of benefits Mags had enjoyed all this time, like knowing what another Herald was doing no matter how far she was from him.

She listened to Lord Leverance describe his two eldest daughters' ambitions, and found his depictions strikingly like what she had heard from the girls themselves. Which was interesting; either *they* had taken their cues from their father, or *he* had actually listened to them.

:It's most likely that they took their cues from Leverance,: Rolan observed. Amily tended to agree. Neither girl struck her as being at all independent or rebellious, so they simply adjusted their wants to fit what their father wanted for them.

"And what about the youngest?" she ventured.

Lord Leverance smiled, but shook his head. "A head full of fancies, that one. And I might have thought to cure those fancies by wedding her to a good, steady, older man who would settle her down but. . . ." His voice trailed off, and he cleared his throat self-consciously. "My wife's father had the same notion, and I was the good, steady, older man. She was only fourteen. My father much approved the match. He advised me to make an early mother of her, so I did. I . . . sometimes think I marred her, rather than made her."

Startled, Amily cast a sideways glance at the man. His expression suggested he was telling nothing less than the truth. She decided to step around that particular sinkhole, most carefully. "So why marry Violetta off at all, at least this Season?" she replied. "It isn't as if she hasn't got years to settle down and become more . . . practical. Your older girls seem as determined to win in the marriage market as you are to have them succeed; they are pretty, accomplished, and I think you have nothing to fear there. I would be more surprised if you did *not* see them both betrothed by Midwinter Day. There's time enough for Violetta."

"That had crossed my mind, and since Violetta seems to be ailing slightly, that may be our best course," he agreed.

"Ailing? She has not come down with a fever—" Amily ventured, though of course she knew exactly what was wrong with Violetta.

"No, I think perhaps she is overwhelmed by all this—" he waved his hand at the street full of palatial homes, no few of them lit up and hosting festivities. "This is nothing like home. She was excited at first, and threw herself into the preparations, but after the Court reception she was exhausted, and now she just seems listless and nervous. She stayed at home for the last two events we were invited to." He laughed a little. "At least if she is tucked up in bed with her little dog and her poetry, she's not finding some handsome devil to break her heart."

Amily did her best not to wince.

"She's staying home this evening too," Leverance continued. "I must confess, if I had my way, I'd stay at home with her, but . . . needs must. There are at least three men who will be at this fete who I am considering for the older girls; they likely won't approach my wife with something as important as an alliance proposal, so I shall have to be there."

"Would you mind if I looked in on Violetta tonight, while you and the rest of your family are away?" Amily asked, cautiously. "I haven't seen her since I brought Lady Dia to you. Perhaps I can bring her some books of poetry I've no use for, to keep her occupied and not missing the dancing so much."

"Oh, by all means! Be my guest!" Leverance exclaimed. Amily smiled a little. Leverance had no idea what she was going say to his daughter; if he had, he would probably have banned her from the house.

Or at least, he would have made certain Violetta was never *alone* with Amily . . . and above all, never, ever, gave her books!

Well, I don't know if Violetta is going to consider these books "proper" poetry or not . . . nor do I have any notion if she'll actually read them once she starts them. But I will at least have tried. Amily had chosen her books very carefully indeed from among the many duplicates that resided in the Palace and Collegium Libraries. People were always giving books to the Collegia or the Royal Family, and no one ever seemed to trouble themselves to find out if they were duplicating existing books.

The first three were books of the "epic" sort of poetry, a story told in one single, very long, poem. Much longer than the epic ballads that Bards had to memorize. The first was the story of a famous female fighter named Taelith Twoswords, who rose to become the Captain of the King's Guard, and, at least according to the poem, accomplished amazing things on and off the battlefield. The second was about a Healer, Vixen, from Vanyel's time; the strange beasties she encountered and the problems she solved were fascinating. The third was the history of the Duchess of Piravale, who, when her father was too sick to join the King's forces against Karse, led them into battle herself, with a bodyguard composed of war-mastiffs that she had trained and raised. The thing that all three of these women had in common was that there was not so much as a *hint* of romantic entanglement in their stories. All three had led very fulfilling lives, and become quite prominent all on their own. The Duchess of Piravale had said quite openly that the more she learned about men, the more she preferred her dogs.

The fourth book was shorter poems, all written by a noted female poet—not a Bard, although some of her works had been eventually set to music. She was a recluse by nature, and in Amily's opinion, a tremendously deep thinker. She spent most of her life never leaving the house and grounds she had been given by a patron, turning out poem after exquisite poem literally until the day she died.

The fifth book wasn't poetry at all; it was a very common book of stories about women and girls *doing* things. Often adventurous things. Usually things that women commonly did not do, and doing them well. Unlike the epic poems, these stories were about women who became master artisans or artificers, who built trade empires, who made incredible artworks, or became famous scholars or teachers. This book was often given to girls just like Violetta to read near the end of their schooling—or at least, that was Amily's experience. She rather doubted it had been Violetta's . . . which was a pity. If she'd had this book to read, perhaps she would not have become as fixated on the idea of true love being the solver of all difficulties and the path to happiness everlasting.

She dismounted at the front door of the mansion, and waited while a boy was sent for the stablemaster himself. The doorkeeper would not hear of her taking Rolan to the stable in person. Apparently that was not to be thought of. She left Rolan in the care of Leverance's nervous stablemaster, assuring him that Rolan would mostly take care of himself, and advising that he just be allowed to stand untacked in a loose box with grain and water and a good warm blanket. Then she stepped inside the antechamber while a servant was sent for. Meanwhile, she waited for Rolan to tell her if things were to his liking. When she was sure her instructions had been followed, she followed another servant into the manse to the ladies' solar, where she was directed to wait for Violetta's nurse.

Hmm. Still has a nurse? Amily had expected a governess, or an aged aunt who would act as a chaperone, not a nurse. Nurses usually stopped tending to their charges well before the children reached the age of ten. *Well, probably they are just keeping the woman on out of kindness. Or maybe she is good as a chaperone. I hope she is the practical sort—*

Unfortunately, when Amily saw her, she knew at once that the nurse was anything but the practical sort. She absolutely babbled about her charge all the way up to the girl's little room, a great deal of it quite personal information that strangers probably shouldn't be hearing. Now, perhaps that was because Amily was a Herald, and the silly old woman trusted Heralds implicitly. But Amily thought not. She had the impression that the nurse would babble this way to *anyone.*

Probably, the family was so used to this that they completely ignored the woman when she started chattering like this, and literally did not hear what she said. But as they climbed the steep, narrow stairs to the third floor, Amily knew the source of at least part of the girl's dreamy and impractical romanticism. In between inappropriate revelations about Violetta and her family, the nurse went on about the hundreds of handsome and charming young men that were sure to fall instantly in love with her charge. It wasn't just romantic poetry that had informed Violetta's world, it seemed.

:You know,: Rolan observed. *:If the girl has any talent herself for poetry . . . she could do worse than follow the example of Lady Adora.:*

:That letter wasn't . . . altogether bad, as a prose-poem,: Amily replied, as the nurse rapped on Violetta's door. *:The gods know there certainly is an audience for fevered and passionate love-poems. More than there is for Lady Adora's work, actually.:*

Violetta murmured something Amily could not hear. The nurse opened the door, stuck her head in, and said something sharp that Amily also could not make out, although the words "your betters" and "when your father gets home" were clear enough. Then the nurse opened the door wide. "Go on in, my Lady Herald," she said with a comically deep curtsey. "If you need anything, there's a bell-pull by the fire; a boy will be up immediately."

At least the foolish woman has the grace to leave us alone,

Amily thought, as the nurse closed the door behind herself. *Of course, she's probably trying to listen at the keyhole.*

The girl's room was tiny, but most of the rooms in this manse were probably tiny. There was just enough room for the bed, a clothes-chest or two, and a small chair at the hearth. Amily dragged the chair over and sat herself down in it, and only then did she look Violetta over.

The girl was pale, with slightly blotchy cheeks that suggested she had been crying a great deal. She looked thinner than the last time that Amily had seen her, but not by much; so at least she hadn't been starving herself. There was a little pile of books next to her pillows, about a half dozen at a guess, and her little spaniel was curled patiently at the foot of the bed. She wasn't actually under the covers; she was in a comfortable-looking thick woolen gown of dove-gray, and there was a handkerchief sticking out of her sleeve, confirming Amily's guess that she had been weeping. All in all, she looked exactly like a young girl who had had both a shock and her heart broken.

On the one hand . . . *Ugh. She's hardly more than a child. She has no idea what a broken heart really feels like.*

But on the other hand . . . *This is the first time anything this terrible has ever happened to her. Just because it is an infatuation, doesn't mean having it crushed doesn't make it hurt less. She's crushed because she poured her heart out to Brand and he threw the letter in the fire. She's devastated because she felt what she* thought *was a lifebond . . . and he didn't. And she's humiliated because she made a fool of herself. And it all hurts, and she has never hurt that much before in her entire life.*

She probably entertained hopes that she would somehow die beautifully and make everyone sorry—especially Brand—but if Amily was any judge Violetta was not the sort to actually pursue suicide. Actually, if Amily was any judge, Violetta was not really the sort to pine until she sickened and died of catching something that would otherwise have been trivial.

Still, I need to make sure that doesn't happen. Dia already raked her over the coals, now I need to redirect her.

"I brought you some new books," she said, handing them over. "These are gifts, you don't need to give them back. Your father told me of your love of reading."

Violetta took them, brightening a little bit. She examined them briefly, but was well aware that to try and read anything would have been a terrible breach of manners, and put them aside. "I . . . I don't know what I could have done to deserve such a generous gift, Herald Amily," she said, with commendable humility.

Amily had decided that she was *not* going to say anything about how much she knew of Violetta's situation. Right now, Violetta thought her humiliation was confined to Brand, Lady Dia and Lady Dia's unknown friend. *Why embarrass her more when my goal is to give her something new to think about?*

So Amily just shrugged and smiled. "It's Midwinter, and time for gifts. Your father said you like poetry, and I thought you might like these. My best friend, Master Bard Lena, recommends them highly."

Violetta's eyes widened, and she curled her legs under her more closely, tucking her skirts in around her feet. "You have a friend who is a Master Bard?" she exclaimed. And then she flushed. "How silly of me. Of course you do, you live here at the Palace. You must know many Bards."

"Sometimes rather more of them than I'd like," Amily chuckled, and so began the stories.

Carefully chosen stories, not unlike those in that last book, of friends and acquaintances, girls she had seen arrive to take classes at the Collegia—not just Bards, Healers and Heralds, but those who were there just to study. All of them went out into the world to become successes. Not so many had romances.

For Heralds, well . . . that was not surprising, although Amily didn't trouble to explain that to the girl. Given the danger involved with being a Herald, it was more unusual when one made a permanent emotional bond than when one didn't.

Bards, well . . . Bards had the handicap of traveling a lot, and never knowing where they would be from one month to the next, and they were often middle-aged when and *if* they got a permanent position somewhere. For Lena to get the position as a Baron's Court Bard so young spoke volumes for her abilities. And to tell the truth, as one of them had told Amily, "Music is a very jealous mistress. Most people don't understand that when they aren't Bards. And when they both are . . . well, then you have two people with *two* jealous mistresses."

Healers were the most likely to settle down with someone . . . so Amily kept her stories about Healers to a minimum. Besides, aside from Vixen—well, and Bear—Healers tended to come in at the end of adventures, they didn't actually have any themselves. And when it came to student hijinks, they generally were the ones standing in the background looking disapproving or apprehensive.

Some of the tales were so funny she actually had Violetta laughing, and not strained laughter either. The third time this happened, Amily wondered when *she* had become such a good storyteller.

:This last year; it was all the practice you got around the fire. After all, you had two Bards giving you the best of examples, and you are a good learner,: Rolan reminded her, with a smile in his Mindvoice. *:I can vouch for that.:*

:Why thank you!: she replied, finding that as time went on, it disturbed her less and less when Rolan revealed he was "watching and listening" as she was doing something. It had seemed intrusive at first, and every time he reminded her he was doing so, she felt very self-conscious. Now it was becom-

ing second nature, and more and more it was proving to be *very* useful.

She stayed about two candlemarks, and by the time she left, she was as confident as she could be that Violetta would at least give the books she had left a try. And if it was even remotely possible to plant the seeds of independence in the girl, well, maybe she had done that, too.

The unexpected visit from the Herald had, somehow, managed to raise Violetta's spirits a bit. Partly it was the assurance that her foolishness had only been noted by three people; Brand, Lady Dia, and Lady Dia's unknown (but thankfully discreet) friend. Partly it was the reminder that, no matter what the poets said, practical people like her sisters were probably right and broken hearts did not remain broken; she had actually *laughed,* quite a bit, at some of Herald Amily's stories. At first, once Amily was gone, she'd been appalled that she had actually forgotten her unrequited love enough to laugh . . .

But then . . . well . . . what was the point of mourning over Brand until she was sick and terrible-looking? Brand wouldn't care, Brand wouldn't even know, and it would only worry her Father. And in the end, nothing would change. Brand still wouldn't love her, he would *still* be the son of her father's greatest enemy, and what would she have to show for all of her spent emotion? Nothing but weeks and months of misery.

After Amily left, she looked through the books the Herald

had given her. Based on reading a few lines, she settled on the one about the Duchess of Piravale, because it had dogs in it. It wasn't like the poetry she was used to—this was one long poem, a story, really, in poem form. But she liked it, and it was easy to like the Duchess, who loved her father the way Amily loved *hers,* and who also loved animals. She didn't seem to care much for pretty things, and she was a lot more boyish than Amily, but it was easy to like her and want to see what happened next in her story.

The poem was *good,* too; she loved the way the words came together, fitted one into another like the gems in a mosaic. Beautiful words really, even when the subject was dogs!

She was still immersed in the book, reading it very slowly to make it last, when the rest of the family came home. She could hear them—or rather, she heard the manor come to life again, and decided to come down to see how the evening had gone.

She found her slippers and opened her door and stood in the staircase listening to the general tenor of the voices— because if things had, for some reason, gone badly, she *really* didn't want to interact with her family until morning.

But she could hear cheerfulness, and her father shouting for food, so things must have gone well.

She padded down the stairs, heading for the dining room, her little dog coming along at her heels. If Father was ordering food, there must not have been much to eat at this fete, so her sisters would be famished too. As she knew, dancing was hard work, especially in the heavy gowns they all wore. But the weight was worth bearing, those gowns were so beautiful!

The servants that were still awake were all scuttling between the kitchen and the dining hall—except the maidservants that were getting ready to help their mistresses out of their gowns and into a warmed bed. So the front of the house was still dimly lit and silent as she slipped through the solar to the dining hall and stood in the doorway.

The Dining Hall had been fully lit, and the fires at both ends built up. The family was down at the far end of the table, with the leftovers from dinner heaped between them. Father wasn't making any of the servants wait on them; everyone was helping him- or herself. Even Mother, who was usually a stickler for manners.

Father saw her as she hesitated in the doorway. "Violetta! You are looking better! Are you feeling as if you might eat something?" The satisfaction in his voice told her that he was happy with *something,* and she smiled.

"I am feeling a little hungry," she said, and joined the rest of the family at their usual spots. They didn't have the literal "high" table here that they had at home, a separate table on a dais above the table where the relatives and servants ate. Here, there was a smaller table at the end of a longer table, like the bar of a "T" and that was where everyone was sitting now. They'd had goose tonight—she had taken little more than a bite or two—and Father had the entire leg and thigh in one hand, a piece of manchet bread in the other. It looked as if Mother had a piece of egg pie. Aleniel had the same, but Brigette, who had a heartier appetite at all times, had cold beef and pickles with her manchet bread. The cousins were not back from wherever they had gone yet, but they generally didn't turn up until long after midnight. Then they would sleep until noon at least, eat like starving beasts, then go out and do it all over again. She had no idea where they were going every night. And no idea why Father had bothered to bring them along. Maybe he hoped some of them would manage to find wives on their own. Maybe he just did it to keep them from getting into trouble back home, or worse, making a wreck of their manor and terrorizing the servants.

Or maybe it had something to do with the feud.

She hoped they were finding parties of their own they could go to, but even if they weren't, Haven was a very big place indeed, the Midwinter Fair (which she had yet to see) was in full roar, and there were probably a lot of ways they could amuse themselves.

"You were saying, Leverance?" her mother said, as Violetta selected a hard-boiled egg and began peeling it carefully.

"Ah, yes. So, when I had a chance to talk with old Spelzan, he told me that Kaltar was *furious.* The Prince not only kept him waiting in the snow until he and his men were practically soaked through, he also 'escorted' them all the way back to their manor to be sure they didn't take any unauthorized detours." Father laughed, and took a bite of goose, putting down his bread to take up his beer. "I swear, it almost makes getting dragged out of the house and down into the city worth it, just to have had all that inflicted on that old bastard!"

Mother primmed up her mouth. She absolutely loathed anything to do with the feud, and if she could have forbidden talk of it, she would have. "Well at least this has done our reputation no harm. In fact, I didn't hear a word being breathed about it, and believe me I was listening."

"It was a quarrel among servants, milady, and had nothing to do with us," Father countered. "And the Prince laid down the law to the miscreants. Why should it do *our* reputation any harm?"

Mother sighed heavily, and gave him a *look* from half-lidded eyes, but Father was either oblivious to it, or chose not to see it. Brigette and Aleniel were now eating ham and pickles hungrily, with their hanging sleeves pinned up onto their shoulders to avoid getting them soiled. They must have been starving for Aleniel to be eating so much. Mother picked at her slice of egg pie with a tiny fork.

"So who did you dance with?" Violetta asked her sisters, knowing that all she had to do was ask that *one* question to get an entire narrative of what had happened that night. In a way, having a conversation with the two of them was extremely relaxing; she never had to ask more than one question, and it didn't matter if her thoughts drifted off elsewhere, because they never noticed.

But tonight she kept her mind on what they were saying. *I am going to try not to be sad,* she decided. *Being sad is not going to bring Brand to me. All being sad will do is make Mother suspicious and Father unhappy. If they find someone for me to marry I will marry him; Brigette and Aleniel are going to marry people they aren't in love with, and it won't be so bad. It might be nice to have my own household and all the books I want. I am going to try and be interested in all the parties. I may never get a chance to come to Haven again, especially if they find someone for me to marry! And how stupid would that be, that I never got a chance to wear my new dresses, or see new dances, never saw the big Midwinter Fair, never went to Court but the once, never really saw the Collegia . . . or anything?*

So she listened to Brigette and Aleniel describe the mansion where the party had been held (much, much bigger than this one, and much older as well), the decorations (this was new; none of the other manses that they had gone to had been decorated for the festivities), the music *(twelve* musicians!), the wine and the refreshments (again, something new; very light little bites of things, rather than the sort of food that would be served at a meal). She was starting to regret that she had not gone. It sounded like something out of a tale. The decorations in particular astonished her; according to the girls huge swags of evergreen and holly hung everywhere, scenting the air with their spicy fragrance. There had been actual trees brought in, covered with apples and nut-shaped sweetmeats, and tables between the trees had been festooned with more evergreen boughs and heaped with cookies and tiny cakes. She loved sweets. What a pity she had not gone!

But then, Herald Amily would not have brought me those books, and been so kind to me.

Her sisters had danced every dance, and at least four men had called them out often enough that it seemed they were interested in pursuing things further. Mother seemed to think so, at least. "Really, it's not just this fete; those same gentlemen asked more than one dance at the last one, too!" she pointed out.

"Well, no one has approached me officially, yet," rumbled Father, and yet he sounded content. "But it's early days yet."

"I hope you weren't too unhappy, missing the fete," Mother finally said to Violetta. "And I hope you weren't too lonely, seeing as we left you all alone, and all the cousins seem to have deserted you." That last sounded as if Mother was getting a little tired of the cousins fleeing as soon as the family was gone. Or perhaps the cousins were not attending nice parties. Perhaps they were taking their entertainment in other ways that Mother did not approve of. Violetta was a bit vague as to what that entertainment could be, but there were hints about "trouble" all the time when maidservants had to be sent away, so she supposed that might be something of the same sort.

"But I wasn't alone!" Violetta exclaimed, making both her sisters look at each other and roll their eyes. "No, it wasn't Nurse. Father gave Herald Amily permission to come visit me when she asked. . . ."

"Wait—" Mother interrupted. "The same Herald Amily who brought us Lady Dia? *The King's Own Herald?* Came to visit you?"

"She brought me some books—" Violetta began, when her father interrupted.

"She was my escort back up here, milady, and asked how Violetta was. She'd heard our daughter was ill." He shrugged. "I didn't want to distract you, and it seemed harmless enough."

"Harmless? It's a *tremendous honor!*" Mother snapped and put the back of her hand to her forehead, theatrically. "Gods defend me! And you didn't think to tell me. I would have made *sure* the servants treated her properly! I would have ordered refreshments! I would have given Violetta instructions! She must think we are worse than countrified, she must think that we are barbarians!"

"She was very nice, Mother, and when she left, she said she'd had a good time," Violetta put in, a little timidly. "She wouldn't have said that if she didn't mean it, surely. Heralds are not allowed to lie, right?"

Mother blinked at her a few times, as if the question stumped her. "Well . . . if you are certain she really said that . . ." Mother took a deep breath, and let it out in a sigh. "I am glad you managed to be a credit to the family, then."

I'm not sure how I managed that . . . But if Mother was under that impression, it was best not to disabuse her of it.

"Leverance," Mother said, and hesitated a moment. "I have something I want to discuss with all of you."

Father sighed. "This is going to involve money, isn't it?"

"You knew that coming here would," she reminded him. "It's this; Guildmaster Ambrose has sickness in his house, and he has canceled his fete—one of the ones we were being asked to attend. There is *just* enough time that we could hold a party in its place . . . and to help satisfy your frugal nature, I did ask of his wife that if we did this, could we purchase the supplies she had laid in. She was actually touchingly grateful, and offered to help me with the organization."

Father put down his goose leg and wiped his hands, for once giving Mother his entire attention. "The advantage to us hosting this party?" he asked.

"Several. It shows the right people that we are willing to step in and provide hospitality as well as being the recipients of it." She was counting off her reasons on her upraised fingers. "It will allow us to pay back those who invited us. Most of all, if there are gentlemen who wish to approach you about the girls, it is *far* less awkward to do so at a fete *we* are hosting."

Father fingered his lower lip, as Violetta slipped a little bit of cheese to her spaniel, who was keeping her feet warm under her skirt. "Good reasons, all of them, but particularly the last. I believe you are right, milady. We should do this."

Brigette and Aleniel clapped their hands in glee. Mother smiled. "With Guildwife Saira to help me, things should go smoothly. I shall pay her the full value for her supplies, but she laid them by at Harvest and they will not be *nearly* as dear as they are now. Brigette, Aleniel, Violetta—you shall be in charge of decorations. You may commandeer as many of your cousins as you care to. I am tired of those layabouts doing nothing but take our hospitality and give us nothing in return."

"My dear," Father said, mildly. "They are our defense, after all."

"Defense against *what?*" Mother retorted. "I have not seen hordes of thieves breaking in, nor any rioting in the streets. No, they can stay at home for a few days, the wastrels, and help the girls make us a credit to your name and House."

Father knew when not to argue with Mother, and this was one of those times. "Very well, my dear," he said, bowing his head to her, a little. "It will certainly do them no harm."

Violetta turned her attention to what Brigette and Aleniel were saying about decorations, since Mother and Father were discussing costs. She was not concerned; Father's tone was not taking on that strained quality it did when he thought something was unreasonable . . . or was going to eat too deeply into household reserves. Mother, it appeared, had gotten things well in hand before broaching this.

Trust Mother to do what she needs to get what she wants. . . .

Aleniel had some decidedly interesting ideas about what to do for decorations. "I was here as a child," she was saying, "And I got up into the attics. There are tournament banners up there, and when I last saw them, they were still sound. If we can beat the dust out of them—"

"Or the cousins can," put in Brigette.

Aleniel sniffed. "The cousins *certainly* can. They can stop talking about how strong their arms are and demonstrate it. At any rate, what if we were to hang those tournament banners up, festoon them with evergreen, and bring out some of the old arms and armor and stand it about? Positioned properly, people will easily see we are meaning to give the party the air of an antique tourney, and not that we just stuck this old stuff up because we didn't know any better."

"What about—" Violetta began, and flushed when they turned to look at her as if surprised she had spoken. "—what about making the sweetmeats in the shape of little shields? And—I don't know what other supplies Mother will be getting, but have the cooks make them look like an ancient sort of feast?"

Her sisters exchanged an astonished glance, then looked back at her. "I never in all my life thought all that reading you do was going to have a use," said Aleniel. "Tell us more? What do you mean by *look like an ancient sort of feast?*"

So Violetta described the sorts of things that people were described eating in her *other* books, the romances and stories from hundreds of years ago. Father had concluded his talking with Mother at that point and gone back to his food, content to listen, while Mother joined their planning. "I know just the banners," she said. "They should be still sound. And we can easily arrange our refreshments to give an *impression* of an antique tourney." She smiled at them all, one of her rare smiles without a hint of doubt in it. "My dear girls, you are showing you have the makings of *very* clever women in you. I shall leave the decorations in your hands, you leave the rest to me."

Violetta went up to her room, accompanied by her little spaniel, much later than she intended to. In fact, by the time they all broke up, plans well in hand, the first of the cousins were trailing in. As Nurse helped her out of her gown and into her nightgown, she took stock of herself and realized that she hadn't thought about Brand for at least two candlemarks.

That was two whole candlemarks when she had not been miserable and sad.

Perhaps tomorrow it will be three, she thought as she climbed into bed.

Brand was moping when Mags arrived.

This was not a surprise. Mags had expected that Lord Kal-tar would probably take out his spleen on anyone who got in his way once the Prince saw him mewed back up in his man-sion. It was a pretty common reaction, after all; whenever something goes wrong, most people seemed to look for any-one to blame other than themselves. That was doubly true for people who were accustomed to having a lot of people around they could blame things on.

He actually expected Kaltar's manse to be full of moping young men, or cowed ones. In fact, the mansion was . . . un-wontedly quiet. The servant that let Mags in was quite beyond "subdued;" Mags would have termed the man "cowed" or bet-ter still, "browbeaten." But the rooms were empty of loungers, and as the servant conducted Mags to Brand, their footsteps echoed in the silence.

Now, if Mags hadn't already known what had happened, he would not have greeted Brand with the salutation he did—

"Good gods, Brand, who died?" he asked, after finally lo-cating the young man slouched in a window-seat in the Great Hall. Brand looked up at him, but did not smile. Instead, he grimaced.

"No one, and that's the problem," Brand replied, not en-tirely in jest. "Evidently our servants and Leverance's decided to have a dust-up, it got broken up, the Prince came down off the Hill to oversee it all, and decided to blame it on Leverance and my father." He sighed heavily, and shook his head. "When Father and the servants got back he lined them up in the Great Hall and lectured them until he was hoarse, and handed out some beatings just to be sure he was understood. Then he drank down a pitcher of wine, gathered up all the rest of us, and read *us* a lecture on . . . well . . . I'm not quite sure. He didn't actually say anything about *not* fighting in public with

House Chendlar. It was more about 'respecting his wishes,' and 'obeying his commands as Lord of the House and your rightful ruler.' In any event, it wasn't pleasant, and it was pretty obvious that no matter what the truth was, in his mind, it was all *our* fault."

"So did his Lordship have anything to do with it?" Mags probed, leaning nonchalantly against the frame of the window-seat.

"Hanged if I know. What I *do* know is that he actually was kitted up for a fight at the time. And the old man doesn't get in much sparring practice when we're not at home. I haven't seen him spar with his Weaponsmaster since we got here. If he wasn't planning on getting involved, it was a damned strange coincidence." Brand shrugged. "He's been spoiling for a confrontation since we got here, so you be the judge. I'm guessing the Prince had the same idea about it being an unlikely coincidence, since he kept Father down there in the snow until Leverance got safely home, *and* escorted him here personally to make sure he didn't make any unauthorized visits elsewhere. I think what added insult to injury is that, if the story I heard was correct, it was Leverance's people who were coming to attack ours in the first place—ours just had advance warning and were going to meet force with force. But because he was caught in armor, he's getting more of the blame. He's been in a foul temper ever since and today he's been taking his temper out on anyone who crosses his path."

Mags considered that. "What did he do to you?" Because it was pretty obvious that Brand had had *some* sort of edict imposed on him. He wouldn't have been sulking, otherwise. And while he was at it . . . since he and Brand were alone for the very first time ever, he decided he was going to try something.

He had noticed that Brand never "leaked" thoughts—not even when he was emotionally wrought up. Lord Kaltar didn't either. Now he decided that, all things considered, it was worth a careful probe. Not to actually *read* what Brand was thinking, but to see if he could, at great need.

"Told me I'm to start attending 'proper fetes' from now on. And that he expects me to find myself a wife before we head home." Brand groaned, and rubbed his temple. "Seriously . . . I thought he was supposed to be doing that *for* me."

Well, well, well. Brand's mind might just as well have been behind a brick wall. It wasn't like the Sleepgivers—something that had been conferred by an outside source, in their case, the bespelled medallions they all wore. And it wasn't like the sort of shield that someone who was Gifted could put up. No . . . no, this was something else entirely. Mags had run into people like this on circuit. They were rare—as rare as the Gifted, in fact! But they were *completely* shielded from being read, or having someone like Mags impose thoughts on them. The trait seemed to run in families, so it made sense that both Kaltar and his son were blocked in this way.

:Well that's disappointing,: Dallen observed. *:If we* need *to know what they're thinking . . . :*

Mags knew from experience that if he absolutely had to, he could probably force his way in, but it would be extremely hard, and might be damaging, and the only time he had done so, it had left *him* feeling knackered for a week. It had taken him a full month to recover his own mental strength as well. It was not something to be tried lightly, particularly not when there were so many other ways to find out what he wanted to know about Brand and Lord Kaltar.

Mags chuckled. "And he thinks he's punishing you, but, old lad, he's done you a favor, can't you see that?"

"How?" Brand asked, incredulously. "How could he possibly be doing me a favor by forcing me to go to these . . . things . . . that no one in his right mind would care to attend? I've gone to enough to know how deadly dull they are! Granted, the afternoon fetes are worse, but it's only a small matter of degree!"

"He's letting you pick the girl yourself." Mags spread his hands wide. "So . . . that means you can look for someone who *lives here in Haven.* "

It took a moment for that to sink in. But Brand wasn't entirely stupid and when he realized what Mags meant, his eyes widened. "So I could actually live *here,* instead of back at that estate. And I would be in charge of the household money, not Father. So—"

"So you could keep Lelage." Mags smiled and nodded. "Now if I were in your place, I know the kind of girl I would look for. Someone with no brothers, maybe no sisters either, for that matter, someone who no one thinks will ever get married." He pressed his point as Brand stared at him in surprise. "Think about it. As long as she has money and will let you do what you want, what do you care?"

"You have a point," Brand said, slowly. "I could live here . . . Father would have the estate all to himself, which honestly, is the way he likes it. You know, I might even be able to make some poor old maid very happy as long as she understood that I wasn't in love with her . . ."

On the one hand . . . it was a terrible thing, talking about these poor women as if they were nothing but pieces of fruit in a market, some past their prime, some underripe, but all for sale. On the other hand . . . that was how it was. It took a girl with spirit to escape from such a system, and it could be done, but *she* had to make the decision to do so. No one could do that for her. In the meantime . . . Brand had just said at least one thing that was kind, if not admirable. *"I might be able to make some poor old maid very happy as long as she understood I wasn't in love with her."* Mags decided to encourage him in that. He knew of plenty of old maids who would be thrilled to get out from under a familial thumb to do what *they* liked, and would consider giving Brand freedom to do as he wished a very small price to pay indeed.

"You'll find a lot of those old maids acting as chaperones to younger cousins or siblings," Mags pointed out. "They'll be at the parties. All you have to do is start making quiet enquiries." He shrugged. "Mind you, it doesn't have to be an old maid. You might find a complacent young thing too, someone bookish, for instance, who would just like to be a scholar and be left alone. Or a girl with ambitions her family doesn't think suitable. Or even a rich widow—although that's chancy. A rich widow can do what she wants, and a rich widow might be very demanding."

Brand shook his head. "No, I'll leave the rich widows to my cousins. They wouldn't at all mind being a rich woman's lapdog, so long as they were in the lap of luxury."

Heh. Sauce for the goose, sauce for the gander. "There's something to be said for that life," he pointed out. "As long as both parties know what they're in for."

Brand made a wry face. "Anyway . . . we've all been ordered to stay away from Flora's. . . ." His face acquired an expression of gloom. ". . . I don't know for how long."

Ah, now there was the real explanation for Brand's sulks. "Pish. It won't be long. Two or three days at most, until something else gets his attention—and if you manage to find some prospective women, it might be sooner than that. Meanwhile, the old man didn't forbid you to take in the Midwinter Fair now, did he?" Mags retorted.

"Well . . . no, actually . . ." Brand looked as if it hadn't occurred to him that there *was* a Midwinter Fair.

"Good. We'll get horses and ride down. The ride will do you good, and there's plenty to see and do down there." Mags had a good idea of where to take Brand. There was not quite the variety of entertainment that there was at the Midsummer Fair, but there was a particular group of traveling players that was performing a bawdy comedy he thought would suit Brand down to the bone.

:You'd better bring me back pocket pies,: warned Dallen.

"All right, as long as we're back in time for me to change for

whatever wretched fete the old man has us invited to." Brand
made a face. "Dear gods, these things are boring. Dance and
drink weak wine. Dance and nibble bland food. Dance and flirt,
but only very politely. Pretend you like the mediocre music. I've
been to village weddings that were more entertaining."

"Get your cloak." Mags gestured to Brand to precede him.
"You forget. These so-called parties aren't supposed to be entertainment for you. They're business. They're horse markets,
and you are the young stallion being trotted out for examination. It's not as if you need to stay there long, just long
enough."

Since Brand's cousins had also been ordered to stay away
from their usual haunts and apply themselves to the serious
business of finding wives, presumably with money, there were
plenty of horses in the stables. Mags reckoned most of them
were at the afternoon parties today, which all could be walked
to. The stablemaster presented him with a horse all tacked up,
a cobby little bay who seemed resigned to being taken out of
the warm stable and into the cold. It felt odd to be riding a
horse instead of Dallen.

Mags knew all the short cuts through the city by now, and
before long he had them both down on the commons, where
a second city of tents and other temporary shelters had sprung
up to support the Fair. He went right past the section of vendors; Brand was not in the least interested in shopping, for
now, anyway. Instead, he brought his charge to the tent of a
wine merchant he knew very well, and with a couple of drinks
of rich, hot, spiced wine inside him, Brand was looking at life
with a little bit more cheer.

From there, Mags took him straight to the "theater," a
rather cunning construction of wood and canvas that allowed
a certain amount of heat to accumulate inside so that the pa-
trons could sit on their wooden benches without feeling any
discomfort through the play. They were in luck; it was just
about to start.

"My treat," said Mags. He paid the entrance fee, and they made their way inside, by luck getting a couple of seats on the end of a bench near the front.

The play was a farce and a highly bawdy one, with people climbing in and out of beds they didn't belong in, getting caught, nearly getting caught, betraying their spouses and being betrayed by them. The audience was mostly young men, which was not surprising, since unlike many acting companies, the ladies were actually played by women and not boys—and although they were never naked on stage (they'd have frozen to death, or certainly caught a fever) they were generally in more of a state of undress than you usually saw outside of an establishment like Flora's. As Mags had thought, Brand was completely thrown out of his gloom, and laughed uproariously at all the antics.

The play itself was witty and cleverly written, with a lot of very good jokes. Even if most of it was not the sort of thing you wanted to quote in polite company.

But the important thing was that it cheered Brand up. Mags knew enough about Brand by now to know this meant he would not go looking for trouble just for the sake of having someone to take *his* ill-temper out on. And it meant he'd go to this evening's fete in a much better frame of mind, prepared to do what his father wanted.

Really, Mags considered that the best thing he could *possibly* do for the situation he was tasked with handling was to get Brand betrothed and his father (if not him) out of the city as quickly as possible. With half the tinder gone, the Chendlar/Raeylen feud could not erupt into a conflagration that might engulf the rest of the Court.

Amily had to admit that the Chendlar manor looked astonishing, and thanks to the fragrant evergreens everywhere, smelled even better. The girls had done a wonderful job of decorating it, and (as their father said with pride) it had all been done with *very* little expense. They'd been resourceful and clever, and had found ways to make use of quite a variety of unlikely materials to excellent effect.

A search for old suits of armor had led to the Guard armory; the Armorer was not at all averse to loaning out as many as the girls wanted—such things were next to useless in his opinion, and only taking up space. According to Aleniel, since Lord Leverance had ordered that the girls could tell their cousins to do whatever they wanted, the first thing they'd ordered was for the young men to polish that armor until it gleamed. The girls had freshened up the look of the suits with surcoats and decorations cut from old curtains and other material found in the attic. There had been plenty of those old tournament banners too, the painted colors faded just enough to make them seem quaint—and disguise how clumsily they had been painted in the first place.

So now, there was a pair of armored figures with tournament lances gracing the front entrance, and more pairs wherever they could be showed to advantage. Huge swags of evergreen framed the front door, with tourney-banners hanging on the walls behind the armor.

Inside, more tourney-banners, now framed in evergreen swags, hung on all the walls of the Great Hall. Every door had a swag of evergreen or of aesthetically faded fabric from the attic above it. The girls had added torches in sconces made from the hands and arms of sets of armor too battered to be salvaged. Ancient braziers, made to warm cold hands outdoors when tourneys had taken place in all weathers, had been repurposed as bowls holding apples. Old helmets graced the center of every refreshment table.

All of the refreshments had been made in decorative motifs that fit the theme. Small cakes had been cut into the shape of shields, little egg-pies had been made to look like round shields with a boss made of crust in the center. There were even fanciful "boar's heads," made of baked bread dough, with currents for eyes, and a baked apple in their mouths. These were laid out on tables placed around the room.

As the guests entered through the decorated front entrance and then proceeded into the Great Hall, their murmurs of appreciation were putting broad smiles even on Lady Leverance's face. She and His Lordship stood just inside the entrance to the Great Hall to receive their guests, and if the relaxation of her rigid spine and a smile that was more gracious and less strained were any indication, she was already completely satisfied with this night's work.

Amily was pleased that Violetta had been so engrossed in helping her older sisters with all of this—her job had been to decorate those old suits of armor after the cousins got done polishing them and setting them up on stands—that she

seemed to have utterly forgotten that her heart was supposed
to be broken. Whether or not she was taking Amily's words to
heart, she had certainly taken Lady Dia's. She hadn't sat in
corners and sighed over her sewing. She hadn't spent as much
time weeping as she did working. She *had* worked hard and
willingly, too; she had sewed her little fingers red, pulling a
stubborn needle through heavy canvas not well suited to
being made into tabards, then made them look like something
planned and not an afterthought by painting fanciful figures
on them in the style of old devices. Amily was very proud of
her, even though she had yet to show that she had taken any
thought about the examples in those books.

Early days yet. No point in trying to force something like
this. The girl was young enough—and, Amily thought, smart
enough—to grow beyond what her parents had tried to drum
into her. There was time enough for those changes, particularly if she could conspire to keep the girl unbetrothed this
year. *Perhaps if I suggest that her parents might find themselves missing their brood if they get rid of them too quickly.
Or perhaps if I suggest that since Lord Leverance is going to
need at least* one *young man to serve as his heir, he should
take more care over the selection of Violetta's husband-to-be
than he does over the other two.*

And if Mags could just get *Brand* safely tied up, and quickly
too, then they'd get House Raeylen out of the city, and Lord
Leverance could get down to the business he'd come here for
in the first place.

*And I can get back to the business of learning to be a
proper King's Own . . .*

She understood, *completely,* why the King had asked her to
give over her appropriate duties and devote herself to being
one half of the effort of keeping this *stupid* feud from blowing
up in everyone's faces. Far, far too many people in the Court
had begun to take sides in the quarrel, and that was never
good. While it was unlikely that anyone other than the mem-

bers of the two Houses would come to blows over it, it *was* likely that decisions were being made that had nothing to do with logic and everything to do with what side someone was on. That was going to make for difficulties down the road, and possibly animosity it might take years to undo.

The effects were already being felt in Council meetings. Subtle, but there. *Actually . . . I'm rather glad Father has taken those over for me for now. I don't have his level of diplomacy and tact.*

But she wanted to go back to what she was starting to think of as "her proper job," let Father go back to regaining his strength and building up his own intelligence network outside of Haven, while Mags built his own inside of Haven. This was putting some delay on experience she should have been getting, during a period of relative calm. There was no war, at the moment, only the usual tense border situation with Karse. And Karse seemed to have learned a lesson they didn't much care for, in dealing with the Sleepgivers. That just left the usual jockeying for power and place in the Court; that was what she needed to learn about first hand, as the King's Own, and that was exactly what she was not getting to see from the inside.

This feud should not have turned into such a . . . mess. Nor should it ever have been allowed to get to the point where it could easily turn into more than that. *So far we've been lucky in that the two sides haven't managed to recruit too many of our younger hotheads, the kind who think getting into fights is a clever thing to do.*

But now, short of putting the two House Heads under arrest and keeping guards on them at all times, there was no way other than what she and Mags were doing to keep it from degenerating. If the two sides started paying for criminal troublemakers . . . if they actively started to court the younger sons of the highborn . . . if they somehow got notoriety among the common folk so that *they* started picking sides . . . then there could be fights in the street and blood shed.

More blood shed, she reminded herself, because there had been a modest amount spilled already, even if the blows had not been fatal.

Mind on the job, she reminded herself. Although she did not expect any trouble of any kind, she was her father's daughter, which meant that just because she didn't *expect* any trouble, she was well aware that did not preclude trouble cropping up anyway.

All three of Leverance's girls looked particularly well tonight, but Violetta was probably the prettiest, not the least because she had gotten some of the color and verve back that Amily had seen in her when they had first met. She *would* dance tonight, as she had not at the Court fete. Her mother had promised her that, and arranged for a few dances with some of the sons of women she herself had become friends with over the course of taking all their offspring to party after fete after party. It would mean nothing, of course; those women were on the lookout for some catch for their boys that would bring them more than Violetta's modest little dower, but it would give her the illusion of romance that she craved.

And it might take her mind off Brand. It was far too soon for her to transfer her affection to someone else, but if she managed to get a little interested in some of these young men, it would help.

The musicians struck up the first tune of the evening, and heads turned. This wasn't a dancing tune yet, but it was very clear to all the guests that the ensemble in the minstrel's gallery above the hall was itself something very special.

Of course, they would have known that already if they could have seen the players.

Amily had seen to it that the family had gotten the services of a little ensemble of Bardic Trainees as their musicians. Since she had the King's permission to do whatever it took to keep House Chendlar occupied with matchmaking, she'd gotten the handful of Trainees who called Haven home to spend a little of their holiday time in rehearsing as a group and taking this job. The fact that they were being paid generously by the Crown hadn't hurt matters, it was true, but it was very good of them to give up their holiday time. Then again . . . none of them were from wealthy families, and she had seen to it that they were being treated extremely well. Being treated, in fact, like the potentially important Bards they could become.

As a result, however, the music was *astonishingly* good when compared to the music that had been played at other comparable fetes. It was certainly turning heads. People were even muting their conversations to listen.

So between the music and the decorations, there was a sense of great excitement in the room that boded well for the reputation of House Chendlar this season. And *that* just might speed things along for Brigette and Aleniel. After all, the sorts of men that both they and their mother wanted were the sorts of men who valued the ability of a wife to put together a successful entertainment almost as highly as they valued the ability of a wife to produce an heir. After all, once you had an heir-and-a-spare you were substantially done. Since most people of wealth and power were not having children as extra labor, but as inheritors of what *they* had, they tended to limit their families. But if you were of wealth, rank, or both, you put together entertainments all the time, and the more successful you were at it, the better your fortunes became.

By demonstrating that they could accomplish this at such a young age—well, Aleniel and Brigette had increased their own value above that of their dower.

And the sooner we get them betrothed and out of the city, the sooner things can go back to normal. That cannot possibly happen fast enough for me. And if Violetta had not managed to start to turn her life around by that time, well Amily had given her every tool she could to do so later. *You can't save everyone,* she reminded herself, a fact which her father repeated to her at least once a day. *You save as many as you can, but you can't save everyone. Particularly if they don't want to be saved.*

Amily had grown up in and around the Court, and it had occurred to her more than once that the Heralds were incredibly lucky in the relative freedom with which they lived their lives. For all of their responsibilities, their lives were not governed by the tyranny of "manners" and "custom." Violetta's letter would have been little more than a cause of teasing at worst if she was a Trainee and it got out. But among her own class . . . Lady Dia had pretty well covered all the ways in which it could ruin her *and* her family.

Well, we avoided that.

She had thought, before going out on circuit with Mags and Jakyr, that it was only the highborn and wealthy whose lives were so constrained. After all, they had titles and money to protect . . . and a lot of leisure time in which to create elaborate codes of manners. But . . . no. No, she had found out that while the common folk *could* have been a bit more lenient in the way they treated each other, for the most part they were just as constrained by custom as the rich.

Although if this had been a little village drama being played out, Violetta's letter would have probably resulted in her father beating her black and blue and forcing her to marry the first cousin that would accept her. Certainly in the eyes of her fellow villagers, the only girl that would write such a thing to a young man was one whose virtue was already gone.

But at least if she was a village girl she'd have had a lot less exposure to silly romances, and more to the other options of what she could do with her life.

:Assuming her parents allowed it, or she had the gumption to run away,: Rolan said, following her thoughts. *:As the third daughter, she'd have had no dower at all and would have been expected to stay home and take care of her parents in their old age. Mind, she might have been able to have her own income, if she—say—raised bees, or was an expert seam-*

*stress. But otherwise, she'd have to get her parents' consent
to have any other sort of life than that—or, as I said, run
away.:*

Amily settled in an out of the way corner, half-obscured by
one of those tourney banners, with a cup of wine in her hand,
and kept not only *her* eye on the proceedings, but the eyes of
several other little unwitting helpers . . .

Like the wren that had gotten in here at some point and
was reluctant to leave. He kept himself out of sight as much
as possible, way up in the rafters and cross-beams of the Great
Hall, but both Amily and one of the maids knew he was there
and made sure there was a hidden supply of crumbs and seeds
tucked out of sight of the people below, but not of the bird
above. And Amily had added her own little supply in the Minstrel Gallery, along with a dish of water she kept filled. She
thought there might be a leak somewhere he was getting water
from as well . . . or possibly there was enough condensation
on the windows to keep him supplied. She made a note that
when all this was over, she was going to net him and bring
him to the greenhouse to winter. It didn't seem fair to expose
him to the frigid winter at this point, since he wasn't accustomed to the cold now, but she could turn him loose in the
spring.

And there was the downstairs cat, allowed to roam the
public rooms freely because she was fastidious, who cared not
at all about the bird (though she was a mighty hunter of mice).
But she was here in the Great Hall because she knew that bits
of cheese and meat were discarded or dropped near the refreshment tables, and knew that this evening would bring her
a round belly as long as she was agile enough to stay out of
the way of the people. She was yet another vantage point—but
far more importantly to Amily, she was a sharp pair of ears.
She could hide under tables and behind banners all she liked,
as long as Amily could hear what she could hear.

And there was the mouse who had made a nest in one of

the evergreen swags, high above the reach of the cat, and was watching the scene, half fascinated by the tantalizing scents of food, and half terrified of all of the people. He was of limited use, but he did give another overhead vantage that was different from that of the bird.

Violetta's little dog had been put to bed in her room—and truly did not *want* to be down here in the crowd and the noise. But Leverance's huge mastiff had been deemed worthy of becoming part of the decorations, and now lounged at his ease along a bench covered with a swath of ancient brocade, kept content by a meaty bone and a bowl of cold water. People seemed delighted by his presence—and he *was* a very mannerly fellow. He was also keeping a benign eye on part of the room that Amily could not see from here. She just hoped that he wouldn't fall asleep. His ears were just about as good as a human's, so he could hear conversations from where he was that she could not.

Then again, if anyone started anything, he would probably be aware of it, even asleep, before she was. He wasn't a guard dog as such, but he would certainly wake up and alert her to something unusual going on.

It was going to be a long night. She just hoped it was going to be a boring one.

Violetta was not exactly *happy,* because even though she was trying with all her might not to think about Brand, she kept thinking of him anyway. It had been easier when she was working on the decorations; then she'd had to concentrate on what she was doing in order to get it all done as quickly as possible. Now that she was here, in the Great Hall . . . she kept wishing that Brand was at her side, about to take her out to dance. She kept picturing how he would look, and what a pleasure it would be to dance with someone so graceful.

But she wasn't *unhappy,* either. She'd been promised the first pavane by some son of a friend of Mother's, and if he wasn't Brand, he also wasn't repulsive.

She had been promised other dances by other young men, and even knowing that they were only doing this because their mothers had arranged it was not spoiling the fact that she was finally going to get to dance with someone who wasn't her cousin.

So unlike that ill-fated Court gala, she was not going to be standing there while her sisters got dance after dance, and she was ignored.

She was wearing her favorite of all the new gowns; red velvet that she had embroidered with her own hands, with a high waist and as daring a neckline as Mother would allow, over a heavenly-soft linen chemise in a deep gold. It was definitely a good color on her. She thought it made her look older, almost as old as Aleniel. She thought Aleniel had made the same observation, since her sister had looked briefly displeased when she had appeared downstairs wearing it.

I don't know why she should care. She doesn't want any of the young men, she wants one of those three old Lords Mother invited specially for tonight! It's not as if they are going to take any interest in me, if they know what my dower is!

Then again, who knew? Maybe Aleniel was not sure enough of their interest to feel confident they would continue it if they got sight of a Violetta who no longer looked as if she *needed* Nurse to take care of her. *Ew. No thank you. I don't want to be married to some old man!*

The musicians up in the gallery gave the signal that they were about to start the dancing. Since *everyone* was excited about having actual Bardic Trainees playing for this, the center of the Great Hall got cleared away very quickly, and that first young man came up and politely offered Violetta his hand.

She took it, and even though he wasn't Brand, it still gave

her just a little thrill. Because he wasn't repulsive, and he was a stranger, and she was, at last, dancing in a beautiful gown at a wonderful party in the capital city.

———————

Brand and Mags had been dragged away from a party that was turning out to be an unmitigated disaster as far as Brand's goals were concerned. Mags hoped he wasn't going to turn surly, but so far he had managed to remain polite to the other attendees, although his asides to Mags were definitely bordering on cruel. Truthful, but cruel.

First, it was dull. Not the usual sort of dull, but *deadly* dull. There were no musicians. There was no dancing. Even the food was dull, the sort of thing you could find at virtually any village fete. *Pocket pies,* for heaven's sake, and it did not matter in the least that these were miniature pocket pies, they were still pocket pies. A great deal of bread and cheese. A minimal assortment of sweetmeats. A lot of apples. The wine was of mediocre vintage, the beer was weak.

And it was clear from the start that the girls here were not interested in *them,* but in the much older, and wealthier, men that had also been invited. Brand's comments about *them* were hilarious. No defect, from a paunch that bulged over a belt to the pathetic attempts to disguise a balding head, went unnoted.

So when a couple of fellows they knew slightly came and gathered them up with a whispered invitation to "come along and have some real fun," Brand was only too happy to go with them. And Mags perforce had to follow. Not that he minded in the least; he was more bored than Brand was, since *he* was accustomed to conversation that varied a lot more than he was getting here.

They got their cloaks and the group of a dozen or so gathered just inside the front door while someone Mags knew only

as "Morin" distributed something, parceling out one of—
whatever this was—to each of them. It was too shadowy in
this little antechamber to see what it was until one was shoved
into his hands. He looked down in blank unrecognition until
he finally realized what it was.

A mask.

His was a black half-mask with a suggestion of a beak.
Morin saw him turning it around in his hands, trying to figure
out how to carry it without damaging it. It seemed to be made
of stiffened fabric, or something of the sort. "Put it on, but
shove it up on your forehead," Morin suggested. "That way
you can pull it down in place when we get there."

Oh! Mags realized, finally, what giving all the young men
masks to wear actually signified. *We're going to go invade a
party uninvited!*

Well, Brand would like that. They hadn't been invited along
on one of these things yet, possibly because Brand was a relative newcomer to the Court, and people weren't sure how he
would behave incognito.

Now this group at least was sure he would behave with the
appropriate level of "impropriety," so he and Mags had gotten
included in the raid.

There was the suggestion of rebellion in this that was going
to appeal to Brand in his current mood, even though the hosts
of the party would probably not care—there was a certain
amount of this sort of thing that went on all during the Season.
Of course, they would most certainly have cared if they were
invaded by common folk from down in Haven! But since it was
the privileged lads of their own class, well it was "all in good
fun" and "part of the Season." There was an unspoken code of
conduct in these "raids." The invaders would not do anything
too outrageous; mostly flirt suggestively and play the fool. The
hosts would not have them thrown out by the servants. The
invaders got a chance to leave *terrible* parties and go to ones
they had not been invited to, on the understanding that they

would leave again after a short time. The hosts got their parties livened up if things had quieted down, and if not, there was a certain cachet that came with being "raided" because the invaders would not stay long at a bad party.

"We're off to Guildmaster Ambrose's manse," said Morin, as Mags tied his mask on and pushed it up, as suggested. "Good food, better wine, and he always makes sure to invite the prettiest girls. He's got good taste in wenches *and* wine. Even his maidservants are pretty little things."

"He's lucky his wife doesn't object," chuckled someone Mags didn't know.

"She doesn't care as long as he just looks," said another, and elbowed Brand. "Trust me, one look at the company Ambrose keeps and you'll stop mooning over Lelage's—*legs.*" He laughed and ducked as Brand mock-swung on him. "Oh, you think nobody knew? The way you were caterwauling in your cups the other night?"

Mags was stumped for a moment, then remembered that another dull party had sent Brand and several other young men out to the "Rose and Thorns," since going down to Flora's was out of the question. The tavern was quiet, but at least the wine was quite good. Brand had done a bit of carrying on about Lelage, and it appeared that Morin, at least, knew the lady by reputation.

"Well, don't let my father find out," Brand said, suddenly sober.

"Bosh, you think he'd care? Every one of our fathers probably has his little tidbit down in Haven," Morin said with a touch of a leer as he held the door open so they could all file out. "Just count your blessings that *his* pretty piece isn't the same one *you* want. I've known that to happen a time or two. Awkward!"

That occasioned some uproarious laughter as they went out into the snow.

Mags kept his mouth shut and listened to their banter, and

it occurred to him—as it had more than once since all this started—that the highborn girls congregated at the party they had just left were not all that different from the ones at Flora's. All of them, the highborn and the girls at Flora's alike, centered their lives on pleasing men. All of them were commodities. If anything, the girls at Flora's were freer to live their lives than the highborn girls were. And really, none of them were *free*.

Not unless they were willing to sacrifice a great deal for an uncertain future. Life at Flora's—or life as the wife of a wealthy man—was comfortable, at least for most of them. Except, of course, when it wasn't. Wealth didn't mean that a man wouldn't beat his wife, or abuse her in other ways.

And what about the girls at the lowest levels of the trade— or the "marriage market"? The ones who sold themselves for enough to eat that night, or a place to sleep . . . whether it was for a coin or as a wife? For them, freedom was a distant and unreal dream. It made him melancholy, and it wasn't until he realized that the group had stopped that he was shaken out of his thoughts.

They had met with a smaller group of three maskers, and Morin was conferring with them. After a moment, the group moved on, but heading down another street. The three they had just met went on their way.

"What's going on?" he asked Morin, pulling his cloak tighter around himself. It was cold, but at least it wasn't snowing, and the wind wasn't blowing. It was dark, and the mansions where parties were being held were lit up like festival lanterns, not only with lights in every window, but with lighting outside as well. Some had lanterns hung out along the paths that led to their doors, some had those *and* braziers to warm the air along the path, but the manse to which they seemed to be heading had torches stuck into the snowbanks on either side of the walkway, and what looked like banners on either side of the door.

And—armored warriors? Who would be mean-spirited and cruel enough to stick a guard in a suit of freezing cold armor out all night to stand next to a door just for the sake of an impression?

But in the next moment he realized these were just empty suits of armor, set out as decoration. Very effective, he had to admit.

"Guildmaster Ambrose has sickness in his house, and the party is being hosted by someone else," Morin replied, as they neared the door. "All right boys! Masks down! Remember, just because you're masked that doesn't mean you won't be in a world of trouble if you make real trouble! Just the usual foolery, make the ladies blush and think they've had a bit of an adventure, don't start a fight, and don't drink *all* the wine. If you're going to be sick, do it outside."

Obediently, Mags pulled his mask down, just as they got to the door, and Brand preceded him inside. Just in time to hear "Welcome, young Lordlings, to House Chendlar."

———

Violetta flung herself through the steps of the bransle in a kind of odd fever. Part of her was enjoying herself; she loved to dance, she loved to dance *fast,* and her partner was tolerable. Part of her wanted to cry, right there, break right down in the middle of the dance, sink down on the floor and weep. This would have been the most perfect night of her life—

If only Brand were here.

Oh, if only he was her partner! She thought she was managing to conquer that desire for him, but every time she thought she had fought it down, it came rushing back twice as strong. She longed for him so much it was a physical ache in her chest. So she danced as hard and as fast as she could, to keep the pain at bay.

And she had plenty of partners to assist her in her efforts.

Evidently this time she had been noticed, and it wasn't only young men who'd been coerced into it by their mothers who were asking to partner her. She only stopped when she was breathless, her cheeks hot, and an ache in her side.

She stepped out of the way and to the sidelines, thinking she would catch her breath and then begin again. Mother was not standing watchdog over any of them tonight, possibly because they were in their own home, and she felt they were safe. Violetta was glad of that, because Mother probably would not have approved of *all* of the men she had danced with tonight. Not that any of them were bad, or they wouldn't have been invited here—just that some were . . . unsuitable. And tonight, she just did not care.

A servant offered her wine, and she took it, sipping it while she looked around at the other dancers and at those who were not yet dancing.

The musicians up in the gallery sounded heavenly; never a missed or sour note, and they were playing tunes she had never heard before. Even Mother had been brought out onto the floor more than once, protesting, but not very hard. Right now Mother was nowhere in sight; exactly how Violetta wanted it.

Brigette and Aleniel were still dancing, though with nowhere near the energy that Violetta had put into it. Well, they were trying to look dignified, even in the fast dances, to create the sort of impression that although they were quite young and attractive, they were older than their years. It was so complicated! It was like putting on mask after mask after mask. Sometimes Violetta wondered where the *real* Brigette and Aleniel were, under all the "impressions" they were trying to make.

Then again, though they shared a home, they were practically strangers. They never shared lessons; they didn't even like the same sorts of things. They saw one another at meals, and sometimes sitting with Mother in the solar to embroider.

She often felt as if she was an only child. The only reason she knew *anything* about them, was because they talked to each other so much, while she listened.

There was a stirring at the entrance. *Quite* a stir, in fact, out of keeping with the way most people had been entering the Great Hall, and out of curiosity she made her way there. *Is it possible Father arranged for some kind of entertainment besides the music?* If they had been at home, where he knew everyone and everything, he sometimes did just that— jugglers, or gypsies, or once, a man with a horse no bigger than the mastiff, that he had trained to do all manner of tricks.

She was just in time to see a crowd of young men, all in masks, bow themselves courteously past her father. Her heart did beat a little faster at the sight. Men in masks! She'd heard of how they would come uninvited to a party, flirt outrageously, steal kisses, and then leave—it sounded so exciting! A little dangerous . . . you could flirt back and no one would tell you that you had made a disgrace of yourself. *I could pretend that one of them is Brand. . . .*

"Welcome gentlemen!" she heard her father say. "You are welcome to our Midwinter fete! Nay, I do not ask you to reveal your faces; well do I remember how *I* once wore a mask and told tales in a lady's ear that made her blush!" He chuckled, and turned to some acquaintance who had joined him for a moment. "How long ago was that? Thirty years?"

"Thirty years, if it is a day," the other man said. "I have not worn a mask and played the rogue since before Prince Sedric was born."

And just at that moment, before she could move closer to the maskers, one of her cousins, Kenteth, came to claim her— somewhat reluctantly—for a promised dance. He was engaged in intense courting right now with a girl called Betrice, and was loathe to spend any time not in that dogged pursuit. But he was a decent partner—and she was hoping one or more of the maskers would notice her if she was dancing, and choose her for a flirtation. *They certainly won't notice me crushed on the sidelines.* She stepped out into the pattern with him; it was a complicated gigue, and one that she had to concentrate on. It was also a lot more acrobatic than any dance she had done thus far. There was a lot of leaping and skipping, and the musicians were playing the melody very fast indeed.

When it was over, she was nearly panting. She moved over nearer to the door where she thought the air might be cooler, just in time to see Cousin Talbot approaching Father with rage on his face.

That startled her. Talbot was hot-headed, but what could have happened that would have set his temper afire?

He looks as if he would like to slay someone!

"Uncle!" Talbot cried, clutching at his side for a sword that was not there, then shaking the empty fist in impotent anger. "Look you, over there!"

He pointed, and the crowd obediently parted for a moment to show one of the maskers. And her heart froze as someone she had never thought to see again tilted his head in a heart-breakingly familiar way. *Could that be—?*

Talbot's angry words confirmed what her heart had told her. "Uncle, that is Brand! Son of Lord Kaltar, of House Raeylen and our enemy! He can only be here to insult our women, stir up our guests against us, and make trouble! Let me—"

No! No, he has done nothing! Do not let Talbot hurt him! Violetta almost cried her fear out loud. But, rather than telling Talbot to get a sword and call for his own, Father looked Brand over calmly. "He behaves like a gentleman. I've heard good things of him—he pays his debts, does no man harm, and holds himself in better repute than that angry dog, his father. Ignore him and leave him be, unless *he* starts a mischief. I would not spoil these festivities with an altercation, and Lady Leverance would not thank us to do so. This is her triumph; good manners and good sense say to let her enjoy it, and revel in the pleasure of knowing she created a fete unmarred by any ill-will or incident. Be content, nephew, and go back and pay your court to the ladies."

But Talbot was anything but content. "This is an outrage! He will make a mockery of us all! I will not endure his presence one moment longer!" he cried, making those near the two of them look at him with alarm.

Without warning, Violetta's father shoved his forearm across Talbot's chest and forced him against the wall behind one of the hanging banners. It startled her a little; she had not known her father was so strong! She slipped through the crowd in an effort to get near enough to listen; for once it was an advantage that she was so small!

"You will endure what I *tell* you to endure!" her father rasped harshly. "Who is the master here, you, or I? You'll cause a ruckus? Start a fight? Ruin the triumph of your aunt? And for what? To prove you are a hotheaded fool that cannot even abide the orders of your Prince for an hour? Do you think the Prince's orders apply only to servants? Do you think that if you quarrel with this boy, he will not send *you* packing? And for what? Do you think this will prove you are a *man?* It proves you are a child! This is *my* house, and I am Lord of it. You eat of my meat, drink my wine, and sleep in my bed, and I say you will endure what I order you to endure! Now! I give you two choices—smile and stay, or frown and growl and fume and go!"

Father stared into Talbot's angry face for what seemed like a very long time before he lowered his arm and let Talbot go. They continued to stare at one another as Father backed up a pace to give Talbot room to move.

A moment later, Talbot stormed off, proving that he preferred to allow his temper to rage, rather than give the appearance he accepted Brand's presence. Her father emerged from behind the banner, dusted off his tunic, and went back to greeting his guests.

Before Violetta could say or do *anything* else, another of

the dances that her mother had arranged began, and her partner came, dutifully, to find her. As she danced, she tried, in
vain, to find Brand amid the crowd. But he was nowhere to be
seen.

Her heart was aching even more now. She wanted, desperately, for him to notice her, and realize that she was not
some . . . stupid little girl. And she wanted, just as desperately, for him to overlook her entirely. She craved his company. She feared his censure, or worse, his ridicule. And he
could say whatever he liked from behind that mask. He could
mock her even more effectively than Lady Dia had.

If he mocks me, I think I will die.

The dance ended, and she turned—

And there he was. Standing between her and escape. Her
heart stopped and all the blood seemed to drain out of her. She
could not have moved if the room had been on fire.

"Is this dance spoken for?" he asked, with a slight smile,
holding out his hand.

She thought she was going to die with pure joy. She couldn't
speak; all she could do was smile and shake her head, then
put her hand in his. Her hands were like ice! Oh, what must
he be thinking?

Whatever he was thinking he didn't seem to mind how cold
her hand was. He took her hand in his, and led her into the
pavane.

She felt as if her skin had become a thousand times more
sensitive. She could not look away from his face, and felt her
cheeks alternately going hot and chill. Her heart raced, and
her mouth was dry, and this was the happiest moment of her
entire life, and the most terrifying. He didn't speak; in all of
her fantasies, he had used the dance as a chance to tell her all
the things she wanted him to say . . . but he didn't say a word.
And it didn't matter. She drank in his smiles, basked in his
glances. She never wanted the dance to end.

But end, it did. As she sank into the curtsey at the end of

the dance, and he bowed, she wished that time would stop, right there, so that she would never have to leave that moment.

But her knees were weak and her legs were trembling as she sank to the floor, and she felt utterly unable to stand—but then his hand appeared before her eyes as if he sensed her weakness. She put her own in his, he raised her from her curtsey, and then she felt so light that she was afraid she would blow away.

"I think you need some wine. And perhaps a little air," said Brand, drawing her out of the crowd and toward the windows. As a servant passed, he took a goblet of wine and gave it to her, then continued to draw her after himself. He pulled her into the bow of the window, and tugged a little at the draperies so that they were sheltered by curtains, where she felt as if they were completely cut off from the rest of the party—the rest of the world. Even the music seemed to come from a great distance. It was as if they were the only two people here.

He let go of her hand, but was standing so close to her she could feel his breath on her cheek. She clutched the goblet of wine in both hands, untasted, holding it just under her chin as if it was a shield that would protect her. And yet, to be protected was the last thing under the sun that she wanted.

"So," he said. "You are the writer of the letter. The lady who wrote to me with such passion the night of the Court Fete."

She felt herself grow hot from her feet to her hair, and her eyes stung. He remembered her letter! He was going to rebuke her, mock her. He was going to tell her she was a little fool, just as Dia had. He had thrown it in the fire . . . he thought it was . . . he thought she was . . .

"The words were beautiful," he said, touching her hand with one finger. "But if I had known that the writer of those words was even more beautiful, nothing could have kept me from coming to you in that moment."

"Oh!" she breathed. "But I would never have asked that of you. Our fathers are mortal enemies, and even masked, you have risked too much in coming here. Only the merest token, a word from *your* hands, would have been enough, more than enough, to sustain me."

"A word only? And only from my hands?" He leaned closer still. "Words fall from lips as well. Would you not rather have had your words from that source?"

She could hardly breathe, and her mind swam. "You know who I am—and I know you. You are Brand, son of Lord Kaltar, and we should be enemies—"

"And who has made that decree? Your father? Mine? Why should their quarrels matter to us?" He bent—she thought for a moment that he was going to kiss her on the mouth, but his lips brushed her fingers where they clutched the goblet, and left a trail of fire where they had been. "Two old men who did not wed for love, do not understand love, and would not know love if their soul-bonded appeared before them. We are not bound by their decrees. Love goes where it will, and comes when it is not called. *You* know that, bright spirit, whose soul knew mine even without knowing my name." His lips brushed her hand again. "You will see me again, and sooner than you think."

And then he was gone, leaving her standing with her hands still clenched so hard around the metal of the goblet that her knuckles were white, but with her heart singing so loudly she was amazed that no one else could hear it.

Amily lost track of Violetta for a little, but before she could worry, the girl reappeared and rejoined the dancers, and she relaxed, and scolded herself for worrying too much. How could the girl get into trouble in her own house, after all?

Probably she had been having a flirtation with one of the maskers—who were bidding goodnight to Lord Leverance even now. Well, good for her; hopefully that would drive all thoughts of Brand out of her mind, one way or another.

She realized at that moment that she was getting . . . very tired of the highborn. And she was not liking them very much. She didn't care for the way they lived their lives, she didn't care for the way that they looked at the world, and she didn't care for how no one was *real* to them unless he or she was in their circle.

Here were two grown men, who should have *known* better, who were continuing a stupid fight over an equally stupid insult that their *grandfathers* had quarreled over. And they were perfectly willing to trample over any innocents that got between them, too!

She wanted to shake them both until their brains rattled in their skulls.

But even if she ever got the opportunity to, they'd never understand why she was so angry at them. It would literally never occur to either of them that there was anything wrong with their self-centered attitude.

:You are so very much like your father,: Rolan observed, affectionately. *:Now you know why I always intended to Choose you when the time came.:*

:It's an honor I would gladly have done without if it meant losing him,: she replied bluntly. *:And it may have caused a lot of problems, but I am so grateful that I didn't lose him that sometimes I can't even breathe.:*

:They are problems I am perfectly glad to weather, for both your sakes.:

:Rolan!: she said, both touched and a little surprised. *:That is so sweet!:*

:I have my moments.:

She turned her attention back to Violetta, who was, by all appearances, enjoying herself. She kept an eye on the girl via the sparrow, who had the best view at the moment, and turned her attention back to Rolan. *:How likely is it that this feud is going to explode into something worse?:*

:Candidly . . . the more fetes and parties the two sides attend, the more people are starting to take sides. Lady Leverance and Lady Kaltar are both very good at manipulating peoples' sympathies, and aside from the maneuvering to get their respective offspring married, they have been quite active in that regard.: Rolan paused. *:It would really depend on* how *it exploded. If it were just brawling in the street with injuries . . . people will shrug and not get involved. But if someone dies . . . well, there are already rivalries within the Court, and people will use the feud to inflate those rivalries into something worse. The problem is, there has been an entire year without anything untoward happening that involved the*

Court. The Karsites are not a tangible threat at the moment, there is no more Sleepgiver problem, and . . . : she got the impression of a sigh *:people are bored. Bored people . . . :*

:Make things up to get worked up about,: Amily replied sourly. She took a goblet from a passing servant and sipped it. *:This is another thing I don't much like about highborn . . . and some wealthy people. They don't have anything to do, so they make up things. Intrigues. Love affairs. Conspiracies. Absolutely none of them are constructive, and at best, they are not* too *destructive.:* She couldn't help but think how Lydia and her circle of friends had been—carefully being *constructive.* Keeping an eye on the Court and the courtiers, because the adults—they had all been youngsters then—never really paid attention to anyone that still had to answer to his or her parents. In Lydia's case, being the pretty little thing all the high-ranking Guildsmen and wealthy merchants ignored, because no girl could ever be pretty and intelligent at the same time. . . .

Amily watched the dancers moving through the intricate patterns of a contra-dance, and tried not to frown. Even here, even *now,* at what was supposed to be a pleasant event, you could see the signs, if you knew what to look for. People whispering, but the looks on their faces were not . . . quite right. There was a slyness to their expressions, a wariness as they tried to make sure they were not being overheard, and a hint that they knew they were doing something that just was not . . . nice. About half the people were here to have a good time. About half were here to conspire over something.

And there was no way of telling just what it was that they were up to. It could simply be malicious interference with someone else's courtship. It could be planting equally malicious rumors about a rival, in love, in business, or in court politics.

Or it could be something more dangerous.

There was simply no way of telling, and even if she'd *had*

Mags' Gift of being able to read almost anyone's thoughts, it was a terrible breach of ethics to actually do so if you didn't have permission, if you weren't ordered to by the King, if you weren't sure someone's life was in danger, or if it wasn't a dreadful emergency.

So the best she could do was what she and Mags and her father were doing now.

:Well . . . what can we do to head things off if *there's an actual armed confrontation?:* she asked.

:Let's consider our options while you keep an eye on the Dancing Dreamer.:

———

Mags decided that the moment they entered House Chendlar, he was going to let Brand do what Brand did and stick tightly to Talbot Chendlar. It wasn't difficult; the moment that Talbot got sight of Brand, it was obvious that he recognized who was in the mask, and he became so enraged he could have been followed by a troop of armed knights and he wouldn't have noticed. Mags was glad that he had made that decision, after slipping in close enough under the cover of a convenient pillar that he was able to overhear Talbot's rant to his uncle.

When Lord Leverance laid down the law to his nephew, Mags was . . . startled. He hadn't realized that the old man had as much of a temper as he did. He also hadn't realized that the old man was as strong as he was; Leverance all but rammed Talbot into the wall, and held him there while he informed the younger man of *exactly* who was in charge of House Chendlar.

That couldn't have gone down well with Talbot. . . .

Mags followed as Talbot wrenched away and left the Great Hall. He was hoping that Talbot would storm off out of the building altogether, but no such luck. Talbot was only heading deeper into the building . . . probably looking for reinforcements among his cousins so that they could find Brand and try and goad him into doing something the old man would find worthy of a beating. Not a good idea. Not good at all.

So he pulled off his mask and left it behind a vase, intercepted a servant coming into the Hall with replacements for the refreshments and purloined two bottles of liquor stronger than wine and two goblets. Then he went after Talbot at the run.

He managed to intercept Talbot *before* he got to any of his cousins, slowed down to a walk, and hailed him. "Ho! Talbot! Just the man I was looking for!" he called, as if he had been searching for the young man since he arrived.

Talbot whirled, and stared at him. "Magnus . . . Thorsten?" He looked startled, as if Mags had somehow managed to jolt him momentarily out of his rage.

Which was just what he wanted. Mags grinned. "You remember me! And here I was afraid that I was utterly forgettable! Listen, Talbot, I need your expertise rather desperately." He took a quick glance around the tiny room where he had managed to corner the younger Chendlar. *Where are we? The Tradesman's Reception Room, I think.* . . . There was nothing here but a table and a single chair. This looked like a place where Lord Leverance's house-master dealt with merchants and the like. He looked around and spotted a window seat, and pointed at it. "Come over here and sit down, I'll pour you something to make it worth your while and plumb your knowledge."

Talbot looked as if he wanted to take any excuse he could think of to escape from any such thing—but then just gave an exasperated shrug. "I'd rather find my cousins and go beat that whelp of a Raeylen, but . . ." The interruption had accomplished exactly what Mags wanted; it had taken the wind out of Talbot's sails. The young man let out his breath in a long sigh. ". . . my uncle has expressly forbidden me to do that, and you've never seen him in a temper. He might look like a kindly old man, but he rules our House with a grip of iron, and no one, I mean *no one,* contradicts him, much less goes against his direct orders."

They both took seats at either end of the window-seat, which was long enough for four or five people to sit side by side. Mags put the goblets down on the wooden seat between them and poured. "Here. Have a drink, it sounds as if you need one. Listen, if that *whelp of a Raeylen* violates the hospitality of the House, it'll be the servants that beat him and throw him out, right?" Mags reminded Talbot. "That's infinitely more humiliating than you doing it. Plus, if the servants do it, that will be them acting on Lord Leverance's orders. And if the Raeylen boy doesn't act like a boor, well, why should you make yourself into the villain here by picking a quarrel with him?"

Talbot looked sour, but nodded. "Give me that goblet and keep pouring. What's your problem and how can I help?" He picked up the goblet nearest him and drank down the contents in a single gulp, holding it out for more.

"Not a problem as such . . . more like information. I need an expert on swords," said Mags, and proceeded to involve Talbot in a discussion of exactly the right sort of sword to give to his purported uncle for a distant birthday. He knew enough about Talbot to know that this actually was something that Talbot was vitally interested in. The selection of a sword was not a minor matter among the highborn, for whom the proper sword meant a very great deal indeed. If you merely went out and bought any old thing with a fancy hilt, no matter how much gilding and ornamentation there was, no matter how impressive the pommel-jewel, if the blade itself was inferior . . . that reflected extremely badly on you. It also reflected badly on you if you presented the wrong *sort* of sword. Where the Heralds trained in a little bit of every fighting style and were generalists, the highborn—at least those who didn't actually lead their men into *real* war—were specialists. Talbot was a rapier-man; he preferred to be armored as lightly as possible, or not at all, and count on his quickness to get him out of trouble. But Mags' supposed "uncle" was trained in broadsword, an entirely different blade.

Fortunately, as Mags well knew, Talbot knew just about everything there was to know about the swords themselves, knew who all the good smiths in Haven were—and for some distance outside Haven as well—and was always ready to display his knowledge. Mags kept pouring, and Talbot kept talking, until Talbot was just tipsy enough that even at his most angry, Mags knew he would never challenge Brand, because even a beginner would defeat him, and Brand was no novice when it came to sword-work. And Talbot knew it too. He carefully put the goblet down at his feet and passed his hand over his face.

"I'm . . . fuddled," he said, enunciating every word with great care. "And I'm man enough to admit when I'm fuddled. I hope I've given you everything you need to know for that present, Magnus, but I think I am going to have to get to my bed before a servant has to carry me there."

"You've been *amazingly* helpful, Talbot, and I'm no end grateful to you." Mags stood up first and offered his arm. And after one attempt to stand, Talbot was not too proud to make use of it, though once up, he was steady enough on his feet to walk with a little assistance from the wall.

He waved Mags off and staggered off in the direction of a staircase. When Mags was absolutely certain that he was actually going to do what he said, he retrieved his mask and went looking for Brand.

He found Morin, who told him that Brand had already left. "He didn't stay long. Just one dance, some wine, and then he said he needed to get back to our original fete before his father found out we'd slipped out."

Well that's a relief. Sensible too. He bade Morin goodnight got his cloak, and followed Brand's example. :*I'm coming home,:* he told Dallen. *:Meet me between here and there. It's been a long night.:*

———————

Violetta floated back to her room, feeling so lighthearted she was almost tipsy. And yet, she had drunk very little; her state was due entirely to her happiness.

Her sisters were still dancing, and the party was still going on, but she wanted to be by herself to savor those few moments with Brand. No one else was back in their rooms; the distant music and murmur of conversation was all that was to be heard as she opened the door to her little room, and once the door closed, even that was cut off. She waved off the maidservants after they helped her out of her beautiful dress and into her shift and told Nurse to go to bed. Since Nurse was . . . well . . . rather drunk, and clearly wanted to get back to whatever little drinking party she and some of the other servants were having, Violetta had no trouble persuading her to leave. The little dog Star was not allowed to be in her room anymore at night, since accidentally being shut in and making a mess he couldn't help. Now he slept in a special basket on the hearth in the solar, where he could get himself to the door the cats used in the kitchen if he needed to go out.

She stuffed a handkerchief in the keyhole to muffle the last of the noise. Then she wrapped a warm shawl around herself and flung open the window; the air in her little room was too close, too still, and she was feeling stifled.

The night was clear and beautiful, and the moon shone down on the snow-covered gardens unimpeded by any clouds. She took deep breaths of the cold air and it tasted better than wine.

And then, as she gazed up at the stars, she heard someone below call her name.

Startled she looked down.

It was Brand. She could see him clearly in the moonlight, smiling up at her.

"Brand!" she said, in as loud a whisper as she dared. "What—how did you get into the garden? Never mind—you shouldn't be there!" She peered down all around the area near her window, now terrified lest someone from the household be within hearing or seeing distance of him. "If anyone here sees you, they'll kill you!"

"I cannot care, so long as I can see you," Brand replied, gazing upward. "Walls and swords are no barrier to one who loves. I told you that I would see you again sooner than you thought!"

"And do you love me?" she asked, hardly daring to phrase the question. "Oh—no! Please do not answer that! What if you lie? Would you lie? Oh—"

"Now how am I to answer that in a way that you'd believe?" Brand asked, with a low laugh that made her shiver with delight. "Should I say that anyone who sees you *must* love you? Should I swear that I love you by my faith, my honor, or by the gods?"

"By your faith?" she replied, her heart pounding and her mouth dry. "But what if you are faithless? By your honor—I do not know enough of you to know! I *believe* in your honor, for you have kept the secret of my letter, and yet I am too confused, I cannot tell . . . if what I believe be true. And by what gods will you swear? At the lies of lovers, they say the gods laugh!"

"I will swear by any thing you desire," Brand declared. Down below her, his face looked strange, white in the moonlight—the visage of a mask, or a corpse . . . she shuddered and thrust the thought away. "Whatever will satisfy you, that, I will swear by!"

"Those who give oaths so easily seldom keep them . . ." Her heart was in her throat. She wanted this, so very badly, and yet . . . *could* she believe him? Dared she?

"How then can I satisfy you?" he asked reasonably.

"Tell me your purpose!" she replied. "It is not enough to swear you love, for so does any man who wishes anything of any maid! I have often heard my father's men and even my cousins swear they loved, only to prove false once their purpose was achieved!"

"I would not harm you for all the world and all the crowns of all the nations in it," he said. "My purpose is to be your love; was that not what you asked of me?"

She couldn't argue with that . . . it was what had been in her very own letter, after all.

"But let me show you—" he said, and a moment later was climbing up the rough stone wall like a squirrel! She gasped, and backed away from the window as he pulled himself up over the sill and dropped down inside. "There you are, my lady," he said with a little bow. "Now you need not fear my being seen, or us being overheard." And with that, he prudently turned and closed the window, pulling the draperies shut.

She backed up again, but there was not much space in her tiny room, and she found her back against the door. He approached her, slowly, smiling. "Do I frighten you, little dove?" he asked, and reached out to stroke one finger down her cheek. "I would not frighten you for all the world."

His touch left a trail of fire down her cheek, and she gasped in a swift intake of breath. This was the nearest she had ever been to a man who was not related to her. And . . . it was certainly the least clothed she had been around any man . . . "You should not be here," she said, faintly. "You should not be . . . so close to me."

"I do many things I should not do. Don't you?" he asked, and took her into his arms. She could not resist, and truth to tell, she didn't want to. His arms around her were hot on her cold skin. "You should. Life is much more exciting when you do things you are not supposed to do. Here. Let me show you."

She shivered at his touch which gave her strange sensations in unfamiliar places all over her body. He held her closer, tilted her head up with one finger under her chin and kissed her.

She went hot, then cold, then hot again, and the shawl slipped from her shoulders to pool at her feet. With one hand he held her against his body as he kissed her, as his other traced patterns on her bare shoulder. Then his hand slipped down off her shoulder and he cupped her breast, his thumb making circles around her nipple, and her knees went so weak she would have fallen, if he had not been holding her up.

Her mouth opened involuntarily beneath his insistent kissing, and then it was much more than just *kissing,* he was doing things with his mouth and tongue and teeth that, together with his caresses, had her fainting with desire for him.

I shouldn't—

But it was too late for second thoughts; he had somehow gotten her onto her bed, and pulled her chemise up and she wasn't thinking anymore at all; her world was composed of strange sensations and things she had *never* experienced before. He moved his kisses down her body until he was doing something down *there* that convulsed her with waves of unbelievable pleasure and made her bite the pillow to keep from crying out. When she had finished shuddering with reaction, she opened her eyes to see that he had stripped his tunic and hose off and . . .

"Don't be afraid," he whispered, and then he was making her go all hot and cold and tingling again before he did what she had gotten a glimpse of some of the servants doing out in the stables or in dark corners, And it hurt, and this time she bit the pillow to keep from crying in pain.

But then he made it better again, whispering comforting things and apologies for hurting her. When he was done, they lay together in her little narrow bed and she fell asleep.

Only to wake and find him gone and the gray light of an overcast morning coming in the uncurtained window.

For one moment she was confused. And then, she remembered.

Suddenly she felt all muddle-headed and bereft. Then she wanted to weep. She wanted to run about laughing like a lunatic. She wanted to cry out into the garden, howl like a dog whose mate was gone. Why had he left her?

Because if it would be bad for him to be caught in the garden, how much worse if he was caught in your bed? she scolded herself.

But he loved her. He would never have dared to do anything like that, dared to enter the garden, dared to climb to her room, if he didn't love her! They *must* be lifebonded soulmates, surely nothing less could have driven him to risk his very life to come to her last night.

She moved, and felt the sore place inside her, and then threw back the covers to stare in panic at the blood on the sheets and her chemise. Stark evidence of her guilt, right there and impossible to hide. *Oh gods—what am I—what do I do? What do I do?*

Before she could even *think* to do anything, the door opened and in came Nurse, with the little dog Star at Nurse's heels. "Time to wake up poppet!" the old woman said, far too loudly. And then she stopped and stared for a moment at the bedclothes, and at Violetta.

And then . . . she *tsked.* "Too much excitement last night, and started your courses two days early, then did you! I might have guessed you would. Well, let's get you out of that mess and get it all cleaned up."

She felt weak with relief. She didn't even have to think of something. She was safe. He was safe. Their secret was safe.

"I'm feeling a little sick, Nurse," Violetta said, knowing that the Nurse would let her stay in bed and sleep or read until afternoon if she thought that Violetta was having female trouble.

"Well then! Let's get you comfortable, and I'll bring you

something for breakfast and a hot brick for your toes and make your excuses to your lady mother," the old woman said, bustling about in her sober brown gown and tabard, stripping the bed and remaking it, bringing Violetta an ewer of warm water, a basin and a sponge to clean off with, and a clean chemise and clout to put on.

Before the sun had gotten much higher, she was tucked up in bed again, clean and with a warm brick at her feet, porridge with cream and honey, and chamomile tea with more honey in it, for her to break her fast with. And when she was done, and everything was cleared away, she leaned back into her pillows and tried to relive everything that Brand had done with her last night.

She knew she should be feeling ashamed for giving herself to him—and they weren't even betrothed, much less married. Her father—what he would do to her didn't bear thinking about. All those terrible things Lady Dia had threatened if he'd discovered the letter would be nothing compared to what he would do if he knew she had slept with Brand. She knew she should be feeling ashamed for consorting so with the son of her father's terrible enemy. She knew she should be worried about a thousand things that could go wrong with this liaison—and she should be contemplating the terrible consequences if they were discovered.

But the gods had brought them together and protected them last night, and she could not help but think that they would continue to do so. This was Destiny! Just like in the great poems! Everything had conspired to mate them, at last, and everything would go right on conspiring to keep them together. He knew it too! Hadn't he said as much? She felt so . . . amazing, so dazzled, that she couldn't think of anything else but this. *If he comes tonight, how can I manage to leave the party early so I can be here when he does?*

———————

Amily awoke to the scent of bacon, hotcakes and honey, and cracked one eye open to find Mags sitting on the edge of the bed, one plate on his knees as he ate, another waiting on the stand next to the bed for her. It had been a long night, she had been so busy keeping track of Violetta and the guests that she hadn't done more than sip at a little wine, and she was ravenous. "Good gracious," she said sleepily, "What's the occasion?"

Breakfast in bed . . . what a luxury. She hadn't enjoyed a non-working breakfast once since she became King's Own, much less one in bed and with Mags. She smiled at him, turned on her side, and started to reach for the plate. More and more she appreciated having the quarters that they did. Being able to cook simple things for themselves and not have to traipse through the snow to the dining hall at Herald's Collegium was lovely.

Perhaps one day when the expansion here at Healers goes in, there will be a dining hall here, too . . .

In the meanwhile, she hoped it would be a long, long time before a Healer was assigned to these rooms.

"I'm hopin' to sweeten your temper so you don' murder me this morning," Mags said, in between bites. "Brand was one'f the maskers that turned up at th' Chendlar do last night."

She almost overset the plate, and him, she sat up so quickly. *"What?"*

" 'Tis all right!" he said, making a placating motion with his fork. "Th' old Lord allowed as how if he behaved, he could stay. Talbot tried t'start somethin', an' th' ol' man ran 'im inter a wall." Mags shook his head. "I'd no notion th' ol' man was so strong. Then I managed t' grab Talbot an' get 'im talkin' an' drinkin', mostly drinkin', till 'e decided 'e had t'get t'bed 'fore 'e fell over." He chuckled, which did not mollify Amily at all. "Even Talbot knows if 'e challenged some'un drunk, 'e's gonna get beat."

She pushed her hair out of her face with one hand and

picked up her fork with the other. She paused for a moment to savor a bite of bacon with a little honey on it. "Yes but . . . I *know* Talbot Chendlar, and he's going to take this as an insult to House Chendlar. He's going to be looking for an excuse to get at Brand, now."

"So?" Mags seemed unimpressed. "I stick to Brand. I see Talbot 'bout to make trouble, me'n'Dallen call fer help."

That was all very well. Except that she was afraid the help might not *get* there in time before someone was murdered. Or Mags might get himself hurt trying to prevent a murder. She tried to remind herself that Mags was not only an *excellent* fighter, but he had the memory-reflexes of his cousin . . . but that was no comfort, thinking of him facing off against Talbot. She'd heard reports from the Weaponsmaster of how good Talbot was in practice, and she had the feeling he wasn't showing everything he had in public.

And she couldn't exactly keep an eye on Talbot.

Mags could clearly read exactly what she was thinking in her face, if not in her thoughts, and his brows creased. Then suddenly, he brightened.

"I'll hev one'f my boys watch 'im. Talbot, I mean. More'n one, I'll hev a couple of 'em watch turn an' turn about so there's allus eyes on 'im. Reckon that'll work t'ease yer mind?" he asked.

She heaved a sigh of relief. "Yes. Yes it will," she admitted. "Very much so. Of all of the young hotheads of House Chendlar, it is Talbot I fear the most. He is the natural leader of the lot, and truth to tell, I think if he were not so closely related to Lord Leverance's girls, one of them would already be wed to him in order to keep the title and estate in the family."

Mags put down his empty plate and brushed some of her hair out of her eyes again. "'E seems t'be th' one a lot'f the young bucks at Court are gettin' behind too, an' that's worryin'," he admitted. "Brand, now, I ain't seen him gettin' people riled up and takin' sides like Talbot does."

"I can't help but think that Brand is playing a very deep game, and there is a lot more to him than the randy young wastrel you've been trailing about," Amily retorted. "I know you feel like you are wasting your time . . . but he worries me."

Mags took her now-empty plate from her hands and set it aside. "I allus listen when yer gut talks, love," he reminded her. "I'll keep on 'im, an' keep sharp watch. Hev ye got a mornin' meetin' with Kyril?"

She shook her head. "Not this morning. He has a breakfast with some of the Lords of Trade."

"Good," he chuckled, and leaned in closer. "Then I got plans."

———

Mags considered his entire "stable" as he made the walk down to Aunty Minda's place. He wanted to consult with the lady herself before he made any actual selections of boys. Or girls, though that was less likely. He wanted to reserve the girls for places the boys couldn't go.

The good thing about the Midwinter Season was that there were messenger boys coming and going all the time, to and from every establishment on the Hill. Especially now. Betrothals were being announced, and those announcements were going out. Small "thank you" gifts were coming from people who had been invited to past parties. Larger betrothal and Midwinter gifts were being sent as well. And although Nikolas himself was pretty much confined to light duty on the King, and forbidden to leave the Palace without the express agreement of the Healers, he still had his finger on the pulse of *everything* going on at Court. All Mags had to do was supply the boys to watch Talbot; Nikolas could supply the reasons for their being at House Chendlar, if they were stopped and questioned.

Mags was trying *very* hard not to be angry at this nonsense, because after all he had been through, it just all seemed so . . . petty. It definitely seemed, to him anyway, to be an extremely poor use of his time.

:It is, it is, and this is what Nikolas does all the time,: Dallen reminded him. *:Petty or not, poor use of your time or not, if this situation gets out of control, people will be hurt, and someone will almost certainly die.:*

:Someone dies all the time down in the bad parts of Haven,: Mags pointed out sourly. *:But ye don't see not one but three Heralds down here, babysittin' feuds.:*

Dallen was silent for a long time. *:It's not fair,:* he admitted. *:It's not fair this gets more attention than Jin Street or Pudding Lane. It really isn't. When a rich man dies, all the world knows; when a poor man dies, more often than not he's chucked into a common grave with five or six others and a fortnight later no one even remembers he lived and died. And we try to have equal justice for everyone but . . . we don't. We just have to do the best we can to make it better.:*

Mags sighed, as he reached the front door of the converted shop. *:Leastwise it's good practice fer Amily. She ain't gettin' throwed inter the river just t'teach her t'swim.:*

He unlocked and opened the door, and closed it behind himself. Aunty Minda was surrounded by four of the children, all of them with bits of slate and chalk, laboriously writing out the words she told them. She had looked up at the sound of the door opening, but now she returned her attention to the children. Mags waited patiently. So far as he was concerned, interrupting their lesson was a sin he'd rather not commit.

When the lesson was over, and she had given them a precious book to share, she got up and walked over to him, slowly, with a care for her aching knees. Too many years spent on hands and knees scrubbing other peoples' floors had left her with joints swollen and painful in weather like this.

But at least now that she was working with Mags, she was seeing a Healer now and again, and things were getting a little better. He tried not to think of all the other Aunty Mindas out there in the city, who could never see a Healer, and who could only continue to endure the pain.

It wasn't fair. It really wasn't fair. They needed more Healers, more Heralds . . .

He stopped the yammering in his mind and concentrated on the job at hand. Because if those two feuding households really did let it all break out into the street, then the people that would be *most* hurt would be the innocents caught in the middle, who'd find themselves involved whether they knew anything about it or not. When a fight became a brawl, and a brawl became a riot, bad things always happened.

He and Minda sat down together on a little bench, and Minda listened carefully as he explained what he had in mind. "You'll want Ash, Sparrow and Detch," she said, nodding her head with authority.

"Ash and Detch, aye, I figgered them. Why Sparrow?" he asked. The two he'd already chosen in his mind were clever lads, could already read and write more than well enough to be given entire lists of people and get their deliveries right. So if Nikolas had to write instructions for them, they'd be fine. But Sparrow—

"Sparrow is known to them up at the big houses," Aunty Minda said, surprising him. "He's already taking orders about from that lady that makes the fine soap over on Deel." She chuckled a little. "Now he's cleaned up, he's a pretty little mite, and the ladies like to see him trottin' about with his parcels. If ye kin git him somethin' nice t'wear, 'e'll look like 'e fits right in."

Well that satisfied that, then. He already knew where Ash and Detch were, and Auntie Minda might have read his mind when it came to Sparrow. "Sparrow'll be here for nuncheon. I'll hold him here till you get back from dealin' with the other two."

Mags gave her a little two-fingered salute and headed off on the trot for the two inns where Detch and Ash were stationed. On the way he Mindspoke with Nikolas to let him know what was needed.

The boys were waiting on their bench in the inn to take messages. And Mags was very glad he had planned for this day from the time he'd first decided to take over the Gripper's gang. He crooked a finger at them from the door of the inn; obediently they got off their bench and followed him.

"Got a special job fer you two," he told them, as he led them toward one of the places where he kept his disguises—a hidden room in the stable of a very busy inn. Carefully he explained what they were to do, and that Herald Nikolas would be giving them further instructions. "So," he concluded, opening the hidden door in the alley for them, "this's why I got ye somethin' you'll look all right in up there."

He lit a candle and stuck it in the holder beside the door before closing it, giving them their first look at the place where he became "Harkon."

Costumes hung on a rack; there was a mirror, a stool, and a table filled with the paraphernalia to turn him from Herald Mags to anything from a blind beggar to a swaggering bravo. There were wigs, and little swatches of lighter colored hair he could insert into his own to give the overall impression it was lighter than it was. But the important thing now was that there were several outfits in several sizes, all of them matching buff-color, that looked like servants' livery.

Now this was the good thing about all of the families up here on the Hill who were only here for the Midwinter Court. It was the next thing to impossible to remember the liveries of all their servants—and indeed, some didn't actually have any livery; they just put their servants in tunics and trews and skirts in buff and black and gray, colors that wore well and did not show stains.

So if these boys were bustling about in buff-colored outfits, people would assume they were *someone's* page-boys or errand-boys or hall-boys, and leave them alone.

"Now, ye find somewhat that fits ye, while I write notes t'get ye in the Palace Gate and on t'Nikolas," Mags told them.

When he had sent them on their way, he heaved a sigh. *Well, that's one problem out of the way.* He'd have three sets of eyes up there, besides his own and Amily. Surely that would be enough.

It was supposedly a routine Council meeting. The Council Chamber was . . . a bit stuffy, and Amily was doing her best to stay awake. Another long night listening to Lord Leverance's private conversations via his mastiff had left her feeling a bit groggy. A ridiculously indulgent breakfast with the King was not helping. He'd decided he'd reward her for her diligence by having some of her favorite treats, but the food threatened to put her to sleep. And although Amily usually appreciated the fact that the chairs in the Council Chamber were very comfortable, today she wished they were a little less so. Amily was sitting beside the King, listening to Lord Hallendale drone on about timber harvesting, concentrating on the great map of Valdemar on the wall opposite her seat at the table, reading the town names and seeing what she could remember from her reading about them one moment—

The next moment, Rolan quite literally shouted in her head—and by the way that Sedric and Kyril's heads snapped up, both of *them* had heard similar shouts from their Companions. *:Chosen! Battle in the street! We ride!:*

"I'll handle this, Father," Sedric said, vaulting over the table in order to get to the door faster. Amily couldn't quite do that, but she was hard on his heels in the next moment. She concentrated on *running*—it still wasn't easy for her, particularly on the slick floors of the Palace—knowing that Rolan could tell her what the situation was when she was firmly in the saddle and could spare attention for something besides where her feet were going. Sedric was ahead of her, but not so far that she couldn't tell which door he was heading for. That one should be her choice as well. Servants and courtiers had already cleared out of the way for the running Prince, and they remained that way as she passed, staring at her in confusion. She barely noted them except as potential obstacles.

I'm just glad something told me to wear my sword this morning. . . .

Kyril called after them, his voice echoing loudly in the Council Chamber to follow them as they pounded away. "Go! You have my full authority!"

They burst out of the nearest door, which was, thank goodness, only two rooms away; Rolan was waiting for her, and Sedric's Companion for him. Neither had had time to get saddled, but that didn't matter, not with a Companion. Sedric paused just long enough to grab Amily and throw her up onto Rolan's back. As Rolan shifted his weight to make sure she was in place, Sedric vaulted onto his own Companion's back like an acrobat or a trick rider, and then both of them were off, side by side, pounding through the gates and onto the road leading down into Haven.

:It's the Raeylens and the Chendlars, having a street-battle,: Rolan told her grimly. *:And almost everything we were dreading. Mags is in the middle of it—:*

She tried not to choke with fear, just twined her fingers in Rolan's mane, and listened to what he was telling her.

:I'm not sure how it started, but swords are out, people are wounded, and there's a mob and I am getting this in bits from Mags. He's up against Talbot Chendlar, trying to keep him from slaughtering Brand.:

And Talbot Chendlar was an expert swordsman . . . she bit her lip and hung on. They'd be there in a few moments. Talbot wasn't the only expert swordsman out there. Mags was good. . . .

But was he good enough to hold off Talbot?

The road between the mansions and small palaces was clear; it was too early for anyone but servants to be out and about in this weather. She couldn't imagine what on earth had brought a bunch of hotheaded highborn men—who should have been sleeping off whatever they had gotten into last night!—out at this time of the morning.

Already they could *hear* the mob, shouts and a few screams ahead of them—but behind them were more mounted Heralds coming to their aid. She could sense them back there, somehow, or maybe this was something she was getting from Rolan. These reinforcements would get to the mob nearly as soon as she and Sedric did.

:And behind them is the Guard,: Rolan told her. *:Nobody's died yet, and we'll make sure nobody does!:*

Then, they turned a corner and barreled into the mob itself. There was a wide place in the road where carriages could pass, and that was where they were battling. Amily had no real time to take in anything but the signs of blood on the snow and the flash of steel before Rolan shouldered right between two combatants and she and Sedric went to work.

Amily pulled her belt free and began laying about her with her sword still in its sheath, using it like a club, indiscriminately, because in a mob like this, there *was* no "wrong" or "right" side, there were just a lot of idiots who needed to have their heads ringing like bells so they'd calm down.

Rolan was shouldering people aside right and left; Amily

could only give thanks to the gods that the ingrained response to seeing a white hide and white clothing was to back off, because otherwise *they* surely would have been hurt. He paused and stood over a young man who was down on the snow, bleeding, until someone—presumably from his own side—yanked on his collar and got him to his feet.

It seemed to take forever before the rest of the Heralds from up on the Hill joined them, and either did what Amily and Sedric were doing with their sheathed swords, or forced their way through the mob, breaking it up into smaller pieces, then separating combatants by reaching down and grabbing hair or collars and pulling them apart. There seemed to be as many fighting with their fists as with their swords. The noise of shouting, swearing men only increased as combatants were driven apart, there were shallow wounds and blood everywhere, but Amily couldn't see anyone down other than that one lad she and Rolan had rescued—

And then, at last, came the Guard. Enough men to get *everyone* separated. And at last, Amily could see Mags off to her right, looking disheveled, and with a minor cut along his collarbone, but otherwise as far as she could tell, he was all right.

Now, finally, the noise died away to coughs, sniffling, and the shuffling of feet. The Guard surrounded the whole lot, penning them in, and virtually daring them to move with their glares. Sedric sent his Companion to the top of the slope so that they would all be looking up at him—and to compound their discomfort the sun was behind him, so they had to squint into its glare.

She wanted to run to Mags, but—no. That would be a very bad idea. Instead she flanked Sedric on his right, and the rest of the Heralds lined up behind them both. She didn't dare even show that she knew him, not when he was in character as Magnus. But she could see that his sword, like hers, was still in the sheath, and he must have been clubbing people rather than meeting steel with steel.

The Guards were angry. Angry enough they were forcing the former combatants to kneel in the snow before the Prince, and Sedric seemed very much inclined to let them do that. People were almost *never* required to kneel before a member of the Royal Family in Valdemar . . . but this was as good a time as any to remind these hotheads who their rulers were.

Finally there was silence and order. Amily looked out over the heads of about forty people kneeling in the snow of the street, all of them men, almost all of them young men . . . *almost.* Because right in the middle of the two sides were Lord Kaltar and Lord Leverance. *And Brand. And Talbot.* On the sidelines were women and a few men who must have come out of the great manors on either side of the road to watch; not all of them were wearing servants' livery. And surely they had been watching rather than participating, because the Guard had not rounded them up with the combatants.

There was complete silence now. Even the Companions were stock-still. Peoples' breath puffed out in white clouds, and that was the only sign that they weren't all statues.

"Good gods," Sedric spat at last in complete disgust, his voice sounding unnaturally loud in the stillness. "Good *gods.* I tell you to curb your servants, and *this* is how you interpret me? As license to brawl in the streets *yourselves?"*

"Prince Se—" Lord Kaltar began, looking up indignantly.

"Hold your tongue!" Sedric roared. "I do not care *who* started this. I do not care *how* it started. I do not care what lies you and Leverance are both spinning in your heads to excuse this barbaric behavior! What I *do* care about is that you both violated the Peace of the City, and the Peace of the Season, and *I will not have it."*

The silence deepened. Amily and the other Heralds sat as quietly as equestrian statues on their motionless Companions, and hopefully that very *stillness* was all the more unnerving to the men who were kneeling, shivering, in the snow.

"This feud ends. *Now,"* Sedric continued, staring from one

Lord to the other. "I have the means to force it to end. First, if *any* of you so much as looks askance at someone from the other family, you'll be cooling your heels in a city gaol until such time as you have the means to get back to your respective estates. Yes, that's right," he added, as heads came up with shocked looks. "The *commoner's gaol.* Where you will be sharing space with pickpockets and thugs and the like. Because if you are going to behave like brawling thugs, I am bloody well going to *treat* you like brawling thugs."

Amily was glad she was well practiced in keeping her expression absolutely neutral, because most of the men were looking at her and Sedric, not at the other Heralds—some of whom were having a hard time repressing their sardonic grins.

"As for the rest of my solution, I'm going to end this feud by ending the reason for it." He turned to Brand's father, his face filled with an implacable anger. "All of this was over a rejected marriage proposition. I'm going to rectify that right now. Lord Kaltar, you will be marrying your son to the eldest of Lord Leverance's daughters, and this will be accomplished within seven days, because I am going to start locking up one of each of your people every day after that if there is *not* a marriage, starting with Talbot and Brand."

Lord Kaltar went white, then red, then white again.

Sedric turned to Leverance. "Lord Leverance, I do not give a horse turd what your plans were, the eldest of your girls marries Brand, and it happens within seven days. Make your excuses if you'd started a betrothal, or send them to me and I'll inform them of the royal edict. You will do this. End of subject."

Leverance went purple. But he didn't even open his mouth to say a word.

Sedric's Companion stamped his hoof twice, to punctuate the order.

"And because your *women* aren't as stupid as you are, and I see no reason to punish *them,* the Crown will bear the cost of the wedding, the Crown will help make it happen, and the Crown will bestow on the new couple a fine estate of their own." He paused; Amily suspected he was conferring with his father in Mindspeech. "It appears that the land and manor of Abendale Hall are unclaimed, as Lord Abendale died this spring and no heir has been found to claim it. It is conveniently located between your two holdings, so that, should either of you idiots decide to march over and molest the other, you'll have to fight your way through the property and people of your own offspring." Sedric's eyes glinted wickedly. "You will now be escorted *one by one* back to your manors. Until a Guardsman taps you on the shoulder to let you know you may rise, *you will remain on your knees in the snow.*" He looked to the Captain of the Guard. "See to it. Anyone who can't follow orders, clap in irons and take down to the city gaol and we'll see what effect a night in straw among petty thieves has on their temper."

His Companion reared up on his hind hooves and pivoted in place. Rolan and the rest did the same a heartbeat later. And they all trotted back up the Hill to the Palace. Sedric did not look back, and Amily followed his example.

But once they got out of earshot, Sedric broke into angry speech. *"What* in the name of all the gods happened?" he demanded of Amily.

"Two nights ago Lord Leverance held a fete," she said, as she waited for Rolan to confer with Mags, who presumably knew exactly what had happened. "Brand got taken up by some maskers, and slipped in. Mags was with them, and he tells me that Talbot was in a murderous rage at the supposed 'insult,' although so far as I or anyone else knows, Brand was perfectly well behaved, danced a few dances, and left."

By this time, Rolan was able to tell her the rest, which she relayed to the Prince. "So this morning, evidently, with his temper not at all improved by a hangover, Talbot gathered up a gang of his cousins and went looking for Brand. And as bad luck would have it, he encountered Brand with a lot of *his* cousins coming down the Hill, heading for the city, as he and his lot came up, looking for them. There were a lot of insults. Mags says Brand was actually pretty conciliatory, mostly, although he also says it was a sort of 'sneering conciliatory,' so I suppose Talbot didn't take any of it as genuine. Then someone pulled a knife, and someone pulled a sword, and Talbot came for Brand." She swallowed hard. "And if Mags hadn't managed to jump in and deflect the first blow, and keep Talbot off Brand, Brand would be dead right now."

The sound of hooves on snow was all there was for a moment as Sedric digested that.

"Or at least wounded," Sedric said, sourly. "Idiots. Bloody idiots. I have no idea if this wedding is going to fix things or make them worse."

:I don't think it can make them worse,: Rolan observed.

"Rolan doesn't know about the fixing part, but he doesn't think it will make things worse," Amily told him. "There's *lots* of precedent for this. I can think of at least three feuds that former Kings and Queens ended with marriages, just off the top of my head without looking anything up. Of course," she added pensively, "in at least two of them, the families had managed to decimate each other to the point where it was hard to get a proper wedding party together. . . ."

Sedric waved that away. "Never mind that. The Council is going to want to know on what authority I ordered this wedding to take place, and I need all the precedent you can dig up." He turned to Amily, some of the anger drained out of him, reached across the space between them and patted her on the shoulder. "So, King's Own, tell me what you know."

———

Mags returned to Amily's rooms after seeing the Healer for the long, shallow cut on his collarbone and the other along his ribs. They weren't bad, but they stung even after actual Healing sessions that sealed them up so they wouldn't keep breaking open and bleeding all over his clothing. He was fervently blessing the reflexive movements he had "learned" from his cousin Bey; all that fancy assassin-technique had kept him from a lot worse. He'd managed to evade Talbot's blade more times than he cared to think about; the man was *infernally* quick, and had reflexes like the King of the Cats. *I'm lucky I got away with a couple of scratches is all.*

But if he hadn't kept engaging Talbot, the man *would* have run Brand through, of this much he was certain.

He opened the door, already sensing that the rooms were empty. He felt a sudden surge of depression that Amily wasn't there, although realistically he knew she must be up to her eyebrows in the consequences of today's near-battle. He felt himself sagging a little as the door closed behind him.

:She's with the King, Sedric and her father,: Dallen informed him. *:They're dealing with all of the repercussions of this nonsense. Lady Dia is going to join them shortly. I told Rolan to tell her you'd seen the Healers and you are all right. She's—:*

There was a knocking at the door, and Mags turned back around, *just* as he had reached his comfortable chair, and went back to it. But his sigh turned into a smile when he saw that there were three Palace servants there, all of them bearing trays with dishes, bottles, plates, bowls and baskets on them.

Without any prompting or directions on his part, they went straight to the largest table in the main room and began setting up their burdens on it. It didn't take them very long at all, for which he was grateful, for the entire mess had wound up with him kneeling in the snow well past lunchtime. Of course he hadn't dared try and get any special treatment. That would have given him away entirely. So he got treated as what he was, a lower-level courtier, somewhere around the lesser cousins in importance. No one asked him why he'd gotten involved, he was treated as just as guilty as the rest of them. Which at least not only maintained, it strengthened his persona, but still. . . .

The servants hurried back out again, hardly waiting to hear his thanks. He sat himself down in a chair and reached for the nearest plate. It was good. It was more than good. It was fantastic. Bread so fresh it steamed when he broke it open, a stew that made him sigh with pleasure, baked squash with honey . . . lovely little iced cakes . . .

When he had finished, he carefully moved everything left over to the hearth to keep it warm for Amily, and went to lie down on the bed. He hadn't expected to doze off, but it had been a very long day, he'd spent a lot of energy out there shivering in the cold, and his wounds more or less stopped hurting as much when he got flat. He didn't realize he was still cold until he pulled a heavy blanket over himself and felt himself relaxing in the warmth. And the next thing that he knew, Amily was shaking his shoulder, and the westering light was coming in the windows, showing it was at least a couple candlemarks later than it had been when he'd stretched out.

"Much as I hate to do this to you," she said apologetically, "I need the eyewitness recitation of events before it gets any dimmer in your mind."

" 'Sall right," he said, rubbing his eyes and wincing as his cuts burned again. He sat up slowly, and perched on the edge of the bed. "It happened like this. . . ."

His account differed substantially from any other she might have gotten in this much: He'd been near enough to Brand—he'd been *protecting* Brand—that he could see the smug expression on Brand's face, and hear some of the low-voiced taunts that Brand had been delivering. Brand had, in fact, been hiding behind him, but egging Talbot on.

"What—what was he thinking?" Amily gasped. "Was he trying to get you killed?"

Mags shook his head. "I don' think so. I don' think 'e intended anythin' worse'n having some'un t' use as a shield whilst 'e poked at Talbot. Not sure 'e even knew it was me."

Brand had been utterly focused on Talbot—as focused on Talbot as Lord Kaltar had been on Lord Leverance. Mags truly did not think that Brand saw anyone other than Talbot—and Talbot had been just as obsessed with Brand. It had been— almost the polar opposite of a lifebond. Like they were bound from birth by hate.

Amily shook her head when he said that. "For all I know, they were. Most things have an opposite, maybe there *is* an opposite to a lifebond. I can't think of any other reason why he'd be so obsessed with someone he never even met until this Midwinter Season."

Well . . . Mags could. Brand and Talbot had been taught from their cradles to hate each other. That was reason enough.

Most of the taunts had gone right over Mags' head; he had no idea what incidents they referred to. All that he knew for certain was that they drove Talbot insane, and he said as much.

But as Amily listened, he saw her eyes widen, and her hand went to her mouth. Finally, when he was done, she let out her breath, as if she had been holding it. "Well. If all that means what I think it does . . . Brand knows that Talbot has been sleeping with Lady Leverance."

Mags nearly tore open his wounds as he jerked with surprise and shock. *"What?"* he gasped.

"I'd begun to suspect as much," Amily went on. "The signs are extremely subtle, but . . . well." She shrugged. "They have to be very, very good at hiding what they are doing from her husband."

He shook his head. "Makes me wonder how Brand figgered it out."

"Same way as anyone else finds out things around here," Amily said with a shrug. "They paid off the right servant. Or they installed a spy in the form of a servant right in the household. You know you can't hide anything from the servants."

"Well, not that sorta thing, anyway," he agreed. And she was right, of course, that was why he himself was going to cultivate servants in selected households. He rubbed his side. "Didja eat?"

"Yes, and thank you for keeping it warm." She sat down beside him—on his good side—and gave him a long, loving kiss. "We ended up not eating much. Stuffing our faces in front of Lady Leverance and Lady Dia would have been rude."

Part of him just wanted to lie back down again. He'd been leading a double and triple life ever since this mess started, and he just wanted to rest. But of course, this was no time to rest. "Anythin' I need to know?"

She shook her head. "Not much. It was the start of wedding planning. Our main problem is we need a neutral spot that is big enough to hold both Houses for the betrothal feast. The King doesn't want it in the Palace and neither does the Commander of the Palace Royal Guard; I think they are afraid hostilities might break out and they don't want that here."

Well, he could see both sides of that argument. On the one hand, the Palace would be the perfect place. Plenty of Guards and Heralds right at hand to break up anything, and the room could be secured. On the other hand . . . plenty of innocents in the form of servants, other residents of the Palace, and Trainees to get hurt.

But the King had the last word and the King had said "Not in the Palace," so. . . . "I expect most of the Guildhalls'd have the same objections," he said, wracking his brain to think of an acceptable venue. Something big. If it were summer, they could pitch a giant pavilion or even hold it out in the open—

"—bloody hell," he said, realizing he'd just recently laid eyes on the perfect spot. "There's a theater troupe down in Haven fer the Midwinter Fair. They got a portable theater down there. Plenty of space. Ye kin heat 'er up with braziers. Off in the commons, so if trouble breaks out, well. . . ." he shrugged.

"The King said, rather acidly, that if trouble broke out during the betrothal feast, and there was no need to rescue innocent bystanders, he was inclined to let them slaughter each other and punish whoever was left standing," Amily informed him.

:I can even hear that in Kyril's voice,: Dallen observed.

"Well, 'e don't mean it," Mags said, with a sigh of resignation. "Or . . . 'e means it, but 'e won't do it. Anyways, go hev a look at it, I think it might do. 'Tis wood walls with a canvas roof, an' ye kin pretty it up however ye like. Hellfire, with Crown money, ye kin hang tapestries over ever' bit of the wall, an' make it look like th' Palace."

"I'll leave that to Lady Dia," Amily said firmly. "But it sounds as if you've found a good compromise solution. It's equally inconvenient to everyone, it is on a neutral spot, and it is far away from the Palace. It's actually *quite* convenient to set up an outdoor kitchen there, which should make serving the feast easy enough."

"Fair'll still be on. Ye could arrange fer a couple of the food vendors t'supply the feast," he suggested, knowing that there were merchants down at the Fair who supplied surprisingly high priced and highly sought-after goods of all kinds, including foodstuffs.

"Even better. I shall leave that part to the King's cook and Lady Dia." She sighed, and put her head on his shoulder. "My poor love, it seems that the one who has had the worst of all of this wretched mess is you."

"An' when it was yer pa that was doin' this job, it was him," he reminded her.

"I don't ever remember him coming home stabbed and slashed—" she began, but he interrupted her.

"You was his little girl. Ye think he would'a let you know thet?" He could not help but notice that his low-class accent was very thick at the moment; a sign he was more tired than he thought. Then again, shivering in the cold was actually pretty exhausting. "He prolly figgered part of his job was t'keep ye from knowin' all the worst parts, so ye wouldn' be afeerd for 'im."

Her mouth quirked up on one side in a sardonic smile. "Yes, that would be just like him, too. Promise me you won't try to *protect* me that way, please."

He had to laugh at that. "Ye think I'd hev a chance in hell of doin' thet, with both of us Heralds? 'Tis a good thing Companions don't outright *talk,* they're the worst at keepin' secrets of anyone I ever saw."

:Hey!: Dallen objected, as Amily laughed unexpectedly.

"Rolan just *harrumphed* in my head," she giggled. "It's . . . the most extraordinary sensation!"

He had to laugh himself. "Bet it is. Well, by yer leave, m'love, I'm beat. Jest fer once, I'm gonna not show up t' keep an eye on Brand. 'E'd prolly be more suspicious of me iffen I did, anyroad, seein' as I was leakin' blood all over afore I was give leave t'go see a Healer."

"Get some sleep, then," she agreed. "I'll be late, I expect."

"Wouldn' argue if ye was t'send round a couple more pages with vittles," he suggested, pulling off his boots and wiggling his toes.

She stood up and kissed him, which made his toes curl, and the rest of him regret that she was going out the door in a few moments. "I'll see about satisfying one of your appetites, anyway," she smiled.

And then she was gone.

———————

Violetta cowered a little in the chair she had been ordered to take. There was no fire in her father's study, and she was cold, despite her heavy woolen gown. She, her two sisters, and their mother were all lined up as if they were on trial, sitting nervously in hard wooden chairs in Lord Leverance's private study. Father strode up and down before his assembled family, his face a study in wrath. Talbot had already been dealt with, and not gently, despite Mother's attempt at intervention. Now, it seemed, there was something Father needed to impart to his family. She hoped that was all it was.

Really, he ought to count himself lucky that Father didn't beat him black and blue—or worse, order the servants to beat him, Violetta thought, hoping against hope that whatever disaster had befallen, Father was *not* going to somehow manage to transfer some of the blame to her and her sisters.

If Mother had anything to do with this, she can defend herself. She indulges Talbot to a ridiculous measure.

At the moment, she was rather vague as to what had actually happened. She had been up in her room, sitting by the window while she worked on her embroidery, and dreamily thinking about last night with Brand, when there had been a commotion downstairs. She had run to the stairs and down to the first floor, only to see Father and some of the cousins hurtling out of the door, armed, while her mother shrieked and wailed at him.

Then there had been a long, long time while her mother collapsed, weeping, on the hearth, and the servants milled about, uncertain what to do.

Then just when everyone was fearing all manner of terrible things, the first of the Leverance household returned. It had been Father, Talbot, and two of the closest cousins. And Father had been in such a perfect rage that Violetta had fled back up to her room with her little dog right at her heels, closed the door, and cowered in her bed, cuddling Star against her chest.

There had been a *lot* of shouting. Some of it had been quite clear. Things like "You would have been better off if that bastard Raeylen had run you through!" and "You insolent puppy, who do you think is the head of this household, me or you?"

By that alone, it was fairly easy to intuit that it was Talbot who was the cause of the debacle, and Talbot who Father was shouting at. Only Talbot dared to push the limits of Father's edicts.

Whatever Talbot had done, it was clear he was in a great deal of trouble. There was no doubt he'd transgressed far past his ordinary behavior, when Violetta had ventured down to get something to eat from the kitchen. That was when she got the sketchy details that there had been fighting, and heard that he had been sent packing, with only his horse and what his horse could carry, back to the estate.

By this point, Mother was weeping hysterically in the Great Hall as Father raged at the rest of the cousins, so Violetta had just taken what the cook would give her and fled back to her room. The cook was thoroughly rattled, and had just pressed things into her hands, shaking the entire time. It had been a very odd meal. A bowl of stewed, dried fruit, half a small loaf of bread, a sausage, and an entire pan of double-cream.

She had hidden up there, until just now, when Father had sent servants for them all and lined them up in his study. Mother's face was still streaked with tears. Brigette and Aleniel sat like a pair of statues. Violetta didn't know *what* to think, but as a precaution, she had locked Star in her room. Having to clean up an "accident" on the floor would be better than trying to protect her dog from Father in a rage. Just because he treated her indulgently, it did not follow that he would spare her his anger. She had discovered *that* quite young.

Finally, he stopped pacing, and abruptly turned to face them all.

He crossed his arms tightly over his chest. His face was quite red. This did not bode well.

"That damned puppy, Talbot, has managed to destroy nearly everything I have worked for," he growled. "I told him to leave the Raeylen whelp alone, but no. He'd have none of that. So we had fighting in the streets, and not just the servants, who we could *dismiss* as being stupid clods who didn't know any better, oh no. This was a gang of the cousins, led by Talbot, acting like a damned lot of street bravos, and not down in Haven, but up *here,* on the Hill, where the King could damned well *not* ignore it! Gods be my witness, I've owned *geese* with more sense!"

Violetta felt the blood drain from her face, and clutched the arms of her chair in sudden faintness. The Raeylen whelp? That could only be *Brand!* And cousin Talbot had gone for him—Talbot, the best swordsman she had ever seen, Talbot, who had left more than one man for dead—

Her vision darkened. She wanted to cry out, to beg her father to tell her how Brand was—was he hurt? Was he dying? Was he dead? But the words stuck in her throat as she tried to keep from fainting. And her father kept right on with his tirade, oblivious to her reaction.

"So! The Prince was sent to sort us out according to the Royal whim, and everything I have been working for the *entire* time we have been here is in shambles!" The anger in his voice made it harsh and grating. "Everything! Gone! And I am left to try and make something in the ruins!"

She fought through her faintness until her vision cleared. When she could see again, her father had turned toward her sisters.

"*You—*" he continued, stabbing a finger at a startled Aleniel "—are ordered to be betrothed to that Raeylen whelp in seven days' time by the Prince himself, Gods save me!"

Relief washed over her—*he's alive! He's all right!*— followed by bewilderment. *What? Aleniel? Marrying* my Brand? *How—why? No! This isn't possible! This can't be!* She put one hand to her temple, feeling as if she had been struck a terrible blow and her senses had all been set askew. This could not be happening! Surely she had heard this wrong!

"And never mind that the ink's not yet dry on the contract to Lord Peramir!" Father shouted. "Hell's Pits! The match of a lifetime, and . . ." he sputtered for a moment, then got control of himself. "Not to mention a violated contract! He could claim your dower, girl, for the insult, and never mind it was the Prince that ordered it!"

"But my lord—he did not—" Mother ventured, and Father calmed himself somewhat. "Lord Peramir has graciously said he understands that a Royal Command is not to be disobeyed, and you should tell the girls how I have arranged matters."

"No, my lord is a reasonable man," Father growled, "And since Aleniel is being given lands and a manor of her own with her marriage to the Raeylen pup, I am not obliged to give one single copper of Chendlar dower into that skinflint bastard Kaltar's hands, and I have no intention of doing so."

Now Father turned to her, and Violetta was still so stunned she could not think, could only stare at him, stricken to the heart. *Brand! My Brand! Given to Aleniel!*

"Lord Peramir has graciously agreed to take you, Violetta, in your sister's place, even though you've none of her talents that make her so valuable to someone like him, and I'll be able to settle what would have been Aleniel's dower on you." Father stared at her as she sat dumb in her chair. "So, you'll be marrying one of the highest lords in the land. You'll be ahead of even the Lady Dia. What do you have to say for yourself, child?"

She stared up at him, stricken with horror. She had only seen Lord Peramir once, but there could not have been a human being who was *less* like Brand in all of Valdemar. He was tall, thin, *old, old, old,* with a face set in a permanent expression of disapproval, and cold, pebble-like eyes. He didn't dance. He didn't converse. He probably disapproved of poetry. He would expect her to care for him, make medicines and potions to soothe him . . . and be in his bed, with his terrible, old body next to hers, doing things—doing things to her that only *Brand* should do! *I'd rather die!* she thought frantically. *I'd rather die!* His skin was like old parchment, his breath stank, he probably had awful things wrong with him—

And he wasn't Brand!

Finally, she shook off her paralysis. *"No!"* she cried out, and flung herself at Father's feet, weeping. She clutched his shoes with both hands, sobbing hysterically. "No, no, no! Oh Father, please, do not ask this of me! I cannot wed—I am too young—I cannot wed—"

"What? *Ask* this of you?" he thundered, grabbing her by the back of her neck and pulling her to her feet. "By all the gods, I am not *asking* you, mistress, I am *telling* you! You are my daughter, you are my property, in law and under the gods! You *will* be wed to this good man, and you will *thank* me for it!"

"I cannot!" she cried, and tried to drop to her knees, but could not, because of the painful hold he had on her. She hung in his hands like a rabbit in the jaws of his mastiff. "Oh Father, good Father, I pray you! I cannot wed this man! I am not worthy! I cannot wed him! I cannot love him! Pray you, pray pardon me! Give him to Brigette, and let me stay unwed! Please, please spare me!" Tears poured from her eyes, which blurred so much that she could not see. Her chest constricted painfully, and she pawed weakly at his chest in entreaty.

"Pray me not! Rather pray to the gods I do not strangle you as is my right!" His face was practically purple with rage. "You thankless tart! You miserable viper! You will go to marry his Lordship with a smile on your face, or by all that is holy I shall drag you there myself by the hair! No!" he interrupted her, as she was about to choke something out, her entire body convulsing with shivering sobs. "Say nothing! Not one word will I hear! You will wed him, or by my right hand I will throw you into the street, or sell you to a bawdy house myself, you vile little brat!"

"My Lord!" Mother gasped out, white as her linen chemise.

"Am I Lord of this house or no?" he roared, and let Violetta go; she dropped groveling and weeping, at his feet. "I say I am Lord of this House, and my word is law!"

She looked up at him through eyes streaming with tears; she hardly recognized him, he was so changed by rage.

"By the gods, this is driving me mad!" he howled, stamping one foot and narrowly missing her hand. "It has been all my work to wed my girls worthily. Talbot undoes the half of that work, and when I come to salvage what remains, and present to you, ungrateful little bitch-dog, a fine man, a worthy man, a man of higher estate than *ever* you could have looked to, what do you do? Do you thank me with tears in your eyes, that he is willing to take you despite the fact that you are nothing more than a feckless, talentless child, unfit to care for him in his old age? No! It is *I will not wed* and *I cannot wed,* and *I cannot love* and *pray pardon me!* Well, I'll not pardon you! I've over-indulged you, I see! I've two good, dutiful daughters who know that obedience is due to their father, and will wed where he tells them! I do not need you! I tell you now, you *will* wed Lord Peramir before Midwinter Season is over, or I will turn you out of the house into the snow in your shift and you will never more call me Father!"

He turned on the others, as Violetta lay in a weeping, hysterical heap on the stone floor. "Leave her! Maybe she will come to her senses! And if she does not, she's no child of mine!"

And with that, he drove Mother and her sisters out before him, and slammed the door behind him, leaving her in the dark.

Somehow Violetta had gotten herself to her room, let her puppy out, and locked the door behind her again. She didn't remember any of it—not getting to her feet, not leaving Father's study, not climbing the stair. She came to herself standing with her back to the locked door, tears still streaming down her face, neck and shoulder aching with bruises, her mind in a whirl of horror. Once safely locked inside, she flung herself into her bed, weeping, weeping, and that was where Brand found her when he came in through her bedroom window.

She only knew he was there when he sat down beside her,

and gently pulled her up to rest her head on his shoulder. "Shhh," he said. "Hush now, sweeting. Why all these tears? Can't you be happy that I managed to survive your murderous cousin?" He chuckled. "The gods themselves know he tried hard enough to kill me, but it is he that is on the road to the country, and I who am still here, unscathed." His arms around her were warm; she sank into them as if they were a haven, and yet, she wept because the haven was so soon to be taken from her.

"You live—but you wed my *sister!*" she sobbed. "And I am to marry that hideous old man she was betrothed to! I hate him! I hate him! He is old, and cold, and ugly!"

"Well, that *is* the Prince's decree," he agreed, and held her even closer than before. "But am I not a clever fellow? And don't you think I have been considering this from the moment the words came from his mouth? And don't you think I have hit upon a solution that will make your evil old man vanish like snow in the spring?"

His calm reply stopped her tears for the moment, and she gulped, wiping her eyes with the back of her hand. "You have?" She moved her head to peer up at him, but her vision was so blurry she could not make out his face.

He tilted her chin up with one hand, and kissed her. "Of course I have. And the first thing you have to understand is that, the truth is, the Prince really doesn't care *which* Chendlar daughter I marry, as long as I marry one of you. But!" He stilled her with one finger on her lips. "He's *said* it must be the eldest, and a Prince cannot be gainsaid. His word is his word, and even if I went to him and explained. . . ." He shook his head. "He would tell me he had given his word. Your father would rail and rage, because even if he was going to be able to give that ugly old man the wife *he* wanted, the very fact that *I* asked for something different would make him oppose me. And no one would ask *your* preference. Besides, if I went and pled our case to the Prince, there would be . . . questions. And certain examinations. And the result of those would be disastrous for you."

"Then I am lost!" she sobbed, looking up into his face, feeling tears scalding her cheeks again, and her heart burning with pain inside her.

He put his hand on her lips, silencing her. "So, I minded me of what I heard an old Guardsman once say, *It is better and easier to ask forgiveness than get permission,* and a brilliant plan came to me, all at once. You and I shall hoodwink them all."

Hope rose in her again. "We will?" she faltered.

"And here is how. First, you will tell your father that you will marry. You will go to him, and beg his forgiveness, and tell him that you were afraid, terrified that Lord Whatever would come to despise you quickly, and that you are afraid, wedding so great a man, that you cannot manage his household, that his servants will be contemptuous of you, and never obey you, and he will leave you in some remote, leaking old tower somewhere all alone." He nodded as she bit her lip. She could all too easily imagine just that happening. *Even if I had not had Brand . . .* She thought of Lord Peramir, and shuddered.

He held her tighter. "You can do this. I know you can. Because it will be for us, little sweeting! It will be to ensure our future!"

"For that . . ." she gulped. "For that, I can do this."

"Good. Now listen to the rest, for here is where I am terribly clever." She held her breath. "There will be a great betrothal feast, of course; the Prince said the Crown is paying for it, so you may be sure it will be as large as your father can arrange on such short notice."

"But . . . if I am to see you and Aleniel . . ." Her voice broke. "I cannot bear it! I cannot bear it!"

He laughed. "You will not have to. *You,* my love, will stay here at home, saying you are not well. And I am sure that no

one will care that you remain here. Why should they? It will
not matter, you are not the intended bride, after all. Your sister
is probably jealous of how young and pretty you are, and will
be glad you are not there to rival her."

"But I do not see—" she began.

"Let me finish," he admonished, and she flushed. "Once
they are all merry and have drunk too much of the bridal wine,
I will make my excuses and slip away. And I will come for you,
and you and I will make our way to a priest I know who will
marry us, and once we are wed, we will present ourselves to
the King the first thing in the morning and beg forgiveness."
His eyes were shining in the darkness, and she listened to
him, awestruck at his audacity and cleverness. "Oh, I shall be
so eloquent! I will tell him of your beautiful letter, how it
moved me, how I was in love with you before I even met you,
and when I met you, I was so smitten I knew that it *must* be a
lifebond! Not even the King himself would gainsay a lifebond,
now, would he, my little violet?"

She shook her head. "I don't think so. . . ." she said, hesitantly.

"So there you are." His voice was full of self-satisfaction.
"The King will be satisfied, because he will have our Houses
bound. The Prince will be moved by our tale of true love. Your
father may be angry with you, but what of it? We will have
our own lands, and the lands of Raeylen when my father dies.
My father is *already* angry, and at the Prince, not at us; at
worst, this will tickle him because it will be tweaking the nose
of the Prince *and* your father. Your sister will have that cold
old man that she wanted in the first place, and I wish her joy
of him." He laughed. "There. Now tell me, am I not the clever-
est fellow in all of the Kingdom?"

She nearly flung herself at him with joy. "You are!" she
exclaimed. "Oh! You are!"

"Then why don't you *show* me how much you appreciate
me," he said, and began to untie her laces.

Lady Dia had taken one look at the theater and declared that it was the perfect venue for the betrothal feast. The acting troupe was perfectly willing to give up their theater, when Mags was able to make arrangements with one of the biggest inns in Haven for them to continue their performances in the central courtyard. With Lady Leverance pretty much giving over complete control of the entire ceremony to her, Dia was able to work at what to Amily seemed to be an insane speed. She arranged for fancy charcoal braziers, fabric to drape the walls, wood to be laid down to form a solid floor, many-branched candlesticks and oil lamps to provide light, cooks and bakers to supply the feast . . . in short, everything that could possibly be needed.

This left Amily to actually *do her job.* Which was a relief. The Leverance household was in an uproar; a betrothal gown had to be fitted to Aleniel at short notice, Brigette was sulking because Lord Leverance had not simply handed the plum potential husband down to *her,* but had bestowed Lord Peramir on Violetta. Instead, it appeared Brigette was going to get Guildmaster Harl Kenton, unless something went drastically wrong, but for now, everything other than the betrothal of Brand and Aleniel was on hold.

Violetta was . . . well, definitely not herself. She was spending most of her time in her room, although no one seemed to notice because they were all so busy preparing for Aleniel's betrothal.

Was she still obsessed, or at least, infatuated with Brand?

I would give it an absolute certainty, she thought, watching Violetta leaf listlessly through a book, looking thinner and paler than Amily had ever seen her look before. *And now . . . she is watching her sister make off with the boy* she *wanted, and the poor little thing is going to be shackled to an old, cold man who was looking for a nurse, not a wife. Poor little thing.*

Amily wanted to somehow reach the girl and give her a hug. Not that this would help in the least.

:She is no worse off than most young women, you know, and much better *off than most,:* Rolan mused. *:He can't live more than ten years, she will still be young when he dies, rich, and with a lofty title—:*

:Rolan, ten years is more than half her current lifespan,: Amily reminded her Companion tartly. *:You might think of it from that perspective.:*

Rolan sighed in her mind. *:She could be poor. She could be starving. She could be married to a man who will beat her. The world is not kind to so many people in it—but we both know if you try to point these things out to her, it will mean nothing in the face of the pain* she *is feeling.:*

There was no good answer. The world was not kind to far too many people.

:So . . . if you will take my advice, you will suggest to Dia that she take Violetta under her wing. At least she will have someone near her age to socialize with. Even if she will not be precisely happy, *she won't be miserable.:* Rolan waited for her answer, and she had to admit, he had a good idea.

:Meanwhile—: he prompted.

:Meanwhile, Violetta is the least of my problems,: she admitted, and switched her point of view to Lord Leverance's mastiff.

After that epic display of temper when he nearly murdered Violetta for daring to object to his plans for her life, she wanted to keep an eye on him.

————————

Mags strolled into Lord Kaltar's hall, to find Brand lounging in front of the fire. "Well, the man of the hour," he said, hoping he didn't sound too sardonic. "What are you doing here? I thought you'd be—"

"Mucking about with betrothal nonsense? Why?" Brand countered. "There's no need for me. All of that is in the hands of my *charming* betrothed's family. I really don't even need a new suit of clothes, and frankly, I don't intend to get one." He shrugged. "I suppose the girl is presentable enough. I'll follow the Prince's orders. And I hope I'll discover when I take control of the lands and manor he's bestowing on me, that it will provide me with the income to get what I *really* want."

"Lelage," said Mags, unsurprised. "So that's why you're not kicking at the traces."

"Nor trying to throw off the collar. Which completely *infuriates* my father." Brand poked at the fire broodingly. "He seems to think we can do something to engineer the downfall of the Chendlars, somehow. I have no idea what he thinks we can do at this stage. Well—I could do *one* thing, I could refuse to get the wench with child, but that would be rather counterproductive as it would leave us without a Raeylen heir, and in the meantime, one of the other two Chendlar girls would be spawning away in service of *their* house. So?" He poked the fire. "I shall let father rage to all and sundry, and plot, and go ahead and marry and get myself out from under his tyrannical thumb at last."

Well, this was new . . . Mags poured cups of wine for himself and Brand, and brought Brand's over to him. Brand took it with a nod of thanks. As Mags had hoped, the wine and his own silence loosened Brand's tongue.

"I envy you, you know," Brand said, with a lifted eyebrow. "I envy the fact that you don't have someone looming over you, day and night, demanding that you live up to some impossible family standard. That you shape your entire life, not around what *you* want, but around what *he* thinks is best for the 'family.' Do you know what he actually screamed at me when we finally all got back up here?"

Mags shook his head.

"He wanted to know why I hadn't taken the opportunity to

kill Leverance when I had it." Brand shook his head. "Never once asked me about how Talbot was trying to cut me to ribbons. All he wanted to know was why I hadn't joined him to take out Leverance and spent a good candlemark shouting at me. The only reason he didn't go at it longer was because he had other people to shout at." His face hardened. "Good gods, I hate him. Nothing I do has ever satisfied him, nothing I *will* do will ever satisfy him. Nothing would please me more than—" He stopped himself. "Never mind. He's off somewhere, probably telling someone what a disappointment I am to him. Once I have lands and money of my own, it won't matter. I'll be able to do exactly what I want."

"That's true enough," Mags agreed.

"Just a few more days," Brand muttered. "Just a few more days."

Since he showed no signs of planning to get up and go anywhere, Mags just poured him another cup of wine and took his leave. He was overdue for checking with his sources down in Haven anyway, and today would be a good day to take care of that.

But Brand's words did seem very curious. Because in "a few more days," he'd be betrothed, not married; he wouldn't be able to take possession of the lands and manor the King was going to give him until the vows were said.

But he shrugged it off. *Maybe he figures on persuading the girl to get married quickly,* he thought. And really, that would not be a bad idea. It would get Lord Kaltar out of Haven, even if it didn't get his rival out as quickly. It would get Brand away from poor little Violetta, who was probably *very* unhappy, not only because her infatuation was getting wed to her sister, but because *she* was about to be tied up to a man old enough to be her great-grandsire. On the latter, he couldn't blame her. It was bad enough that these people regarded marriage as a sort of dynastic and financial contract, but it was worse that they

ended up putting together couples who were so wildly un-
suited for each other.

And worst of all? That they treated their women like some
sort of superior livestock whose only purpose in life was to
breed and to serve.

Cole Pieters was like that, too.

It occurred to him that maybe he and Amily could convince
the King to do something about the girl's match . . . but what
could they do? And wouldn't that still be treating her like potential breeding stock, just suggesting she be bartered off to a
slightly more desirable man?

He wished the poor thing had some interest other than
sappy poetry. Or . . . well . . . some backbone. Then, maybe,
they could convince the King or the Prince to become her pa-
trons and get her more education, give her a chance to have
an independent life, and then she'd have some choices, informed choices, not a life forced on her. . . .

Might as well wish for the moon, he thought glumly. And
he had to remind himself of something he'd been told over
and over in so many lessons. . . *you can't save everyone, so
save the ones you can.* Easy to agree with, though, when you
were nodding along to what the teacher was telling you. Hard
not to feel guilty when you saw so much misery. And really,
how "miserable" was she? She was unhappy, certainly, but
there was real misery down in the slums of Haven, where
people were trying to figure out where their next meal was
coming from.

*But hell, for all I know, she'll be happy, once she gets over
bein' unhappy. Never heard nothin' bad about the old man.
Might jest be reserved, not cold. Might open up to 'er. They
might come to like each other just fine.*

He could hope, couldn't he? And meanwhile he could get
down to his lads in the city. *Them,* he was certainly able to
save.

Squashed into the carriage with her mother and her two sisters, Violetta rubbed her temple, and not at all surreptitiously. Brand had told her to make some excuse to get away once the betrothal ceremony was done, but she was not actually having to feign feeling ill. She actually *was* feeling ill. Her courses had started—they had begun late, but thanks to the blood on the sheets the night Brand had first loved her, Nurse thought they were early, and that they had come early due to all the excitement. There was a dull ache in her gut and a pounding in her head. While they were dressing Aleniel, she'd said something about it, quietly, but no one had noticed except Nurse, who'd done her best in the middle of all the fuss but—

Well, no one was paying any heed to her or how miserable she really, truly felt. Everyone's attention was on Aleniel.

Aleniel was in fine fettle, with rose in her cheeks, and her eyes sparkling, clearly relishing her chance at being the center of everything. Candlemarks had been spent on making sure her new gown—deep blue velvet with sleeves lined with fur and a fur collar, over a chemise of creamy lambswool as soft as silk—fitted perfectly. Another had been spent on her hair and the wreath of wax flowers that sat on it. She'd had a special betrothal bath full of scent, rose scent had been liberally applied to her, she had been gowned and coiffed, and a magnificent fur cloak, gift from Lady Dia, had been placed over her shoulders. She'd been bathed and dressed in the ladies' solar, after all the men had been chased away from that part of the manor. Then there had been the fuss of getting her into a carriage and down to the remade theater.

No one paid any attention to anything else. So far as everyone else in her family was concerned, Violetta had been, more or less, excess baggage.

When they arrived, Violetta saw that the theater was surrounded with guards, but they were not of the Valdemar Guard, nor her father's men, nor those of Lord Kaltar. No, these were paid men, hired by the Crown, and presumably that was because they would be absolutely neutral and not take any sides if some altercation broke out. They looked very odd, with their helms and lances wreathed with holly and ivy. Comical in a way, though Violetta had been feeling too uncomfortable to laugh at them.

When Violetta trailed after her sister into the refurbished theater, she was astounded at the transformation that Lady Dia had made to it. First of all, it blazed with light. The somewhat shabby walls were hidden behind hangings of green baize. Panels of tapestry had been pinned on the soft wool at intervals, and the upper selvages were hidden with garlands of holly, ivy, and evergreen branches. Braziers stood along the walls, not only warming the air, but adding the perfume of pine cones. Hundreds of candles and dozens of lanterns added both heat and light, and underfoot was a laid wooden floor she could not have told was not gracing some home. Only the canvas roof gave the origin away, and even that was bedecked with more garland swags, draped from the center (where the centerpole propped up the canvas) to each corner of the structure.

There were two tables—one for the members and allies of each House—and Violetta took her place where she was told. You could not see the table itself, it might have been boards laid over trestles for all she could tell, for it had been draped with more green baize, and whatever supports were under it had been swathed in more of the stuff. Candles and lanterns stood in centerpieces of nuts, apples, and pears all along its length, and trencher-bread was already at each place, waiting to hold the feast meats.

There was also a smaller table at the far end, set at right angles to the rest. That would be for Aleniel. . . .

. . . and Brand. . . .

It was like a knife to the heart every time she had to think of the two of them together. Tears sprang to her eyes as she took her place on the stool she had been shown to, and she bowed her head and reminded herself that all this was just a farce, a show. And tonight she would be Brand's bride, and *nothing* would undo that.

But it was hard, so hard, to sit through the betrothal ceremony.

It began as soon as all the seats at the tables were filled. Brand and Aleniel stood behind their table, as the Prince presided, solemn-faced. This was only a betrothal, of course, not a wedding, so there was no priest, just the reading of the contract, and the recitation of promises to hold to the contract.

It's tawdry, Violetta told herself, desperately. *It's not about love, it's about business, and ending a stupid feud. They don't love each other, the only thing Aleniel cares about is the title, the manor and the lands.*

But it was so hard, listening to Aleniel recite her vows in a proud voice, and hearing Brand repeat his, sounding much more subdued. It got harder, as they put their names to the

contract . . . and as the Prince declared them formally betrothed it felt worst of all. Her insides were twisting up, and it
was all she could do not to break down in tears right then and
there. *That should have been me!*

It was cold comfort to know that the moment the Prince
held up the signed contract should have been the moment for
enthusiastic applause—and that moment was marked only by
tepid handclapping, quickly cut short.

That seemed to satisfy the Prince however. He waited until
Aleniel and Brand took their seats at their little table, and took
his leave with his entourage.

The serving of the feast began. At the table across the way,
Lord Kaltar was holding forth on horses, and pedigrees, with
some sly glances at her father. Father was ignoring him, and
holding forth on trade. The two families might just as well
have been at two different feasts.

No one had been allowed anything larger than the tiny
little eating knives that were at each place. The only people
armed were the guards.

The first course came in; bowls of pottage, a Boar's Head,
baked waterfowl, and custard tarts. The carvers began on the
Boar's Head (one for each table) and the waterfowl; the one at
Violetta's place, which she would share with five other people,
was a goose. But the entrance of the servers with their platters
of food at least distracted the two antagonistic groups from
each other.

That gave Violetta her chance. She got up from her seat and
went to her mother's, really and truly feeling ill, now. Between
the strain of the ceremony, the frantic beating of her heart at
the very sight of Brand, and the aching of her head and gut,
she wasn't having to pretend anything. She felt drained, and
sick, and her carefully-braided and coiled hair felt as heavy as
a helmet.

From her mother's reaction when she finally got Lady
Leverance's attention, she looked as ill as she felt. "Violetta?"

she said, more than a little sharply, as if she somehow thought her daughter had gotten ill deliberately. "What ails you?"

Violetta bent and whispered "My courses," and her mother's face cleared and became at least a little sympathetic. Violetta spoke a little louder, so that her father, whose attention had finally been caught, could hear her as well. "My head aches fearfully, and I had rather not eat . . ."

"Then go back to the manor, child," he said, instantly, which told her that she really *must* look pitiable. "You won't be missed." He signaled to a page, and gave the young lad instructions. "Take the lady to our carriage, see she is safely back home, then return with the carriage immediately." He turned back to Violetta, but already she could see his attention was wavering. "Go on, child, get better. Follow the boy."

I cannot leave this place quickly enough, she thought, as she hurried out in the wake of the child in Chendlar livery. The cold air outside the tent was a blessed relief; the silence in the carriage even more of a relief. The little boy sat solemnly across from her and said nothing. She leaned back in her seat and closed her eyes, trying *not* to think of Aleniel's smiling face. *It isn't you he wants, it's me,* she thought, spitefully. *You can have your nasty old man once I have Brand. I'll live in a cottage if it is with Brand.*

It seemed to take forever for the carriage to make its way back to their door; the page hopped out and helped her out, opened the manor door for her, then jumped immediately back into the carriage before she was even inside.

She went in and closed the door behind herself. The heavy *thud* it made echoed through empty rooms. Every servant that could be spared was down at the theater, and the rest—mostly kitchen and cleaning staff—were probably already asleep.

She trained through the silent house to the kitchen, and found it equally empty. But there was a store of custard tarts in one of the pantries, and shortbread cakes with their tops all encrusted with sugar crystals, and she had hidden away apples and a knife in her room. She was craving sweets, so she helped herself to a plate of tarts and cakes, and a bottle of mead, and carried them all back up to her room without seeing or hearing anyone else.

Once there, she struggled out of her feast-dress and into the more practical garb that Brand had told her to wear; a warm woolen hunting-dress, soft and loose, with a split skirt. Then she curled up on the bed with her stolen sweets and her little dog, and began the interminable wait.

––––––––

Mags was more than happy to have the evening "off," so to speak. He had not been invited to the betrothal feast; "Magnus" was neither lofty enough in rank nor close enough to Brand in friendship to warrant an invitation, it seemed. Or perhaps Brand was afraid that the tale of how he had *hidden behind Magnus for the entire fight* might have been revealed if Magnus was invited.

That suited him just fine. He'd already had one taste of flinging himself into the fray to keep the warring parties separate, and he wasn't eager for a second. Even if the fray was purely verbal.

Besides there were *more* than enough invitees on both sides to subdue any hotheads. That theater was crammed. And he had real work to do.

In the afternoon, while Flora's girls were primping themselves in anticipation of customers, he'd had a chance to do a long-overdue interview of both Flora and his chief informant among the girls themselves. There wasn't anything at all urgent that they could tell him, but he didn't like to leave them unspoken to for as long as they had been.

From there he had gone to a tavern that Harkon was known to favor, and simply ate and drank, waiting for people to approach him.

And that was where things got a little . . . odd.

He felt eyes on him the entire time.

This wasn't unusual; people were afraid of Harkon, but they also generally wished they had something to sell him at the same time, because he was known to be prompt and generous when some bit of information was particularly good. But tonight it felt as if people were uneasy, but didn't know *why* they were feeling uneasy, and dropping into a slightly more receptive frame of mind, with some of his shields down and others thinned, didn't get him anything much in the way of stray thoughts. He got the sense that something was brewing, and some people here knew that, but didn't know *what* it was. And you didn't get any money out of Harkon by coming up to him and telling him "Well, I hear there's something up, I heard it from a cousin who heard it from a friend, but I don't know what it is."

In fact, you were far more likely to get cuffed across the ear for wasting his time.

Finally, he gave up, and went on to his third stop of the night, Aunty Minda's. Here, he was met with considerably more enthusiasm than in the tavern.

His "lads"—he called them all "lad," even the girls— swarmed him, eager to let him know their new accomplishments. There were a handful still out, the older boys, who could safely stay out later, since thanks to more experience, muscles, and faster reflexes they could be expected to be able to keep themselves out of trouble.

And one was out on a special mission; Coot, who was coming along *nicely*. Mags had filched Chendlar livery for him, and left him down at the betrothal feast with orders to stay close to Violetta and her parents. Coot was just small enough to pass as a page, though he was actually older than most serving pages were. Mags was exceptionally pleased by the boy; once he'd come to realize that he actually had support and a home again, he'd proven to be fanatically loyal and very intelligent.

Mags had every intention of making him a regular "plant" among household servants, eventually. That would require a lot more training than this—actual *servers* would be dealing with the food; the little pages would just be set around the tent for errands and the occasional pouring of wine. He'd make a good set of eyes there, get plenty of practice in being just that, and all without any risk of being uncovered, because tonight things would be tense enough that no one was going to pay attention to a little page.

"Eh, lads, settle," he told them, as he took a seat next to the hearth, across from Aunty Minda, who just smiled and kept knitting. "Ye all know how't goes. So let's hear yer tales."

Now that he had a full evening, he intended to use it right here. As the youngest member of his "gang" stood beside him to recite what he'd learned—and what he'd picked up by listening to all the customers gabble while he waited to run messages—Mags felt himself relax from the tension he'd felt back at the tavern. The feud mess was almost over. It was time to get down to real business again.

Amily was startled during her late dinner by a tickling at the back of her head that she associated with Violetta's little dog. Between bites of pork pie, she relaxed, and allowed her thoughts to unfocus and reach out to the puppy. *It's probably nothing,* she thought. But on the other hand . . . the Chendlar manor was all but empty, and now would be a good time for any of the Raeylen adherents charged with mayhem to slip in and wreck the place, making it look as if it had been ransacked by a gang of thieves, perhaps. If that was happening, she could tell Rolan and the Guard could be sent before they got away.

But when she was able to settle into the dog's mind, and see through his eyes, she was surprised to discover he was on the bed in Violetta's room being fed bits of sweets by the girl herself.

Now . . . that's odd. Violetta was no longer in the feast gown that she'd been wearing when Amily left the Chendlar manor late this afternoon.

Then again, when Amily had left the manor, Violetta had been looking decidedly ill. She'd hesitantly said something that Amily hadn't entirely understood to her nurse, and the nurse had *tsk'd* and said it was probably due to excitement. Whatever "it" was. Then everyone had ignored her and gone back to fussing over Aleniel.

Well now, here she was in her own bed again. She must have left the feast, but since she wasn't in tears—although she was looking anxious, and still a bit pale and uneasy—she probably hadn't misbehaved in any way, but had been sent home because of illness.

Well, she just watched her infatuation get contracted to her sister, Amily reminded herself. *That can't have been easy.*

Odd, though. Amily would have thought she'd change into a bedgown and snuggle in under the goosedown comforter, not still be dressed. If you were home for the night, why get out of your feast gown and then into what looked like a walking gown meant for cold weather?

All of her instincts alerted. There was something very odd going on here, and she didn't like it. Not one bit.

The little wretch was up to something.

With an irritated sigh, Amily pushed her dinner aside and settled into her chair. Until she knew what it was that Violetta was up to . . . well, she was just going to have to live in the head of that silly little dog.

———————

The door to Aunty Minda's burst open, and everyone, Mags included, jumped in startlement and turned to stare. Those that had weapons, like Mags and Minda, had automatically put their hands on them.

But it was Coot standing there, cold air pouring in around him; panting, looking around wild-eyed. As soon as he spotted Mags, he gave a wordless bleat of relief, and ran for him, shouting as he came.

"Boss! Somethin' ain't right! Somethin's real bad! People are fallin' over an' passin' out!" he gabbled, grabbing Mag's wrist and trying to tug him to his feet.

It might have taken precious time to untangle what the boy was trying to tell him, between his gutter-speech and his very real fear, but his thoughts were pouring out, with all the force of emotion behind them, and within moments, Mags knew what he'd seen.

He'd been sent to escort Violetta back to the Chendlar manor; he had done so, and returned as fast as the carriage driver was prepared to go. Which was not very fast at all, and with a stop at a tavern on the way for at least three drinks, while Coot fretted. But eventually they got back on the way again, and the driver had pulled in his carriage with the others and prepared to doze on the driver's box while Coot scrambled back to his post. The only thing on his mind was to get there quickly, and hope he wouldn't be chided for being gone so long—and then recognized as someone who wasn't part of the household.

But . . . when he got there . . . the guards that *had* been watching the tent were gone.

Coot's instincts, honed by living all his life in perilous situations on the street, immediately shrilled alarm. Back when he'd *been* on the street, missing guards would have sent him in the other direction, heading for Mags. Once he'd settled— well, now he'd have run inside to see what was wrong, because surely *something* must be, and the first thought was that the feasters had become fighters and the guards had gone inside to separate them. But careful coaching by Mags made him go to the door and take one cautious peek inside before running back to report.

Mags had no trouble seeing clearly what was in Coot's mind. The image was practically branded into his memory. Everyone at the feast was unconscious, sprawled over tables into their food or actually fallen to the floor. Even the servants were unconscious. The man nearest Coot was still breathing— so at least they weren't dead, which had been his first, horrified thought.

—and then the sounds of someone walking quickly for the tent door made him scamper away from the entrance, to hide in the shadows.

That was when he saw Brand shove the tent door aside and come striding out, taking a cautious look to either side before heading for the line of picketed riding horses.

Coot was taking no chances at that point; in his memories he took to his heels then, and ran with every bit of speed and skill he had, making for Aunty Minda's. Mags could read the thoughts in his head, clear and cogent despite his terror. *Watch won' lissen t'me. They'll wanna know whut I was doin' in this livery. But they'll lissen t'Boss!*

"Well done, Coot, well done." He clapped Coot on the shoulder, sprang to his feet and ran for the door, pausing only long enough to make sure his short sword and dagger were securely tied down for his race to the Commons. Meanwhile Dallen was sounding the alert, and he knew he could count on Dallen to pass the word to all the Heralds, and the Heralds would muster the Healers. Because whatever else was going on, there would be a tent full of people who'd been drugged or poisoned, and that alone required Healers.

He thanked the gods that the Commons weren't all that far from where he was now—

He dashed out into the back yard of Aunty Minda's. Roofrunning would be faster, but he wouldn't have time to get up there. So he would have to do the next best thing; run straight through the maze of yards and walls rather than following the streets until Dallen could catch up. If he could . . . right now Dallen was in a stall in an inn that he'd have to get himself out of. Every moment that Mags wasn't moving as fast as he could toward that tent might mean the difference between life and death for someone.

So he ran. And it was a good thing he had done this very route in the past, and more than once, just for practice. And yes, at night, like now. Every shadow that loomed up in front of him was something he knew well. He knew where the sound footing was, where good holds on walls were, which storage boxes and barrels would hold his weight and which wouldn't, what animals were in which yards, and most especially, where the dogs and hogs were. His mind plotted out his run about three wagon-lengths ahead of him, and the cold air burned in his lungs as he leapt, climbed, tumbled, ran, and leapt again.

All he could think of was those images in Coot's mind; what the *hell* was going on? If everyone except Brand was unconscious, what did that *mean?* Was the man running away? Brand wasn't the sort he'd have taken as being willing to strike out on his own—and anyway, wasn't he *getting* exactly what he wanted from this betrothal? Why would he run?

And if he wasn't running from his betrothal, why in *hell* had he drugged everyone else there? Because that was the only explanation for why he had walked out of that tent on his own two feet.

He leapt for a wall, caught the top with both hands, and was over it. Pounded across a dirt yard, up a rain-barrel and over the wall on the other side. Dashed a few lengths down the alley, and leapt for another wall, ran along the top of it and jumped down, pounded down the narrow gap between two buildings with his shoulders brushing either side.

And then he sensed Dallen nearby. *:Near you, Mags. Help's coming, but we'll be there first,:* Dallen said grimly. *:By the gods, I do not like this, Mags! Lady Dia is down there!:*

Mags knew, from all his time with Bear, exactly why Dallen was grimly concerned. Even if the feasters hadn't been poisoned, there was no way of telling how *much* of a drug any of them had in him, and too much of anything that would put you to sleep could also easily kill you.

He ran across the street, squeezed in between two more buildings, and leapt up onto the top of another wall. They met at the next alley, and he jumped from the top of the wall right down into Dallen's saddle and they were off, at *real* speed, pounding down the street to the Commons, then into the chaos of the Winter Fair at night.

People cleared away from them, but there weren't that many at this late hour. There were only a few tavern tents, and shows still running at this time. Most of the tents were dark, and he and Dallen shot down between the rows of darkened and closed merchant-tents, hurtling for the Theater Tent.

He spotted it at the end of a row, looking like a festival lantern all lit up, standing in lone splendor, surrounded by waiting coaches and horses.

Dallen skidded to a halt as Mags flung himself off Dallen's back, landed and tumbled to his feet, and then went into a crouch.

The only sounds were the occasional snort of a sleepy horse, and the jingle of harness. Nothing else.

The tent itself was eerily silent. And there was no one on the coaches. No waiting drivers.

There were also no servants moving about the two pavilions that had been pitched to hold the food and keep it warm for serving after it had been brought from the cooks of the Midwinter Fair.

His first instinct was to charge in through the tent flap.

His second, and the one he followed, was to creep up to it, pause in a careful crouch beside the tent door, and open his mind.

There were half a dozen men in there; he identified the leader, and seized on the man's thoughts.

". . . got no stomach for killin' then get gone." The words echoed the thought, which came from the mind of a hardened murderer. "I got it from here."

Mags saw out of the man's eyes; saw the ruffians, scarred and weathered-looking—but they were also well-dressed ruffians, showing that whatever else these fellows were, they were prospering. He didn't recognize any of them, which made him think that they weren't ordinary thieves.

Were these the guards that we hired? If they were, they'd done a good job of concealing what must be extensive criminal pasts in order to get the job!

And did Brand have anything to do with that, I wonder?

The men lined up before their leader, and silver exchanged hands. Mags tried to get as good a look around as he could while the leader was occupied with paying off his men. There were bodies piled on the tables, and each other; servants and the coachmen heaped on top of their masters. It looked as if they had been dragged in and just left there, and they must have been deeply unconscious to not have woken up in the process. However this had been accomplished—

—some drugged drink. Some coshed- whispered the leader's memories –

—as he guessed, he saw in those memories that they had all been brought here, solving the mystery of where all the servants were. There had been a toast to the betrothed couple that all the servants had been brought in to join, at Brand's insistence, of course. When would servants ever refuse a good cup of wine? It wasn't often they got wine, let alone good wine. This just made Mags even sicker inside, because that wine must have been *heavily* dosed for it to drug all the servants with just one cup each. That meant that there were, almost certainly, some dead already. . . .

"Take yer pick of the horses, and scatter," said the leader, and the others saluted him and left without a word. Mags threw himself back into the shadows, and Dallen kited around the side of the tent out of sight, as they all came running out. Each of them took a horse. In moments, they were gone.

Meanwhile the leader's mind moved on to the next set of his instructions. And in a bright, terrible burst of vision, Mags knew what the rest of the plan was.

And knew he was the only one close enough to stop it.

———————

Violetta heard the sound of a snowball hitting her window, and ran to it. Brand's beloved face stared up at her from the snow-covered garden, pale and white in the moonlight against the dark blue of his cloak. "Can you leave by the garden door?" he called, softly, so as not to disturb the sleeping servants.

"Yes!" she called back, closed the window, then threw on her own cloak, slung the roll of clothing Brand had told her to bring over her back, picked up the basket with her valuable jewelry in it, and coaxed Star to jump inside. Then she ran down the stairs to the solar, and out through the garden door, into the snow, and into Brand's arms.

"Come on," he said, releasing her after too short a moment, and taking her hand. "We need to be quick, before they notice I haven't come back yet."

She nodded and ran hand-in-hand with him to the stables. The horse he had taken was still standing there, tied to the door of an empty stall, and it whickered curiously at them when he pulled her to it. He mounted, then pulled her up behind him.

Then they were off.

She held her basket in her lap with one hand and wrapped her free arm around his waist, hiding her face in his cloak and holding herself as close to him as she could. Her heart sang with joy to be near him, with him at last. She felt giddy with happiness, as if she had drunk far more of the mead than the few sips she had taken.

She had thought they would gallop away, but in fact, they moved at a sedate walk, and once down off the Hill, blended with the evening traffic. There were more people here than she was used to seeing in streets; this first street off the Hill seemed to be lined with inns, judging by the signs over the doors and the sounds and smells at either hand. There was a lot of coming and going between these inns too. As walkers and riders and the occasional carriage crowded in around them, she grew anxious, and tugged at his sleeve.

"What, my dove?" he whispered over his shoulder, as a hot-chestnut man cried his wares under an awning to her right.

"Shouldn't we be running?" she whispered back, her anxiety gnawing at her, as they turned into a street full of shops that still seemed to be open, even this late at night. Did Haven never sleep?

"Not at all," he assured her, and patted her hand as his horse snorted in reaction to a boy running under its nose, heading for a door just ahead of them. "If we run, we'll draw attention to ourselves. If we just go with the crowd, we'll just be part of the crowd. Right now, we're well away, no one knows we are gone yet, and we absolutely don't want anyone remembering something as potentially suspicious as a man and a woman on a galloping horse."

Satisfied with his answer, she cuddled up against his back again, and watched as they made their way from the street of shops into another, quieter street, and then yet another, a street that seemed to be full of silent workshops. All the buildings were dark, the windows shuttered, the doors firmly closed. There were some faint lights in windows overhead, but not many of them. She guessed—from what she knew of the Chendlar manor's home village, that the craftsmen lived above their workshops, and likely were asleep by now, or about to sleep.

They were the only people on this street, at last and when she craned her neck and looked around him, in the distance she could see what was probably the city wall.

Finally, he tapped his horse with his heels and urged it into a faster walk. They made it all the way to the end of the street without seeing a single soul, then they passed through a gate that was manned by Guards and Watch that paid no attention to them at all, and were out onto the open road.

There was nothing outside the wall here, not even a single house. Just the road, stretching on before them, crossing several fields before plunging into a dark mass of what she thought must be trees.

That was when she realized that they *weren't* going to the street of Temples as she had assumed. But—weren't they going to get married right away? He'd promised—

She sat up straight again. "Brand!" she said, a little more sharply than she had intended. "I thought—"

He had urged his horse into a trot now. "I don't trust any priest of any faith in Haven not to betray us," he said. "I know a fine fellow I trust implicitly in a village a little away from here. I've already arranged things with him. He's waiting for us now, at the inn. He'll wed us on the spot, and we can wait until the hue and cry dies down. It's a fine little inn there, very comfortable, and the innkeeper serves the best sweet pastry you have ever eaten." Once again, he patted her hand before returning his attention to the road. "Won't that be wonderful?"

For the second time, her anxiety ebbed, and she laughed at herself. What was she so afraid of? That he'd not marry her after all? That he'd spirit her away, like some scoundrel in a song, and murder her? Well, *that* was truly absurd; he loved her! The last thing he wanted to do was harm her! And as for not marrying her, well, if he wanted that land and manor the

King promised, he'd have to marry *one* of the Chendlar girls, and she would be a better wife to him than Aleniel!

Then she chided herself for even *thinking* that he'd be wedding her for the sake of the property. He *loved* her! And she loved him! *Silly girl,* she told herself, as the horse trotted further and further from Haven, and the noise and lights of the city receded behind them. *This is like a song in good truth, the one in which the lovers live happily together forever.*

17

Amily had fallen asleep "watching" Violetta, it had been so dull. All the girl did was eat pastry, pet her dog, stare into the fire and drink a little mead. She had decided, after a while, that the reason the girl had changed into another dress and not into her bedgown was because there were no servants awake to bring her anything, and she didn't want to be wandering about the place in a night rail if she decided to go back down to the kitchen for more food. After all, if she hadn't eaten much today, which was possible with all the excitement, she was probably starving, and pastry was not going to assuage that for long.

Trust a child to go straight for the sweets, she had thought. In so many ways, Violetta was *still* a child, which made her father's plan to marry her to that old man rather . . . nauseating to be fair. *Somehow, I must do something about that,* Amily had decided. What that would be, she wasn't sure, but it had to be something that would benefit, not just Violetta, but every girl in her position. *I must speak to the King, once*

Brand and Aleniel are married and we've got this stupid feud behind us. Wasn't that what the King's Own was supposed to do? Advise him on matters that his Council would not think of?

At least Violetta had shown some common sense in this, enough that Amily's instincts had let her drowse off. She clearly understood that it wasn't a good idea to be ghosting about a mostly-deserted manor in something as flimsy as a bedgown. There were far too many young men living here at the moment who might lose whatever inhibitions they normally had when drunk. Oh, it was true that her rank should keep her safe. And yes, certainly, anyone who transgressed would pay and pay dearly for molesting one of the Lord's daughters. But that would be after the damage had been done. And that sort of forethought doesn't usually come to a man deep in his cups.

Especially the sort of men that the cousins were, who thought that their rank entitled them to anything they wanted. In her bedgown, she could be a kitchen maid taking advantage of the situation to help herself to kitchen dainties she would never otherwise get. But if Violetta was properly and appropriately dressed, a cousin would likely mind his manners. Even drunk, it was easy to tell the difference between a fine lady's gown and the common chemise and skirt of a maid.

Which led her to thoughts of how *unfair* it was that just because a girl was a menial, she didn't have the same protection against being molested as the lord's daughter. And Amily's thoughts went around and around and around.

And it had been a long and exhausting several weeks, what with everything she was expected to do. Keeping track of Lord Leverance. Keeping track of Violetta, just in case. Morning sessions with the King, learning what her father knew. Council sessions in the later morning and afternoon. Dinner with the Court, attending the evening Court functions at Lydia's side, and maybe, if she was lucky, some time before bed with

Mags. Even if she was lucky, she still felt impelled to check on Lord Leverance and Violetta at intervals over the evening. It made for a long, long day, and she'd had long, long days for quite some time now.

So . . . she'd dozed off.

Until Rolan awakened her.

Instead of words, images flooded into her mind. The feast-tent, and all the collapsed bodies of both clans. Brand striding out the tent door. Mags, running at top speed through the dark, heading for the tent and its victims. It all rushed into her head at once, and for that moment she understood *exactly* what it must have been like for him to share his thoughts with his cousin Bey. It all came in exactly as if she herself had experienced it, it was all coherent and just *there*.

Because with the images came the knowledge of what each of these things meant, as if she and Mags momentarily shared every thought he'd had. Disorienting, and yet, at the same time, because she had so much experience in lurking in the minds of animals, not disorienting at all.

It was like a pail of cold water to the face, and she came completely awake all at once. Rolan released her mind, and for a moment, she sat there in paralysis, and had no idea what to do. Her heart was pounding, and she felt breathless, cold, and afraid. If Brand had left that tent full of victims—what of Violetta? Was *this* why she had left early? Was *this* why she was dressed suitably to go outside again?

Then, just on the wild chance that she *might* learn something, she sought for the puppy, Star's, mind.

He wasn't where she'd "left" him. She searched further, and found him at last. He was in the dark, and lying quietly in the bottom of some sort of small container not much bigger than he was. His nose told him—and thus her—more or less where he was. Outdoors, and by all the "country" smells, no longer in Haven. By the sounds, on horseback. And there was someone with him besides Violetta. Someone male.

He poked his head up then, as if he understood that she needed him to get at least a glimpse of where he was.

Snow-covered fields. Grazing fields, farm fields, all under a blanket of snow in the moonlight. So much open space surprised and actually frightened the little dog, who was used to rooms, and enclosed gardens that were like outdoor rooms. He didn't like it at all, whimpered, and ducked his head back down again.

There was only one road out of Haven that cut through empty fields, and not the Commons (currently occupied by the Fair) or houses and workshops that had been built outside the walls.

South Road.

Even as she thought that, the pup whimpered again, and a man's voice she *knew* spoke sharply and incredulously.

"In—for the love of the gods, Violetta, did you bring that damned muff-dog?"

Brand. . . .

She was shocked out of her trance. Violetta was with Brand, riding out of Haven. Surely Violetta had *no* idea of what he had just left!

Good gods, what is he going to do with her? She was surely a potential hostage at the least. Had he taken her to protect himself? Dear gods, what was going on here?

:Rolan!: she cried, but before she even said anything, she already knew from the information pouring into her—every Herald and every Healer was either speeding down to the Commons or mounting up to do so. There was no one to chase after Brand and Violetta.

Except me.

Again for a moment, she was paralyzed with indecision, as her heart continued to pound. Go with the others?

No. What if Violetta knows nothing of this? Surely she knows nothing of this! What if. . . . Brand had been so duplicitous, fooling them *all*—who knew what he was going to do with her? He didn't know his scheme had been uncovered, and when he realized it, yes he would *surely* use her as a hostage! There was no one to send. The Guard would never get to them in time. *We have to get her away from him!*

:Meet me outside!: Rolan cried, and she leapt to her feet, and grabbed for her bow and arrows as she sped out the door. No time for a cloak. She had to rely on Rolan to tell—anyone—where she was going. As she hit the cold air, an enormous white form skidded to a halt next to her and collapsed to its knees. She rolled onto his bare back, twined her fingers in his mane, and he lurched to his feet and was off in a single motion.

It was *freezing,* but Rolan radiated heat like an oven, and she just crouched as low on his back as she could to take advantage of that. Her mouth was dry, and her hands in Rolan's mane shook. She had never done anything like this alone before. But she was the only one who could *find* Violetta. She had to go.

:I'm telling others, the Trainees, the ones who aren't already on the way down to the tent. They'll follow my guidance.:

Well that was a small comfort. There would be people coming. Just . . . not immediately.

Other Heralds were mounting up, or already galloping down to the Theater Tent around her, in front of her, behind her, some carrying Healers doubled up behind them.

Rolan joined the river of white. They all poured down the street that wound through the mansions and palaces like an avalanche—but then she and Rolan dashed alone down a side road that would take her to the South Road.

Clutching her fingers in Rolan's silky mane, she closed her eyes again and sought the puppy. Gods, it was cold, so cold. Her unprotected ears were freezing.

He was no longer in the carrier. He was floundering through snow too deep for him, whimpering, trying to follow the fast-fading scent of his mistress.

Brand must have grabbed him and tossed him aside.
And what did *that* mean for Violetta?
She shuddered, and Rolan put on a little more speed.

———————

:Help is coming!: Dallen cried again, but Mags knew that help was not going to arrive in time. Not for what he had just seen in the killer's mind. For the next part of the plan was to tip over all the braziers, all the lanterns, all the candles, and set the tent and its contents on fire with everyone in it.

He didn't even have to think about what he was going to do; he was going to have to surprise the killer and buy time. So he stood up and strode right through the door of the tent as if he owned the place, startling the killer—who was standing between the tables full of unconscious guests—into jumping back a pace or two.

The murderer stared. Then he grinned, crookedly, as if he was entirely amused, and at that moment, Mags realized something.

He wasn't wearing his Whites. He wasn't even wearing his disguise of "Magnus." He was dressed as Harkon, a cheap bully-boy from the bad part of Haven. So he wasn't going to have the murderer as intimidated as he might have been if he was facing off against a Herald. In fact, the man probably thought that he was a cheap tough who had noticed the silence and come in here looking to see if there were some quick pickings to be had. That he was someone easily intimidated, or easily killed along with the rest.

"Well . . . what've we got 'ere?" the killer drawled. "I don' recall you bein' on m'roster." The grin turned cruel. "Well. One more set'a burned bones ain't gonna matter one way or t'other."

:I can't get to you!: Dallen said frantically. *:I can't get through that door! It's too small, and if I try to kick it down*

the whole tent might come down!: Mags knew immediately that would be a very bad idea, The canvas would come down on all that flame, and he *and* the killer *and* everyone unconscious would burn together.

:Don't worry about it,: Mags replied, most of his attention on the murderer. *:All I need to do is hold him off and keep him busy until help comes. All I need to do is keep him from starting fires. . . .:*

So he grinned, as cocky as Harkon was, out in the streets, when he knew that he had a foe outmatched. "Could be them bones'll be yours, cobber," he replied arrogantly. "Ain't found a match fer me in Haven yet."

The killer chuckled nastily. "Oh, I'm gonna laugh when I put m'blade in yer gut," he replied, and lunged.

But of course, Mags wasn't there. He'd already leapt back out of reach, but as the killer reached the limit of his lunge and had not yet recovered, he dashed back in, and smacked the other's extended blade aside, slashing down with his dagger at the killer's sword-hand.

Only the fact that he was *fractionally* faster than Mags saved him from a severed wrist. He managed to pull back, and Mags' dagger hissed along the edge of his sword as the killer leapt out of the way.

But he'd lost that smile. And Mags could see his thoughts as clear as if they were his own.

As always, since he had shared the Sleepgiver's thoughts, Mags went into a cool and detached frame of mind the moment he began fighting. Oh, he was *afraid,* but the fear was locked away behind a mental wall. What was in charge now was calm, calculating, and above all, *observant.* Nothing escaped him, not the tiniest squint of an eye or the fractional movement of a hand.

Mags lunged before the killer could get his hands on a table-lamp, but there were *dozens* on either side of him and it was only a matter of moments before he was able to grab one and send it crashing into the canvas of the tent, or the flammable baize—

Dallen *screamed* in his head. *:Mags! I grant you leave!:*
Time froze.

———————

"So . . . I s'pose I could . . . like . . . take over somebody's head?"

He and Dallen were walking along the riverbank near the Waystation just outside Bastion. They'd been talking about his Gift, how strong it had become. How Dallen thought that after that session with the Sleepgiver drugs, and trading memories with his cousin, he might be the strongest Mindspeaker in all of Haven. And it had occurred to him, more than once, that if he could put words *into someone's head . . . he could probably put* thoughts *there, too. And maybe . . . actions?*

:You can, I am sure of it,: was Dallen's reply, though it sounded troubled. And Mags knew why. To do something like that . . . it was dangerous. He could get lost in someone else's head. It was bad enough when he was simply listening to what they were thinking, but to go right inside *like that was courting great peril. You didn't know what was in peoples' heads, what their secrets were. Ugly things could overwhelm you, knock your feet right out from under you. Like being trapped in someone else's nightmare. He'd gotten a sense of that with the first Sleepgiver ritual when the talisman had tried to take him over; he'd nearly lost himself then. To open himself deliberately to that sort of thing would be perilous.*

It was also very wrong. Listening without asking was bad enough, though certainly there were plenty of extenuating circumstances, like if someone was trying to kill you or other people. But taking over their thoughts? Or taking over their body entirely? That was . . . well, it was wrong in so many ways he couldn't count them all.

On the other hand . . . killing people was very wrong too.

"So how do I know when it'd be all right?" he asked after a long, long moment. "If I even can, that is."

More silence on Dallen's part. And then came the answer.

:You'll know, if I give you leave,: *the Companion said, almost too quietly to be heard.*

———————————

Time unfroze, and so did Mags' thoughts. He saw the killer reaching for a lantern.

And as if he was plunging a sword into the man's body, he plunged his mind into the man's head.

The man screamed in sheer terror, sensing that something was terribly, terribly wrong, but Mags was already on his knees, grabbing his own head in both hands. A moment later, the killer was mimicking his pose, though not voluntarily. Mags had put him there.

And now Mags was fighting to keep his sanity in a sea of horror.

For all that they were assassins and murderers, the Sleep-givers were curiously . . . clean. Bey, in particular, had a high sense of honor. And aside from that one insane one, when they killed, they killed cleanly, quickly, and dispassionately. They didn't enjoy killing, although they enjoyed the skillful exercise of their talents. They didn't torture. They didn't enjoy inciting fear. In fact, when they did their work right, the victim never even knew they were there until it was too late.

This man loved to kill, reveled in it, reveled in the fear of his victims and their pain. When he got a chance to torture, he took it, and his mind was full of those memories and how he had enjoyed every one of those experiences. His one regret on this job was that he wouldn't be able to stand here and gloat while his victims burned. Being inside his mind was like drowning in sewage.

And this time Mags didn't have the luxury of curling his "self" up and just riding it all out. He had to keep control of this man's body, keep him down with every muscle locked in place. Had to hold him until help came. The images, the memories of what this man had done in the past surged through him, threatening to shake him loose with their foulness, for it was exactly as if *he* had done these things, rejoicing in the pain, thrilling to the terror.

He sweated and wept and gagged—and held, and held, and held.

———————

Amily and Rolan galloped at full speed through the Old South Gate. Everywhere her body didn't physically touch Rolan's she was painfully cold, and she'd had to try keeping her ears warm by putting first one side of her head, then the other, against his outstretched neck. Her muscles were cramping as she fought to stay on his back without a saddle. Her stomach was a knot, and the cold air seared her lungs.

The moon was high overhead, and the road a ribbon of dark through the white snow. She blessed the road-clearing crews, and Rolan's night-sight. Was her bow still on her back, her quiver of arrows on her belt? She freed a hand to check. *Yes.* She sent her mind ahead, searching now for a single horse, somewhere out there, probably deep under that mass of darkness that was an orchard.

Suddenly, she found them, felt them. Found the horse's mind, anyway. He was not happy; confused at being asked to go outside the city at night, confused by the darkness of the road, confused by everything about this journey he found himself on.

There they are . . . Brand was shifting in his saddle, looking back over his shoulder. Could he hear the galloping hoofbeats in the distance? The horse certainly could. He kept flicking his ears backward, anxiously, hoping for another of his kind.

Of course Brand could hear Rolan coming nearer. Companion hooves rang like bells; they were unmistakable. Brand put spurs to his horse; the poor beast bucked and resisted; it couldn't *see,* and it didn't want to go dashing off into the dark.

Violetta was crying, and her seat on the back of the horse shifted precariously. *"Brand!"* she was sobbing. *"Brand, why did you do that? Brand!"*

She must be crying about her dog. Poor child, she loved that little pup, and Brand had essentially thrown it into the snow to die. It was only luck that it wasn't dead already; luck that it had hit soft snow and hadn't broken its neck or its legs in the fall.

He ignored her, fought with the horse, and got him to canter. Then, impatient, he jabbed the beast with both spurs, viciously, digging them in as hard as he could. The pain lanced through Amily as the horse was roweled. The poor thing cried out, stumbled, broke into a run—

She felt him trip over something, and felt his terror as he started to fall.

Oh gods! She fled his mind before he hit the ground, knowing that he was going to be hurt at best, and at worst . . .

Her heart beat like a bird's wings as she came back to herself. Oh, gods, what had almost happened! *:What would happen if I was in his mind when he died?:* she asked Rolan, leaning over his neck as he put on yet more speed.

:I don't know,: Rolan said, soberly. *:With humans . . . it is a shock. I don't know what would happen with an animal.:*

She shivered all over and resolved never to have to find out.

But at least now she knew where they were. On this road, up ahead, in the orchard. And she and Rolan were within a few heartbeats of the edge.

And what do we do when we catch them?

The tiny part of him that was watching for others, for Heralds, felt them burst into the tent. Mags felt hands on his shoulders, familiar hands, and a familiar mind wordlessly supporting his. *Nikolas . . .* he thought, and let go of the killer's mind, falling back into his own. And then Nikolas held him as he retched, and spit bitter bile, and retched, and spit, right there where he was crouched. It was all dry, and that didn't make it any better. His stomach felt as if it wanted to throw itself out of his mouth. His chest and stomach muscles strained to the tearing point. He felt as if he would never be clean again. He felt as if he would never, ever be free of those horrors.

But then . . . as someone brought him a cup of cold water, as body after limp body was carried out of the tent—people *he* had saved—he fought back. He remembered how he had dealt with the memories that the Sleepgivers had forced on him, and with Dallen's help, he did the same to these. He . . . neutralized them. He'd never be able to forget them, but he and Dallen pushed and pushed at them until they weren't *his* anymore. And the less they were his, the more they would fade.

Finally, both mind and body stopped being in revolt. He sat up, with a nod of thanks to Nikolas, and drank the water down in a single gulp. He felt Dallen in his mind, still pushing the terrible memories into the background.

Because they weren't done yet. There was another emergency to deal with.

"Amily," he choked, and staggered to his feet, stumbling out of the tent. Dallen was right by the entrance; Mags hauled himself into the saddle, and Dallen launched into a gallop. Amily was out there . . . on the South Road. He wouldn't reach her by the time she reached Brand—but damned if he still wouldn't try.

:They're all safe. Mags is coming. More behind him.:

Amily nodded as relief gave her new strength. Now she could just concentrate on Brand. She had thought her heart couldn't beat any faster, and yet, it did. She still didn't know what she was going to do when she caught them; she only knew she had to keep Violetta safe, and keep Brand from escaping until he could be captured.

Rolan leapt over the stiffening body of the poor horse and charged into the heavy snow under the trees. Amily could hear Violetta wailing somewhere ahead of them.

A moment later, Violetta's cries broke off, and she could *see* them. Brand had stopped trying to escape; he had his back to a tree, and Violetta held in front of him, like a human shield.

Rolan came to a halt, the heavy snow helping, rather than hampering that. She stayed on his back, straightening up— not yet reaching for her bow and arrows. She needed to stay *on* Rolan, at all costs. It was her greatest advantage against his greater strength and more practice fighting against *real* opponents rather than in practice bouts. And she didn't want to goad him into something terrible by drawing down on him.

"Our fathers sent you, didn't they?" he said, bold as brass, though he was panting with the exertion of trying to run through the snow. "Well, we love each other, and we're not going to go through with that sham of a marriage. You can tell your King that. He can't force us to marry anyone we don't love. Right, my dove?"

"Yes!" Violetta wailed, tears running down her face. "Why should Aleniel marry him? *She* doesn't love him, and I do, with all my heart! Just let us go! All the King wants is for *one* of us girls to marry Brand, he can't possibly care which one! Why should it matter? And I don't care what my father says! Aleniel will be happier with Lord Peramir than I ever would be, and she's better suited to him! We aren't doing anything wrong, we were going to get married in the next village! Just let us *go!*"

Amily was suddenly filled with an inarticulate rage at the way this young man had manipulated the poor child every step of the way. Taking advantage of her naïveté . . . what had he been doing to her in secret? From the way she acted, surely he had seduced her, slept with her, although that scarcely seemed possible. And now he had virtually kidnapped her, in a way that would make it look as if his murders of her family and his own was merely an "accident." Things were starting to come together in Amily's mind, very *ugly* things. "Violetta . . . step away from Brand," she said, trying to keep her voice steady.

"No!" the girl cried, pressing herself closer. "He hasn't done anything wrong! He hasn't stolen me away! I came with him because I *wanted* to! I told you, we are in love and we are getting married!"

Amily realized, as she saw Brand's slow, sly smile, that *he* didn't know that his plan had been foiled.

There was no way of getting the girl away from him at the moment without telling her what was going on. How her parents had nearly been burned to death at his orders. And Violetta would never believe anything that *she* said.

But what if Brand said it?

"You don't know what you're saying, Violetta," she replied, speaking very slowly, stalling for time, as she half-closed her eyes, and recited that little rhyme in her head. Nine times; she had to get through it nine times, all the while envisioning that wisp of blue fog with blue eyes in the middle of it settling over Brand. "You know nothing about this man. You don't know what he is, or what he is capable of, Violetta. He's nothing but a mask over something terrible; a monster that was able to fool us all into thinking he was just an ordinary young man." As she finished the last of her nine repetitions, Brand began to glow within a nimbus of dim, faintly pulsing, blue light. She had set the Truth Spell, that would show whether or not what he said was the truth. But that wouldn't be enough. She would have to turn it coercive. She steeled herself, then she did what she had never done before.

She envisioned that nimbus of light closing down on his head, the blue eyes superimposing themselves over his. She felt Rolan's will joining with hers. *Speak True, Only True, Even that which you shall rue!*

"Tell her, Brand," she said, harshly, as the blue eyes opened and looked right into hers, and she got the *distinct* sensation of some strange intellect nodding at her. *"Tell her what you did to all the betrothal guests. Tell her your plan."*

Brand made a strangling noise, and then . . . suddenly started talking.

"You can thank this stupid little goose for my plan," he said, as Amily slowly got her bow off her back and nocked an arrow to it. She might need it. He would be forced to *tell* the truth, but if he realized what she was doing, he might try something. Violetta was still in his clutches. "If it hadn't been for her ridiculous letter, I'd never have given her a second look when we invaded her father's fete. But of course, when a girl throws herself at your head with such incredible enthusiasm, and your father has cut you off from the whorehouse, well, you take what you can get. I said sweet things at the fete, and sweeter things under her window. She wanted me, and who can blame me for taking advantage of that? She let me into her bedroom, then she let me into her bed, the silly little tart."

Violetta started, and tried to twist in his grip to look into his face. Her eyes grew as big as young plums when she saw the blue glow about him. "Brand—" she stammered.

"Tell her how you really feel about her, Brand," Amily ordered . . . wishing with all her heart that she didn't have to. But Violetta needed to know the truth. She felt sick, physically sick, as Brand began to speak.

"Feel? I don't feel anything," Brand replied. "She's a pair of legs to spread, a passably pretty face, and an empty head.

But she's more tractable than that virago of a sister, and younger, so she'll be easier to train to do what I want. I can get her to do pretty much anything I want as long as she thinks I love her. So long as the King's gift comes with her, she'll make a passable wife. And other people will think the story is all so very romantic."

Violetta's face went white. "Brand?" she whispered.

"When the Prince ordered you betrothed, what did you decide to do?" In the distance, Amily could hear Companion hooves at the gallop. Mags was coming. Beneath her, Rolan was as steady as a rock, and although she felt energy draining from her to fuel the Truth Spell, she felt energy flowing from Rolan to her to replace it.

"I wanted to look over the intended bride first. One Chendlar bitch was as good as another, the way I saw it. But after I got a look at the sister, and realized what trouble she was likely to give me about having my whores, I started to think—why not figure a way to have the silly one instead? I thought, the King's gift will come with her, no doubt of it. Then my dear father got into his cups and started talking about poisoning all the Chendlars at the betrothal feast or the wedding feast, so I'd have the Chendlar lands as well as the King's gift. And like always, he bullied me about it, laughed that I wasn't clever enough to have thought of that idea, taunted me that I wouldn't be ruthless enough to pull it off." His face contorted into a sneer. "Dear gods, how I hated that man. How I hated him. I wish I could have seen him burning alive. And that was when I thought, why should I settle for one estate, or two, when I could have three? Of course, there was the small matter of getting rid of the families in a way so that I wouldn't get blamed. But when I saw that tent that they decided was perfect for the betrothal feast—it all came together."

Violetta looked as if she was going to faint at any moment. Brand was paying no attention whatsoever to her.

"And how did you come to the notion of drugging the

guests and then setting the feast tent on fire with them all in it?" Amily asked, quietly.

"Well, I thought about poison, as father had. But poison . . ." He shook his head. "The Healers are too good at finding poison. And someone might survive it. But if I put a sleep drug in the special wine for the toasts, I knew I could send them all unconscious and the Healers likely wouldn't be looking for that, so then . . . it was just a matter of figuring out how to kill them when they were asleep." He paused, and his eyes stared off into the distance. "When I was a child there was a traveling show that worked out of a tent just like that one we took for the feast. One night, someone knocked a torch into a pile of hay next to it. The entire thing was engulfed in no time. They said that the wax that was used to waterproof the canvas turned it into a giant torch instead. You could see it for miles. Almost everyone inside was killed." The unblinking blue eyes of the Truth Spell . . . thing . . . stared into hers. Behind them, Brand's eyes were as hard and glittering as glass. "And that was when I knew what to do. Just hire a few killers, drug the betrothal toast wine, escape with this little tart so I had a lot of distance between me and the tent when it went up, and we'd be two, poor, pathetic orphans only deserving of pity. Everyone would probably assume a fight broke out, someone knocked over a torch, and they set fire to themselves. My wretched father would be dead at last. And I'd have three estates instead of two."

Amily heard and felt Mags ride up next to her and dismount. She wasn't sure what he was planning to do, but she was starting to sense control of the spell slipping from her.

"After all, no one was going to miss any of those idiots," Brand concluded. "The King certainly wouldn't; he'd never have to worry about the damned stupid feud again. I certainly would be happy to see my father in his grave. Leverance was a useless old man who couldn't even keep his wife out of Talbot's bed. And as for this stupid wench, I knew that all I needed to do to keep her quiet was to keep putting children in her belly. She'd be convinced I loved her, she'd mawk all over the brats the way she fawned all over that stupid dog, and I'd be free to spend most of my time here in Haven, rich enough to keep Lelage and any other whores I wanted."

And then, between the time he said those words and his next breath, Amily's control over the spell broke.

The blue eyes closed. The blue light faded and was gone. And Brand's face underwent a terrible change, from calm and complacent to infuriated. "You—what did you do to me?" he screamed, trying to tighten his grip on Violetta.

But he was too late. Rolan must have warned Mags that the spell was about to break. Mags was rushing him, and tackled, not him, but the girl, ripping her out of his grip. Mags turned the rush into a tumble, curling so that he took most of the fall himself, then managing to roll to his feet and put Violetta behind him.

Brand screamed in fury, and pulled his sword from its sheath, charging after him.

Only to stop, and look down, and stare, stupidly, at the arrow in his heart. He stood there for only as long as it took for Amily to draw a breath, then he dropped to the snow, blood staining the ground in a slowly growing pool beneath him.

The antechamber to the Greater Audience Chamber was cold and empty except for her. Thin, gray winter light came in through the windows on Violetta's right. There was no place to sit, but then, she didn't think she should sit; if she did, she was afraid she would never have the courage to stand up.

Then came the words she had been waiting for, and dreading, delivered in a high, clear, boy's soprano. "Lady Violetta of House Chendlar, come into the Court!"

The page in royal livery who had made the announcement opened the carved wooden door to the Greater Audience Chamber, and stood aside. It seemed to be a league from where she stood to the open door. There were two banks of seats there, one on either side of the strip of carpet leading to the dais. She would have to pass between them to reach the foot of the dais, and both sides were packed for the inquest. One side had been designated as for House Raeylen, the other for House Chendlar, but every spare seat was taken. Violetta took a long, shuddering breath, clasped her hands together inside her muff, and took comfort in the presence of dear little Star inside it. Everyone had advised her to carry the muff, and the puppy, when she went to testify before the King, telling her that Star would help keep her steady. Well, "everyone" being Lady Dia and Heralds Amily and Nikolas.

She kept her eyes on the floor, and took slow, careful steps as she walked up the strip of carpet to the throne, thankful that her footsteps weren't echoing on hard floor. That would have been . . . very uncomfortable. *As if I could possibly be more uncomfortable than I am now.* She passed between the two ranks of seats for the courtiers, stopping at last at the dais. Only then did she raise her eyes.

The entire Royal Family was there; the King, Prince Sedric, and Herald Nikolas on her right, the Queen, Princess Lydia, and Herald Amily on her left. The contrast was . . . striking. And not because it was all women on the left, and all men on the right. To the right, everyone was dressed in Herald's Whites. Extremely elaborate and ornamented Herald's Whites, but absolutely recognizable instantly as the uniform. To the left, the Queen was in Royal Blue, the Princess in mourning black, and only Herald Amily was in Whites.

She studied their expressions, looking for a clue as to how they felt about *her,* even though it was not she who was on trial here. They were sober-faced, but . . .

What would they have looked like if everyone had died?

A few people *had* died, despite the best efforts of the Healers; the drug that Brand had used had been too strong for them, or else they had drunk too much of it. Lord Kaltar, ironically enough, had been one; the rest had been cousins on both sides. The survivors were just lucky that the Healers had decided to purge them instead of letting them sleep off their dose.

Actually, everyone was just lucky Herald Mags got there and stopped that awful man from burning them all alive.

She shivered, thinking about how near a thing it had been,

and glanced to the side, where her parents were. Both ranks of seats, to the right and to the left, were mostly full of people in mourning. Even though the Chendlar cousin that had died had been relatively remote, the House was still in full mourning for him.

I wonder what Talbot is thinking now? Would he be gloating, because he had been right about Brand? *Probably.* She was glad he wasn't here. She was not looking forward to encountering him again, and not just for that reason.

She hardly knew how to look at her mother, who not only was in head-to-toe black, but was veiled in black as well, and had found a black cloak somewhere. Brand had been under the Truth Spell, forced to tell the exact truth as he knew it. And what he thought he knew was that Violetta's mother had been going to bed with . . . Cousin Talbot. What was she supposed to think of her mother now?

I know she doesn't love Father; I've always known that. She wondered now if that was partly why she'd wanted true love so badly; in everything she had ever read, if you had true love, you were sheltered forever.

Except that . . . now she knew that true love didn't protect you from betrayal, if the person didn't love you back. And how would you know he didn't love you back if he feigned it as well as Brand had? The first you would know, was the moment you discovered that you had been betrayed.

And her mother proved that formal contracts didn't protect you from betrayal either. Nor did vows. What would?

She looked back at her father. Her father, also in black, nodded encouragingly at her.

Herald Nikolas cleared his throat and she brought her attention back to the dais, turning to look apprehensively at him. She knew what was coming; they'd told her exactly how this part of the inquest would go, but that still didn't stop her from being afraid.

"The King's Own is about to set the Truth Spell on you, Lady Violetta," he said, gravely. "Are you prepared?"

She shivered again, but nodded, and caressed Star inside the muff. "Aye, Herald," she whispered. It sounded very loud in the silence.

"Keep your answers very short, no more than a few words. Just answer exactly what you are asked," Lady Dia had told her, over and over. *"No more. No less, but no more. If they want an explanation, they will ask for it. Trust me, girl. The less you say right now, the better."*

She couldn't tell any difference when Herald Amily signaled to the King that the spell had been set, but evidently everyone else could, because of the swift intake of breath across the room. Nothing felt different to *her.* Star didn't stir or whimper, just nudged her hand with his nose. Nothing looked different to her. She relaxed just the tiniest bit. Perhaps this would not be so bad.

"When did you first see Lord Brand?" the King asked.

No, this was going to be bad. Tears welled up in her eyes. If only she had somehow known the kind of terrible person he was! If only she could go back in time, and make other choices!

"The Royal Midwinter Fete, here, in the Palace, your Majesty," she said, bowing her head to hide her expression and fight for control.

"I tell you again, keep your answers short and simple, and try to keep from being too emotional," Lady Dia had warned. *"If they want more, they will ask more questions, and tears won't do anything except to make it hard for you to answer."*

"Did he pay any attention to you, ask you to dance, pay court to you?" was the next question. She looked up, a little. The King did not display any particular expression at all; he was sitting straight up in his throne, just looking at her dispassionately. Beside him, the Queen looked grave, but the Princess gave her a little nod, as if to encourage her.

She shook her head. "No, Majesty," she said, her voice going a little hoarse with unshed tears. "Not at that time. He danced with many ladies, but not with me. He did not even look at me."

Why didn't I realize what he was, then? The only people he paid court to were the prettiest of the ladies. Anyone who wasn't beautiful, he ignored. That should have told me what he was!

"And what did you think of him?" asked the King.

"I thought—I thought—he was glorious," she whispered. "I thought—I thought I must be in love with him, just looking at him made me feel so strange, happy and giddy and as if I never wanted to be out of his presence. The passion was so sudden, so sweet—I thought it must be a lifebond. I could not think why I should feel this way, so suddenly, if it were not a lifebond."

The questions came, short, carefully phrased. They asked her about her letter, and she cried with humiliation, but told the truth; told how she had taken refuge in the library, used the palimpsest she had found there, and poured out her heart to him, then contrived a way to get it into his hands.

She didn't dare look at her parents through that. This was the first they would have heard of the letter. She wasn't sure how the King had come to hear of it . . . unless Lady Dia had told him.

Oh, silly goose, of course she did. She'd have to. This is a murder inquest. She would have told the King everything she knew.

She just wished it hadn't been that letter.

And it isn't as if Lady Dia didn't warn me then. Oh, why was I so stupid?

They asked her if he had answered it, and she shook her head. "No, Majesty," she said. "I was . . . told . . . that he threw it in a fire."

They didn't ask her who had told her that, which confirmed to her that it had either been Lady Dia or Lady Dia's still-unidentified friend who had told them.

The only thing that she could think was that, in light of everything else that had happened, and given what Brand had done, her letter was probably a very minor transgression at worst. She hoped, anyway.

They asked her about the next meeting, at the House Chendlar fete . . .

"He came with a band of masked young men," she said. "And he actually looked for me, and sought me out."

"And what did he say?" the King persisted.

"Very flattering and most loving things, that he loved me in return, and had since reading my letter, and that I would see him again," she faltered.

"And did you?" came the inevitable question.

Here it comes. Here is where I ruin myself forever. "Aye, Majesty. I was looking out my window after the fete, and Brand appeared in the garden below my window and called to me."

She braced herself for the next questions, dreading what they would lead to—how he had climbed to her window. How she had let him into her room, and let him kiss and caress her. How she had let him into her bed.

But those questions never came.

"So, then, he appeared beneath your window," the King repeated. "We will assume he said the usual lover-like things. Did he make you any promises?"

She felt stunned. Because, so far as those listening were concerned, Brand had never left the garden. She had remained chastely in her room, and he on the snow below.

"Aye, Majesty," she stammered.

The King asked her in detail about the promises Brand had made to her—but not *where* those promises had been given.

"And did you believe him?" This time it was Herald Nikolas asking the question. She turned toward him.

"Oh yes. I wanted to, so much, I think I would have believed him no matter what," she sighed. Star nudged her hand again, and she caressed him. At least she still had Star.

"Would you have believed him even if he'd had a reputation as a rake?" Nikolas persisted.

"Aye," she said mournfully. "But—he didn't."

"That is true, Majesty," the Prince put in. "Brand's reputation was no worse than any other young man of the Court's. It is true he was known to frequent certain—establishments—but he had no reputation for great debauchery. In my opinion, there is no reason why the lady should have doubted him when he made promises of love and marriage."

Gravely, the King thanked his son.

And the questions moved on, past that point of terrible exposure. They asked her how she had felt when the Prince had decreed Brand should wed her older sister. They asked about Brand's plan for the two of them to flee together and be married. Once again, they did not ask *where* or under what circumstances he had made those promises. She realized with a sense of shock that these questions were deliberately setting the impression that she and Brand had never really so much as touched—that all their contact and talking had been as he stood below her window, in the snow-covered garden.

She could scarcely believe this. It seemed a miracle. How had they managed to avoid—

And then, she looked up into the King's eyes. He held her gaze for a very long time, then slowly, gravely, nodded.

She felt herself going hot all over. He *knew!* He *knew!* Herald Amily must have told him!

Well, of course she did. He is the King. And she is the King's Own. She had to tell him everything.

And yet . . . yet he was deliberately trying to keep her tattered reputation as safe as he could.

In that moment . . . she decided that she would do anything for her King. Anything. He must have seen the sudden devotion in her eyes, because he smiled, very briefly, and very faintly, before going on with his questions.

Finally, the King dismissed her, and she curtsied, and backed away, turning at the last moment to leave by the door she had come in. The page closed the door behind her, shutting her off from the sight of all those people, and every bit of energy that had sustained her drained out of her in a single moment.

Lady Dia and her nurse were waiting there, much to her relief. Lady Dia took her muff and Star, and the nurse let her weep out her nerves and grief on her ample shoulder, patting . her back and murmuring comfort. She could scarcely believe she had escaped disgrace so easily. . . .

And yet . . . there was still the terrible betrayal. She would never forget those cruel words that Brand had spoken when compelled by the Truth Spell. She would have them scorched into her memory for the rest of her life.

There was still the moment Brand had been killed before her very eyes, a sight that came between her and sleep any time she closed her eyes.

There was still knowing how easily she had been led. *I have escaped disgrace. But I can never escape what I know. I can never escape myself . . .*

"Come along, sweeting," the nurse murmured. "Come and sit down. You've done all you need to do now."

She nodded, wearily, and let them take her off to another room, knowing that nothing was ever going to be the same ever again.

———————

Amily was mortally glad to have the inquest over. Not that she was concerned about how it was going to go—Brand's guilt was sealed. There was no question of it. Even Brand's mother accepted it the moment that the thug Mags had captured identified Brand as the man who had hired him to burn the tent and everyone in it. It was confirmed when no less than two dozen apothecaries from within Haven and the Fair came forward to show records of Brand's purchasing a very specific sleeping potion from them. Not even the most fervent believer would have doubted.

No, the case was probably the most conclusive she had ever seen. She was just tired to death of all of this.

"We find," the King said, gravely, when Amily finished giving her own testimony, "That Brand Kaltar of the House Raeylen did willfully and with malice aforethought contrive to bring about the murders of all the members of Houses Chendlar and Raeylen excepting only himself and Lady Violetta. We find that the Lady Violetta is to be held blameless in this, and that she had no knowledge of his plot." He bent his gaze to the Raeylen side of the Court.

Lord Kaltar's widow braced herself. It was entirely possible that the King could declare their lands and holdings forfeit, and she knew it.

But Amily knew her King, and knew that was not what he had in mind.

"We declare that the head of House Raeylen is to be Lady Porthia, widow of the late Lord Kaltar, on condition that she declare the feud between the two houses to be at an end for all time, and make an effort to negotiate marriages between the two houses. I do not say that you *must* accomplish these weddings, only that you at least try. How say you, my lady?"

For a moment, Lady Porthia closed her eyes, as if she could hardly believe what she had heard. Then the lady stood up, dressed in deep mourning, her face full of grief. "I say that this foolishness has claimed enough blood, Majesty. And that when son turns against his own father . . ." She faltered for a moment. "When son turns against his own father, that hate has become a disease that must be cut out. If any man, woman, or child of this House attempts to foster this feud, I shall banish him to the Pelagirs and drive him there myself. And to foster ties between our houses is precisely the way to end this madness."

She sat down. The King nodded. "Well said, my lady." He turned to the House Chendlar side. "And you, House Chendlar.

I have some words for you. First, I command you to follow the same edicts regarding this feud. How say you?"

Lord Leverance stood up. "I say aye." He looked across the space between the two banks of seats to Lady Kaltar. "I say that I am deeply sorry that it came to this. I say that should the Lady Kaltar find herself in need of advice and not like what she finds in her own House, I will gladly send her my Steward, my Seneschal, or hire for her any other man—or woman—she is in need of." He closed his eyes for a moment. "I cannot imagine how terrible it must be to lose your spouse and your only child in the same moment, and know that the one conspired to slay the other. And . . . I say I wish that it had been true, what my poor, silly daughter dreamed. That she and Brand *had* been in love, and lifebonded, and were only fleeing to wed. I wish this feud had been drowned in love, and not blood."

He sat down abruptly, and with a look of surprise and shock on her face, his wife impulsively embraced him.

Amily felt a shock of surprise, herself. *Well . . . perhaps Cousin Talbot's position in the House is not as secure as he had thought . . .*

The King nodded. "Then hear the rest of my edict. Your daughter Violetta has behaved poorly. She certainly did things she should not have done. She lied to you, her parents, by omission if not commission. She went behind your back to consort with a young man, and she is fortunate that she came to no harm from it. She was, in short, a besotted little fool."

Lord Leverance nodded. "You will hear no dissent from me on that score, Majesty. What would you have me do with her? Send her into the country? Send her to a Temple? Find her an older and wiser husband?"

The King shook his head. "None of those. It may have been the promise of an *older and wiser husband* that sent her into the arms of a young and headstrong man in the first place. I do believe she needs a seasoned and practiced hand on her, someone who can give her experience of the world and common sense without indulging her. But I do not believe that sort of schooling will be found in the country, in a Temple, or at the hands of any man. It is my experience that overly romantic young people are best cured with an immersion into the work of the world."

Lord Leverance looked puzzled. "I shall do whatever you propose, Majesty, since I am at a loss as to a solution for what you suggest."

King Kyril nodded. "I do have a proposition. Lady Dia has offered to take her in fosterage, and I decree that she should remain here, in Haven, for a year. Lady Dia will take her on her works of charity, see to it that she has work to occupy her hands, and otherwise school her in the ways of the world. After that, we will see how she has matured."

Violetta's parents bowed their acceptance of this. This had been Amily's idea. Violetta was going to get *exactly* the sort of education Dia and Lydia had. She'd get lessons in practical matters, and in weapons-work as well. No more excessive daydreaming. . . .

Not that she's likely to be longing after that, now.

But also, this would be getting her out from under the eye of her parents and older sisters, the former of whom might be inclined to indulge her even more after this, and the latter of whom would certainly do their best to persecute her for nearly ruining their own plans.

"And with that, we declare this inquest is at an end," the King said. And he and the rest on the dais filed out through the little door behind them, leaving the courtiers to sort themselves out and leave.

On the other side of the little door was a sort of lounge. And once the door was closed, all six of them flung themselves down into comfortable chairs. The Royals cast off the heavy fur-lined cloaks that came with their regalia, and set aside their crowns.

"I saw no reason to bring up the fact that Brand had seduced that child," the King said, once they were all comfortably disposed, and Lydia had poured them all wine. "It wasn't relevant to the inquest. She's going to be in enough trouble for sending him that idiotic letter as it is, let's not add shaming to the mix."

"There's still going to be shaming," Lydia pointed out. "People will speculate. There will be a period where everyone will feel sorry for her, but it is inevitable that people will wonder about all those midnight meetings, and some people will assume the worst."

Amily sighed, and nodded. "But we can't stop people from talking," she pointed out. "No matter where she goes, there are going to be people speculating, and making up their own minds."

"Which is why I want her here," Kyril said firmly. "If we stand behind her, the speculations will die for lack of being fed. Dia can certainly teach her how to hold her head high and shame the devil."

There was a tap at the door, and Mags entered. The King smiled. "And here is the hero of the hour."

Mags blushed. "Me an' everybody else that come runnin'," he replied. "Not like I was alone down there."

He entered, and sat down on the arm of Amily's chair. "You ask me, this'un's the hero. Made all the right moves. And went chargin' after Brand 'xactly the right way—made sure we all knew where she was, stayed on Rolan where she was safest, an—glory!—hit 'im with the coercive Truth Spell! She ain't never done that fer real afore, an' how many times did ye practice on me? Three?"

"Four," she corrected. "All in the last sennight. I just had the feeling I was going to need to know how to do it."

Lydia went around, refreshing everyone's wine, and sat down with Sedric again as the King cleared his throat.

"Well, I want you two to know, that although I was concerned when we nearly lost Nikolas, I am concerned no longer. Amily, Mags was right. You acted in every way possible exactly as the King's Own should. You and Rolan properly understood that Brand had to be stopped, and you acted when no one else could. And while I was dubious as to how useful your Gift was for the King's Own, it's turned out to be surprisingly handy." He paused for a moment. "I am curious, however, about two things. The first—what were you going to do if that poor horse hadn't broken its neck and sent them down?"

"Shoot it," she said, bluntly. "I intended to take whatever shot I could get. If I could lame it, I would, but if I had to, I would have killed it. The further Brand got from Haven, the harder it would have been for Mags and the others to arrive in time if I got into trouble." She had already thought that through, when the horse stumbled and she fled from its mind.

"The other question I have is this. Did you have to shoot to kill Brand?" The King leveled a steely gaze on her, but she met it fearlessly.

"Yes, sir," she said. "Mags was protecting Violetta, and was already exhausted. If he was murdered, Dallen would die. I had Brand's confession, and I could not risk losing a valuable Herald and his Companion. In that light, I could not be sure of a lesser target, so I took the body-shot."

She had not forgotten how she had missed, when she had tried to shoot the Sleepgivers during the siege of the Bastion and had been unwilling to shoot to kill. *I am not making that mistake, and taking that risk, again. Not when it's Mags.*

The King nodded, satisfied, and turned to Mags. "I am *very* impressed with your little gang of runners," he said, bringing a smile to Mags' face. "In fact, I am so impressed that I'd like you to keep me informed about them. And should any of them show any sign of being especially intelligent, or inventive, or inquisitive, I'll see to a sponsorship as an Artificer, and see that they are enrolled in the Collegia."

Well that brought a smile to *Mags'* face. Amily squeezed his hand, happy to see him so pleased.

Kyril looked around at all of them. "Well," he said, at last. "We have somehow managed to come to Year's End. We will have a great deal to be grateful for, tomorrow night."

Amily nodded. And realized that this would be her first Midwinter's Eve Feast with the King and his immediate family and friends. *Something new . . .*

"And we will have a very important question to be answered in the New Year," the King continued, with a twinkle in his eye that had not been there since the entire disaster of the two feuding Houses had begun.

"And that would be, Kyril?" Nikolas asked, looking as if he had no idea what his old friend and King was about to say—though Amily was pretty certain she knew.

And that was confirmed a moment later.

He laughed, probably anticipating her father's stunned reaction. *"How soon can we get these two married?"*

The look on Nikolas' face . . . was beyond price.